PENGUIN

THE SECRET FRIEND

Chris Mooney is the author of four previous thrillers. *Remembering Sarah* was nominated for the prestigious Edgar Award for Best Novel, and his most recent bestselling novel, *The Missing*, was the first to feature CSI Darby McCormick. He lives in Boston with his wife and son.

The Secret Friend

CHRIS MOONEY

PENGUIN BOOKS

PENGUIN BOOKS

Published by the Penguin Group
Penguin Books Ltd, 80 Strand, London WC2R 0RL, England
Penguin Group (USA), Inc., 375 Hudson Street, New York, New York 10014, USA
Penguin Group (Canada), 90 Eglinton Avenue East, Suite 700, Toronto, Ontario, Canada M4P 2Y3
(a division of Pearson Penguin Canada Inc.)
Penguin Ireland, 25 St Stephen's Green, Dublin 2, Ireland (a division of Penguin Books Ltd)
Penguin Group (Australia), 250 Camberwell Road, Camberwell, Victoria 3124, Australia
(a division of Pearson Australia Group Pty Ltd)
Penguin Books India Pvt Ltd, 11 Community Centre, Panchsheel Park, New Delhi – 110 017, India
Penguin Group (NZ), 67 Apollo Drive, Rosedale, North Shore 0632, New Zealand
(a division of Pearson New Zealand Ltd)
Penguin Books (South Africa) (Pty) Ltd, 24 Sturdee Avenue,
Rosebank, Johannesburg 2196, South Africa

Penguin Books Ltd, Registered Offices: 80 Strand, London WC2R 0RL, England

www.penguin.com

First published 2008
1

Set in Monotype Garamond
Typeset by Rowland Phototypesetting Ltd, Bury St Edmunds, Suffolk
Printed in England by Clays Ltd, St Ives plc

978–0–141–03087–6

For Pam Bernstein,
mentor and friend.
You're one in a million.

I

Darby McCormick had finished hanging the last of the bloody clothing inside the drying chamber when she heard her name called over the loudspeakers. Leland Pratt, the lab director, wanted to see her inside his office immediately.

Darby stripped out of her latex gloves and lab coat and used the sink in Serology. As she scrubbed her hands, she glanced in the mirror. On her left cheek and underneath her eye was a thin, jagged scar partially hidden by makeup. The plastic surgeons had done a remarkable job, considering the amount of damage Traveler's axe had caused. She removed the rubber band holding her ponytail, her dark red hair falling against her shoulders, and dried her hands with a paper towel as she left the room.

Standing behind Leland's desk and talking on the phone was a thin woman impeccably dressed in a sharp black business suit – Boston Police Commissioner Christina Chadzynski.

The woman placed a hand over the phone's mouthpiece.

'I'm sorry, I was looking for Leland,' Darby said. 'He paged me.'

'Yes, I know. Come in and shut the door.' The commissioner returned to her phone call.

Christina Chadzynski was the first woman to hold the commissioner's job, the highest position inside the Boston Police Department. When her name had been thrown into the ring as a potential candidate, the Boston media had anointed her as the 'great hope' to build a bridge between Boston police and community leaders in high crime areas like Roxbury, Mattapan and Dorchester, where she had been born and raised.

Three years into her term, Boston's homicide rate had soared to its highest level in decades. Politicians decided to offer up Chadzynski as the sacrificial lamb, and the Boston media took the bait. Newspaper columnists and other so-called media experts were calling for her resignation. Chadzynski had failed, they said, because she wasn't devoted to her job, because she was no longer in touch with the common man since she had married Pawel Chadzynski, a former investment banker turned power broker who was active in Boston's political circles. There were rumours Chadzynski was planning a run for mayor's office.

'I've got to go,' Chadzynski said and hung up. She motioned to the pair of stiff chairs set up in front of Leland's government-issued desk. 'Miss McCormick, are you familiar with CSU?'

Darby nodded. The newly formed Crime Scene Investigative Unit was a specialized group made up of the department's top investigators and forensic technicians who responded to the city's homicides, rapes and other violent crimes. Appointment to the unit was by the police commissioner. Darby had applied for one of the forensic positions. She wasn't asked for an interview.

'Emma Hale,' Chadzynski said, opening a file. 'I assume you know who she is.'

'I've being following the case in the papers.' Last year, in March, the freshman Harvard student disappeared after attending a friend's party. Eight months later, in November, the week before Thanksgiving, her waterlogged body had washed up on the bank of the Charles River in a section of Charlestown locals called 'The Oilies'. Emma Hale had been shot in the back of the head.

'I take it ballistics didn't match the slug to a former case,' Darby said.

'We didn't find a match.' Chadzynski put on a pair of thick-framed designer glasses. A significant amount of money had been invested in her hair, makeup, clothes and jewellery. The diamond ring was at least three carats.

'When Emma Hale disappeared, CSU thought it might be a kidnapping – her father, Jonathan Hale, is very wealthy,' Chadzynski said. 'Then another college student disappeared this past December.'

'Judith Chen.'

'Do you know what happened?'

'The papers say she vanished on her way home from the campus library.'

'CSU is investigating a possible connection.'

'Is there one?'

'They're both college students. That's the only connection we have. The slug we recovered from Emma Hale's skull isn't connected to any cases, and all her time spent in the water washed away any trace evidence. The only piece of evidence we have is a religious statue. I'm sure you read about *that* in the papers.'

Darby nodded. Both the *Globe* and the *Herald*, citing an anonymous police source, said a 'religious' statue had been found inside the victim's pocket.

'Have you heard anything about the statue?' Chadzynski asked.

'The word around the lab is that it was a statue of the Virgin Mary.'

'Yes, it is. What else have you heard?'

'The statue was sewn inside Emma Hale's pocket.'

'Yes.'

'What did NCIC have to say?' Darby asked. The National Crime Information Center, a nationwide database maintained by the FBI's Criminal Justice Information Services, was the de facto clearing house for all open and solved cases involving murder, missing persons, fugitives and stolen property.

'NCIC didn't contain any homicides involving a Virgin Mary statue sewn into the victim's pocket,' Chadzynski said.

'Did you talk to the site profiler at the Boston office?'

'We consulted him.' Chadzynski leaned back in her chair and crossed her legs. 'Leland told me you recently completed your doctorate in criminal psychology from Harvard.'

'Yes.'

'And you've studied at the FBI's Investigative Support Unit.'

'I've attended lectures.'

'Why do you think the killer – whom we are presuming is male – took the time to sew this statue inside a dead woman's pocket?'

'I'm sure the site profiler shared his theories with you.'

'He did. Now I'd like to hear what you have to say.'

'The Virgin Mary obviously holds some special significance for him.'

'Obviously,' Chadzynski said. 'What else?'

'She's the primal archetype for the loving, caring mother.'

'You're telling me this man's got mommy issues?'

'What man doesn't have mother issues?'

Chadzynski let out a tired laugh.

'On some level the killer cared for her,' Darby said. 'Emma Hale was kept alive for several months. When her body was found, she was wearing the same clothes she had worn on the night she disappeared. And she was shot in the back of the head.'

'Do you think that's significant?'

'It suggests that he couldn't face Emma Hale –

that he felt some sort of shame or remorse for having to kill her.'

Chadzynski stared at her for what seemed like several minutes.

'Darby, I'd like to place you on CSU. You can appoint anyone from the lab to your team. In addition to your forensic responsibilities, I'd also like for you to act as the second lead on the unit. You'll share investigative duties with Tim Bryson. Have you met him?'

'Just in passing,' Darby said. She didn't know much about the man beyond the fact that he had once been married and had a daughter who died of a rare form of leukaemia. Bryson didn't talk about it. He was intensely private, didn't fraternize with the crew outside the job. Other cops said Bryson was fiercely dedicated to his work, a quality she deeply admired.

'This is a tremendous opportunity,' Chadzynski said. 'You'll be the first forensic technician in the history of the department to be placed in an investigative position.'

'Yes, I realize that.'

'So why do I sense some hesitation?'

'If you really felt this way, why did you reject my application?'

'After your . . . encounter with Traveler, the department offered you counselling and you refused it.'

'I didn't see the need.'

'And why is that?'

Darby folded her hands on her lap. She didn't answer.

'You survived a traumatic event,' Chadzynski said. 'Some people think –'

'With all due respect, Commissioner, I don't care what other people think.'

Chadzynski's smile was polite. 'You caught Traveler. He was on the run for three decades. The FBI's top profilers couldn't find him, but you did. I could use your experience here.'

'I'll need access to all the information – murder book, autopsy records and pictures.'

'Tim will have copies delivered to you today.'

'Have you discussed this with him?'

'I have. His ego is bruised, but he'll be fine. You know how men are.' A conspiratorial grin now. 'I also think these two cases could benefit from a fresh look at the evidence, what little of it we have. Who would you recommend from the lab?'

'Coop and Keith Woodbury,' Darby said.

'Coop . . . Do you mean Jackson Cooper, your lab partner?'

'Yes.' Jackson Cooper, known around the station as 'Coop', was, in addition to being Darby's friend, the closest thing she had to family since her mother died. 'Coop was involved with the Traveler case. I could use his help here.'

'I don't know Mr Woodbury.'

'Keith's only been with us for a few months – he's our new forensic chemist.' Darby had worked with him on a recent shooting case. Woodbury was thorough and, without a doubt, one of the brightest people she had met.

'Then let's bring them in so I can welcome them aboard,' Chadzynski said.

'Coop's off today, and Keith's at a seminar in Washington.'

'Then I'll let you deliver the good news.' Chadzynski, using a gold fountain pen, wrote on the back of a business card.

'I may need additional lab resources,' Darby said.

'You'll have them. I discussed the matter with Leland. You have his full support.'

Chadzynski slid the card across the desk. 'The top number is my cell phone. Tim's numbers are below it. He's expecting your phone call. Do you have any other questions for me?'

'Not at the moment.'

'Then I'll let you get to it.' The commissioner picked up the phone and started dialling.

2

Darby left voicemail messages for Coop and Keith Woodbury. Tim Bryson didn't answer at any of his numbers. She left a message at his cell phone number asking him to call and then checked out Emma Hale's forensic file.

From the evidence locker, Darby checked out Emma Hale's clothing and carried the sealed evidence bags to the back benches in Serology, where she would have plenty of space to spread out.

Darby placed the file on the bench but didn't read it. She wanted to examine the clothing herself and see if her analysis matched the report compiled by Paula Washow, the forensic technician assigned to CSU.

Emma Hale's clothes, caked with dried mud and algae and stained with blood, were ripped and torn in several places from the weeks she spent bumping up against rocks, sticks and whatever debris lined the bed of the Charles River.

Lying on the sheets of butcher paper were a Dolce & Gabbana cocktail dress, size 2; a camel-hair winter topcoat by Prada; and a single pair of Jimmy Choo high-heel pumps, size 6, the heel broken. The lacy black thong and matching bra were imprinted with the name of a high-end lingerie boutique on

Newbury Street – Boston's equivalent to Rodeo Drive.

Darby owned only one designer treasure: a heavily discounted black Diane von Furstenberg dress she'd accidentally discovered on a clearance rack. Emma Hale had spent an *extraordinary* amount on this outfit – the lingerie alone was a few hundred dollars.

The Harvard student's body was discovered by a local pit bull off its leash, buried underneath two inches of frozen snow. Hale was brought to the morgue and photographed. Darby studied the photos.

Hale's coat belt was tied and knotted around her waist. One of her shoes was missing, the other hanging on to her ankle by a single strap. Her hands and feet, Darby noticed, weren't bound.

Dried bloodstains, diluted from Emma Hale's time in the water, were visible on the back of the coat. Blood had soaked through the coat's fabric. The flow pattern suggested that, after she was shot in the back of the head, Emma had lain on her back for a period of time, the blood seeping through her jacket and onto her dress. The drag patterns indicated she had been moved.

Had Emma simply landed on her back after she was shot, or had her killer rolled her over to allow her to bleed out before moving her? With no crime scene to analyse, no blood splatter patterns to interpret, it was impossible to know. Either Emma was shot near the dump site – maybe even at the dump site – or she was shot at another location and then transported to the place where she was dropped into the water.

If Emma had been shot outside, how had her abductor managed to keep her calm? Did he tell Emma she was going home and make her change into her old clothing? Wearing her old clothes, Emma would feel comfortable. She might take him at his word. Did he blindfold her? If Emma wasn't gagged, she might scream. If she wasn't bound, she might run. Someone might hear the gunshot and call the police. Someone might see him and call the police. If Emma was killed outside, in a public spot, and then dragged or rolled off something like a bridge, blood would be left behind. Someone might stumble across it and decide to call the police.

And when did her killer sew the statue in her dress pocket? Did he do it when she was alive or after she was dead? Would he take the time to sew the pocket shut outside where he might be seen? Doubtful.

The more likely scenario was that Emma Hale was killed at the place where she had been kept for several months. Her abductor would have privacy and control over his environment. After she was dead, he could take his time sewing the statue inside the dress pocket. He could let her bleed out. Then he could move her body to his vehicle and drive to the dump site. Darby wondered if Emma's body had been wrapped in something like a plastic tarp.

Darby took her own set of pictures of the clothes

and then, using the light magnifier, began the long, painstaking hunt across the fabrics looking for any overlooked evidence. Small, rectangular-shaped cuts were visible on the clothes – the places where Washow had collected bloodstain samples for DNA testing.

As she worked, her thoughts kept drifting to Judith Chen's parents. They had flown up from Pennsylvania and for the past three months lived in a shabby hotel waiting for the phone to ring with news of their youngest daughter. The Boston press followed their every move.

Darby finished her initial review shortly before 11:30 a.m. Next, she examined the clothes using various light sources and checked the blood patterns and tears under a stereo microscope. She found no other trace evidence – no fibres, threads, hairs, glass or any biological fluids.

From the last evidence bag, she removed the five-inch ceramic statue of the Virgin Mary. The Blessed Mother, dressed in a blue robe, stood in the classic pose Darby remembered from church and catechism books – hands outstretched in a loving embrace and head titled slightly to the side as she looked downward, the woman's expression frozen with eternal sorrow.

The man who shot Emma held this same statue in his hands. He placed it in her dress pocket and then sewed it shut. He wanted to make sure the statue stayed with her. Why? What was the significance of the statue and why was it so important that it stayed with Emma after she died?

During lunch, Darby read over Washow's forensic report. Washow hadn't found any trace evidence on the clothing, which wasn't surprising. Floaters were notoriously difficult. All the time spent underwater had washed away any trace evidence, if there was any to be found.

The clothing had been treated with luminol to enhance the diluted bloodstains. The collected blood samples matched Emma Hale's DNA profile. Testing on the thread used to sew the statue inside the dress pocket came up negative for blood.

No blood or fingerprints were found on the statue. The underwear was sprayed with a chemical marker for traces of semen. Negative. No foreign pubic hairs were found. Vaginal and anal swabs failed to reveal any DNA evidence.

The bottom of the Virgin Mary was stamped with the words 'Our Lady of Sorrow' – a charity organization started in 1910 that used the proceeds from the sale of religious statues, rosary beads, prayer cards and religious note cards to help fight world hunger. The charity disbanded in 1946. No reason was given. The statue was manufactured by the Wellington Company based out of Charlestown, North Carolina. The last production run for this particular Virgin Mary statue was in 1944. The company went bankrupt in 1958. Since the statues weren't manufactured any more, there was no way to trace them.

Washow, assuming the statue may have some worth as a collectible, conducted an exhaustive search with several Boston-based antique dealers specializing in religious items. The Virgin Mary statue amounted to nothing more than a cheap trinket.

Standing inside her office, Darby thought about the lingerie. Did Emma Hale have a boyfriend or someone special she was meeting that night?

And what had happened to Emma Hale's purse? Had it been dumped or had her killer held on to it as a souvenir? Darby considered the question as she left the lab, on her way to an appointment.

3

Moon Island, situated in Quincy Bay, was once the site of a sewage treatment plant. It is now owned by the city of Boston. In addition to an outdoor firearms range, the forty-five-acre site is also used for bomb disposal and as a training facility for the Boston Fire Department.

Moon Island is not open to the general public. Access is through a causeway which is blocked off by a gate.

Darby stood under a cold, grey sky at the outdoor firing range along with six recruits from the Boston Police Academy. They all wore the same navy blue baseball cap, safety glasses and padded earmuffs. They each wore the same black jacket with a single bright blue stripe running down the sleeve.

The recruits, all men, were training with a Ruger .38 special. Darby, having completed her range test and state-certified firearms safety class, now used her own weapon, a 9mm SIG P-229 with a .40 S&W cartridge. She had selected the handgun for its relatively compact size and comfort. She was still getting used to the weapon's hard recoil.

The firearms instructor, Steve Gautieri, was demonstrating the classic Weaver stance, the position where the shooter, using a pyramidal base or 'boxer's stance' with one foot in front and the other behind, leaned slightly forward. This stance, Gautieri explained, was the key to accuracy. If the shooter's feet were parallel, the shot would be either too high or too low.

Darby had adopted a strong stance technique where her legs were spread further apart, almost in a V-shape, her shoulders more forward than the male recruits'. She had also adopted a different grip. Instead of securing her free hand, her left hand, around the fingers holding the handgun, she formed a fist and placed the grip of her handgun against her wrist before firing. It had helped tremendously with her accuracy.

The targets were ready. Darby reminded herself not to jerk the trigger, just squeeze it.

The bell rang. Darby fired the gun, her mind flashing snapshots from Traveler's underground basement of horrors – the human bones on the floor and dried blood on the walls; the nightmarish maze of wooden corridors of locked and unlocked doors leading to dead ends; women screaming for help, women crying and begging, dying. She could recall every image, every texture and sound.

Darby fired the last shot and straightened, the muscles in her forearms aching. She felt oddly relaxed, as though having just completed a long, satisfying run.

The recruit standing next to her, tall and rugged,

kept glancing at her while the firearms instructor examined the results. The sky had grown darker, and it had started to snow. Light flakes swirled in the wind.

Gautieri held up a paper target. 'Take a look at this shooting, boys. See the nice, tight pattern right here in the centre? This belongs to Darby McCormick, the girl standing at the end there. Nice job, Darby. Want to know why she beat the rest of you? Because she's got her stance down and she knows to squeeze the trigger and not to jerk it. You're dismissed. Darby, I'd like a word with you.'

Gautieri waited until after the recruits left before he spoke. 'What kind of ammo are you using?'

'Triton .40 S&W, one thirty-five grain,' Darby said. 'The one-stop shots approach ninety-six per cent.'

'That's some serious firepower.'

'A lot of law enforcement agencies use it.'

Gautieri looked back to the paper target and grinned. 'You pissed off at anyone I know?'

Darby's clothes reeked of cordite. When she stepped into the parking lot she saw her lab partner, Jackson Cooper, leaning against her black Mustang.

With the exception of his short, blond hair, Coop bore a striking resemblance to Tom Brady, the quarterback for the New England Patriots. Coop wore jeans and a black North Face fleece jacket. He was adjusting the brim of his Red Sox baseball hat when Darby stepped up to him.

'What are you doing here?' Darby asked. 'I thought you took the day off.'

'I did. I spent it with Rodeo.'

'You were at a rodeo?'

'No, that's the name of my girlfriend. Row-day-oh. I got your message about your meeting with the commissioner. I tried calling but you weren't answering your phone.'

'I turned it off.'

'I called the lab. Leland told me you were here, so I decided to swing by. He also wanted me to tell you the files you requested have been delivered to the lab. Fill me in on what's going on.'

For the next twenty minutes Darby filled him in on her meeting with Chadzynski and her review of Emma Hale's clothing.

'What do you want me to do?' Coop asked after she'd finished.

'Tomorrow morning, I'd like for you to take a look at the Virgin Mary statue and see if anything was overlooked.'

'I'll do it now.'

'Don't you want to get back to Row-day-oh?'

'No. I had to fake an emergency to get out of her place.'

'How did you do that?'

'I used her phone to page myself, then told her I had to go to a crime scene.' Coop grinned, pleased by his cleverness. 'I'm going to break up with her. It's not working out. She's into all this artsy-fartsy shit. Last night she made me watch *Bareback Mountain.*'

'I think you mean *Brokeback Mountain.*'

'Given what those two dudes are doing up in the mountains, I think I was right the first time.' Coop smiled. 'Did you talk with Bryson?'

'I left him a message, but he hasn't called back.' Darby took out her car keys. 'Do you know Tim?'

'Does anyone know Tim?'

'What do you mean?'

'You know what I mean. Bryson's real private. Do you know his partner?'

'Cliff Watts.'

Coop nodded. 'Cliffy has worked with Bryson for almost a decade and he doesn't know anything about the man. Has never been to his home, never went out drinking with him. Cliffy is solid. Appointing Woody was a good choice, by the way.'

'What is it with guys and nicknames?'

'It's how we show affection, Freckles.' Coop pushed himself off the Mustang. 'We should get going. Weathermen are saying we're going to get a nor'easter. They're predicting two feet.'

'I'll believe it when I see it. Last Monday they said we're going to get a foot and I woke up to two inches.'

'I bet that's not the first time you woke up to two inches.'

'Tell me about it. Remember last month when you passed out on my couch? I saw you in your boxers and let's just say there's a whole lot of truth to that Irish curse thing.'

'Very funny. I'll see you back at the lab.'

Seated behind the wheel, Darby started the car and turned on her phone. There was one message: Tim Bryson had returned her call. He said it was urgent. She dialled his number.

'Bryson.'

'Tim, Darby McCormick. I just got your message. I'm on my way back to the lab, but I was wondering if we could set up a time to meet and talk.'

'A call came in about a body floating in the Boston Harbor behind the Moakley courthouse.'

'Is it Judith Chen?'

'The clothes seem right,' Bryson said. 'I'm on my way to the morgue. We can talk there.'

4

At 5:30 p.m. Hannah Givens stood under the roof of the Macy's department store at Boston's Downtown Crossing, waiting for the bus. This afternoon's light snow had turned into a powerful storm. She wished she had taken an earlier bus instead of working overtime at the deli, helping clean up and do some food preparation for tomorrow morning's weekend breakfast crowd – provided the city was open for business. The weathermen were predicting several feet of snow.

Hannah tucked her hands deep in her down parka and looked over Macy's lighted window displays where mannequins with perfect figures wore spring dresses. One caught her eye – a beautiful black cocktail dress with a revealing but tasteful slit up the leg. Northeastern University's spring formal was coming up in three weeks and no one had asked her.

In a strange way, she was relieved. Even if someone asked her, she couldn't afford a new dress – not unless she was willing to pull extra shifts at the deli as well as dipping into her grocery money for the next two months. The idea of eating Raman noodles for breakfast, lunch and dinner wasn't appealing, and besides, it wasn't like she could fit into any of these dresses. She would never be thin, not like the girls in the magazines, not like this mannequin or even her two roommates, Robin and Terry, who got up every morning to work out at the gym and ate nothing but salads sprinkled with goat cheese.

Hannah knew she wasn't much of a looker. She was tall, almost six feet in heels, a big-boned, curvy woman with nice hair and a pleasant face. She didn't have much of a chest, thanks to her mother's genes. From her father she had inherited SIS – Shitty Irish Skin that freckled from the sun. The Givens lineage had also given her a lazy eye that, despite her mother's assurances, hadn't corrected itself over time.

The real problem, Hannah suspected, was her personality. She was boring. She was smart, hardworking and good with the books, real good, but that didn't count for much until you got older, when the tables turned and things like brains and a high salary made men stop and take a second look. While Robin and Terry drank dollar drafts at dive bars on Thursday nights and worked the fraternity party circuit Friday through Sunday, Hannah was either working or studying. She wanted to have fun – honestly, she did – but with her two jobs and her course workload, she didn't exactly have a lot of free time.

While she waited for the bus, Hannah passed the time imagining herself five inches shorter and fifty pounds lighter wearing the black dress in the window and a stunning pair of Manolos as Chris Smith, the handsome lacrosse player from her Shakespeare class, escorted her to the spring formal. She'd look like Cinderella going to the ball.

A car horn honked behind her. Hannah turned and saw a black BMW parked against the kerb on the corner of Porter and Summer Streets. The passenger's side window was rolled down.

'Hannah? Is that you?'

A man's voice. She didn't recognize it. She couldn't see who was sitting behind the wheel. The car's interior was dark.

'I'm in Professor Johnson's calculus class,' the man said. 'I sit in the far back.'

Hannah stepped up next to the open window. In the soft blue light coming from the dashboard, she saw the man's face.

He had been in some sort of accident, like a fire. His face was severely scarred, covered with makeup, his nose an awful, crooked mess of skin. His left eye was damaged, wide open and unblinking.

Hannah pulled away from the window. The wind, wild and fierce, whipped curtains of snow across the streets.

'I'm sorry, we haven't been formally introduced. I'm Walter. Walter Smith.'

'Hello.'

'You ready for Johnson's midterm next week?'

'I'm going to do a little studying once I get home.'

'I hope you're not waiting for the bus. They're running *waaaay* behind schedule on account of the storm. I just heard it on the radio. Hop in. I'll give you a ride.'

Hannah wanted nothing more than to get out of the cold, to get home and slip into a warm bath. She had a long weekend of studying, and she planned on getting a head start tonight, but the thought of getting inside the car with this stranger filled her with anxiety.

'Thanks for the offer,' Hannah said, 'but I don't want to put you out of your way.'

'You're not. I'm heading over to Brighton anyway to visit a friend.' Walter Smith was already moving the backpack and textbook into the back seat.

He wasn't a stranger, not exactly. He was in Professor Johnson's class. She didn't recognize him, but that didn't mean anything. The calculus class was held in a big, musty lecture hall. There were well over a hundred students.

'You'll freeze to death out there,' Walter Smith said. 'Hop in.'

A small statue of the Virgin Mary was mounted on the dashboard. Seeing the statue sent the anxiety away. Hannah opened the door and hopped in, grateful to be out of the cold wind.

The inside of the car was warm and smelled of new leather and cologne.

'I live at one twenty-two Carlton Road,' Hannah said, buckling her seatbelt. 'Do you know how to get to Allston?'

Walter Smith nodded as he pulled away from the

kerb. 'One of my friends lives around there,' he said. 'Speaking of which, do you mind if I swing by and pick up him up? It's on the way.'

'No, of course not.'

The city ploughs were out, busy trying to clear the streets and highways. Traffic was slow.

'So,' Hannah said, 'what's your major?'

Walter Smith was majoring in computer science. He wanted to design computer games. He grew up on the west coast – he didn't say where – and told her he was living in the Back Bay although he was seriously considering moving to someplace like Brighton or Allston where rent was considerably cheaper. When Hannah asked him how he liked Northeastern, he shrugged and said he wanted to go to MIT but couldn't afford it.

Hannah thought it was odd he could afford a BMW and to rent a place in the Back Bay but couldn't afford to take out a college loan. If you could go to MIT, why waste your time and money on Northeastern? Hannah didn't want to come across as nosy, so she didn't ask.

By the time they hit Storrow Drive, Walter had grown quiet. He was doing this weird thing with his tongue – gently chewing it on one side of his jaw, then moving it over to the other side. She tried talking to him about music and movies but he seemed distracted. Maybe he was concentrating on the road. The snow was bad, and the roads were pretty slippery. She spotted more than one accident.

Walter took the Allston exit. Ten minutes later he pulled into a small strip mall with a Radio Shack and two other buildings that looked abandoned. The parking lot was empty. He drove behind the building and parked in front of a loading dock. Crates and trash were stacked up next to several back doors. There was nobody back here.

'Dave must be waiting inside,' Walter said. 'Reach inside the glove compartment and grab the yellow sheet of paper. It has Dave's cell number on it.'

Hannah leaned forward and opened the glove compartment. Walter smashed her face against the dashboard.

'I'm sorry,' Walter Smith said as he pressed a bandana against her nose and mouth.

At first Hannah thought he was trying to wipe away the blood; then she inhaled some bitter odour that smelled of spoiled fruit. She struggled to move away but she was caught against the seatbelt.

'I didn't mean to hurt you.' His voice trembled, and he started to cry. 'I'm sorry.'

She grabbed his wrist with both hands and tried to yank it away, but Walter Smith's grip was too strong. She could taste blood – *her* blood – on the back of her throat and she started to gag.

He was crying harder now. 'I'll make it up to you, Hannah, I promise. I'm going to make you very happy.'

Hannah slumped back against the seat, hearing the

windshield wipers going back and forth, back and forth, the Virgin Mary's mournful eyes looking at her with arms wide open, ready to comfort.

5

Walter Smith popped the trunk. He unfastened Hannah's seatbelt and then headed out into the wet, heavy snow, quickly making his way to the passenger's side.

Hannah was heavier than Emma and Judith, and considerably taller. Instead of picking Hannah up and cradling her in his arms, Walter gripped her under the armpits and dragged her to the back of the car. The blankets were already set up.

Walter placed her in the trunk. He brushed the snow from her face and tucked a pillow under her head. Hannah's nose was bleeding in a slow, steady trickle. He hoped it wasn't broken.

From his pocket he removed the baggie holding the tiny Ambien pills he ordered online from Mexico and wedged three of them down her throat. Hannah moaned, swallowed. Good. He moved her arms behind her back and handcuffed her wrists. Then he handcuffed her ankles.

Walter stared down at Hannah. Her face was remarkably warm and open. Her face was what had attracted him. He had seen her waiting for the bus and Mary spoke to him, told him Hannah Givens was THE ONE and Mary was right, she was always right.

Walter rolled Hannah onto her side so the blood wouldn't trickle down her throat and make her sick. He'd have to stop and check on her at some point.

Walter tucked a blanket under her chin. He kissed Hannah on the forehead, then shut the trunk and got back behind the wheel.

The wet snow was coming down at a fast clip. Walter drove slowly, carefully, with both hands gripping the wheel. A lot of cops would be out tonight.

As he drove, Walter kept glancing at the statue on the dashboard. Mary's voice was clear in his head. His Blessed Mother told him not to worry.

6

The dead woman lying on the autopsy table didn't look like a woman any more – she didn't look human, in fact, but more like one of those creatures from an old black-and-white horror movie, a frightful, angry thing that had clawed its way out from a grave. The teeth were bared, the lips and surrounding facial tissue and missing eyes picked away by postmortem fish feeding. The rest of the body was covered by a blue sheet. A white card with a case number was placed under her chin.

The face was unrecognizable. Darby wondered if the woman was Judith Chen.

A heavyset man from ID, the section of the lab that dealt exclusively with crime scene photography, took close-up pictures of the bloated face. Coop stood behind him, watching. The small white-tiled room reeked of disinfectant mixed with the overpowering metallic odour of the Boston Harbor.

Darby had already taken her own set of pictures. As she waited, she reviewed what little she knew of the case, most of which came from newspapers.

Two and a half months ago, on a Wednesday night during the first week of December, Judith Chen, a freshman at Boston's Suffolk University, was studying for her chemistry midterm at the campus library. Five minutes shy of 10 p.m., Judith, dressed in pink nylon running pants, a pink sweatshirt and Nike sneakers, decided to call it a night. Somewhere between the library and the apartment she was renting in Natick, the nineteen-year-old chemistry major disappeared.

It was now mid-February and the body lying on the table wore the same clothing.

The ID man gave her the nod. Darby, dressed in scrubs, put on a surgical mask and a face shield and approached the body.

The woman's pink sweatshirt and pink nylon running pants were wet, caked with mud and twigs. The feet, still laced with sneakers, hung over a sink dripping with water. Darby was glad to see Bryson had tied paper bags around the woman's hands.

The right running-pant pocket was sewn shut with the same black thread used on Emma Hale's dress pocket. Darby peeled back the waistband, and through the transparent pocket lining she saw the same five-inch statue of the Virgin Mary she had held in her hands at the lab.

On the back of the woman's head was a puckered hole – the muzzle stamp from a handgun. There was no exit wound. Darby recalled that the .22 calibre slug found in Emma Hale's skull hadn't produced an exit wound either.

Coop removed the paper bags and examined the woman's hands. The fingers were gnarled into claws, and the skin, white and puckered with wet wrinkles known as washerwoman's syndrome, had started to slough off the body. The fingernails were painted a bright pink.

'They're pretty shrivelled,' Coop said.

'Which way should we go? Tissue builder? Injecting water under the skin?'

'Since the body's already showing epidural detachment, the best method would be to use the glove technique. Your hands are roughly the same size, so we can print her here.'

Darby collected grit and fingernail samples. After she finished, Coop slid the skin off the right hand and transferred the 'skin glove' to a dish holding alcohol.

She didn't see any evidence to indicate the body had been weighted down. It didn't matter, really – the putrefaction gases would cause even a weighted body to float to the surface eventually. Did the killer know this?

Darby plugged in the portable Luma-Lite and waved the alternate light source across the clothing. She found several hairs. After she collected them, she adjusted the wavelength and found stains that fluoresced – blood or semen. She marked the areas and then cut off the clothes.

The saturated bloodstains on the back of the sweatshirt resembled the same pattern she had seen on Emma Hale's jacket and dress. Like Emma Hale, this woman had lain in her blood for a period of time before she was dumped into the river.

Darby unlaced the sneakers and carefully removed them. River water, sand and grit fell into the sink. She cut off the socks. The toenails were painted the same bright pink as the fingernails. She packed each item of clothing into its own bag and then, using a hand-held magnifier, examined the Virgin Mary statue. It was the same size and colour. 'Our Lady of Sorrow' was stamped on the bottom.

The evidence packed and sealed, Darby turned her attention to the body.

The veins were a dark purple and stood out against the bleached white skin. Darby examined the facial abrasions. There was no way to tell with any certainty if the abrasions were postmortem or antemortem.

When a body sinks in water, it's knocked around the ocean or river floor. The head is battered against rocks, and fish and crustaceans pick apart the soft flesh in the face. When the body finally surfaces, it is most often mangled; the face, like this one, is practically unrecognizable.

Above the right breast was a moon-shaped tattoo. The colour was from chromogenic bacteria – *Bacillus prodigiosus* and *Bacillus violaceum*. They invaded the dermis and produced patterns resembling tattoos.

Part of a Snickers candy wrapper was stuck to the inside of the thigh. Darby bagged it and then swabbed the vagina and anus for possible DNA evidence. She ran a comb with wool through the woman's pubic hairs and transferred it to an evidence bag.

Darby had finished making her notes when Coop signalled for her.

She carefully fitted the woman's loose skin over her gloved hand. Then she pressed each fingertip against the inkpad and transferred the prints to the print card.

'There's no hair growth on the legs or under the arms,' Darby said. 'Her pubic hair is also trimmed.'

'So her killer allowed her to shave before she died?'

'Maybe.'

'You think the perp might have done it? I ask because there was this case not so long ago, in Philly, where this guy washed his victims in his bathtub after he raped and strangled them. He shaved their legs, arms, even their heads.'

'To remove evidence,' Darby said.

'Exactly.'

'A true psychopath doesn't have empathy for his victims. They're objects, a means to fuelling a fantasy that's often based on sadism. Women who are used as sexual objects are tossed like trash. They're not allowed to shave their legs and put on nail polish. He cared for this woman.'

'If you say so,' Coop said.

Darby fitted a headset equipped with a magnifier lens and light and examined the body for any trace evidence. What she found was mostly silt and twigs.

'Darby?'

She looked up from the body.

'Twelve-point match,' Coop said. 'It's Judith Chen.'

Darby felt a hot, tearing sensation work its way through her chest as she went back to work.

Like Emma Hale, Judith Chen had disappeared for weeks, being held somewhere until her captor decided to put a bullet in the back of her head. Like Emma Hale, Judith Chen had been dumped in the water dressed in the same clothes she was last seen wearing, a small statue of the Virgin Mary sewn into one of her pockets.

'I'll tell Bryson,' Darby said.

7

Darby found Detective Tim Bryson standing in the hallway, talking on his cell phone and looking magazine-cover slick in a camel wool topcoat buttoned over a sharp navy blue suit. Clothing aside, it was impossible not to take notice of him.

The majority of men she knew in their early fifties had gone to seed – big beer bellies and jowls; greying, receding hairlines. Bryson had a sharp jaw line and a youthful face that gave him the look of a man somewhere south of forty. She had seen him at the police gym on more than one occasion. Like Coop, he was a health nut with an amazing body – lean and muscular. In addition to the gym routine and running, she had heard Bryson did yoga once a week at a studio in Cambridge.

Bryson saw her. 'I'll call you back,' he told the caller and hung up.

'It's Judith Chen.'

Bryson nodded and stared at the floor for a long moment. He seemed disappointed, as though he had been holding out hope.

'I think we should check for any recent abductions or missing persons involving female college students,'

Darby said. 'It also wouldn't hurt to warn the local colleges.'

'That's the commissioner's call.'

'I'll talk to her about it.'

Bryson took a long breath through his nose. Times may have changed in terms of equal opportunities for women, but the Boston Police Department still had a frat-house mentality, and Darby knew her new role would rankle many of the boys. She wondered if Bryson felt that way. Time to find out.

'You have a problem with me being appointed to your unit?'

'It wasn't my call,' Bryson said.

'So that would be a yes.'

'Everyone says you're one hell of a lab rat.'

The term was meant as an indirect slap. Bryson was saying she belonged to the lab.

'I'm not interested in playing the whole alpha-dog game,' Darby said. 'It's boring and counter-productive.'

'Excuse me?'

'Save the swinging dick routine for the locker room.'

'You talk to your boyfriend like this?'

'I'm not as polite. I'm trying to be more sensitive to your male sensibilities.'

Darby moved closer, invading his personal space, and saw the fine web of lines around his eyes. 'I know the papers have been pissing all over you for not finding Emma Hale. For the record, I think they're wrong.' She kept her voice calm. 'When we find this asshole, if you want to be the poster boy for the department and smile and wave to the cameras and get the credit, be my guest. Until that moment comes, we need to work together on this. If you don't want to, then by all means keep playing the passive-aggressive victim. It's your choice.'

Bryson didn't answer. Darby left him standing in the hallway.

Darby arrived at the lab and hung Judith Chen's wet clothes inside the drying chamber where they would stay during the weekend. She wasn't holding out hope of finding anything significant. All that time spent underwater had, as with Emma Hale's clothing, washed away anything of value.

Sitting on her desk was a cardboard box containing copies of the murder books and pictures. Darby wanted to get caught up but wanted to read without being distracted. She decided to go home. Coop stayed behind at the lab to work on the statue. He promised to call her later.

By the time she reached her Beacon Hill condo, a good foot of snow had already covered her street. Darby opened the door, placed the box on her couch and deactivated her alarm. She took a long shower, standing under the hot water until it ran cold, and then dressed in jeans and her father's old U-Mass sweatshirt.

Inside the kitchen, she poured herself a generous glass of Booker's bourbon. Her windows faced Suffolk University. The college was directly across the street. Last fall, Judith Chen had been attending classes inside that building. Now her corpse was lying inside the cold room waiting to be autopsied.

Darby took a long sip of bourbon. She refilled the glass and carried it to her office.

The former occupants had used the space as a nursery; one wall was still painted a light blue with clouds. She had only lived here for three months, and during that time, she had purchased an L-shaped desk for the corner, a bookcase and comfortable leather chair she set up by the window overlooking her back porch and the neighbour's tiny backyard.

Darby grabbed the box from the couch, set it up on her desk and removed a copy of Emma Hale's murder book.

8

Darby took out the autopsy pictures and crime-scene photographs and tacked them to one side of the wall. On the other side she tacked the pictures she had taken of Judith Chen along with the copies ID had given her. Chen's murder book was incomplete. Tim Bryson was at the station filling out the report.

Vaginal and anal swabs for Judith Chen had tested negative for semen. All that time spent underwater had washed away trace evidence and DNA – if there was any DNA to be found. There was no way to tell for certain if Chen's abductor had sex with her. With floaters, the usual evidence – tearing and abrasions – was gone, devoured by decomposition.

The good majority of crimes involving women more often than not contained some underlying sexual component. If that was the case here – and from a statistical point of view, it should be – then why did he sew a Virgin Mary statue in their pockets?

Maybe this wasn't about sex. Maybe these two college girls were chosen to fill some psychological need. Darby grabbed the murder books and settled into the chair with her bourbon, the dead women hanging on the wall behind her, looking down, watching.

Judith Chen was nineteen, the youngest daughter of a middle-class family from Camp Hill, Pennsylvania. Her father was a plumber. She decided to attend Suffolk University because the college had offered the best financial aid package. Boston was an expensive city to live, and with student housing tight, Judith Chen and a roommate rented one half of a duplex in Natick – a forty-minute commute by train. She took out a college loan and paid for her living expenses with the money she earned from her two jobs – the first as a waitress at a Legal Seafood restaurant in Boston's theatre district, the second job as a sales assistant at the Abercrombie & Fitch store at the Natick Mall.

Emma Hale was also nineteen, the only child of Jonathan Hale, Boston's top real-estate developer. Emma lived in a multimillion-dollar Back Bay penthouse with its own parking garage for her convertible BMW. A pop star from the eighties lived in the second penthouse suite.

Jonathan Hale was a powerful man with a Rolodex full of important names eager to provide favours. When his only child was reported missing, the operating theory was a possible kidnapping. Boston police acted swiftly and contacted the FBI.

Commissioner Chadzynski ordered the CSU lab members to examine the penthouse. It was a ridiculous request – Emma Hale was last seen leaving the apartment of her friend, Kimberly Jackson. Darby knew the real reason behind the commissioner's agenda. Thanks to the proliferation of hit TV shows depicting forensic technicians as gun-toting investigators who ran around interviewing suspects, their testimony carried a lot of weight with juries. Lawyers called it the 'CSI effect'. Seeing TV footage of real crime scene investigators heading into the building would play well with the public, making it look as though everyone was cooperating, working hard and pooling their resources to find the missing Harvard student. It was great PR.

Darby read through the pages listing all of Emma's belongings – the walk-in closet full of designer dresses, shoes and handbags; the four jewellery boxes containing necklaces, earrings and bracelets purchased at upscale stores like Cartier and Shreve, Crump & Low. One box held nothing but watches.

On paper, the two women appeared to live extremely divergent lifestyles. Emma was rich, Judith lower middle-class. Tim Bryson and his CSU team had produced an exhaustive list of the women's movements and activities to see if they intersected at one common point – a bar, charity group, gym or dance club. Bryson had examined each woman's computer to see if they belonged to a similar chat room or a social networking site like Facebook. No connection was found.

Both women had shared the loss of a family member. Emma's mother died of melanoma – the same skin cancer that had killed Darby's mother. Emma was eight when her mother died. Judith's older sister was killed by a drunk driver. Neither woman was seeing a local psychiatrist or campus counsellor.

Both women were college freshmen. Bryson had investigated the possible connection that they had applied to the same college. Emma Hale had applied to Harvard, Yale and Stanford and was accepted to all three. Judith Chen hadn't applied to those colleges.

At the moment, the only common trait the two women had was that they had disappeared on their way home. There were no witnesses to either abduction. Did they know their abductor, or had they, for some reason, accepted a ride from a stranger? Or were they both forced into his vehicle?

Family and friends were interviewed. Darby read each interview carefully. When she finished, she read through them again, hoping to find a common thread. She didn't find one.

Darby put the murder books on the floor and went to the kitchen to refill her glass. She stepped back inside the office and turned her attention to the women hanging on the wall.

Her gaze automatically shifted to the crime-scene photographs. The dead, she had discovered, were much easier to handle. Everything was black and white. The living contained too many shades of grey.

The killer didn't care how they looked dead. What drew him to these two college women was something in the way they lived.

The physical differences between the two women were startling.

Emma Hale was nearly model perfect, with a stunning face and body shaped by a strict diet and physical regimen overseen by a private trainer at the exclusive LA Fitness Club in the lobby of the Ritz Carlton on Tremont. She had a nose job a month after her sixteenth birthday. The Manhattan surgeon who performed the rhinoplasty also did her boob job when she was eighteen.

Judith Chen was slim and flat-chested. She didn't belong to a gym. Friends and family members described her as quiet and reserved, serious about her studies. She had graduated at the top of her high-school class. She had applied to and had been accepted to some of the top colleges in Massachusetts – Boston College, Boston University and Tufts. Those schools couldn't offer the same financial aid package as Suffolk.

According to the interviews, Emma Hale was the polar opposite. She was outgoing, popular and gregarious. The young woman wanted for nothing. Daddy provided everything – the penthouse, the clothes and jewellery, the convertible BMW.

Darby felt the sting of class resentment – not because Emma Hale was born into a rich family but because the young woman didn't have to work for anything. Darby had little use or patience for a pretty party girl who went through life shopping and going on European and Caribbean vacations; summers spent in Nantucket and weekend nights spent drinking at the clubs; long days recovering from her hangover on friends' boats, her rich daddy picking up the entire tab.

Here was a picture of Emma Hale attending some ritzy party. An antique platinum locket dangled above her ample cleavage. Here was another picture of the pretty co-ed with her arm around a good-looking man with dark hair and brown eyes – the boyfriend, Tony Pace, a Harvard sophomore.

Something twitched deep in Darby's mind, a twinge of familiarity. Was it something about the boyfriend? No. Bryson had interviewed Pace. He hadn't attended the party. He had the flu and stayed in his dorm room. All of his alibis checked out. Pace agreed to a polygraph and passed. What was it, then?

Here was a picture of the couple standing on a boat, their skin deeply tanned, smiles perfect, not a wrinkle on them. Darby wondered why she was focusing so much on Emma Hale and switched her attention to a picture of Judith Chen dressed in sweats, a black Labrador puppy held in her arms as she smiled to the camera. Here was a picture of Chen with her roommate.

Darby paced inside her office. Every few minutes she stopped and looked back to the wall to see if something in the pictures or the women's faces grabbed her attention. When it didn't happen, she went back to pacing or stopped to pick up trinkets and held them in her hands for a moment before putting them down. She kept neatening her desk, making sure everything was in its proper place and alignment.

The wind blew, shaking the old windows. Blinding white sheets of snow whipped across the old brick buildings. Darby finished the last of the bourbon. She felt relaxed, calm. She thought about spring. It felt years away. Emma Hale had a summer home on Nantucket. She played tennis and golf and spent days on the boat. She wore designer dresses and lots of jewellery.

(the locket)

What about it? The locket, Darby knew, contained a picture of Emma's mother. What else? Jonathan Hale had identified the locket, which Emma was wearing when her body was found. She was wearing the locket when her body surfaced. She was wearing the locket . . .

'Oh Jesus,' Darby said out loud, hands trembling as she reached for the murder book.

9

Darby flipped through the pages, stopping when she reached the one containing the list of items found in the jewellery boxes located in Emma Hale's walk-in closet. Here it was: 'Oval antique locket with platinum chain, middle drawer, jewellery box #2.'

She grabbed the phone and called Tim Bryson. The phone seemed to ring forever. She felt a surge of relief when he picked up.

'A week after Emma Hale's abduction, you and your team went through her house and catalogued her jewellery.'

'That's right,' Bryson said.

'I'm looking at the list of Emma's jewellery. It says an oval antique locket with platinum chain was found in the middle drawer of the second jewellery box.'

'Where are you going with this?' Bryson sounded put out. Was he still sore from their talk at the morgue?

'When Emma Hale's body was found, she was wearing a platinum chain and locket,' Darby said. 'It's listed on the inventory page.'

'The woman owned a lot of jewellery. It's possible she owned a similar locket. I remember seeing a lot of necklaces that looked the same.'

'This necklace is unique. Hale gave it to his daughter for Christmas a few years ago, when she was sixteen.'

'Why would her killer go back to her penthouse for a necklace after she had been abducted? It doesn't make any sense.'

'Did your team take pictures?'

'Tons of them,' Bryson said.

'They're not included in the file you gave me.'

'They're back at the station.'

'Where?'

'ID has them. I never asked for copies since the whole thing was a monumental waste of time.'

Darby checked her watch. It was after seven. ID was closed. Coop was at the lab but he couldn't access the ID office. It was a separate department.

'I'll call Hale and see where he stored Emma's things,' she said.

'She's been in the ground for, what, five months? You think he's held on to her jewellery?'

'There's one way to find out.' Darby found Hale's numbers listed in the file. 'I'll call you if I find out anything. Thanks for your help, Tim.'

Darby hung up and dialled Jonathan Hale's home number. Hopefully the man would allow her to view his daughter's belongings, all of which had been released back into his possession. Hale didn't have a high opinion of BPD. The man had openly criticized the department in the press.

A woman with broken English answered the

phone. Mr Hale wasn't home, she said. She wouldn't elaborate.

Darby explained who she was and why she was calling, and then asked for a number where he could be reached. The woman didn't have a number – she was just the housekeeper, she said – but offered to take a message. Darby left her numbers.

Darby tapped the phone against her leg, wanting to do something. The matter, she knew, could wait. There was no urgency.

Emma Hale had lived in the Back Bay – a quick ride on the T, which was still running. Darby wondered if the young woman's belongings were stored inside the building, maybe even in her home. A building like that probably had someone who worked the front desk.

Darby didn't want to wait, wasn't good at waiting. She needed to know. She stuffed Emma Hale's murder book into her backpack and grabbed her coat.

10

Emma Hale's building had a concierge who, in addition to tending to the needs of the thirteen owners, also acted as security guard. The man's name was Jimmy Marsh. He sat behind an ornate front counter with two crystal vases on each end holding lilies. Soft, decorative lighting offset the glare of the six security monitors.

Darby introduced herself and then asked about Emma Hale's penthouse.

'Mr Hale hasn't cleaned it out yet,' Marsh said. He saw the look of surprise on her face and added, 'Some people grieve differently, you know?'

'So everything's still upstairs.'

'I can't say for sure. Nobody is allowed up there. After Emma's body was found, Mr Hale asked me to change the locks.' Marsh sighed and rubbed a liver-spotted hand over his bald head. He was a big man, thick and hard with fat, with a crooked nose that had been broken one too many times. 'Emma was such a beautiful girl, beautiful and charming,' he said. 'Every Sunday morning she'd go out for coffee and bring me back a blueberry muffin from the place I love right around the corner. I'd offer to pay her, but she always said no. That's the kind of girl she was.'

'Sounds like you two were close.'

'I wouldn't say that. She was a good kid, and I kept an eye on her. I promised her dad. Mr Hale owns this building – he owns half the buildings here in the Back Bay. He's a very powerful man.'

So I keep hearing, Darby thought. 'Do you work here full time, Mr Marsh?'

'Yeah, me and this other guy, Porny – Dwight Pornell is his name. Dwight generally takes the night shifts, but his old lady had a baby, and I've been covering for him. We see everyone who comes and goes. That's why this desk is set up here right by the front door. Every guest who comes in is required to sign in right here.' Marsh tapped the open leather guest book set up on the counter for emphasis. 'We check licences and make photocopies of 'em. Security here is tight, Miss McCormick.'

'How long have you been keeping this guest book?'

'Ever since nine-eleven,' he said. 'That changed everything. You can't go anywhere without signing your name and flashing your licence.'

'Do you keep all the copies?'

'Yes ma'am.'

'The security cameras,' Darby said. 'How long have you had them?'

'They were put in place when Mr Hale was rehabbing the building back in, oh, ninety-six or so. They watch the front doors, the delivery area – we got a camera inside the private parking garage. We take security here very seriously.'

'You keep mentioning that, Mr Marsh. Is there something you want to get off your chest?'

'Me? No, I'm just a lowly security type. Your buddy there, Mr *GQ* Detective, he thought I might have had something to do with what happened to Emma. You ever walk around with a microscope up your ass?'

'Can't say that I have.'

'Well, let me tell you, it don't feel too comfortable. I think if Detective Bryson put the same amount of effort into the investigation as he does how his hair looked on camera he would have found Emma. Are you any closer to catching the son of a bitch who killed her?'

'We're investigating several leads.'

'Which is cop-speak for you don't have jack shit.'

'How long have you been retired from the force?'

'I worked patrol in Dorchester for twenty years. That's why Mr Hale gave me this job. It's a great gig. I don't have to wonder if some dipshit I pull over is going to pop a cap in my ass.'

'Mr Marsh, you said you put new locks on Emma's home.'

'That's right.'

'Do you have a set of keys?'

'The penthouse was released back to Mr Hale.'

'You didn't answer my question.'

'I have a spare set, yes, but no one is allowed up

there. I'm sorry, but I can't let you up there without his permission.'

'Then you better get on the phone.'

'Mr Hale's out of town.'

'How do you know that?'

'He was here Wednesday or so and happened to mention it to me.'

'Why was he here?'

'He wanted to go up to his daughter's home.'

'Why?'

'I don't know, and I didn't ask.' Marsh leaned back in his chair, the spring squeaking under his weight, and clasped his hands behind his head. 'Tell you what. Why don't you come back here Monday morning and –'

'Maybe I wasn't clear,' Darby said. 'I need to get inside Emma's penthouse tonight.'

'I don't have his number.'

'But you *do* have an emergency number to call in case there's a problem.'

'The number I have goes to his answering service,' Marsh said. 'You think I have the man's home phone number? You know how many people he employs? Come back Monday.'

'I can have a court order here within the hour.'

Marsh stared at the makeup-covered scar on her cheek. Darby took out her cell phone and started dialling.

'I'll see what I can do,' Marsh said, standing. He

walked into the back room behind the desk and shut the door.

Darby paced the small lobby, listening to the wind howling outside the front doors. Why had Marsh given her such a hard time? Was it because she was a woman? She wondered if Tim Bryson would have received the same treatment. Maybe Marsh was simply acting in what he believed was the best interest of his employer.

Darby turned her attention to the security monitors. One camera monitored the front door. Two swept the street, what little of it she could see; the snow was coming down at a furious clip. Another one was installed above a large bay door – probably the delivery area for bulky items such as furniture. The other two cameras kept watch on the garage door and the parking garage. If Emma's abductor had, in fact, come back for the necklace, how did he manage to get through without being caught?

Twenty minutes later, Marsh came out of his office. 'Emma's place is on the fifteenth floor,' he said, handing Darby a set of keys.

'Alarm?'

Marsh glanced at a computer console. 'It's off. I think it's been turned off for a while now.'

'Is that unusual?'

'I remember Mr Hale had it shut off when you people were running in and out of Emma's place. You'll need to talk to him about it.'

'Did you speak to him?'

'No, I spoke to his assistant, Abigail. She spoke to Mr Hale. He wanted you to know you have his full cooperation.'

'I'd like Abigail's number,' Darby said. 'I'll collect it when I drop off the keys.'

Darby rode the elevator to the fifteenth floor. She stepped into a dimly lit hallway containing two doors. At the end she saw a delivery elevator.

Emma's door was on the right. Darby unzipped her coat and then slipped on a pair of latex gloves. She checked the two locks and didn't see any signs of forced entry. She unlocked the door, reached inside and found the light switch.

Emma Hale's home was two floors of blonde oak hardwood floors and windows that stretched from floor to ceiling. Darby was taken back by the enormous amount of space. The main room, twice the size of her condo, was magazine-showroom perfect, from the modern-type furniture and rugs to the Jackson Pollock-inspired oil paintings and knock-off Greek statues. The kitchen had black granite countertops, a Viking range and a Sub-Zero refrigerator. Nice living for a Harvard student.

The air had a stale quality to it, and the heat was on, as though Emma was expected to return. Darby wanted to roam through the rooms to get to know Emma better. First, she needed to find out about the necklace.

The master bedroom was most likely on the second floor. Darby climbed the spiral staircase. The penthouse, she had read, had four bedrooms and two bathrooms, one of which held a Jacuzzi tub and a plasma-screen TV. She was about to step into the hallway when the lights went out.

11

Blackout, Darby thought. The snowstorm must have knocked out the building's power.

This wasn't the winter's first blackout. The endless cold days and even colder nights with their mean, freezing winds had knocked down power lines all over the city, sometimes for hours. Darby hoped that wasn't the case here. She hadn't brought a flashlight.

She did, however, have some light. Directly across the hallway was a bedroom. The door was open and Darby saw a large bay window overlooking Arlington Street and part of the Public Garden. The street lights were on, as were the lights for the Ritz Carlton. The hotel must have had a backup generator – no, wait, the lights were on in the brownstones across the street. The storm must have knocked down the power lines for this side of the street. Wonderful.

Looking down the hallway, Darby saw another opened door; a dim rectangle of silver light spilled onto the hardwood floor and across the wall. She doubted the walk-in closet had windows. To examine the jewellery boxes would require a flashlight.

Two choices: she could wait here in the dark until the lights came on or she could go back downstairs and see if Marsh had a flashlight she could borrow.

Darby placed her hands on the railing and made her way down the stairs. Her eyes had adjusted to the dark, and she could see well enough.

The creak of a floorboard above her made her stop. Darby spun around, heart racing, and looked to the second-floor hallway. It was empty. She was alone.

Darby moved up the steps, another part of her mind taking control, reminding her of the night over two decades ago when she was fifteen, leaning over the second-floor banister of her home and staring down into the semi-dark foyer convinced an intruder had somehow broken into the house. Her rational mind told her she was being ridiculous. All the downstairs doors and windows were locked. She was alone and she was safe. Then she saw a black-gloved hand grip the railing.

Darby reminded herself she wasn't fifteen; she was thirty-seven, an adult. The creak she had just heard was probably nothing more than the sound of a big empty home settling in a particularly cold winter.

Still, she didn't move. Something about the hallway was off. It took her a moment to recognize it.

The rectangle of street light she had seen earlier on the floor and wall outside the room down the hall was different. The light was narrower now – not by much but there was a perceptible difference. The door had been wide open. Now it was three-quarters shut. Someone was in here, she was sure of it.

Only one way to play it.

Mouth dry and heart hammering against her ribcage, Darby removed the SIG from her shoulder holster. Her other hand was inside her jacket pocket. She took out her cell phone, and as she dialled 911, she kept her eyes focused on the bedroom door.

'This is Darby McCormick from the Boston Crime Lab.' She spoke loud and clear. 'I'm calling to report an intruder at four-six-two Commonwealth Avenue. I need you to send multiple backup units. Have them cover all of the exits.'

Shoving the phone back inside her pocket, she climbed the remaining steps. She stepped into the hallway, stopped. No movement, no sound. She spoke into the silence.

'Put your hands behind your head and step into the hallway, nice and slow.'

'I have no intention of harming you.'

The deep, male voice had a slight accent – British or Australian, she wasn't sure which. It came from inside the room down the hall.

'Step into the hallway with your hands behind your head,' Darby said.

The door opened and the intruder moved into the square of light, his hands clasped behind his head. The man stepped back, his face covered in shadows. He was tall, well over six feet, and wore a long topcoat and black shoes.

'You're much taller than I expected, Miss McCormick.'

'Do I know you?'

'We haven't officially met.'

'What's your name?'

'I'm not ready to share just yet.'

'How do you know me?'

'You're Boston's Persephone, the queen of the dead. Or is it queen of the damned?'

His topcoat was open. Underneath his suit jacket Darby caught a glimpse of a shoulder holster under his left arm.

'This is what you're going to do,' Darby said. 'With your left hand, I want you to take out your weapon. Make a sudden move and you'll be on a feeding tube for the rest of your life.'

The intruder wore black leather gloves. He slipped a finger inside the handgun's trigger and slowly lifted it out of the holster – a nine-millimetre. He dropped it to the floor.

'Now kick it over to me.'

He did.

'Keep your hands behind your head and kneel down on the floor. Then you're going to lie on your stomach.'

'I hope you're not going to shoot me in the back of the head.'

'Why would you think that?'

'I understand Emma Hale was shot in the back of the head.'

'Why are you interested in Emma Hale?'

'I might be inclined to answer your question if you answer one of mine.'

'You're not in a position to trade.'

'Then I'm afraid I'll have to leave.'

'That's not going to happen.' Darby cocked the trigger and stepped forward. 'Down on the floor. I'm not going to ask you again.'

'I saw you this past weekend at your parents' gravesite. Were you asking your father the beat cop for advice? Or were you seeking inspiration from your mother, the coupon-clipping housewife? I bet it was your mother. She kept a lot of secrets hidden underneath her apron, didn't she?'

Darby heard sirens. A moment later, flashing blue and white lights reflected off the windows and walls.

His hands clasped behind his head, the intruder stepped forward, into the street light shining outside the bedroom door. Darby got a good look at his face and her breath caught.

12

The man's eyes were completely black, devoid of colour. His facial skin was unnaturally pale, stretched tightly across the bone.

'Stay where you are,' Darby said.

The intruder kept walking. Darby backed up into the doorway of the bathroom.

'Emma is fortunate to have someone so dedicated working on her behalf,' the intruder said. 'You could be sitting at your new home in Beacon Hill, and yet here you are searching through the dark for answers. I wonder why that is.'

He stepped into the spare bedroom and gently shut the door as if he was retiring for the night. She heard him click the lock.

Next she heard a rattling sound – the window, he was opening the window. Why? *There must be a fire escape.*

Darby made her way down the spiral staircase. When she reached the living room, she saw a thin sliver of light near the bottom of the front door. The hallway lights were on. *He must have tripped the circuit breaker.*

She took the stairs. Marsh was sitting behind the

desk, reading a magazine, when he looked up and saw Darby racing down the stairs.

'Where does Emma's fire escape lead?'

'To the alley around the corner,' Marsh said, standing. 'What's going on?'

Darby didn't answer. She was already out the front door, running down the steps and through the heavy snow. Patrol cars were trying to edge their way through the traffic. She ran around the corner, past the ramp for the building's garage. The alley was empty. Snow whipping across her face, she shielded her eyes as she moved down the alley, the SIG out, ready to fire.

When she reached the end of the alley she saw the fire-escape ladder rattling in the wind near a dumpster. Fresh footprints were in the snow under the ladder. Darby followed them as they curved to the right onto Arlington Street.

Cars were stuck in traffic, drivers and passengers gawking at her as she moved into the street, looking through the blowing curtains of snow for the intruder. Darby couldn't see him. The man with the strange eyes was gone.

Jimmy Marsh said the electrical box for Emma's penthouse was inside the walk-in closet. Armed with a flashlight borrowed from a patrolman, Darby pulled back the row of dresses and found the main circuit breaker. She flipped the switch. The lights were back.

The closet was long and narrow, packed with seemingly endless rows of clothes and shoes meticulously arranged in professionally crafted organizers made of polished oak. The jewellery boxes were actually four small cabinet drawers lined with red velvet.

In the second drawer Darby discovered an empty space between two stunning diamond necklaces. She flipped to the page in the murder book, found the listing for the contents of the jewellery box. The antique locket and chain was listed between a gold diamond necklace and another necklace with a platinum chain. The necklaces were here; the locket and chain were missing.

Still, she wanted to see the pictures CSU had taken of the jewellery boxes.

Darby called Coop. He was still at the lab. She explained what had happened and what she needed. Coop offered to wait at the lab until someone from ID came to unlock the office and retrieve the pictures. He promised to deliver them to the Hale building.

Tim Bryson didn't answer his phone. Darby left a message about the missing necklace, hung up and then went to work on the spare bedroom where the intruder escaped. The door was locked, so she had to crawl up the fire escape to enter the bedroom. There was no sign of forced entry on the window. She searched around the floor and through the snow for any evidence the intruder might have dropped.

13

Walter Smith carried Hannah down the cellar steps. When he reached the door to her room, he switched Hannah to his shoulder.

The key card was tucked in his front jean pocket. Walter stepped up next to the card reader. It beeped. He punched in the four numbers. The electronic locks clicked back. He opened the door and gently set Hannah down on her new bed.

Walter turned on the small lamp on the night-stand. Hannah's nose had stopped bleeding but blood had stained the front of her wool jacket. He took off her hat, jacket and gloves and folded them on top of the washing machine down the hall. Then he went upstairs.

His first stop was the garage. He opened up the trunk and removed the extra blankets Mary had told him to pack. His Blessed Mother said that if he ever got stopped by the police, they would search the trunk. *If the police find blood, Walter, they'll take you away and you'll never see me again.* Walter threw the blankets into a garbage bag.

The bathroom was on the second floor. Walter opened the medicine cabinet. He heard a car engine racing down the street.

Was it the police? Had they found him? Panicked, he turned off the bathroom light and looked out the tiny window.

A big truck was ploughing its way through the snow. It came to a stop at the end of his street, and in the street light he saw the words 'AJ Movers' printed on the side of the truck. The big engine coughed as it turned right and headed up the steep hill, stopping in front of a grey clapboard ranch that had been vacant for well over two years. Someone was moving into the Peterson home.

Walter relaxed. He grabbed the bottle of hydrogen peroxide and a roll of toilet paper and headed back to the basement.

For the next half hour he cleaned the blood from Hannah's face. Her nose was swollen but it wasn't broken. Good. He didn't want her disfigured in any way.

Walter made one more trip upstairs, to the kitchen. He filled a large Ziploc bag with crushed ice and placed it on Hannah's nose. Her clothes were wet and smelled of fried food. Her sweatshirt was rolled up; he could see her stomach. She had a small, strawberry-coloured birthmark on her waist. He touched it. Her skin was warm and smooth.

Walter rubbed his hand across her stomach. He realized what he was doing and yanked his hand away, disgusted with himself.

'I'm sorry, Hannah. That was wrong.'

Hannah didn't stir, didn't move.

'I'm sorry I hurt you. It was an accident.' Walter hoped she could hear him.

The ice had melted. He took off Hannah's boots and socks. She had pretty feet.

Walter shut off the light, about to head upstairs, when he thought of Hannah's wet clothes. He wanted her to be comfortable.

In the dark, with his eyes shut, Walter slipped off her jeans then worked the sweatshirt and T-shirt over her head. Walter opened his eyes when he reached the hallway. Mary would be proud of his self-control.

He put the wet clothes in the washing machine. When he came back into the bedroom, he saw the outline of Hannah's body in the soft light from the hallway. She wore nice cotton underwear – the simple kind good girls wore, not the sinful stuff he saw in magazines and on TV. Emma had worn that kind of underwear – expensive, promiscuous. Hannah wasn't like that. Mary said Hannah was a good girl, with a good heart.

Hannah's breasts swelled beneath her bra. Walter stared at her chest, wanting to touch her again. The time would come for that later, after they got to know each other, after he showed Hannah how much he loved her and how happy she would be here with him.

His Blessed Mother was trying to speak to him. Mary's voice sounded far away. He closed his eyes and concentrated.

It's okay, Mary said.

Walter didn't move. His skin felt hot, the scars covering his face and body throbbing with heat.

Here, let me help you.

Walter felt his Blessed Mother working through him. Mary unbuttoned his shirt. Mary pulled off his T-shirt and unbuckled his belt. Then she gently guided him to the opposite side of the bed and moved back the sheets. Mary didn't have to tell him what to do next.

Walter climbed on top of Hannah and laid his head against her chest. He could hear the soft beating of her heart. He closed his eyes, knowing he could stay here forever, just like this, pressed up against her skin. He buried his face in her soft hair.

'I love you, Hannah. I love you so much.' Walter kissed Hannah's cheek and, unable to contain his joy any longer, started to cry.

14

Darby stood inside Emma Hale's closet, holding the photograph ID had taken of the second jewellery box. An antique locket with a platinum chain lay on the red felt between the two diamond necklaces. She handed the photo to Bryson.

'I checked everything against the photographs and the inventory list. Everything's here except the antique locket. There's no question Emma's killer came back for it.'

Bryson stared at the photograph for a long moment, his expression clearly pained.

'Marsh pulled tonight's security tapes,' Darby said. 'I've already got them bagged. They only keep a month's worth of tapes here. The rest are stored in Hale's security office in Newton. Hale's supposed to be home sometime over the weekend, but I don't want to wait that long. Hale's personal assistant is a woman named Abigail. I want to talk to her and see if we can get inside the office first thing tomorrow morning.'

Bryson placed the photograph back inside the small evidence box sitting on top of a leather ottoman. 'Patrol's still sweeping the area for the intruder, but I'm sure he's long gone,' he said. 'Darby, this man you met, you said his eyes were entirely black.'

'It was like I was looking at a Halloween mask.' Thinking about it again, even in the light, made her shiver.

'The power was out,' Bryson said. 'It was dark, so maybe you saw –'

'The man's eyes were black, Tim. No colour whatsoever – no pupil, no iris, nothing, just black. Everything he wore was black – his coat and shoes, his pants, shirt and gloves. He's between six one and six three. His face was very pale and his black hair was cut short. I could pick him out of a lineup.'

'Do you know him?'

'No. Why?'

'He knew your name, he saw you at your parents' gravesite,' Bryson said. 'I got the feeling he knew you.'

'I have no idea who he is or what he was doing here.'

'Did he seem familiar in any way?'

'I definitely would have remembered meeting someone like that.'

Darby felt cold all over. Her palms were damp. She shoved them in her jean pockets.

'I talked to Marsh,' she said. 'He swears he doesn't know anyone matching that description.'

'You think he's telling the truth?'

'My gut instinct says yes. Still, it wouldn't hurt to hold his feet to the fire.'

'I agree. For the moment, let's assume Mr Marsh is

telling the truth. If that's the case, then the intruder didn't walk through the front door, he found another way in. You said he left by the fire escape.'

'I already checked the window,' Darby said. 'There's no sign of forced entry. He found another way in – maybe the same way Emma's killer found. I doubt either of them walked through the front door.'

Bryson turned his attention to the electrical box. 'You must have surprised him coming up the stairs. He probably shut off the power hoping the darkness would make you leave – at the very least it would give him enough cover to slip away. Then he moved behind the door and waited in the bathroom. Problem was you had already spotted him. He heard you call the police and realized he was trapped.'

'That's the way I see it,' Darby said. 'Has Jonathan Hale hired anyone to look into his daughter's death?'

'Not to my knowledge. You don't think this man you met is working for Hale, do you?'

'I'm trying to find a reason as to what he was doing here.'

'If this man is, in fact, working for Hale, why didn't he tell you? Why go through all this drama and subterfuge?'

'That's a good question,' Darby said. 'Either he's working for Hale or he's working independently for reasons we don't understand.'

'How are you doing?'

'I'm fine.'

'You look a little shaky.'

'I'm coming off the adrenaline high. I'm going to get to work.'

'Hold on.' Bryson eased the closet door shut. 'I think we got off on the wrong foot back at the morgue.'

'Forget about it.'

'No, I want to clear the air.' Bryson scratched his chin. 'Look, I was a bit of an asshole. Am I pissed about how this whole thing went down? I'd be lying if I said I wasn't. But what you said about me wanting the credit, that's bullshit. I'm not looking for the limelight. The press is up my ass, putting my name and picture in the papers. I can't control that. If you can help me find this guy, that's all that matters.'

'Good, then we're on the same page.'

'You said Hale has a personal assistant.'

'Marsh did. He said the woman's name is Abigail. I'll get the number.'

'I can do it.'

'Actually, I want to go and take a look at the security system.'

Bryson opened the door. 'Nice work on the necklace,' he said.

The master bedroom held modern-type bureaus and a beautiful canapé bed. Like the spare bedroom, the floor-to-ceiling window overlooked Arlington Street and part of the Public Garden. Darby imagined what it might have felt like to go to bed every night with this stunning view of the city. She wondered if Emma Hale took the time to appreciate the view and her good fortune. Like many rich kids, the young woman probably took it for granted.

Darby knew she harboured a grudge against the rich. The truth was she didn't know Emma Hale. Maybe the young woman did appreciate her good fortune. Darby suspected her anger had something to do with a comment the intruder made about her mother being a coupon-clipping housewife. After Big Red died, Sheila McCormick worked double shifts at her nursing job and managed not only to keep a roof over their heads and food on the table, but had saved every extra penny to help Darby pay her way through college.

Coop stood in the hallway, working a wad of chewing gum between his front teeth while someone from ID photographed the handgun, a Beretta.

'The serial number is still on it,' Coop said to her. 'Hopefully the trace will lead somewhere good. You happen to check out the ammo?'

'No.'

'Armour piercing,' Coop said. 'You're lucky the son of a bitch didn't try and shoot.'

'I need to go downstairs. When I come back, I want to process the closet first. Then I want to check the CSU inventory list to see if our boy took anything else besides the necklace.'

'I'll come with you.'

Darby saw the look of concern in Coop's eyes. She had an idea what was coming.

Coop waited until they were alone in the hallway.

'I'm staying with you tonight,' he said. 'Please, no arguments.'

'I'll be fine.' Darby pressed the elevator button. 'There's no reason for you to –'

'Look, Wonder Woman, why don't you hang up the cape and give it a rest, okay?'

'Wonder Woman doesn't wear a cape. Besides, I'm sure you'd like to get back to Row-day-oh. Maybe you can sleep in and then watch another one of those uplifting cowboy-in-love movies.'

Coop blew a bubble, popped it.

'I know men look at you as some, I don't know, some wonderfully delicate, fragile bird that needs protection,' he said. 'I don't look at you that way. I've worked out with you. I've seen you spar in the boxing ring and work the speed bag. Half of them don't know you could kick their ass sideways over the course of a weekend and not break a sweat. I'm not debating your superhero status. I want to stay over because I'll sleep better knowing you're safe.'

Once again, Coop had managed to scale her protective walls and see into her true feelings. She was glad he made the offer. She didn't want to be alone.

'This is the part where you graciously thank me,' Coop said.

'I don't have an extra bed.'

'But you do have a queen-size bed.'

'Forget it.'

'I was going to suggest you take the couch. Why are you always thinking about sex? It's very disturbing.'

15

Jimmy Marsh was seated behind the front desk, giving his statement to Tim Bryson's partner, Detective Cliff Watts.

Darby looked to the monitors set up behind the desk. 'Tell me about the security cameras,' she said.

'The two above the front door cover the door and the street,' Marsh said. 'There's another camera for the delivery area, and the other two watch the garage – one for the garage door, the other for the parking lot. We see everyone who comes and goes inside this building.'

'But you don't have a security camera on the alley.'

'No. I know where you're heading. This person you met, whoever he is, he might have left by the fire escape but he couldn't have gained access that way. You can't stand on top of the dumpster and reach the ladder. It's too high.'

'Let me ask you this. If you wanted to get inside the building without being seen, how would you go about doing it?'

'You can't.'

'How do you gain access to the parking garage?'

'You need a garage door opener.'

'So if I had one and drove up to the door, I could open it.'

'Well, yeah, in theory,' Marsh said.

'And if I have a garage door opener and entered the garage, you wouldn't see me.'

'No, but I'd see your car on the monitor.'

'Do you know the make and model of every car?'

'You have to register your car at the front desk.'

'Do you know the make and model of every car?'

'I've got a pretty good idea. Twenty-two people live inside the building. About half of them have cars.'

Darby looked at the security monitor aimed at the garage door. 'That camera is pointed at a passenger's side window,' she said. 'If a car pulled up to the garage, you wouldn't be able to see who is behind the wheel.'

Marsh didn't answer.

Darby turned to him. The man was staring at the monitor, rubbing his tongue over his teeth.

'Mr Marsh?'

'You're right,' he said. 'I couldn't see who was behind the wheel.'

'Can you *hear* the garage door open?'

'I watch those monitors very carefully, Miss McCormick.'

'I'm not questioning your dedication to your job or your abilities. Every security system has a flaw, and the person who entered Emma's penthouse tonight found it. Now, can you hear the garage door open?'

'No.'

'Do you have someone posted inside the garage checking people as they come in?'

'No.'

'And if you were occupied with something else, like a delivery or a phone call, you wouldn't necessarily see someone who entered through the parking garage.'

'I guess it's possible.'

'And if I didn't have a garage door opener and was, say, hanging out around the corner of the building, I could sneak inside once the garage door went up, correct?'

'I suppose,' he said.

'Does the security camera inside the garage record what goes on in there?'

'Yes, it does.'

'Okay. Now if I was a resident, after I parked my car, how would I get to my unit? Do I have to come back out and come through the front door?'

'There's a private elevator inside the garage which takes you up to your floor.'

'That would be the delivery elevator I saw at the end of Emma's hallway.'

'Yes.'

'Is there a camera installed inside the elevator?'

'No.'

'What about on the individual floors?'

'We just monitor the outside of the building.'

'That's what I thought,' Darby said. 'Thank you for your help, Mr Marsh.'

16

Walter Smith woke during the early hours of Saturday morning trembling with anticipation. So much to do, so much to do; he threw off the covers and raced out of his room.

The spare bedroom, stacked with barbells and weight benches, was dark. The shades were always drawn to block out the sunlight. He didn't turn on the lights. He could see well enough.

For the next hour he worked out in the dark with the heavy weights slowly, feeling the muscles burn. Despite the scarring and multiple corrective surgeries, he had achieved decent definition in his chest, arms and shoulders. He thought his legs had improved dramatically.

Sweating and fatigued, he stepped into the dark bathroom and took a long shower. He dried himself off, wrapped the towel around his waist and stood on the damp bathmat.

This was the part he hated. Looking in the mirror always upset him.

Walter summoned his courage and turned on the light.

Ropes and mats of brown and maroon-coloured scars covered his entire chest. Scars did not have any elasticity; they had halted his best efforts at building significant muscle definition.

The fire had burned over ninety per cent of his body. The remaining healthy skin had been used to rebuild his eyelids. The plastic surgeons had done what they could.

Walter had replaced the toupee provided by the Shriners Burn Center with an expensive and realistic-looking hair system. His left ear had been rebuilt using pig cartilage. His left hand didn't work, the tendons permanently damaged, his fingers nothing more than a claw.

A wave of despair gripped him. His Blessed Mother reminded him that Hannah would never see most of these scars, just his face.

Still, his face needed a lot of work.

The makeup artist at Shriners was very patient. She had shown him the best methods to hide what he really was.

First, he applied a special moisturizer that provided oxygen to the skin. It was very important to let the medicine work its way into the scar tissue, so he sat down on the toilet and flipped through the latest issue of *Details*.

Walter studied the advertisements of good-looking male models posing in expensive underwear; in nice jeans and T-shirts; in suits. For inspiration he had taped some of the ads to the wall of his workout room.

As he flipped through the glossy pages, staring at

the tanned faces with sharp jaw lines, perfect noses and piercing eyes, he wished for exercises to improve the appearance of his face. For that he had to rely on makeup.

Walter checked his watch. Half an hour had passed. He tossed the magazine on the floor, stood and grabbed the bottles he needed from the medicine cabinet.

The oil-based foundation took a long time to apply because he only had one good hand to work with. While the makeup dried, he took out a jar of American Crew pomade and worked the waxy substance through his black hair. The pomade gave his hair the same wet, messy look he had seen in the magazines. It took a bit of time, but the result was worth it.

To complete the transformation, he used a pressed powder, applying it with a brush.

Walter stepped back from the mirror. The face staring back at him in the unforgiving light wasn't as scary. Not as good looking as the male models in the magazines, but not frightening. He looked human.

Walter fussed with his appearance for a few more minutes, studying his face from different angles, applying touch-ups where needed. He checked to make sure his hair covered his missing ear and then put on a pair of Diesel jeans and a long-sleeve black shirt. He checked himself in a full-length mirror that didn't show his face. He looked good. Very stylish.

He slipped on a pair of black Coach loafers and headed downstairs to the kitchen.

The basement door was open. He could hear Hannah crying.

Walter so very badly wanted to go down there and hold Hannah, tell her everything was going to be okay. He hadn't meant to hurt her. What happened last night was an accident.

Mary told him to leave Hannah alone. It was best to wait, Mary said. Let Hannah cry and scream out her anger and fear, get it all out of her system.

He needed to pray for strength. He opened the closet door, got down on his knees and lit the candles. Dozens of statues of the Blessed Mother looked down on him, smiling, arms wide open, accepting. Walter made the sign of the cross, closed his eyes, and with his hands pressed firmly together, prayed to his Blessed Mother for thanks.

17

Saturday morning. Darby stood at her kitchen window, sipping coffee and watching a snowplough trudging its way down Cambridge Street under a bright, clear sky. According to the news, yesterday's storm dumped two and a half feet of snow along eastern and northern Massachusetts. New Hampshire got the worst of it – as much as three feet in some areas.

Coop was still in the shower. Darby checked her watch. It was almost noon. She was itching to get to the lab to see if AFIS, the FBI's Automated Fingerprint Indexing System, had found a match on the single latent print lifted from Emma Hale's jewellery box.

They had spent last night and a good part of the early morning hours examining every inch of Emma's home, paying close attention to the walk-in closet and the spare bedroom where the intruder had escaped. The only evidence the man had left was a wet shoeprint which Darby had lifted from the floor in front of the window.

How had the intruder gained access to the penthouse? Darby wondered if Bryson had discovered anything on the building's security tapes. Finding the man on one of the tapes would answer the question of how he had accessed the penthouse but it wouldn't explain what he was doing there or what he was looking for.

The serial number for the Beretta was traced back to Joshua Stein from Chicago. His home was broken into in 1998. The thief stole crystal and a lockbox holding cash and a Beretta. It was possible that last night's intruder was a thief – finding a way to slip inside Emma's home undetected was by no means an easy task – but the more likely scenario was that the man with the strange eyes had purchased the handgun from a pawn shop. Some pawn shop owners dealt stolen handguns as a side-business, based on referrals. It was also possible the intruder had bought the Beretta second-hand on the street or through a private dealer. The list of possibilities was endless. The handgun was a dead end.

With the exception of the missing locket, every item listed in the CSU inventory was found inside the penthouse. Emma Hale's abductor had come back for the necklace but he apparently hadn't taken anything else. Did he wear gloves to hide his fingerprints? Had he touched any of the other jewellery? Coop was planning on spending the rest of today fuming each piece of jewellery inside a superglue chamber to see if Emma's abductor had left behind any partial latent prints. With luck, they would find one and a matching print in AFIS.

Pouring herself another cup of coffee, her mind turned to the question that stood above the others:

Why would Emma's abductor risk breaking into her home and risk being caught to retrieve a locket?

Darby didn't have a definitive answer, but she had several theories, all of which pointed back to her original assumption that the man who had abducted these two women and kept them alive for months had, in fact, cared deeply for them.

Darby carried her coffee mug through the living room, on her way to her office. Coop was no longer in the bathroom. Her bedroom door was cracked open a few inches. She moved down the hallway in her socks, about to knock on the door to tell him that the coffee was ready, when she saw Coop, shirtless, slipping into his jeans.

She told herself to look away but kept staring. The hard, knotted muscles in his chest and stomach rippled under his smooth, pale skin as he buttoned his jeans in the bright sunlight pouring through her windows. It was easy to see why so many women took notice of him – the hard body and perfect outline of his jaw; blond hair and blue eyes. But she had seen his other side, the one he kept buried under the charisma and constant joking. She had spent many weekend afternoons with Coop, just the two of them, drinking beer and watching football.

They were friends, she reminded herself and, feeling embarrassed for gawking, quickly ducked into her office.

Emma Hale and Judith Chen hung on the wall, the two young women happy, smiling, eyes bright with hope. Darby was staring at the pictures when her cell phone rang. She removed it from the charger and answered the call.

'I've finished reviewing last night's security tapes,' Tim Bryson said. 'Your friend slipped in through the garage at eight thirty-three and took the delivery elevator to the penthouse.'

'There was no sign of forced entry on the door or the deadbolt.'

'Either he had a key or he picked the lock. There are devices on the market that you can use to slip inside the keyhole and rake the locks. If you know what you're doing, you can open them in a matter of seconds. Or maybe he bumped the lock.'

'Bumped it?'

'You take a key, place it inside the lock then slam it with a hammer, rock, shoe, whatever, and break the lock drum. It's called lock bumping. I'll have someone from burglary take a look. Where are you?'

'I'm at home. I'll be at the lab in about half an hour.'

'Do you have internet access? I want to email you a picture.'

Darby told him to send it to her lab's email address. She could access her account from home.

Her laptop had broadband access. In less than a minute, she was logged on to her Outlook account. She saw Bryson's email with a jpeg attachment and downloaded the picture.

On the screen was a colour headshot of a man

with short black hair and pale skin. He had the same black, cadaverous eyes as the man she had met last night.

18

'Where did you get this?' Darby asked.

'Is this your man?'

'It's him, no question. Who is he? Do you know?'

'His name is Malcolm Fletcher. Does the name ring any bells?'

'No. Should it?'

'Fletcher is a former profiler from back when the Investigative Support Unit called itself Behavioral Sciences,' Bryson said. 'He's also the FBI's number four man on their Most Wanted List.'

'What did he do?'

'According to what I've read on the internet, Fletcher attacked three federal agents in eighty-four. One is brain dead. The other two disappeared. Their bodies were never recovered. The interesting thing is the Feds didn't place Fletcher on their Most Wanted List until 2003.'

'What's the reason for the delay?'

'Good question. If I had to guess, I'd say the Feds wanted to handle the matter internally.'

What a surprise, Darby thought. 'How did you find him?'

'My first job out of the academy was as a beat cop for Saugus. There was this case back in eighty-two where the bodies of two strangled women were dumped along Route One. The detective in charge of the case, this guy named Larry Foley, called the Behavioral Sciences Unit, and BSU sent a profiler to study the cases. I never met Fletcher personally, but his name was tossed around a lot – everyone kept commenting on his strange, black eyes. I was on my way into the station when I remembered his name and thanks to the power of Google, there he was on the Most Wanted List.'

'What's the deal with his eyes? Is it some sort of hereditary condition?'

'I have no idea. Like I said, I never met the man. I have a federal friend in the Boston office. I'm going to call him and see what I can find. Maybe he can give us some idea as to what the hell Fletcher is doing here.'

'Do you trust this person?'

'You're worried the Feds might decide to get involved?'

'The thought crossed my mind.'

'Mine, too,' Bryson said. 'Let's talk to the commissioner and see how she wants to play it.'

'I'd like to review the Saugus cases you mentioned.'

'Hold on, I've got another call.'

Coop stepped into her office wearing a T-shirt that said 'I Like Boobies'.

'How old are you again?' Darby asked.

'My mother gave me this for my birthday.' Coop

rubbed a hand over his wet hair and looked at the pictures hanging on the wall. 'I'm glad to see you're not taking your work home with you.'

Bryson came back on the line. 'That was Jonathan Hale. He wants to talk about what happened last night.'

'What did you tell him?'

'I told him you and I would meet and discuss the matter with him at his home at two. He lives in Weston. I'm at the station right now. You want me to swing by and pick you up?'

Darby gave Bryson her address. She hung up and filled Coop in on Malcolm Fletcher.

Coop sat in the leather chair by the window, squinting in the sunlight. 'I think it would be wise if I stayed with you for a bit,' he said.

Darby felt relieved. She didn't want him to go home. Not yet.

'I'll swing by my house and pick up some stuff,' Coop said.

'Are you going to wear any more of those ridiculous T-shirts?'

'It's either that or I sleep in the nude.'

A snapshot of him slipping into his jeans flashed through her mind. Her face reddened.

'Please,' he said. 'Don't fight me on this.'

'You can take my car.' Darby opened her desk drawer and removed the spare set of house and car keys. She tossed them and stood. 'I'm not going to cook for you.'

'What about backrubs?'
'Keep dreaming.'
'Not a problem,' Coop said.

19

Weston is Boston's suburban version of Nantucket, an exclusive enclave of predominantly rich whites who live in jaw-dropping multimillion-dollar mansions surrounded by acres of beautifully manicured lawns and woods. The town's poorest residents live in million-dollar shacks in order to take advantage of the school system, the best in the state of Massachusetts. Almost every high-school graduate is guaranteed acceptance into a top-tier Ivy college.

Jonathan Hale lived at the end of a private road. His mansion, a sprawling mass of modern architecture, sat on top of a hill. Workers sitting on John Deere lawnmowers equipped with ploughs were clearing snow from the long driveways.

A limo was parked in front of a garage, its bay door open, the interior lights on. Darby spotted a vintage Porsche, a convertible BMW and a car that looked like a Bentley.

'What do you think?' Tim Bryson asked as he pulled his old diesel Mercedes up to the front gate.

'Seems awfully cold,' Darby said.

'I was referring to the house.'

'I know.'

Bryson rolled down the window and pressed the intercom button.

A crackle of static, then a woman's voice said, 'Hello?'

'This is Detective Bryson. I'm here to see Mr Hale.'

'One moment, please.'

Standing inside the foyer, dressed in a pin-striped suit without a tie, was a tall man with a thick head of grey hair and a strong, handsome face pale with grief – Jonathan Hale. Darby recognized him immediately from the press conferences on TV.

Hale looked and carried himself like an old blue blood, only the image wasn't accurate. He had dropped out of Harvard during his sophomore year to build computers out of his parents' garage in Medford. Eight years later, he sold his mail-order computer company to a competitor and used the proceeds to buy residential property in Boston's highly desirable Back Bay.

With the income generated from his rental properties, he created a successful start-up business that developed financial software for investment firms. During the height of the dot-com craze, Hale sold the company for a staggering amount of money which he invested in commercial real-estate opportunities in Massachusetts. The man was Boston's version of Donald Trump, minus the bad hair, trophy wife and megalomaniac desire for self-promotion. According to the papers, Hale, who had never remarried following the death of his wife, was a huge contributor to a number of Catholic charities.

Bryson did the introductions.

'Maria is preparing lunch,' Hale said. His voice was raspy, tired, the words slightly slurred. 'Would either of you like something to eat or drink?'

'That's very kind of you, but we don't want to take up your time,' Bryson said. 'Is there a place where we can talk privately?'

Hale suggested his office.

Darby trailed behind the men, taking in the home with its vaulted ceilings and artful lighting. Japanese antiques were prominently displayed on walls and stands. Inside a restaurant-sized kitchen, an older Hispanic woman was busy working at the stove.

Jonathan Hale slowed his pace and looked over his shoulder at Darby. 'McCormick ... You're the one who caught that killer that was all over the news.'

'Traveler,' Darby said.

'It's Dr McCormick now, isn't it?'

'Keeping tabs on me, Mr Hale?'

'It's rather difficult not to, young lady. You've become somewhat of a media sensation.'

Unfortunately, he was right. The Traveler case, the focus of national TV programmes like *Dateline* and *60 Minutes*, now lived in perpetuity on cable shows such as *Forensic Files*, *Court TV* and A&E's *Notorious*. Darby had never given an interview but, because of her connection to Traveler, her name was constantly mentioned in the pieces along with pictures taken by photographers hiding in bushes or their cars. Her movements were even the focus of the 'Inside Track', a gossip column published by the *Boston Herald.*

Hale's office was spacious and bright, with bookcases and leather armchairs straight out of the Harvard Club. A fire was going. The warm room smelled of woodsmoke and cigars. Hale waited until they were seated.

'I talked with Mr Marsh this morning,' Hale said, stubbing out his cigar. 'He gave me the description of this man. Do you know who he is?'

Bryson took the lead. Darby wanted to take a back seat and observe.

'We don't,' Bryson said. 'What about you? Do you know this man?'

Hale appeared puzzled. 'Are you suggesting that I know the man who broke into my daughter's house?'

'It's just a routine question, Mr Hale.'

'No. I don't know who he is.'

'Have you ever seen a man matching the description?'

'No.' Hale picked up a highball glass containing what appeared to be bourbon. 'What was he doing there?'

'We're investigating several leads. Have you –'

'Detective Bryson, when I spoke to you this morning, you said it *appears* someone broke into my daughter's home. Did this person break into Emma's home or not?'

'We found no sign of forced entry on the door.

We're wondering if the man had a key. How many people besides yourself have access to your daughter's place?'

'I have a key, as does Mr Marsh.'

'Have you made any other copies?'

'No.'

'Have you given your keys to anyone?'

'No, I haven't. I don't want anyone inside Emma's place.'

'Then why did you give Mr Marsh a key?'

'He has keys to every unit. He's the building's security administrator. He needs a key in case there's a problem.'

'Does Mr Marsh know Emma's alarm code?'

'I would assume so. He has access to the building's security system. The computer lists the alarm code for each unit. Emma's alarm has been turned off since her . . . abduction. I had it turned off, at your request, when you had people coming in and out.'

'Why haven't you turned it back on?'

'To be honest, I haven't really thought about it.' Hale finished his drink. 'Pardon me for saying this, detective, but I have the feeling this is turning into some sort of interrogation.'

'I apologize,' Bryson said. 'I'm trying to understand, as I'm sure you are, what this person was doing inside your daughter's home.'

Hale shifted his attention to Darby. 'I understand you spoke with this person.'

Darby nodded.

Hale waited for her to speak. When she didn't, he said, 'Are you going to tell me what he said? Or are you going to keep me in the dark?'

20

Tim Bryson answered the question. 'It's part of our investigation.'

Hale's gaze never left Darby. 'Why did you want access to my daughter's home, Dr McCormick?'

'I've recently been assigned to your daughter's case,' Darby said. 'I wanted to get a feel for her, to try and get to know her.'

'Mr Marsh paged my answering service. When I spoke to my assistant, she said you were rather adamant in wanting to get inside Emma's place. There was talk of a court order.'

'I wanted to investigate a new lead.'

'Which is?'

'It's part of our ongoing investigation.'

'See, this is the problem I have with you people.' Hale's tone remained courteous. 'Every time you come here you expect me to answer your questions but you refuse to answer any of mine. Take this religious statue you found inside my daughter's pocket. I've asked you what it is and you won't tell me. Why?'

'I don't blame you for your frustration, but we need –'

'My daughter's home was released back to me.

I allowed you access. I think I have a right to know why.'

'We're not the enemy, Mr Hale. We're after the same goal.'

Hale went to take another sip of his drink, realized the glass was empty and looked around for the bottle.

'I noticed that you haven't cleaned out any of Emma's things,' Darby said.

Hale put the glass down on the table, leaned back in his chair and crossed his legs.

'It's rather difficult to explain,' he said after a moment. He cleared his throat several times as he brushed lint off his pants. 'Emma's house, the way she left things . . . it's all I have left of her. I know this is going to sound irrational, but when I'm in there, looking at her things, the way she left them, I feel . . . I can still feel her. It's like she's still alive.'

Bryson said, 'When was the last time you were inside Emma's place?'

'Last week,' Hale said, standing.

'Have you hired a private investigator to look into your daughter's death?'

'I wouldn't call him that.' Hale walked to the corner of the room, picked up a bottle of Maker's Mark bourbon from the small bar and refilled his glass. 'Dr Karim is a forensic consultant.'

'Ali Karim?' Darby asked.

'Yes,' Hale said as he sat back in the chair. 'Do you know him?'

She knew the name. Ali Karim, a former pathologist for the city of New York and, without a doubt, one of the best in the field, now ran his own consulting firm. Karim had been hired as an expert witness on a number of prominent criminal cases, most of which were in the media. He had written several bestselling books and was a staple on the talk-show circuit.

'Why did you hire Dr Karim?' Darby asked.

'I wanted someone to tell me the truth,' Hale said.

'I don't understand.'

'My daughter was shot in the back of the head with a twenty-two calibre weapon. Detective Bryson told me she died instantly. That's not exactly true. The way the bullet entered her skull, Emma was alive for several minutes. My daughter suffered. Horribly.'

Bryson spoke up. 'Mr Hale –'

'I understand why you said it, and I don't blame you.' Hale sipped his drink. 'I didn't know about your daughter, Detective Bryson.'

'Excuse me?'

'I was told your daughter died. From leukaemia.'

'Your point, Mr Hale?'

'You know what it's like to lose a child. You know that kind of pain. And while I appreciate your intentions to spare me the details of my daughter's death, I've asked you, repeatedly, for information. I've asked you to tell me the truth. I want to know how she died, what this person did to her – I want to know every detail. That's why I hired Dr Karim. They're looking at this case from a fresh perspective.'

'They?'

'Karim has recommended the names of several investigators to review the evidence.'

'What are the names of the investigators you've hired?'

'I haven't hired anyone yet.'

'Have you met these people?'

'No.'

'How did you find Dr Karim?'

'I've seen him on talk shows over the years. He has experience in these types of homicides, so I decided to call him and he agreed to review Emma's autopsy. He supported all of the medical examiner's findings, by the way.'

There was a knock on the door. When it opened, the housekeeper poked in her head and in broken English said, 'Mr Hale, police are on the phone. They said it emergency.'

Hale excused himself and picked up the phone from his desk. He listened for several minutes, then said 'Thank you' and hung up.

'I'm sorry, but I'm going to have to cut this meeting short,' Hale said. 'One of my buildings has been burglarized. Is there anything else I can help you with?'

'Yes,' Bryson said. 'Mr Marsh told us that backup copies of the building's security tapes are stored at your Newton office.'

Hale nodded. 'The tapes are burned onto DVD. It saves on storage space.'

'I'd like to look at them.'

'I don't suppose you'll tell me why.'

'We're pursuing a theory.'

'Of course,' Hale said, sighing. 'You might as well follow me to Newton. That's where I'm going. It appears someone broke into the building.'

'What's the address?'

Hale wrote it down on a sheet of paper. 'I'll meet you there,' he said, ripping the sheet off the pad and handing it to Bryson. 'If you'll excuse me, I need to make some phone calls.'

Darby placed her business card on his desk. 'If this man approaches you, or if you think of anything else, you can call me or Detective Bryson. Thank you for your time, Mr Hale. I'm sorry for your loss. I truly mean that.'

21

The afternoon sun reflected off the rolling sheets of snow and ice. Darby put on her sunglasses to cut the glare. She waited until she was seated inside Bryson's car before she spoke.

'Did you know Hale hired Karim?'

'No.'

'You don't seem surprised.'

'It's what the rich do. They buy their way out of everything.' Bryson started the car and leaned back in his seat, probably wanting to give the engine a chance to warm up. 'Take the JonBenét Ramsey case. Their little girl is murdered, and what do the parents do? They hide behind lawyers and hire top-of-the-line forensic consultants. They get all these so-called experts involved, and wouldn't you know, they put up enough roadblocks to prevent that case from ever going to trial.'

'The Boulder police were sloppy at the crime scene – and don't get me started on how the district attorney behaved.'

'My point is the rich think they operate on a different playing field,' Bryson said. 'And guess what? They do.'

'Do you want to talk to Karim?'

'You're a peer. He might be more willing to share information with you.'

Darby wasn't expecting much. Legally, Karim didn't have to share anything.

'What do you think about our conversation in there?' Bryson asked.

'When we spoke about the intruder, Hale kept fidgeting – stubbing out the cigar, shifting in his chair and looking at his drinking glass. He barely gave us any eye contact.'

'It could be that he's pissed off at us because we won't share information and we haven't been able to give him any closure.'

'He seemed nervous.'

'I picked up that, too. Then again, I'd be nervous if I employed the services of the nation's number four Most Wanted felon.'

'That's quite a leap, Tim.'

'Maybe.' Bryson put the car in gear and drove down the driveway.

'He seemed genuinely surprised about the break-in,' Darby said.

'It's awfully convenient.'

'It is. Still, Fletcher might be working alone.'

When Bryson reached the end of the driveway he said, 'Do you have kids?'

'No.'

'I had one, my daughter, Emily. She had this really rare form of leukaemia. We took her to every specialist under the sun. Seeing everything she went through, I would have sold my soul to the devil to spare her life. I know that sounds overly melodramatic, but it's the honest-to-God truth. You'll do anything for your kids. Anything in the world.'

Darby thought of her mother as Bryson turned onto the main road.

'The other thing they don't tell you is that the pain never goes away. It hurts as much now as it did the day she died.'

'I'm sorry, Tim.'

'Guys like Hale aren't used to living with question marks. The man can buy anything he wants. His net worth, I hear, is somewhere north of half a billion dollars.'

'You think he's made some sort of Faustian deal with Fletcher?'

'His daughter was kept somewhere for half a year, endured only God knows what and then the son of a bitch decides to put a bullet in the back of her head,' Bryson said. 'Hale's been very vocal in the press about his opinions of us. He believes we've done a shit job. If he feels he can't get justice from us, maybe he's decided he can get it somewhere else.'

22

Jonathan Hale stands in front of the living-room window, rubbing the antique locket holding Susan's picture between his fingers. During the day he carries the locket in his pant pocket; at night, he wears it to bed, afraid that if he places it inside a drawer he will somehow be leaving Emma, putting her on the same shelf as Susan, his dead wife, and start the process of forgetting.

Only you can't forget your children. You won't ever forget the frantic phone call from Kimmy, your daughter's best friend, Kimmy asking why Emma is skipping class and not returning any phone calls. Is she sick, Mr Hale? Is everything all right? You'll never forget that agonizing moment when you discover your daughter's empty home or how you forced yourself to keep swallowing the fear minute-by-minute as those first few days bled into a week then stretched into two, then four, then seven, and yet you keep believing the police will find her alive as the months roll by, there's still time, there's still time. You're still clutching that hope and your faith in God when the doorbell rings and you see the detective standing on your front step. You won't forget the painful look on Detective Bryson's face when he tells you the news that a woman matching your daughter's description has been found floating in the river. He opens a folder and you see a picture of a woman's bloated face, the skin waxy and white, picked apart by fish. She is wearing a platinum chain and antique locket – the same one you gave your daughter last Christmas. You remember Emma sitting in the chair tucked in the warm folds of her bathrobe, sunlight pouring through the window and the backyard full of fresh snow. You see her opening the locket and you remember the look on her face when she sees the picture of her mother, dead all these years. You remember that moment and a thousand other ones as you stare at the picture inside the folder, at the white card with the morgue number lying below her chin, and yet you still believe it's a mistake, it has to be a mistake.

The detective waits for you to say, 'Yes, this is my daughter. This is Emma.' Only you can't say the words because once you do, you are saying goodbye.

Hale turns his attention to the groundskeepers clearing away the snow. He wishes it was still fall, his favourite season. He pictures the leaves blowing across the front lawn, that wonderful crisp, clean smell in the air, and it triggers a memory of Emma at seven – she's running across the colourful leaves, screaming, a shoebox gripped in her hands. Inside the box is a blue jay. One of its wings is injured; the other flaps frantically, trying to seek flight.

You need to help the bird, Daddy, he's hurt.

Wanting to wipe away that look of fear from his daughter's face, Hale grabs the phonebook and calls veterinarians as the bird makes high-pitched, painful sounds. Finally, he finds one that treats birds – it's in Boston, a short distance away.

Hale knows how this is going to end. He is hoping to spare Emma but she insists on going with him.

When the vet delivers the news, Emma turns to him to solve the problem. He tells her how God has a plan for all of us, even if we don't understand it. She cries and he holds her hand on the way back out to the car without the bird and she doesn't talk on the way home. A year later she would hold his hand again as he led her away from her mother's grave, reciting the same speech.

Hale remembers deeply believing in those words, in his faith. He doesn't believe any more.

He reaches for his glass. It's empty. He refills his glass with fresh ice. Susan's old cookbooks sit on a shelf next to the stove. When she was alive, she always cooked. Now he has people who cook for him. Several times they have followed the recipes Susan had scrawled on index cards or marked off in her favourite cookbooks but the food never tastes the same.

On more than one occasion, he has tried to throw out the cookbooks. Each and every time he felt as though a part of him was being torn in half. He donated all of Susan's clothing without a problem but he can't part with the cookbooks. Dumping them

– even giving them to a friend – it was like saying goodbye in pieces. *I can only give you away in pieces.* Hale thinks of all Emma's things waiting to be packed up and wonders what items would tug at him, beg and plead not to be thrown away, to hang on to be remembered.

Glass in hand, Hale stumbles back to his office – he is intensely drunk – opens the door and sees Malcolm Fletcher sitting in a leather chair.

23

Jonathan Hale had met the man earlier this month. The meeting, at the Oak Room bar inside the beautiful Copley Fairmont Hotel, was arranged by Dr Karim.

It was difficult to sit still. His blood pounded against his ears, and every colour and sound inside seemed bright and loud – the murmured conversations of the business lunch crowd mixed with the clink of forks against china; the deep maroon of the table linens; the afternoon sunlight pouring through the windows, reflecting off liquor bottles sitting on the shelves behind the bar with a mirrored wall.

Eyes watching the front door, Hale sipped his drink and replayed the previous day's conversation with Dr Karim.

'Mr Hale, I've talked about your daughter's case with a consultant. This person is on his way to Boston. He'd like to speak with you privately.'

'What's his name?'

'He's very skilled at finding people who don't want to be found. He's had great success in these sorts of cases.'

'Why won't you tell me his name?'

'It's . . . complicated,' Karim said. 'I have known this man

for thirty years. He's been working exclusively with me for the past decade. He is, without a doubt, the best in his field. He found the men responsible for my son's death.'

Hale was confused. During their initial conversation in which Karim outlined how his group worked on one case at a time until it was resolved, Karim had shared the painful loss of his oldest son Jason, an accidental victim in a gang shooting in the Bronx. New York police, Karim said, had never solved the case.

'I thought you told me your son's case was still active.'

'That's what the police believe,' Karim said.

Hale grew still as the knowledge of what Karim was possibly suggesting sunk in.

'Do we understand one another, Mr Hale?'

'Yes.' Hale's mouth was dry, his skin tingling with an electric sensation. 'Yes, we do.'

'When you meet him you're to answer all of his questions,' Karim said. 'If he agrees to work on your daughter's case, you're to do everything he asks. Whatever you do, don't lie to him.'

A man wearing sunglasses and dressed in a sharp black wool topcoat over a black suit stepped up next to the table. The man was tall, well over six feet, with the kind of powerful build Hale associated with boxers. The man's thick black hair was cut short, his pale skin looking bleached in the sunlight.

'Dr Karim sent me,' the man said. His voice, deep and rumbling, carried a slight Australian accent. The dark lenses hid his eyes.

Hale introduced himself. The man, wearing gloves, shook his hand but didn't take them off as he slid into the opposite seat. He didn't offer his name.

'What can I get you to drink?' Hale asked.

'I'm fine, thank you.' The man rested his forearms on the table and leaned closer. Hale smelled cigar smoke. 'I'd like to talk to you about the religious statue found in your daughter's pocket.'

'What about it?'

'Was it a statue of the Virgin Mary?'

'I don't know,' Hale said. 'The police refuse to tell me anything.'

'Have you cleaned out your daughter's apartment?'

'No. Dr Karim told me to leave everything alone. He's thinking of hiring investigators to come in and take a look at Emma's things.'

'What have you removed from her home?'

'I haven't ... I can't bring myself to remove anything.'

'Don't remove anything, don't touch anything,' the man said. 'With your permission, I'd like to look through your daughter's home.'

'The building has a concierge. He'll provide you with a key. I'll call him.'

'I want you to listen to me very carefully, Mr Hale. If we agree to work together, you're not to tell the police about my involvement. For all practical purposes, I don't exist. That condition is non-negotiable.'

'I don't even know your name.'

'Malcolm Fletcher.'

The man waited, as if expecting some sort of reaction.

'And what do you do for a living, Mr Fletcher?'

'I used to work for the FBI's Behavioral Science Unit.'

'And now you're retired?'

'In a manner of speaking,' Fletcher said. 'I'm sure you have people who perform background checks before you hire an employee.'

'It's standard procedure.'

'For your own safety, I insist you keep my name private. If you send my name bouncing through any of the computer databases, I'll find out, and I'll disappear. Dr Karim will swear under oath that he never mentioned my name. He'll also stop working on your daughter's case. Are you a man of your word, Mr Hale?'

'I am.'

'Make me a copy of your daughter's keys and mail them to Dr Karim. I'll be in touch with you shortly.'

'Before you go, Mr Fletcher, I need to speak to you about something.'

Hale put down his glass and tried to look into the man's eyes. All he could see were the dark lenses.

'When you find the man who killed my daughter, I want to meet him. I want to talk to him alone before you deliver him to the police.'

'Dr Karim told you about what happened to his son.'

'He did, yes.'

'Then you know I'm not going to involve the police.'

'I want to speak to him.'

'Have you ever killed a man, Mr Hale?'

'No.'

'Have you read *Macbeth*?'

'That condition is non-negotiable.'

'I don't think you fully understand the implications of what you're asking. You need to give the matter some serious thought. In the meantime, remember what I said about involving the authorities.'

Hale kept his word. He didn't conduct a background check. What he knew about the man he had learned from the internet.

In 1984, Malcolm Fletcher, an FBI profiler, was suspected of assaulting three federal agents. One agent, Stephen Rousseau, was still on a feeding tube in a private hospital in New Orleans. The bodies of the two other agents were never recovered.

In 2003, the former profiler was placed on the FBI's Most Wanted List. Hale could not find a reason for the gap in time.

Now Malcolm Fletcher was inside his home office, sitting in one of the leather chairs.

The man had called this morning. Hale told him about the police; Fletcher stated he wanted to be present during the conversation. Not wanting to arouse any suspicion among the staff, Hale suggested he enter the house through the balcony doors leading to the office. The woods would provide excellent coverage.

Hale shut the office door. Fletcher had listened to the entire conversation from inside the coat closet.

'I told them everything you told me to say.'

Fletcher nodded.

'They wouldn't tell me about the statue,' Hale said.

'I know.' Malcolm Fletcher stared at the fire. 'Please have a seat. I want to talk to you about the man who killed your daughter.'

24

Jonathan Hale took the chair across from Fletcher. Everything the man wore was black – his suit and shirt, his shoes and socks. The colour was an odd choice for someone so pale.

'Last night,' Fletcher said, 'while Miss McCormick was standing in the dark wondering why the lights went out, I was trying to ascertain the reason for her impromptu visit. I knew she would never tell me, so before I was forced to reveal myself to her, I took the liberty of planting a small listening device on top of the crown moulding above the closet door and another one inside the spare bedroom. Fortunately, I had the necessary surveillance gear inside my car, so I listened to Miss McCormick's conversation with Detective Bryson. I know the reason for her sudden urgency to gain access to your daughter's home.'

Fletcher turned his attention away from the fire. Hale could not look away from the man's strange eyes. For some reason they made him think of the mystery stories he read when he was a boy – Hardy Boys stuff where they hunted for buried treasure hidden in dank old castles full of cobwebs and skeletons, rooms full of terrible secrets.

But there was something calming behind the man's eyes. Hale felt his heartbeat slow.

'When Emma disappeared,' Fletcher said, 'the operating theory shared by both the Boston police and the FBI was that she had been kidnapped.'

'That's right.'

'The photograph Detective Bryson showed you to identify your daughter, do you remember it?'

'Yes.' Hale could see the photograph clearly in his mind's eye. He remembered wanting to reach through it and brush away the soot and sand from her face, pick out the twigs tangled in her wet hair.

'In the picture, Emma is wearing a platinum chain with a locket,' Fletcher said.

'I gave it to her for Christmas.' Hale reached inside his pocket and squeezed the locket between his fingers.

'The locket and chain were inside your daughter's home *after* she was abducted,' Fletcher said.

'I don't understand.'

'The man who killed your daughter came back for the necklace. The police believe he's on one of the security tapes – that's why they asked for access to your Newton office building. They want to review the backlog of tapes. They're now in my possession.'

'You're the one who broke into the office?'

'Yes. I want the police to believe I'm acting independently.'

Malcolm Fletcher handed him a cell phone. 'Keep

this with you at all times. The phone is disposable, so there's no way the police can trace the call. If you have any questions, dial the number programmed into the phone's memory. There's only one. Do you know Judith Chen?'

'The missing college student from Suffolk,' Hale said.

'Her body was found yesterday. The police discovered a religious statue sewn in her pocket – a statue of the Virgin Mary. The same statue was found with Emma. I heard Miss McCormick talk about it last night. It reminded me of something, so I decided to investigate. I've come across some information that could be problematic for the Boston police.'

'What kind of information?'

'I'd rather discuss it with you later, after I've had a chance to review the security tapes. I want to see if my theory is, in fact, correct.'

'Marsh told me the police took last night's tapes. I'm sure you're on them.'

'I have no doubt.'

'Then it's only a matter of time before they find out who you are.'

'Yes, I realize that,' Fletcher said, standing. 'I'm going to create a diversion.'

'With what?'

'The truth,' Fletcher said.

Hale's Newton office building was conveniently located off the Mass Pike. The parking lot, cleared of snow, contained a single patrol car. The front door, made of glass, was shattered. Darby saw a brick lying on the lobby floor.

The place was trashed. Computer monitors were smashed against the floor, desk drawers overturned, contents spilled everywhere. Plants had been thrown against the white walls, some of which were spray-painted with bright neon swastikas and the phrases 'Jews Go Home' and 'White Power'.

The patrolman, short with thick shoulders and a doughy face, stifled a yawn. 'Assholes came in here and, as you can see, tossed the place to shit,' he told Bryson. 'The little bastards were pretty smart. They cut the wires for the alarm.'

'Why do you think kids did this?'

'Every time we get one of these hate-crime things, teenagers are always behind it. Probably one of those Aryan Brotherhood groups from Southie. They came here last year, broke into a synagogue and spray-painted the same lovely phrases all over the walls. It's an initiation thing.'

'And now they're ransacking office buildings?'

'Hey, I'm just throwing out ideas. You're the detective, so why I don't let you go and detect?'

'Who called it in?'

'One of the plough guys,' the patrolman said. 'The two of 'em got here this morning at around nine. When they made their way around to the front, they saw the door, took a quick peek inside, called it in and here we are.'

Bryson nodded, looking at a security camera mounted against the ceiling.

'You can forget that,' the patrolman said. 'The tapes were removed from the recorders.'

'Show me.'

The door to the security room had been pried open. Given the marks, Darby suspected something like a crowbar was used.

Like the lobby, the small room had been ransacked – recorders, computer monitors and cheaply made pressboard bookcases were smashed against the floor covered in hundreds of DVDs stored inside clear jewel cases. Some of the DVDs were smashed into pieces. Darby noticed pieces of equipment that transferred VHS tape to DVD.

Bryson picked up one of the cases. It was neatly labelled with the building's name, month and year of the recording.

'How much you want to bet the recording we need is missing?' Bryson asked.

'That's a sucker's bet,' Darby said. 'Still, we should get people here to catalogue the DVDs and see what's missing.'

'I'll make the call. We're going to have to process this. I'll call Ops, get some people here.'

'I'm going to get back to the lab. I'd also like to look at Chen's place.'

'She's renting in Natick. They have a key. I'll let them know you'll be calling.'

'I'd like to view last night's security tape.'

‘I already made you a copy. I put it in the overnight drop-off.’ Bryson sighed as he tossed the DVD case onto the floor. ‘I’ll have patrol drive you into town.’

25

The lab's overnight drop-off box contained only one item: a sealed padded mailer. Darby saw her name written across the front. She opened the mailer on her way to the conference room.

The VHS security tape showed, in grainy colour, Emma Hale's parking garage. Sitting on the edge of the table, Darby watched a man with short black hair, pale skin and a black wool coat walk quickly across the garage to the delivery elevator. He pressed the button and waited, his back facing the camera. The man's hair colour and clothing matched the intruder she had met last night – Malcolm Fletcher.

When the elevator doors opened, Fletcher stepped inside and moved to the right, out of the camera's view. The doors shut.

If Fletcher was working for Hale, he wouldn't have to sneak inside the building.

Darby rewound the tape and watched it again.

What were you doing inside the penthouse? What were you looking for?

She watched the tape three more times and, failing to find anything useful, left the conference room.

Coop and Keith Woodbury were working inside

a small evidence room. Pieces of Emma Hale's jewellery sat inside a clear fuming cabinet slowly filling with a cyanoacrylate vapour. Off-white latent fingerprints appeared on the jewellery.

'How's the humidity level?' Coop asked.

Woodbury, tall and sleek, with a shaved head and a runner's build, examined the gauge. 'It looks good,' he said, his voice, as always soft and pleasant. He saw Darby, said hello and then turned his attention back to the gauge.

Coop put down his clipboard. 'The AFIS results came back – no good news, I'm afraid,' he told her. 'The partial thumb we found on the jewellery drawer's metal handle not only failed to find a corresponding match, it couldn't even find a *probable* match. We'll need a better-quality print.'

'Any luck with the jewellery?'

'We've only done one tray. So far, all the prints belong to Emma Hale. It's going to take a few days to get through this.'

Darby nodded. Fuming with cyanoacrylate, the main chemical in superglue, yielded great latent prints but the process was slow. Then there was the additional step of dusting the prints to preserve them so they could be lifted.

'How did the meeting with the father go?' Coop asked.

Darby hopped up on the back counter and filled them in on her talk with Hale and the subsequent burglary.

'Nice timing,' Coop said. 'You think Fletcher knows about the missing necklace?'

'The only way he could know about it is if he had access to our evidence file,' Darby said. 'Hale doesn't have a copy.'

'So what the hell was Fletcher doing there?'

'I have no idea. I want to talk about the Virgin Mary statue.'

'No prints.'

'I know,' Darby said. 'Either our man wiped it clean before he placed it in the pocket or he was wearing gloves. But wearing gloves while holding a sewing needle would be tricky, don't you think?'

'Depends on the type of gloves he was wearing. If they were ski gloves or ones made of thick leather then, yeah, it would be hard to hold a sewing needle and thread the pocket. But if he was wearing latex . . .' Coop shrugged.

'What if he wasn't wearing gloves at all?' Darby said. 'What if he sewed the pocket shut with his bare hands?'

'I see where you're going. Trying to lift a latent print from clothing . . . it rarely happens. Fabric doesn't hold a print's ridge characteristics.'

'That's true. Generally,' Darby said. 'Chen's running pants are made of nylon, and the area around the pocket was spotted with blood. What if he left a print?'

'Then the question becomes how to lift it without damaging the blood sample for DNA testing.'

'There are some chemicals we can mix together that won't damage the core STR loci.'

Woodbury, who had been quietly listening, spoke up. 'If you go that route, I wouldn't recommend using a peroxidase-reaction chemical. For one, they're not easy to use. Second, there's a toxicity issue.'

'What about using a solution based on a general protein-staining dye?' Darby asked.

Woodbury thought it over.

'That would be safer,' he said after a moment. 'I'll have to do some research and see if I can find the appropriate, ah, recipe.'

'And we'll have to wait until the clothes are dry,' Coop added.

'I want to examine Chen's skin,' Darby said. 'I want to see if our man touched her with his bare hands.'

'I'd say the chances of a latent print surviving that long underwater are slim to none.'

'Coop, what's the first rule you told me when it comes to fingerprints?'

'There are no rules.'

'Exactly,' Darby said, hopping off the table. 'Let me tell you what I have in mind . . .'

26

Coop needed to finish processing the jewellery inside the fuming cabinet. He agreed to meet them at the morgue. Keith Woodbury helped Darby carry the items she needed.

Judith Chen's nude body lay on a steel table. While Woodbury set up the equipment in another room, Darby plugged in the portable Luma-Lite and, wearing a pair of orange-tinted goggles, moved the wand of light over Chen's body.

At 180 nanometres, Darby found diluted bloodstains on the woman's face and chest. On Chen's forehead was a smear shaped like the letter 't.' Darby thought the smear resembled a crucifix.

She paused several times to adjust the light's wavelength. At 525 nanometres, she discovered a full latent print. She called Coop.

'Bingo.'

'You're shitting me.'

'I shit you not,' Darby said. 'I have a nice latent print on her forehead. It's at the tip of – get this – a cross.'

'There's a *cross* on her forehead?'

'My guess is he baptized her before dumping her

into the water. Don't you remember anything from Catholic school?'

'I've tried to block it all out,' Coop said. 'How are we going to lift the print?'

'My recommendation is to use superglue – Keith's setting up the fuming chamber right now. We'll put Chen's body in the chamber, and once the cyanoacrylate has set, we can dust the print using an ultraviolet powder and then develop it with something like Ardrox dye. Since you're the fingerprint expert, I'll let you make the call.'

'Thank you.'

'You're welcome,' Darby said. 'Now haul your ass over here, and bring that partial latent thumbprint with you.'

Darby left Coop and Woodbury to lift the print from Chen's forehead and drove to Natick.

Judith Chen lived with a roommate in a duplex, on the corner of a crowded street. A Natick patrol car sat in the driveway. The rest of the street was quiet. Good. The media wasn't here.

Darby showed her ID to the patrolman.

'Bedroom's on the second floor, right at the top of the stairs,' he said, stepping out of the car. 'Parents were here earlier. They didn't take anything.'

'What about Chen's roommate?'

'I don't know. She moved back in with her parents – she's from Long Island, I'm pretty sure – she left here must have been in early December. She's taking a semester off. Got all spooked about Chen's disappearance and didn't want to live here alone. I'll get you her name and phone number.'

The house was dark. Darby turned on the light and climbed the stairs.

A bathroom was on the top floor. It was spotless. Darby wondered if the roommate had cleaned it before leaving.

She opened the medicine cabinet. The left half was empty. The right side contained items which most likely belonged to Chen – vials, tubes and containers of various makeup and lotions; a lot of Alka-Seltzer and cold medications. There were two prescription bottles – Paxil, an antidepressant, and something called Requip.

Darby walked down the hallway. It took her a moment to find the light switch for the bedroom.

Hanging on Judith Chen's wall was a framed picture of her holding a Labrador puppy – the same photo Darby had tacked to the wall inside her home office.

Some of the picture frames were on the floor. Darby wondered if the parents had taken them off the wall earlier in the day. The bed had a pink comforter and matching throw pillows. Darby saw the indentation marks where the parents had probably sat.

Darby was glad the room seemed to be in order. She wanted to see how the woman had lived.

A small Dell laptop sat on a tiny desk. She turned

on the lamp. Three large chemistry textbooks and several spiral notebooks were staked in the corner. Everything was coated in dust.

Darby put on a pair of latex gloves and flipped through the notebook pages full of complex chemistry and calculus equations.

An hour had passed when her phone rang.

'You're going to love this,' Coop said. 'The print from Chen's forehead matches the partial print we recovered from the handle of Hale's jewellery drawer. I'll put the forehead print into AFIS. Keep your fingers crossed.'

The notebooks didn't contain any 'To Do' lists, Post-It notes or handwritten reminders like where to meet friends for dinner. The desk drawers contained computer manuals and several paperback copies of Jane Austen novels.

Darby turned on the laptop, relieved when it didn't ask for a password.

Chen used Microsoft Outlook for email and the calendar to keep track of appointments. Darby sorted through the months leading up to her abduction and found only entries containing Chen's class schedules and the dates that certain projects were due.

Her phone rang again. The caller was Tim Bryson.

'We've catalogued the security DVDs. Care to guess which ones are missing?'

'The ones from the day Emma Hale disappeared to the day her body was found,' Darby said.

'You got it. I vote we put people on Hale and see if Fletcher shows up.'

'I saw the security tape. If Fletcher is working for Hale, why did he sneak inside?'

'I don't know. Maybe he isn't. Maybe Fletcher is going to try and approach Hale, or maybe he's simply acting alone. All I'm saying is that we should cover all the bases.'

'I agree. You think the commissioner will go for it?'

'That's the next hurdle. What do you have on your end?'

Darby told him about the latent print found on Judith Chen's forehead and the matching print recovered from Hale's jewellery drawer handle.

She hung up and turned her attention back to the laptop. The files saved in Microsoft Word contained homework assignments and several essays for an English composition class.

There was a small folder holding digital photographs of Chen with what appeared to be her family and female friends. There were several photos of her with the dog and a white cat with black fur around its eye and chin.

Darby was examining Chen's internet search history when her phone rang again.

'Good afternoon, Dr McCormick.'

It was the intruder, the man with the strange eyes, Malcolm Fletcher.

27

'I didn't think I'd hear from you again,' Darby said, wondering how Malcolm Fletcher had got her number.

'I want to talk to you about the man who killed Emma Hale.'

'Do you know something?'

'I might.'

'And why do you want to share this information with me?'

'If you cannot get rid of the family skeleton, you may as well make it dance.'

'Another quote by Shaw?'

'Very good. I thought your generation had abandoned reading. What do you know about Themistocles?'

'He was an Athenian political leader.'

'Impressive,' Fletcher said. 'Themistocles led his people to victory over the Persians and was later banished by the same people he saved.'

'You've lost me.'

'In the end, it always comes down to a matter of degrees – how far you are willing to go, how far you're willing to push your way through the dark. I shouldn't have to warn you, of all people, that the truth is, more often than not, a terrible burden. You may want to give that some thought.'

'What are you suggesting?'

'I'm extending an invitation to meet the man who killed Emma Hale and Judith Chen.'

'How do you know the same man killed Hale and Chen?'

'Judith Chen was shot in the back of the head, like Emma Hale – at least that's what the papers are reporting. Are the cases connected, Dr McCormick? Or may I call you Darby? After reading so much about you, I feel as though I know you.'

'What should I call you?'

'Think of me as your secret friend.'

'How about you tell me your first name?'

'What would you like to call me?'

'How does the name Mephisto sound?'

A quiet laugh. 'Are you worried I'm going to hurt you?' Fletcher asked.

'The thought had crossed my mind.'

'I didn't hurt you last night.'

'Hard to do when you have a gun pointed at you.'

'I suggest a private meeting at the Sinclair Mental Health Facility in Danvers. I'll contact you in two hours.'

'And if I say no?'

'Then I wish you the best of luck finding the man who killed Judith Chen and the other women. I have no doubt of your abilities. You're certainly much more dedicated, and considerably brighter, than

Detective Bryson. He should have discovered the missing necklace months ago.'

Click. Malcolm Fletcher was gone.

Darby called Tim Bryson. She filled him in on her conversation. Bryson listened without interrupting.

'I don't understand why he wants you to go to Sinclair,' Bryson said after she finished. 'The place has been abandoned for, Christ, it must be at least thirty years now.'

'I've never heard of Sinclair.'

'Before your time, I guess. The hospital was built sometime in the late eighteenth century. It was used as an asylum for the criminally insane. In the seventies, a private company took it over for a bit, and then it went back to being a state-run hospital. It's going to be torn down next spring to make way for condos, I think.'

'Fletcher said, "I wish you luck finding the man who killed Judith Chen and the *other* women." Maybe he knows something about another victim, someone we haven't found.'

'I think he's jerking your chain.'

'He knows about the missing necklace.'

Bryson didn't answer.

'The only evidence we have at the moment is an unidentified latent fingerprint,' Darby said.

'You haven't examined Chen's clothing yet.'

'Which is going to have to wait until Monday. I don't want to spend Sunday sitting around with my thumb stuck up my ass.'

‘I don’t suppose I can talk you out of this.’

‘I want to know why Fletcher called.’

‘I’ll meet you at the hospital,’ Bryson said. ‘And I’m going to bring backup, just in case.’

28

Danvers, located north of Boston, was an hour's drive from the city. Darby used the Mustang's GPS navigation system. She took Route One North and made good time until she hit the mall traffic in Saugus. She ducked and weaved her way through the lanes, and when the traffic finally broke free close to Lynn, she tore up the highway.

Access to the hospital was through a single road, long and steep, that twisted its way through the woods. A beat-up Ford truck was parked at the bottom. Painted on the side panel were the words 'Reed Associates'.

The man sitting behind the wheel was a young Italian kid with a smooth, dark face and black hair spiked up with a lot of gel. A diamond earring and two gold hoops were in his left ear. He closed his *Maxim* magazine when Darby knocked on the window.

'I want to take a look around the hospital,' she said, showing him her laminated ID.

'You guys having a convention here or something? You're the second cop who's asked for a tour.'

'Someone else has been here recently?'

'This afternoon,' the security man said. 'Mr Reed gave him a tour.'

'Did this cop leave his name?'

'I have no idea. I didn't talk to him. Chucky did. I came down here to relieve Chucky of his shift. By that time, the dude was already talking to Mr Reed.'

'What did he look like?'

'Let's see . . . He was tall, at least six feet or so, black hair. He seemed pretty dressed up, nice shoes and stuff. He drove a Jag. Pay must be nice in Boston, huh?'

'He drove a Jaguar?'

'Yeah, a black one, real nice. It's one of the new models.'

'How can you tell?'

'I checked it out when he was up there with Mr Reed. I have a thing for nice cars. I own a Beemer.'

'Is Mr Reed here?'

'Yeah, he's up at the top somewhere.'

'I need to speak with him.'

'Hold on.' The security guard picked up a walkie-talkie. 'Mr Reed's on his way down.'

'What's your name?' Darby asked.

'Kevin Salustro.'

'Did you happen to see the Jag's licence plate?'

'No.'

'After I'm done with Mr Reed, I'm going to come back and ask you a few questions. While you're waiting, I want you to write down everything you remember about this cop including what you saw inside his car.'

'Like I said, I only caught a glimpse of him.'

'Just write down what you remember. You got a pen and paper?'

'No.'

'I'll get it for you,' Darby said.

Bryson arrived half an hour later, along with a van containing six cops. It was after six and the evening sky was pitch black.

Nathan Reed, the owner of Reed Associates, the company that provided security for the hospital, was a tall, wiry man with crooked yellow teeth and fingers stained by nicotine. Darby guessed the man was somewhere in his sixties. He wore a check flannel jacket and an orange hunting cap with fur flaps that covered his ears.

'It was the oddest thing, this cop showing up here out of the blue,' Reed told them. They were standing at the bottom of the hill, their backs to the wind. 'He spoke to one of my guys, Chucky, and I just happened to be here, so Chucky got on the horn and called me. We can't have anyone wandering through the hospital without an escort for liability reasons.'

'How did you know he was a cop?' Darby asked.

'He showed me his badge.'

'What was his name?'

'I don't know. He didn't tell me.'

'Did you ask?'

'No, ma'am, I didn't. Cop comes knocking, you do what you're told and don't ask too many questions.'

'Did he have an accent?'

'As a matter of fact he did. British or something,' Reed said. 'He showed me his badge and said he needed to get inside and take a look around the C wing. I told him the place had been cleaned out – there's nothing up there. He said he wanted to take a look so I took him up.'

'Mr Reed, this is going to sound like an odd question, but did you see his eyes?'

'His eyes?'

'Did you notice what colour they were?'

'Haven't the foggiest,' Reed said. 'He was wearing sunglasses. I don't mean to be a Nosy Nelly, but why are you asking me all these questions? Don't you know why he was here? I assume you people work together.'

'This cop you met, we don't know who he is,' Darby said. He sure as hell sounded like Malcolm Fletcher. The description was dead-on. 'Anything you can tell us will be extremely helpful.'

Reed cupped his hand over a lighter and lit a cigarette. 'You ever see that Clint Eastwood movie *High Plains Drifter*?'

'Several times,' Darby said.

'This guy gave off that same type of menace. You know, do exactly what I ask or there'll be hell to pay. That's why I didn't ask any questions. I took him up there to C wing and let him look around for a bit. Truth be told, I was glad when he left.'

'What time did he leave?'

Reed thought it over for a moment. 'Around four, I'd say.'

'Did he find anything up there?'

'No. Like I said, there's nothing up there. The whole place has been cleaned out. I took him to C wing, he looked around for a bit, then he thanked me and left.'

'He specifically asked you to take him to the C wing,' Darby said.

'Yes ma'am. C wing's the place where they once housed the violent offenders, the real nasty ones like Johnny Barber. You remember him?'

'Can't say that I do.'

Reed took a long drag off his cigarette. 'Johnny Barber – his real name was Johnny Edwards or something – Johnny was a serial rapist back in the early sixties. Worked at a barber shop and cut up women's faces with a straight-edge razor – hence the name. Court found him guilty by reason of insanity so he was shipped off here.' He pointed his thumb to the long road winding its way through the woods. 'Turns out he was also a great artist. They hung some of his paintings on the walls, and I've got to say, they were pretty damn impressive. Then he attacked a doctor – tried to stab him with a paintbrush of all things – so they took his art supplies away and you know what the crazy son of a bitch did? He started using his own turds as crayons. The pictures weren't that bad. Smelled horrible though.' Reed's laugh echoed over the wind.

'I need you to show me where this cop went,' Darby said.

Reed flicked his cigarette into the woods. 'I managed to plough out the main road here before my truck shit the bed, but the top of the campus is a mess,' he said. 'I hope you two are in the mood for some exercise 'cause we got a lot of walking to do.'

29

Bryson already had a flashlight. Darby grabbed the spare she kept in the trunk of her car and then followed Reed, along with Bryson and the six other men, up the steep access road.

A slick layer of ice covered the pavement. She walked carefully, watching each step. The hill, bordered with pine trees, their branches weighed down with heavy, wet snow, seemed to stretch for miles with no end in sight.

'The campus is in the process of being torn down,' Reed said, his breath pluming in the cold air. 'I told your cop friend the same thing. There's nothing in there, nothing at all. The whole place has been cleared out.'

'When did the hospital close?' Darby asked.

'An electrical fire in the morgue gutted the Mason wing back in eighty-two. The lackeys on Beacon Hill decided it was too expensive to fix – the hospital is over two hundred years old – and with the state-wide budget cuts in mental health, the hospital closed the following year.'

'There's a morgue in this building?'

'At one point in time, this place was a research hospital. When a patient died, the doctors would study their brains – this was back at the turn of the century when such things were allowed. Anyway, after the fire happened, the place shut down permanently – lack of funding and all that. I can't say I disagree with the decision. It would have cost a pretty penny to fix this place up.'

Darby nodded, not really listening, her focus turned inward on Malcolm Fletcher. What was his interest in an abandoned hospital? If he was, in fact, looking for something, why didn't he sneak in? Maybe he couldn't find another way in and decided to ask Reed for help.

When they reached the top of the hill, Darby was out of breath, her legs shaking with fatigue. Reed lit another cigarette.

The Sinclair Mental Health Facility, a massive Gothic structure of ancient brick and barred windows, was set around a wide courtyard holding the remains of a water fountain and several trees which were probably even older than the hospital. Some of the stained-glass windows were still intact.

'That there's the Kirkland building,' Reed said. 'Place is over two hundred years old.'

Darby had never seen anything so massive in both size and length. Going in there one could get lost. Forever.

'How big is this place?'

'About four hundred thousand square feet,' Reed said. 'There are eighteen floors not including the basement, which is a maze in and of itself. Kirkland is divided into two wings – Gable and Mason. You can't go inside Mason. The floors are pretty much rotted away, and the fire did a lot of damage, so we had the place sealed off back in eighty-nine. In another few months, everything you see here will be gone to make room for condos. Truth be told, I'm a little sad. This building's a historic landmark, the last of its kind. See those two buildings to your far left? Those used to be the tuberculosis buildings. They had one for male patients, one for female. There's a lot of history here.'

Darby waded through knee-high snow covering the courtyard. The place had the look and feel of a New England college campus from the early fifties – quaint and secluded, a sprawling mass of brick buildings tucked inside a heavily wooded area sitting on top of a hill overlooking Boston, eighteen miles to the south.

'Kirkland's become sort of a local tourist attraction ever since that movie *Creepers* came out,' Reed said. 'You see it?'

Darby shook her head. She was not a fan of horror movies any more. They hit too close to home.

'The Morrell book was much better,' Reed said. 'The story's about a group of urban explorers known as creepers who break into old historic buildings. The movie producers used the hospital as a location. We've had to increase security over the past five years. We have guards posted around the property twenty-four hours a day. Majority of people we arrest are teenagers and college students looking for a spot to drink and get high and screw, if you can believe it.'

Reed took out his keys and walked up the stairs to the main doors. The glass behind the steel security grate was cracked.

'You brought him through the front door?' Darby asked.

'Yes ma'am.'

'Is this the only way you can access the hospital?'

'The front door is the *safest* way to enter the hospital,' Reed said. 'There are some other entrances through the basement ducts and some old tunnels that lead out into different parts of the property, but half of 'em have collapsed or are about to. You try and go in that way, you're risking your life. That's why we got all this security around here. Place is a liability. Back in ninety-one, some asshole broke into the property, fell and cracked his head open. He sued and won a nice little settlement for himself. If you saw the legal bills, your head would spin.'

Beyond the front door was a hallway that opened up into a large, rectangular-shaped room stripped clean of its furniture. There was nothing in here but bare floors and walls covered with flecks of chipped white paint.

'This used to be the reception area,' Reed said. 'Grab a hardhat from that box over there. You two don't scare easily, do you?'

'If he gets scared, I'll hold his hand,' Darby said, glancing to Bryson. Tim didn't hear the comment.

He was moving the beam of his flashlight around the room.

'This one time, I took a group of ghost hunters through here for some TV show,' Reed said. 'They were carrying these weird gadgets that looked like props from that movie *Ghostbusters.* One of them thought they saw a ghost and the stupid son of a bitch ran away screaming and fell through a hole and fractured his foot. Stay behind me and watch your step.'

30

The adjoining room was as long and wide as a football field, with a vaulted ceiling and mouldy, water-stained wallpaper printed with tiny red and blue roses. The back wall had custom-made picture windows, many of which were broken or missing. The linoleum floor was covered in snow and patches of melting ice.

'This used to be the main dining room,' Reed said. 'Back in the forties, they had professional chefs that cooked all this fancy food. Brought in lobsters during the summer, had these big cookouts for the patients on the front lawn – there used to be a small golf course here, too, believe it or not. I wouldn't have minded staying here during those days. Place sounds like a resort. How much you know about Sinclair?'

'We don't know much,' Darby said.

'You want, I can tell you about the history. Might help pass the time. We got a lot of walking to do.'

'Sounds good.'

Reed walked through the dining room, his footsteps crunching over the snow and ice. 'When the hospital was first built back in the late eighteenth century, it was called the State Lunatic Hospital,' he said. 'The place was known for its humane treatment of patients. Dr Dale Linus – that would be the first hospital director – he believed in a humanistic approach to treating mental illness – fresh air, healthy food and exercise. It was a pretty radical idea at the time. Linus kept the number of patients to five hundred, making sure each patient got the help and treatment they deserved. In the beginning, they treated all types of people, not just criminals. A lot of the patients came here from all over the world because of the progressive therapies Linus invented.'

'What sort of progressive therapies?'

'Let's see . . . Well, there were the water therapies where they'd dunk patients into freezing cold water to try and cure their schizophrenia. Then they tried something called insulin comas. That was supposed to help calm patients down. Sinclair was the first hospital in the country to perform a lobotomy.'

'I don't know if that's necessarily progressive.'

'It was at the time. Now it seems barbaric, given the fact that you can pretty much pop a pill to treat almost any mental disorder. Sinclair was so successful, so revolutionary in its approaches to treating the mind, two buildings were devoted strictly to teaching doctors who came in from all over the world – they had to build a dormitory to house them all.'

Darby followed Reed into a cold corridor – same concrete, same chipped paint. A lot of the walls were covered in graffiti. One hallway was sunken in with debris.

'When did the hospital name change over to Sinclair?' Darby asked.

'Dr Phinneus Sinclair became the hospital director back in, oh, sixty-two, I think. That was around the time they started taking in only criminals. The more normal patients, for lack of a better term, went over to the McLean Hospital, which was gaining a reputation for treating the rich, rock stars and weirdo writers and poets, people like that. McLean was the place to go if you had money. Sinclair became the place to come to if you wanted to pursue studying the criminal mind. Dr Sinclair was trying to discover the origins of violent behaviour. He did a lot of studies involving children who came from broken homes.'

Darby had never come across Sinclair's name during her doctorate work. Maybe the studies were considered radical at one time. Now, in the twenty-first century, finding the origins of violent and deviant behaviour rooted in childhood trauma seemed commonplace.

Reed ducked underneath a beam and took them down a long corridor that opened up into a large, rectangular area with doors on both sides. Darby moved the beam of her flashlight through the rooms of broken windows. The rooms were various sizes. All of them were empty.

'These are the doctors' offices,' Reed said. 'Man, you should have seen the furniture in there. All antiques. Some guy bid on all of it, hauled it away and made a small fortune.'

He paused in front of a big room holding an ornate stained-glass window. 'This was the hospital director's office. Your cop friend stopped here for a moment, just stared for a bit like he was reminiscing or something. He didn't say anything but . . .'

'What?' Darby prompted.

'It's not important, really, just sort of odd. I just remembered he didn't take off his sunglasses. I mentioned he might want to take them off, given where we were heading, and he just ignored me and walked off like he knew where he was going.'

Darby followed Reed down three flights of dusty stairs, the ancient building creaking and moaning around her. Ten minutes later, Reed stopped in front of an old steel door and shined his light on the faded red lettering: WARD C.

'This is where they did the prefrontal lobotomies,' Reed said, opening the door. 'Watch your step in here. Moisture collects on the tiles, even in the winter. Place is sealed tighter than a flea's ass. It's slippery as hell.'

No windows, just pitch-black darkness. The cold room reeked of mildew. Mounted against the wall was an old General Electric clock covered in rust. Darby spotted several spigots. *They probably hooked up hoses to them to wash away the blood.* She wondered how many patients had undergone what was considered, at one point in time, to be a progressive medical solution to treating mental illness.

Reed's boots squeaked across the tiles. 'When I

first took the job, the steel tables with the leather restraints were still in here. They used to do shock treatments in here, too.'

A creaking sound as he opened the door at the far end. The adjoining hallway was in a state of partial ruin. Darby followed the man through another hallway and then it opened into a wide space full of two floors that reminded her of a prison. Cells were on either side, each steel door equipped with locks and a grating so doctors could look in on their patients. The doors were rusted, the small rooms stripped clean.

'This here's C wing,' Reed said. 'The cop walked over to this room here.'

Reed moved the beam of his flashlight inside and jumped back from the door. Darby moved past the man and looked into the cell.

Thumb-tacked to the wall underneath a windowsill was a photograph, a headshot of a woman with long blonde hair parted in the middle and feathered. She had piercing blue eyes in a deeply tanned face and wore a white collared shirt.

'That wasn't here this afternoon,' Reed said. 'I'll swear on a stack of bibles.'

Darby's attention was on the windowsill. Standing above the photograph was a statue of the Virgin Mary – the same statue that had been sewn inside Emma Hale and Judith Chen's pockets.

She turned to Bryson, who was staring at the statue, mesmerized.

'Do you know this woman?'

Bryson shook his head.

Darby examined the picture. It was printed on thick, glossy paper. There was no writing on the back, no date or time-stamp anywhere on the paper. Darby wondered if this picture had been printed on a computer. Every photography and drug store had kiosks where you could slip in a memory card and print out digital pictures in a matter of minutes.

'Mr Reed, would you excuse us for a moment?'

The caretaker nodded. He stepped away from the cell and joined the other men who were wandering around the vast room, beams of light crisscrossing over one another as they searched the cells on the two floors. Darby turned to Bryson.

'I've got evidence bags in the trunk, along with a spare kit. I can process this room myself, and you can be the witness to anything we find. It will be quicker than having to get people from the lab in here.'

'What about a camera?'

'I've got a Polaroid and a digital.'

Darby's cell phone vibrated against her hip.

'What do you think of Sinclair?' Malcolm Fletcher asked. 'It's like walking through purgatory, isn't it?'

31

'I wouldn't know,' Darby said, motioning to Bryson. 'I've never been to purgatory.'

'Haven't you read Dante?' Fletcher asked. 'Or don't they teach that in class any more?'

'I've read *Paradiso*.'

'Yes. The good Catholic girls always learn about heaven first, don't they?'

Fletcher laughed. Bryson stood behind Darby. She held the phone an inch from her ear so Bryson could listen.

'The nuns should have made you read *Purgatorio*,' Fletcher said. 'It's where Dante describes purgatory as a place where suffering has a real purpose that can lead you to redemption, if you're willing to go the distance. Are you willing to go the distance?'

'I found the room with the photograph.'

'Do you recognize the woman?'

'No. Who is she?'

'What do you think of the Virgin Mary statue?'

'Is it supposed to have some sort of meaning?'

'Now is not the time to be coy, Darby. The moment of revelation is at hand.'

'Let's talk about the woman in the photograph. Why did you leave it here?'

'I'd be more inclined to answer your question if you answer one of mine,' Fletcher said. 'Is the statue on the windowsill the same one you found on Emma Hale and Judith Chen?'

Darby wasn't about to give the former profiler any specifics about the case. 'Why did you place it here?' she asked. 'Why did you want me to find it?'

'Tell me about the statues and I'll give you the name of the woman in the photograph.'

Bryson shook his head.

'I'm afraid I don't know what you're talking about,' Darby said.

'Why don't you ask Detective Bryson? Or would you rather put him on the phone?'

How did Fletcher know Bryson was in the room?

He must be watching.

Bryson moved away, drawing his weapon, and ushered Reed inside the cell. Darby covered the phone's mouthpiece.

'Don't tell him a goddamn thing,' Bryson said, and then signalled his men.

Darby's gloved hand gripped the SIG and slid it from the shoulder holster. She looked past the door, into the dark, decaying room cut with blades of light and steaming breath, wondering where the former profiler was hiding.

Darby pressed the phone back to her ear. 'Tell me about the woman in the photograph.'

'You can't find this woman alone,' Malcolm

Fletcher said. 'But if you're willing to take the journey, I'll be your guide.'

If this was some sort of trap, why would Fletcher stage it in an abandoned mental hospital with a room full of cops? It was too elaborate a setup. Could the man possibly be telling her the truth?

'I think you need to explain your agenda,' Darby said.

'There's no reason to fear me. We're both after the same goal.'

'Which is?'

'The truth,' Fletcher said. 'I'll lead you to the woman in the photograph, but once you open Pandora's Box, there's no turning back. You may want to give that some thought.'

'And you're going to guide me to her out of the goodness of your heart.'

'Think of me as the boatman Charon guiding you across the river of hate.'

'Where is she?'

'She's waiting for you downstairs.'

Darby's breath caught. It took her a moment to regroup.

'She's here,' she said.

'Yes. Are you ready to meet her?'

There was no menace in Fletcher's voice, none of that jovial taunting from the previous conversations. What Darby heard was a cool, neutral tone that conjured a memory from her childhood – ten years old and taking a shortcut through the Belham woods and seeing three boys from her class. They had found a dead coyote. One of the boys, Ricky something, the fat one with the mean eyes, asked her if she wanted to see it. Darby said no. They called her a chicken, a frightened little girl.

To prove them wrong, she marched down the embankment, tripped and fell. She came to a hard stop, dimly aware of the buzzing sound of flies behind the boys' laughter, and when she pushed herself up, she felt something hot and alive squirming between her fingers. Maggots, hundreds of them, roiled inside the carcass. Darby screamed and the boys laughed harder. When she started to cry, the fat one, laughing, said, 'Hey, don't get mad at us. You're the one who decided to go down there.'

The memory vanished when Fletcher said, 'I don't mean to be rude, but I'm pressed for time. I need your answer now.'

Why was Fletcher doing this? Was this a ruse in order for him to try to get information about the case? Or did the former profiler actually know something?

Darby's attention shifted to the Virgin Mary statue on the windowsill. *Where the hell did you get it?*

Don't tell him a goddamn thing, Bryson had said.

Stay or go? Call it.

'Call me when you're ready to share,' Darby said and hung up. She turned to Reed, who appeared visibly shaken. 'How many floors are below us?'

The old caretaker took off his glove and wiped his

face with a liver-spotted hand. 'Four,' he said, 'and that's not including the basement level.'

'Have you been down there recently?'

'Nobody's been down there in years.'

'We may need to search the hospital. I'll need you and your men to help us.'

'You want us to help you search the *entire* hospital? I can't allow that, Miss McCormick. There are too many areas that are unstable. It's not safe.'

Darby was staring at the photograph of the young woman. Was she somewhere inside the hospital? Was she alive? Was she hurt or injured?

'Please stay inside this room, Mr Reed, until I come back.'

Darby, her pistol drawn, stuck close to the walls. Above her and across the room, Bryson's men slammed back cell doors, searching for Malcolm Fletcher. She doubted they would find him. The former federal agent was too skilled at hiding. He had eluded capture for decades.

Tim Bryson stood at the end of the hallway, breath steaming in the cold air above the beam of the tactical flashlight mounted underneath his handgun, a 9mm Beretta. She got Bryson's attention and nodded to an empty room. The window had bars on it, the broken glass protected by a mesh grille. Snow had collected on the sill.

'I think we need to organize a search party,' Darby told Bryson.

'You think the woman in the picture is waiting for us somewhere in here?'

'He wanted to lead us downstairs. I think we need to take a look.'

Bryson thought it over for a moment. He was sweating.

'You may be right,' he said. 'I'll organize the search. Process the room, and get back to the lab. I want to know what the son of a bitch is up to.'

32

With the aid of a flashlight, Malcolm Fletcher carefully made his way down a hallway with rotted floorboards, far away from the Boston police.

Fletcher had an excellent visual memory. He remembered the layout of the hospital, having roamed through its corridors lives and lives ago when he was employed as a special agent for the FBI's newly formed Behavioral Science Unit.

In 1954, Hurricane Edna had ripped one of the massive oaks in front of the hospital and sent the tree crashing into the roof, the falling debris crushing most of the floors. Given the exorbitant cost of fixing the floors, the board of directors decided to seal off the passages.

When an electrical fire gutted a good portion of the Mason wing in 1982, the hospital was already under state care. Lawmakers, sensing a potentially lucrative payday, put the land up for sale. A historical society looking to save the hospital, considered by many to be an architectural landmark, the last of its kind, filed petitions and injunctions. Potential buyers were scared off by the threat of significant legal costs and a long, protracted court fight.

For twenty-odd years the hospital had been abandoned, and during that time, the long New England winters had caused significant rot and water damage to the walls and floors. It had taken a considerable amount of patience and skill to find a safe passage to the top floor; the amount of decay and ruin was severe.

Fletcher slid into a room with broken windows. He removed his cell phone, found a signal and called Jonathan Hale.

'I believe I know the man who killed your daughter,' Fletcher said.

Darby had left her car unlocked. Her kit was in the trunk. Reed radioed Kevin, the young man parked in the pickup at the end of the road, and asked him to bring the orange box in the trunk to the C wing, which he did, half an hour later.

She took pictures then decided she wanted help processing the hospital room. She bagged the photograph and statue and called Coop from the road.

'Fletcher left us two gifts,' Darby said. 'A photograph and – get this – a Virgin Mary statue. I'm pretty sure the statue is the same one we found with Hale and Chen.'

'Do we know where or how Special Agent Creepy found the statue?'

'We do not.'

'Why lead you to an abandoned hospital, though? What's the point? He could have dropped the photograph and statue in the mail.'

'It's not as dramatic.'

'True.'

'And maybe Fletcher wants us to discover something about that particular room. He deliberately left the statue and photograph inside a patient room that housed violent offenders – the same room he had been to earlier in the day.'

'How long did you say the hospital has been closed?'

'At least twenty years,' Darby said. 'Probably more like thirty.'

'And you think you're going to find the name of the patient or patients who occupied that particular room? Good luck with that.'

'I'll see you in an hour.'

As Darby drove, she thought about Coop's parting words.

When Sinclair closed, the truly violent offenders were most likely transferred to other psychiatric hospitals. The schizophrenics, the patients who were bipolar or manic depressive, would be evaluated and then, thanks to the ever constant squeeze of mental health dollars, treated on an outpatient basis and pushed back into the street. The files had been floating through the state's mental health system for decades. Trying to track down a patient file, even with a specific name, was tantamount to finding the proverbial needle in the haystack.

*

Coop was waiting for her inside their office.

'Where's Keith?' Darby asked.

'He went home to have dinner with the wife and kids and then is coming back to the lab to help us process the room. Let's take a look at the photograph first.'

After taking pictures, Coop examined the paper. It didn't contain any marks or distinguishing characteristics.

'The woman in the picture, with the hairstyle and clothes, I'm guessing it was taken in the early eighties,' Darby said. 'What are you going to use to treat the paper?'

'Ninhydrin mixed with heptane,' Coop said, flicking the switch for the ventilation unit.

Darby put on the safety goggles and a breathing mask. Coop, wearing a pair of nitrile gloves, sprayed the back of the paper. It turned purple. They both examined the paper, waiting for the ninhydrin to react with the amino acids left by the human hand.

There were no fingerprints.

Coop sprayed the side holding the photograph.

'No prints,' Coop said. 'Lucky for us we already know who he is.'

33

Hannah Givens sat on the bed with the tray of food – toast and eggs – that the man named Walter Smith had left inside the sliding food carrier. She didn't have a clock or a calendar, but this was her second breakfast. Today must be Sunday.

She didn't have windows, either, but she did have plenty of light. Two pretty Tiffany-style lamps were inside the room – one on the nightstand next to the bed, the other set up on a small reading table full of thumbed-through issues of *People*, *Star*, *Us*, *Cosmopolitan* and *Glamour*.

The most interesting item was the big white armoire. The shirts were small and mediums; Hannah was a large, a size 12. Shoes were arranged neatly at the bottom – Prada, Kenneth Cole and two pairs of Jimmy Choos, all of them a size six. Hannah wore a size ten. Clearly the shoes and clothes hadn't been picked out for her.

Hannah thought about the clothes and magazines with their wrinkled pages and again wondered if another woman had lived in here before her. If so, what had happened to her? The question left a cold space in her stomach.

She wrapped the down comforter around her even

though the room was warm. The fear was still there but it wasn't holding her hostage any more. It had drifted to some other place and, for a reason she couldn't quite explain, she didn't feel the need to cry or scream. She had done all of that, anyway.

Waking up in the dark for the first time, her head foggy, Hannah had a brief moment where she believed she was at home. Then the memory of what had happened descended on her like scalding water and she was out of the bed and stumbling through the strange dark, bumping into foreign objects as her fear reached a hysterical pitch and then she was screaming, screaming it all out until her throat was raw.

Finally, she summoned the nerve to face the dark and searched the room as a blind person would – slow, cautious steps; hands feeling over each object to register its shape. Here was a table. Here, a chair – leather, judging by its cool, smooth feel. Next a nightstand, and what was this? It felt like a lamp. She found the switch and turned it on.

The first thing she noticed was her pyjamas – soft, pink flannel. They were her size but these weren't her pyjamas. The man named Walter had undressed her. He had come in here while she was unconscious and taken off her jacket and clothes. He had seen her naked.

Walter, Hannah was sure, hadn't raped her. The two times she had had sex, she had woken up the next morning feeling slightly sore. Walter hadn't raped her but he *had* undressed her. Had he touched her? Taken pictures? What? What was he going to do to her? *Why* did he want her?

One thing was clear: Walter didn't want her to leave. The room had one door but no doorknob. Mounted on the wall was a keypad unit much like the ones she had seen in office buildings; you needed a keycard and a code to open it. Drilled into the door was a one-way peephole. Walter could see in but Hannah couldn't see out.

Clearly Walter wanted her to feel comfortable. The room was the size of a small studio apartment, windowless, with a small kitchenette and walls painted a warm yellow. A beautiful red cashmere throw blanket was draped over the back of a leather reading chair with matching ottoman. Behind the chair was a bookshelf holding well-read paperback romance books. A cloth shower curtain hid a toilet but there was no bath or shower. The room even had its own thermostat.

The two cabinets above the kitchen sink held boxes of cereal and Saltine crackers. There were no dishes. No stove. The drawers didn't contain any silverware or anything sharp, just paper and sanitary napkins, tampons and an odd assortment of make-up. The refrigerator was stocked with cartons of milk, orange juice, yogurt, plastic bottles of Poland Spring and almost every type of soda – Coke, Pepsi, Mountain Dew, Dr Pepper and Slice.

Hannah's attention shifted to the centre of the

room, to the white roses in a plastic vase sitting on top of the small, circular dining table. The petals had started to wilt.

A rapist wouldn't leave flowers for her. A rapist would come in and have his way with her.

Walter hadn't come into her room (*yet*, she reminded herself). Every time he brought her meals (three times a day) he placed a plastic tray in the food carrier and slid it through without saying a word. For lunch (or was it dinner?) he had made chicken with mashed potatoes and gravy.

Hannah rolled over in her bed and shut her eyes. Her roommates had to be wondering why she hadn't returned home. Monday morning she was scheduled to work the early shift at the deli. If she didn't show up, the owner, Mr Alves, would call her at home and leave a nasty message on the answering machine. Robin or Terry would hear the message and call her parents. Her parents would call the police. People would start looking for her. She needed to find a way to hold on and survive until she was found.

What if they couldn't find her? Wouldn't there come a point where the police would stop looking?

She couldn't think about that. She needed to stay positive, as impossible as it seemed, and keep her head clear so she could think.

Yesterday, after breakfast, Hannah searched the room for something she might be able to use as a weapon. No microwave or coffee pot. The small colour TV was bolted to its small wooden stand. No hot water in the sink, only cold. The refrigerator's produce drawers had been taken out. Apparently Walter was afraid of her using one of the drawers to try and knock him over the head or something. He had used chains and padlocks to secure the two dining chairs to the table legs. She could move the chairs out to sit but she couldn't use them as weapons. Walter had foreseen that option. The table legs were too thick and sturdy; she couldn't break one off unless she had a saw.

At some point Walter would want to have his way with her and she needed to be prepared. Taking a deep breath, Hannah forced herself to look at the room again.

34

Okay, Hannah thought. *What places haven't I searched?*

The mattress and chair cushions.

Needing to do something, Hannah got out of bed and moved her hand between the mattress and box spring. Failing to find anything, she moved to the leather chair, removed the seat cushions and searched the dark crevices with her fingers. They bumped up against something hard. *Please God let it be a knife*, she thought, and pulled the item into the light.

It was a small spiral memo pad, the kind that could easily be tucked inside a shirt pocket. Hannah opened the notebook and saw pages written in faded pencil. She read the first page.

I found this notebook on the floor under the bed. A small pencil was tucked inside the spiral. Walter must have dropped it – when, I don't know. Maybe during one of the times we fought. The notebook must have slipped out of his pocket or shirt and he forgot about it. He was using it as a grocery list. Now I'm using it to write down my thoughts. If I don't do it, I'll go insane.

I don't know how long I've been here. After three months, I stopped tracking time. Time has no meaning down here, and thinking about it fills me with terror.

I can't fight him any more. I don't have the strength. Now I've decided to be polite. I do everything he asks. When he brings me gifts, I always thank him (he loves bringing me nice clothes). Walter brings me anything I want (except the phone). All I have to do is ask. Walter, my ugly genie. One time, early on, I must have been here a month, we were talking about Christmas and he asked, 'What was the best gift you ever received?' I told him about the platinum chain and locket with the picture of my mother. My father gave it to me last Christmas. He asked me where it was, and I told him. I didn't think much about it. We were just talking.

A week later, he gave me the necklace. I was shocked.

'I borrowed your keys – they were in your purse,' Walter said. 'Do you now see how much I love you?'

Walter never appears upset or sad or angry – he doesn't appear to feel anything, *which is what scares me the most. It's like there's nothing living behind his eyes, at least nothing any normal person would recognize. I picture his mind as a dark attic full of cobwebs and nasty, crawling things that bite if you get too close. Walter talks like we're the best of friends. I share everything with him, making up stories, whatever, so he'll feel close to me. I pretend, just like I did in the acting classes. I pretend I care. I pretend to understand him while taking in my surroundings, looking for the perfect moment to escape.*

I've convinced him to give me a bath twice a day. He always stands outside the door, which he leaves open a crack so he can talk to me. HE NEEDS TO TALK. *That's what feeds him – talking, human contact. I know this now.*

Walter has just left my room. We watched a movie together, Pretty Woman. *He likes to watch romantic comedies every night after dinner. He brings wine (always in a plastic container, never glass; he knows, if given the opportunity, I'd smash the bottle across his head). This time he sat with me on the bed. I was wearing a dress and shoes he had picked out (Walter insists on getting dressed up every night, like we're a couple going out on the town). I styled my hair the way he likes it and put on nail polish. He even gave me a small bottle of the Chanel perfume I love so much. I wore it for him. I'm his doll – his personal, private living doll. During the entire movie, I could tell he wanted to hold my hand.*

When the movie ended, Walter went to remove the DVD (keeping a close eye on me, of course) and the idea I've been nursing for weeks came to mind.

'Don't leave yet,' I said.

Walter looked pleased. He loves it when I ask him to stay.

I smiled and swallowed back my fear. As revolting as it was, I had to go through with it.

I stood. This was my last chance.

'What is it, Emma?'

I unbuttoned my dress.

'What are you doing?' he asked.

I let the dress drop to the floor and stood in front of him, naked, except for the chain with the locket holding a picture of my mother. I had to wear it for courage.

'What are you doing?'

I tried hard to keep the hatred and disgust out of my voice. 'I want to make love to you.'

Walter didn't answer. He looked away, embarrassed.

When I touched him, he pulled away.

'Don't be scared,' I said.

'I'm not.'

'Then what is it?'

Walter didn't answer.

'Are you . . . a virgin?'

'Having sex with someone when you're not in love, it's a sin,' Walter said, 'an abomination in the eyes of God.'

But kidnapping someone and keeping them prisoner apparently wasn't. 'How can it be a sin if I want to make love to you?'

Walter didn't answer, but his eyes moved up to my chest. I grabbed his good hand and placed it on my breast. He was shaking.

'Make love to me.' If I got him on the bed with me, he'd be vulnerable. Get on top of him and poke his goddamn eyes out with my thumbs. I was nursing enough hatred to know I could go through with it.

'It's okay,' I said, moving his hand across my breasts. He was breathing hard but he wouldn't stop shaking. I moved his hand down across my stomach and he yanked it away and stormed out of the room.

He came back later and gave me a small plastic statue of the Virgin Mary. It's on my nightstand right now. He made me pray with him for strength. We pray together every night, kneeling on opposite sides of the bed, and give thanks to HIS Blessed Mother. Walter never shuts his eyes. I pray along with him, of course. I don't tell him I don't believe in those things any more.

After he left, I held the statue in my hand, hoping it would bring me comfort. It doesn't. I used to think of hell as some dark place full of fire and eternal pain. Now I think of it as a place where you'll be alone forever, a place where you feel a total lack of anything. I know I'm going to die alone in this room. I just don't know when.

Hannah heard a beep, followed by the sound of locks clicking back. She shoved the notebook under the chair cushion as the door swung open.

35

The man named Walter Smith came into the room with his head bowed in either shame or embarrassment, maybe both. Hannah had a chance to look him over in the soft light.

His face had been badly burned. Even under all the makeup, she could see thick, bumpy scars. *That's why he's keeping his head bowed*, she thought. *He doesn't want me staring at his face.*

Knowing he was physically damaged made him seem inferior for some reason, less threatening. Hannah felt as though she might be able to reason with him. She could reason with anyone.

Walter held a wicker basket packed with an assortment of muffins and croissants. Tissue paper overflowed from the sides of the basket and the handle was decorated with ribbons. It reminded her of the get-well basket her father had bought on the morning after her mother's hysterectomy.

Hannah felt a sense of unease as she watched Walter place the basket on the table and retreat to the shadows near the sink. His hair was long, wet and messy. It looked too perfect. If it was a wig or a hairpiece, it was the best one she had ever seen.

Walter, his head still bowed, stared at the floor and cleared his throat.

'Your nose is looking better.'

Was it? She didn't have a mirror, but she had felt her nose with her fingers. It was still swollen. She wondered if it was broken.

'I'm sorry about what happened,' Walter said.

Hannah didn't answer, was afraid to answer. What if she said the wrong thing and set him off? If he came at her with his fists, she couldn't protect herself. He was too big, too strong.

'It was an accident,' he said. 'I would never hurt someone I love.'

A cold sweat broke across her skin.

You can't love me, she wanted to say. *You don't even* know *me*.

It was as though Walter had read her mind.

'I know all about you,' he said. 'Your name is Hannah Lee Givens. You graduated from Jackson High School in Des Moines, Iowa. You're a freshman at Northeastern University. You're majoring in English. You want to be a teacher. When you can afford it, you like to go to the movies. You go to the library and check out books by Nora Roberts and Nicholas Evans. I can bring you some of those books, if you'd like, and movies. Just tell me what you want and I'll get it. We can watch movies together.' Walter looked up and forced a smile. 'Is there something you'd like to see?'

How long had he been following her? And why hadn't she seen him?

Walter seemed to be waiting for her to answer.

What had the writer in the notebook said? *That's what feeds him, talking. He needs to talk, needs to connect.*

Hannah wanted him to leave so she could get back to the notebook and read what else this woman had written about Walter. Maybe there was something in there that could help her figure out a way to escape – and she *would* escape. She *would* find a way. Hannah Lee Givens knew she wouldn't live down here forever – and she sure as hell wasn't going to be used as a punching bag. She just needed to figure out a way to survive until she was found.

'You're still upset,' Walter said. 'I understand. I'll come back later with your dinner. Maybe we can talk then.'

He took out his wallet and waved it in front of the card reader. The lock clicked back. He didn't punch in a code. He opened the door but he didn't leave.

'I'm going to make you very happy, Hannah. I promise.'

36

Monday morning, while driving to work, Darby received a phone call from Tim Bryson. The commissioner wanted to meet at nine.

'I've also got a copy of the murder books from the Saugus cases Fletcher worked on back in the eighties,' Bryson said. 'Why don't we meet early? That way you'll have a chance to read it over.'

Darby found Bryson seated in the waiting area outside the commissioner's office. On his forehead was a gauze pad wrapped under two Band-Aids. The previous night, while searching one of Sinclair's lower levels, Bryson had whacked his head on the edge of a steel beam.

'I'm guessing six stitches,' Darby said, sitting next to him.

'Try ten. How are you feeling?'

'My back and legs are sore. I've never done so much crawling and bending in my entire life.'

Along with assistance from Danvers police, a dozen search groups, aided by Reed and his security men and architectural blueprints of the hospital floors, had examined a portion of Sinclair's lower levels all night Saturday and throughout Sunday, calling off the search at a few minutes past midnight. Absolutely nothing was found.

'I told you he was playing us,' Bryson said.

'We still haven't searched the basement fully.'

'You really believe that woman is lying somewhere inside the hospital.'

'I believe Fletcher wants us to find something.'

'I still think you're wrong.'

'If I am, I'll buy you a drink.'

'No, you'll buy me dinner.' Bryson's smile wiped away his years. He handed her a thick folder. 'Here are copies of the murder books for the two strangled women from Saugus. Go ahead and read. I'm going to get some coffee. How do you like yours?'

'Black,' Darby said, opening the cover.

On the evening of 5 June 1982, nineteen-year-old Margaret Anderson, from Peabody, was last seen leaving a friend's party. The next morning her partially nude body was discovered along the Route One highway in Saugus. Three weeks later, a twenty-year-old Revere woman named Paula Kelly left her shift at a diner. Kelly's body was found dumped on the highway less than a mile away from Anderson's, a man's leather belt, size 38, wrapped around her throat. Both women were raped, but no semen was found.

Nineteen-year-old Sam Dingle lived at home with his parents and his younger sister and worked at the Saugus mall at a music store that both women frequented regularly. The store manager said Dingle had spoken at length to both women on several occasions and had even asked Paula Kelly for her phone number.

Saugus police had recovered a partial thumbprint from the belt around Kelly's throat. The print came from Sam Dingle's right thumb.

The belt never made it to the state lab for further testing. The evidence room at the Saugus police station had lost its key piece of evidence. Sam Dingle was never arrested.

While Saugus police tried to build a case against him, searching for more evidence, Dingle, according to his sister Lorna, suffered a nervous breakdown and was admitted to the Sinclair Mental Health Facility. Six months later, Dingle was discharged. He lived at home with his parents for a week before hitchhiking out west.

Bryson came back and handed her a cup of coffee with a plastic lid. 'You're the first woman I've ever met who drinks her coffee black.'

'Why ruin a good thing?'

Bryson nodded with his chin to the murder book. 'What do you think?'

'I think I'd like to talk to Sam Dingle.'

'So would I,' Bryson said. 'We're looking for him. His parents are dead, and his sister doesn't live in Saugus.'

'I'll call the state lab and see what they have for evidence.'

Bryson sipped his coffee. 'A call came in this morning from two girls living in Brighton,' he said. 'A college student named Hannah Givens was reported missing. Her roommates called it in. They all go to Northeastern. According to the report, Hannah Givens was supposed to come home after her Friday shift at some deli in Downtown Crossing. They called her cell and left messages. Givens hasn't come home or called.'

'Is she local?' Darby was thinking maybe the student had gone home for the weekend to visit her parents.

'Her parents live in Boise, Idaho,' Bryson said. 'I don't know all the details yet, it's just a preliminary report. Watts is on his way to Brighton to look into it. We have some other missing-person reports from the past month, but none involving female college students.'

The commissioner's secretary was a thin, neat man with long, manicured fingers and blond highlights in his gelled brown hair. 'The commissioner will see you now.'

37

Christina Chadzynski sat behind a wide mahogany desk, reading a file under the soft light of a lamp. Her office, wide and airy with windows overlooking the grey sky hanging over Boston, was decorated with nautical antiques and replicas of old wooden sailing ships.

Four chairs were set up in front of the desk. Darby took the seat next to Bryson and waited for the commissioner to finish reading his report detailing the events from Friday night until Sunday evening.

Chadzynski closed the file. 'I don't even know where to begin.' She took off her glasses and massaged the bridge of her nose. The corners of her eyes were lined with wrinkles. Even with makeup, the woman looked tired. 'Let's start with the man you met Friday night at Emma Hale's home.'

'Malcolm Fletcher,' Darby said.

'You're sure this man is Fletcher?'

'Detective Bryson showed me his picture from the FBI website. That's the man I met. Fletcher was here in eighty-two, consulting on two strangling cases for the Saugus police. We're investigating a possible connection.'

'And we still don't know what Fletcher was doing inside Emma Hale's home.'

'No. Mr Hale claims he doesn't know the man.'

Chadzynski's brown eyes were as cold and unforgiving as an X-ray. 'Are you suggesting that Jonathan has hired the services of a known felon?'

'Do you know Mr Hale?' Darby asked.

'We travel in the same social circles. My husband knows him very well. They do a lot of charity work together.'

'We know Malcolm Fletcher accessed the building through the garage,' Darby said. 'He took the service elevator to Emma Hale's floor and entered her apartment. Burglary examined the locks. They weren't picked. He had a key. I think it would be prudent to place Jonathan Hale under surveillance.'

'Darby, the man is a respected member of the community. I can't have him followed without a valid reason, and I certainly can't bring him in for questioning. The press would crucify us.'

'Hear me out. Malcolm Fletcher is the man I met inside Emma Hale's home. I don't know what he was doing there. Either he's working alone, for a reason we don't yet understand, or he's working for Hale.

'For the moment, let's assume Fletcher is acting solo – and that may, in fact, be the case,' Darby continued. 'We know Fletcher was here once before, back in the early eighties, when he was working as a profiler. Is it possible he's independently investigating a connection between the strangulations and the murders of Chen and Hale? Yes. We also know Hale's Newton office was broken into and the surveillance tapes, the DVDs, for Emma Hale's building are, in fact, missing. So we do have some evidence to suggest that Fletcher's acting alone. However, given what we know about the man's history and his status on the Most Wanted List, don't you think it wise to place Hale under surveillance for his own protection?'

'Darby has a valid point,' Bryson added.

Chadzynski put on her glasses. 'How many times have you spoken with Malcolm Fletcher?'

'I spoke with him inside Emma Hale's home,' Darby said. 'So far, he's called me twice – Saturday afternoon while I was at Judith Chen's and then later while Tim and I were at Sinclair.'

'And he hasn't called you since?'

'Not yet.'

'Do you think he'll call you again?'

'I think it's a strong possibility.'

'What do you base that on?'

'He's inserted himself into our investigation. He led me to Sinclair where we found, in a room inside an area where they supposedly held violent offenders, a picture of a woman and a statue of the Virgin Mary – the same statue we found inside the pockets of Hale and Chen.'

'Where did he get the statue? Do we know?'

'We have no idea.'

'And the woman in the photograph,' Chadzynski

said. 'Is she connected to these strangled women from Saugus?'

Bryson answered the question. 'Cliff Watts passed her picture around the Saugus station. They don't know who she is. She's not listed in any of their missing-person cases. I'm going to give a copy of the picture to our Missing Persons Unit after this meeting.'

'My understanding is you searched the hospital and failed to find anything else,' Chadzynski said.

'We only managed to search part of the hospital,' Darby said. 'The basement itself is a maze. Some sections are sealed off because they're unstable. Other areas are locked. The place is massive, and it took a good amount of time to map out the areas we searched. We only had a day and a half.'

'So you think we should continue the search?'

'I do.'

'Tim?'

'I don't see the need.' Bryson explained his position.

Chadzynski turned back to Darby and said, 'What do you think Malcolm Fletcher wants you to find? You can't honestly believe a living woman is trapped inside the hospital.'

'The last time I spoke to Fletcher, he mentioned a quote by George Bernard Shaw – "If you can't get rid of the family skeleton, you might as well make it dance." I don't think he was being clever. I got the sense he was warning me. He mentioned opening

Pandora's Box. I think there's something inside that hospital, and he wants us to find it.'

'Or, as Tim suggested, Fletcher is simply jerking us around.'

'That very well may be true,' Darby said. 'The fact is he's involved himself in this case. He left us the same Virgin Mary statue we found in Hale and Chen's pockets. I'd like to know where he got it.'

'You think he wants to help our investigation?'

'I don't know what the man's motives are,' Darby said. 'What little I know about him came from the FBI website, which isn't much.'

Bryson said, 'There's also another theory: What if Malcolm Fletcher murdered Hale and Chen?'

'That's not Mr Fletcher's style,' Chadzynski said.

'Do you know something about him?'

'How many people have you told about Malcolm Fletcher?'

'I told Watts,' Bryson said, turning to Darby.

'Jackson Cooper and Keith Woodbury know,' she said. 'I haven't told anyone else.'

Chadzynski crossed her legs. 'What I'm about to say I'd like to stay inside this room.'

38

'This is the second time Malcolm Fletcher has resurfaced in Boston,' Chadzynski said. 'The first time was roughly nine years ago. Do you remember the Sandman case?'

'It was big news.' Darby had followed the story in the papers.

A serial murderer named Gabriel LaRouche had murdered a family in Marblehead, a North Shore town north of Boston, and called the police. LaRouche, watching the house through sophisticated surveillance equipment, waited until all the police were gathered inside and then detonated the bomb he had left at the crime scene. Two more families were killed before he was captured.

'Do you know Jack Casey?' Chadzynski asked.

'The former profiler,' Darby said. 'He's the one who caught Miles Hamilton, the "All-American Psycho".'

'Yes. Casey had retired from the Bureau and was working as the chief of detectives for Marblehead, where the first family was murdered. Boston SWAT was called in at one point – there was a hostage situation on a highway. I have a personal friend at the Bureau, someone who works in Investigative

Support. Jack Casey brought Fletcher in as a behind-the-scenes consultant. After the Sandman case was solved, Casey left Marblehead and hasn't been seen or heard from since. Fletcher disappeared. Several years later, he was placed on the FBI's Most Wanted List.'

'Fletcher attacked the agents in eighty-four,' Darby said. 'Why did the Feds wait so long to place him on the list? Do you know?'

'The Bureau wanted to handle the matter quietly.'

'What a surprise.'

'Malcolm Fletcher was one of their best profilers,' Chadzynski said. 'His clearance rate is unprecedented. The problem was he crossed the line into vigilantism. The last dozen or so serial cases he worked on, each killer died. The last four cases he worked, the suspects disappeared. My friend didn't say how long this had been going on, but when the Bureau found out, they sent in three agents to apprehend Fletcher and you know what happened next.

'After the FBI placed him on their list, a task force was formed to apprehend him. The problem, from my understanding, is that nobody knows much about him. For a man on the run, he lives quite well. He stays in good hotels. He enjoys fine wine and cigars. He prefers driving luxury cars.'

'The security guard at Sinclair said Fletcher drove a Jaguar,' Darby said.

'He's also a clothing snob,' Chadzynski said. 'I remember my friend saying Fletcher was ordering hand-made suits and shirts from a well-known tailor in London's Mayfair district. Nobody knows anything about the man's family life or if his eye condition was caused by some genetic defect or disease. I was told the man isn't a psychopath. He kills for specific reasons. Are you familiar with *The Shadow*?'

'The movie with Alex Baldwin? It wasn't very good.'

'Actually, I was referring to an old pulp-magazine character. The Shadow was a vigilante. He skulked around in the dark, fighting for justice.'

'"Who knows what evil lurks in the hearts of men? The Shadow knows,"' Bryson said. He saw Darby's expression, and with a slight grin, added, 'Before your time.'

'Malcolm Fletcher is the same way,' Chadzynski said. 'He only targets people whom he believes have committed some grievous offence. I heard speculation – and, at the moment, that's all it is, idle speculation – that Fletcher was working independently on some of his unsolved cases. Maybe these Saugus cases are connected to Hale and Chen in some way. I'll need to make some phone calls.'

'You're going to bring the Feds into this?' Darby asked.

'We need to consider the possibility. They have access to information about the man that we don't.'

'I think that's a mistake.'

'I agree with Darby,' Bryson added. 'The Feds will come in, take over the case and when things go wrong, they'll start pointing the fingers back at us, get their PR machine to cover their ass.'

'Let me call my friend and see if I can make some subtle inquiries,' Chadzynski said. 'I doubt the task force would come here based solely on a sighting. They'd want concrete evidence before they mobilize. In the interim, we need to take some proactive measures. Darby, since he seems to be focused on you, with your permission I'd like to place a trap-and-trace on all of your phones. I'd also like to place you under surveillance.'

Darby nodded.

'Tim, you have surveillance experience,' Chadzynski said. 'Can you head it up?'

'I'll take care of it.'

'Good. As for continuing to search through Sinclair, I'd like to suspend the operation until we have something more concrete. I want our focus on Judith Chen.'

'We may have another potential victim,' Bryson said. He told Chadzynski about Hannah Givens.

'Have either of you spoken to Dr Karim?' Chadzynski asked.

'I've left a message at his office over the weekend,' Darby said. 'I'm hoping he'll cooperate.'

'I'll take care of it,' Chadzynski said. 'Karim likes to push, and I like to push back. Keep me informed at every step.'

The commissioner stood. 'Good work on the necklace, Darby. Let's see what else we can find.'

39

When Darby arrived at the lab, she immediately went to Serology. Coop had set up in the back, near the grouping of windows with the strong light. Keith Woodbury was taking pictures.

The pink sweatshirt, nylon running pants, socks and sneakers were laid out on sheets of butcher paper. Like Emma Hale, Judith Chen's dirty clothing was ripped and snagged in several places from rocks, branches and other rough, sharp things she had bumped up against during her journey across the cold, dark bed of Boston Harbor. The clothes were dry but still carried the water's polluted, metallic odour.

Coop handed her a mask. 'Paperwork's all done, and Keith is almost finished the Polaroids,' he said.

'What about digital?' Darby always used digital pictures to augment her files.

'How long have we been working together?'

They each took an item of clothing and began the painstaking process of examining the fabric under the illuminated light magnifier.

Inside the running pants Coop found a long black hair. He examined it under a comparison microscope. The hair didn't contain a root bulb, which ruled out DNA analysis. Given the length, texture and colour, chances were the hair belonged to Judith Chen. He placed the hair inside a glassine envelope and went back to work.

The sweatshirt was stained with blood. The splatter pattern suggested that Judith Chen, like Emma Hale, was shot first and then transported to the destination where her body was dumped into the water. Darby wondered if their killer had used the same vehicle both times. She also wondered if Chen and Hale had known they were going to die. Given the advanced decomposition of the bodies, it was impossible to know if either woman had struggled or put up a fight.

'This is interesting,' Darby said. Using a pair of tweezers, she pointed to a tiny pale smudge on the right shoulder of the sweatshirt.

'What is it?' Coop asked.

'It looks like makeup.'

'What's that stuff you chicks put on your face and cheeks?'

'It's called foundation. Chicks use it to even out their skin tone.'

'Okay, so Chen smudged some of her makeup on her shoulder.'

'Look at the placement. It's too high on her shoulder. She couldn't have done that.'

'Maybe she wiped her hands on her sweatshirt.'

'Women don't wipe their hands on their clothes, Coop.'

'I think it's safe to assume she was being held under less than favourable circumstances.'

'If she wanted to wipe off her hands, she'd wipe them on her pants or the front of her sweatshirt. Why reach up and wipe it on her shoulder?'

'Good question.'

'This is probably oil based.'

'You've lost me.'

'The makeup is oil based as opposed to water based. If it was water based, we probably wouldn't be able to see it. All the time in the Harbor would have washed it away.'

Darby swung the illuminated magnifier over the stain. 'The colour is too pale,' she said. 'Chen's skin was darker. She wouldn't have used this shade. It's made for pale Irish chicks.'

'Emma Hale had pale skin. Maybe it belonged to her.'

'Then how did it get on Judith Chen's shoulder?'

'Maybe the guy who abducted Chen made them wear makeup.'

'Or maybe he wears makeup to cover a scar or a defect,' Darby said. 'Don't give me that look, Coop. I know plenty of men who use concealer to hide a pimple or a scar.'

'You mean guys like Tim Bryson?'

'I don't think Tim wears makeup.'

'He gets his hair cut at some fancy place on Newbury Street *and* he does yoga.'

'For the record, yoga is an amazing workout. You should try it sometime.'

'I'm strictly free weights, sister.'

'Which way would you go?'

'Sorry, but I don't swing that way.'

'Good for you. I was referring to the sample. Mass spectrometer or FTIR?'

Woodbury answered the question. 'FTIR has the better library.'

Darby nodded. While the mass spectrometer could isolate a sample's components, Fourier Transform Infrared Spectroscopy was a more sophisticated test. It would identify the organic and inorganic compounds found in a sample and compare them against its library in search of a 'molecular fingerprint'.

Darby took several close-up photographs of the smudge and then prepared the sample.

'I'll keep working on the clothes, see if I can find the print in the pant pocket,' Coop said. 'You two kids have fun.'

FTIR had failed to find a unique match in its makeup library, but that didn't mean one didn't exist. The lab's FTIR system was only as good as its library.

On the FTIR computer screen was a bar graph listing the sample's various chemical properties.

'There's a large concentration of titanium dioxide,' Woodbury said. 'We also have paraffinum liquidum, cera alba, talc, isopropyl palmitate, magnesium carbonate, allantoin, propylparaben and copernicia cerifera. We also have one listed as unknown. Let's make sure we have the latest version of the makeup library.'

Woodbury checked the system. The makeup library had been updated early last month. He checked to see if there were any additional updates to download. There were none.

'Maybe it's not makeup,' Darby said.

'These are chemicals found in makeup, but which brand?' Staring at the monitor, Woodbury leaned back in his chair, rubbing a hand across the stubble on the back of his head. 'The problem is the sample listed as unknown. It's throwing the system off. We'll need to isolate it first.'

'Could FTIR give us a possible list of brands?'

'It could, but you could be talking hundreds of samples. The level of titanium dioxide is interesting.'

'Meaning?'

'It's rather high,' Woodbury said. 'Makeup – and that covers everything from foundation to products used to camouflage scars or pimples – contains traces of titanium dioxide, mica and iron oxides. Here, we have a higher than normal level of titanium dioxide. Did Chen have any scars on her face?'

'I don't think so. I'll have to check the photographs.'

'Did she use makeup?'

'She had some things in her medicine cabinet.'

'If I had the makeup she used, I could take samples and run tests against what we have here.'

'I'll make sure you get them.'

'Are you going to get them yourself or are you going to send someone there to retrieve them?'

'Why are you asking?'

'I don't know how to say this without sounding sexist, so I'll just say it. You're a woman.'

'Thank you for noticing,' Darby said.

'What I mean is you're more familiar with makeup than, say, a male patrolman who might rifle through her medicine cabinet or makeup kit and overlook something. For all I know, this sample is a zit cream with a camouflage tint.'

'Understood. I'll collect the samples myself.'

'The other thing is we may be talking one or more different samples of makeup – meaning you could have two different brands here. You may also want to get Emma Hale's makeup. If both of these women were held in the same place, maybe Chen used one of Hale's products.'

'How are you going to identify the unknown sample?'

'Let me see what I can do.'

That was Woodbury's way of saying he wanted some time alone to think. Darby knew he didn't like to work with someone hovering over his shoulder asking questions.

'I'll get you the makeup,' Darby said.

She was standing in her office, putting on her coat when she received a call from the station's front desk.

‘I’ve got a woman named Tina Sanders here who wants to speak to you,’ the desk sergeant said.

The name wasn’t the least bit familiar. ‘What does she want?’ Darby asked.

‘She says you have some information on her missing daughter, Jennifer. I told her to go to Missing Persons, but she said the detective she spoke to told her only to speak directly to you and no one else.’

‘What’s the detective’s name?’

‘Hold on.’ The desk sergeant spoke in a murmured conversation for a moment and then came back on the line. ‘She doesn’t know the guy’s name but said he was working with you on the Sinclair case. Does that mean anything to you?’

‘Send her up,’ Darby said.

40

Tina Sanders was ravaged by osteoporosis. Protruding from her back and hidden underneath the red fabric of a ratty down coat was the classic dowager's hump. The woman was hunched forward, her bony, gnarled fingers clutching the rubber grips of her walker. Her hair, tied up in rollers, was partially hidden underneath a blue silk scarf.

'Did you find Jenny?'

'Let's talk in the conference room,' Darby said.

Tina Sanders shuffled across the floor in her walker and black orthopaedic shoes. Darby held open the door. She had already left messages on Tim Bryson's cell and office voicemails asking him to call her immediately.

Darby helped the woman into a chair. Cigarette smoke was baked in her clothes and hair.

Hand shaking, Tina Sanders reached inside her purse. She came back with a folded piece of paper and placed it on the table.

The glossy 8½ × 11 sheet contained a picture of a blonde woman with feathered hair – the same picture Darby had seen tacked to the rotted wall inside Sinclair.

'Where did you get this, Miss Sanders?'

'He left it in my mailbox.'

'Who left it in your mailbox?'

'The detective,' Tina Sanders said. 'He told me to come down here and find you. He said you knew what happened to Jenny.'

'What was this man's name?'

'I don't know. What's going on with Jenny? Did you find her body?'

'You'll have to forgive me, Miss Sanders, but I'm confused. Bear with me a moment.' Darby opened her notebook. 'First tell me how you got this photograph.'

The old woman struggled with her impatience. 'I got a call this morning. It was a man saying he was a detective from Boston. He said Darby McCormick from the Boston Crime Lab found out what happened to my daughter. I asked him what it was, and he told me to go out to my mailbox. That's where I found the picture. When I came back to the phone, he wasn't there, got disconnected or something. That's what happened. Now tell me about Jenny. What did you find?'

'Where do you live, Miss Sanders?'

'Belham Heights.'

Darby grew up in Belham and knew the Heights section well – triple-deckers with views of clotheslines fastened to porches and postage-stamp sized backyards separated by sagging chain-link fences.

'And this is your daughter in the picture.'

'I said that, what, six times now?' Tina Sanders

removed a pack of Virginia Slim cigarettes from her purse.

'I'm sorry, Miss Sanders, but you can't smoke in here.'

'I just want to hold this.' She had turned the cigarette pack over; tucked underneath the cellophane was a gold crucifix. 'I've been praying for this moment for twenty-six years,' she said, voice breaking. 'I can't believe it's finally happening.'

'Tell me what happened to your daughter,' Darby said. 'Start at the beginning and take your time.'

41

On the evening of 18 September 1982, twenty-eight-year-old Jennifer Sanders, a psychiatric nurse for the Sinclair Mental Health Facility, had left the hospital to meet her mother at a bridal store in downtown Boston. They were scheduled to meet at 5 p.m. and then have dinner.

By six, when Jennifer hadn't shown up at the bridal store, Tina figured her daughter, coming into the city from the North Shore, was stuck in traffic. There was no way for Jennifer to call and say she was going to be late. This was 1982, a time when cell phones were big, bulky expensive toys owned by the wealthy.

By 7:30 p.m., and with still no word from her daughter, Tina Sanders had grown nervous. Maybe Jennifer got into a fender bender. Maybe her car had crapped out and she had left to seek out a pay phone to call AAA. If that was the case, Jennifer would have called the store to let her mother know what had happened. Maybe she was in an accident. Maybe she was seriously hurt and on her way to the hospital.

Or maybe, Tina thought, Jenny had gotten the dates mixed up. Or maybe she had simply forgotten. Jenny was very forgetful lately. She worked long hours and was always tired. Jenny was under a lot of stress – planning for the wedding and possibly having to find another job. An electrical fire had destroyed part of Sinclair, and in the midst of the chaos of moving patients to other hospitals, there was constant talk that Sinclair might be forced to close its doors.

Tina used the bridal store's phone and called her daughter at work. Her boss was still in his office and said Jennifer had left a few minutes before five.

Jennifer's fiancé, Dr Michael Witherspoon, an oncologist, was home. They had recently bought a house in Peabody, close to where Jenny worked, and decided to move in together.

Tina had the correct date, Witherspoon said. Was there a problem?

Tina Sanders told her future son-in-law Jenny was late. She stayed at the store until eight, when it closed, and drove back home to Belham, telling herself there was a rational explanation for this. There was no reason to worry.

Dr Witherspoon didn't share his future mother-in-law's optimism. By midnight, and with still no word from Jennifer, he was sure something had happened. Pacing the rooms waiting for the door to open or the phone to ring, his imagination conjured up all sorts of grisly scenarios.

He also had another reason to worry: Jennifer was two months pregnant. She didn't want to tell anyone the news just yet – it was too early in the pregnancy, she insisted, and anything could happen. She knew of too many friends who had suffered miscarriages.

There was another reason Jennifer didn't want to tell her mother. Given her staunch Catholic background, Jennifer felt a measure of shame for getting pregnant before she was married.

Sinclair was a massive place, and Jennifer worked in a world of emergencies. The patients she treated were violent offenders. Sometimes they killed themselves or another patient. They attacked the staff. There had been an incident the previous year when a paranoid schizophrenic punched Jennifer in the face. The young man believed Jennifer was trying to poison him.

Witherspoon called the hospital's emergency line and asked to speak to someone in security. He explained the situation and asked the man on the other end of the line to look into the matter. The security guard called Witherspoon back an hour later.

'They found her car in the lot,' Tina Sanders told Darby. 'That's all they ever found of her.'

'Does Michael Witherspoon still live in Peabody?'

'No, he left . . . it must have been ten, fifteen years ago. Moved out to California, I think. We lost contact. He kept in touch with me in the beginning, those first few years, and then he came to me one day and said he couldn't live like this any more, not knowing, the stuff with the police.'

'What stuff with the police?'

'They thought he had something to do with

Jenny's disappearance, but that was ridiculous. The man was devastated. They put him through hell. He wanted to get on with his life. I didn't blame him. You don't have that luxury as a parent.'

'Were you and Jenny close?'

'Of course we were.' The woman seemed insulted by the question. 'Growing up, it was just the two of us. Jenny's father was in the Marines, stationed in China. He wrote me one of those Dear Jane letters saying he fell in love with some Chink. I never heard from him again.

'I helped Jenny with all the wedding stuff, you know, going with her to look at dresses, picking out flowers. She was paying for the whole thing herself. Jenny was working a lot of overtime at the hospital to help pay for the cost of the wedding. God knows I couldn't help her, not on a waitress's salary.

'Michael's family was real rooty-toot; thought their shit didn't stink,' Tina Sanders said. 'Jenny didn't say this, mind you, but I think Michael's the one who pushed for the big wedding. His parents offered to pay, but Jenny said no. She was proud that way. She was going to pay for everything herself. She wanted a nice, simple wedding, not some fancy ballroom gala. Michael's parents weren't too happy about it. He was a nice guy. Kind of uppity, I guess, 'cause he was a doctor and all, but he treated Jenny real well.'

'What was Jennifer like?'

Tina Sanders clutched the cigarette box between her palms as she spoke.

'She was a good kid, obedient, did what she was told. I never had any problems with her. She had a real positive outlook on life, never complained, was real passionate about her job – she really believed she was helping people at McLean's. That's the first mental hospital she worked at. I don't know why she left. The patients were much better there, kind of easier to manage, she said. Jenny, she loved to help people. She shouldn't have taken that job at Sinclair.'

'Why do you say that?' Darby asked.

'During the last year, she became real moody and withdrawn. She didn't call as much. When we got together, she barely talked. She said she was having problems sleeping. She said it was the stress of the job plus working overtime to pay for the wedding, the talk of layoffs and the possibility of the hospital shutting down for good. I didn't know she was pregnant – that explained the mood swings.' The old woman rubbed a finger over the crucifix. 'She could have told me. I wouldn't have judged her for getting knocked up.'

'Did she normally keep secrets from you?'

'No. No, she didn't. We were close, like I said. Jenny not telling me about the pregnancy, it really bothered me for a while, but I understood. She wanted to get married in a Catholic church. Getting knocked up before you're actually married, well, I don't have to tell you how the Catholic Church frowns upon such matters.'

'Did your daughter ever talk about or mention a man with black eyes?'

'You mean like they were bruised or something?'

'I was referring to the actual colour of his eyes,' Darby said. 'This man, his eyes are completely black. He's tall, about six feet or so, has pale skin and dresses very well.'

'I don't know anyone like that.'

'Excuse me for a moment, Miss Sanders.'

42

Darby left the conference room and from her office retrieved the computer-printed photograph of Malcolm Fletcher, the one from the FBI website.

'Have you seen or met this man, Miss Sanders?'

'Is this the man who killed Jenny? Are you telling me you found him?'

'No, we haven't. Have you seen or met this man?'

'No.'

'Did Jenny ever tell you about meeting or seeing such a man?'

'If she did, I don't remember. Did you find her body?'

'We found this photograph in connection with another case,' Darby said. 'I'm sorry, but that's all I can tell you.'

'I don't understand. The man I spoke to specifically told me *you* had information on what happened to Jenny. He said you would tell me the truth.'

'I am telling you the truth.'

'It sounds to me like you got nothing. Why did he tell me to come all the way down here for this?'

'Miss Sanders, what you've told me is extremely helpful. I'm sure a detective will want to stop by and speak to you about your daughter. Will you be home later today?'

'What else do I have to do? You think I'm going dancing?' Tina Sanders reached for her walker. Darby stood to help but the woman waved her off. 'I can do it myself, thank you.'

'Has anyone else besides yourself touched this piece of paper?'

'No.'

'Before you go, I was wondering if I could take your fingerprints.'

'For what reason?'

'I need a comparison set of prints,' Darby said. 'I want to see if anyone else has touched this picture.'

Darby's cell phone rang. It was Tim Bryson. She told him where she was and what had happened. Bryson asked her to keep the woman there.

'Detective Bryson is on his way up,' Darby said. 'He'd like to speak to you for a moment.'

'If you find the man who killed Jenny, I want to talk to him. I want this man to know I forgive him.'

'You forgive him,' Darby repeated.

'You can wipe that look off your face. I'm not some crazy old bat.'

'Miss Sanders, I don't –'

'I don't expect you to understand, but I'm going to tell you anyway.' Tina Sanders gripped her walker. 'After Jenny died, I decided to go back to my Catholic faith. I go to St Stephen's almost every day. Father Donnelly said I had to let go of the hate, and the only way to do that was to forgive this man. That way I can keep Jenny alive, keep her close to me and remember the good parts. That's what I'm left with now, the good parts.' Tina Sanders eased back into a chair. 'It took a long time to get to this place, a lot of crying and anger, but once I decided to forgive this man – I mean *truly* forgive him – the good Lord Jesus took away the pain. Now every day I'm surrounded by Jenny's love. When I die, Jenny and I will be reunited in heaven.'

Darby wondered what the woman had managed to discover on the other side of her grief to inspire that type of faith.

43

Boston detectives worked out of the fifth floor in an area called the bullpen. Pairs of desks sat facing each other down a long, gymnasium-type space lit up with crummy fluorescent lighting that glared off the computer monitors. Phones rang day and night.

While the police department's top slot was held by a woman, the ranks of beat cops filled with women of every shape, size, age and colour, the detective bullpen was still boys only. No matter what time of day Darby came here, no matter what the season, the bullpen always smelled to her like a men's locker room – sweat and testosterone masked by too much aftershave and cologne.

It was 5 p.m. on Monday. Detectives filling out paperwork, typing on their keyboards and talking on the phone watched her as she walked down the aisle.

Tim Bryson sat in the corner near one of the coveted window spots, elbows propped up on his desk and chin resting on his folded hands as he read through a NCIC file for Jennifer Sanders.

'How did you make out with the photograph?'

'Tina Sanders' prints are all over it,' Darby said. 'I sent Coop over to dust the mailbox, but I'm not holding out any hope.'

'Here, take a look.' Bryson pushed himself away from his desk and stood. 'I'm going to get some coffee. You want one?'

'I'm all set, thanks.'

Darby felt the warm spot he had left in his chair. On the corner of his desk was a framed picture of a young girl with long blonde hair and a gap-toothed smile. His daughter looked no older than ten.

The first part of the NCIC file was pretty much a rehash of what Tina Sanders had told them. Darby scanned through the text, stopping when she found the investigative notes.

For the first six months, Danvers investigators had worked the patient angle. Maybe one of her former patients had abducted her. Jennifer Sanders was an attractive woman.

By the end of the year, with no witnesses, evidence or leads, detectives decided to investigate the murder-for-hire angle, the theory being that Witherspoon, wanting to break off the engagement but feeling trapped by the pregnancy, had hired someone to murder his fiancée. Witherspoon was an odd duck, they thought, cold and guarded. Witherspoon submitted to several polygraphs. Each time he passed. Detectives kept working on their theory, interviewing known contract killers.

Two years later, the trail went cold. The case was still listed as active.

Bryson sat on the edge of his desk. 'Anything jump out at you?'

'No. I called the state lab. The only evidence they had was Jennifer Sanders' car. Judging by what I was told over the phone, they really went through it – vacuumed the carpets, everything. They found some interesting fibres but they didn't lead anywhere. They said they'd send over copies of what they have.'

'Great. More shit to read to read through. This asshole is going to bury us in paper.' Bryson stood and grabbed an empty office chair.

'I spoke with Danvers PD,' he said, rolling the chair across the floor. 'The Sanders case wasn't transferred to their computer system, it's somewhere in storage. If we're lucky, we'll get a copy by the end of the week.'

'How did your interview with the mother go?'

'The pregnancy thing bothers me.'

'Not all pregnancies are planned.'

'I'm talking about the fact that she didn't tell her mother. Could be she was ashamed, you know, Catholic guilt about having a baby out of wedlock.'

'Wedlock,' Darby repeated. 'Where did you pick up that word, Tim, the *Dictionary for Old Farts*?'

Bryson tossed his paper coffee cup into the trash. 'Watts went over to Brighton and interviewed Hannah Givens' two roommates. Givens' backpack is inside her room. He went over to Northeastern and got a copy of her class schedule. Hannah failed to show up for her Shakespeare and history class. Nobody has seen or heard from her.'

'What about the parents?'

'Watts talked to the mother this afternoon. She was worried. Hannah calls and talks to her mother every Sunday. The mother says Hannah always calls. Watts is interviewing Hannah's boss, flashing the picture the roommates gave him to people who work in the area. The picture's going to run on all the news cycles and it will be in tomorrow's papers.'

Was Hannah Givens being held in the same place as Hale and Chen? A trickle of fear ran through Darby, cutting through her fatigue.

'Chadzynski is holding a press conference tomorrow morning to address what's going on with Hale, Chen and Givens,' Bryson said. 'She's debating about releasing Fletcher's name. Personally, I think it's a good move. It might force him to crawl back under his rock. This asshole has us jumping through hoops and, frankly, I'm getting sick and tired of it.'

'I don't blame you. I feel the same way.'

Bryson wasn't finished. 'He sends us to Sinclair, and we waste a day and a half searching empty rooms and hallways for what? Because he left a picture of a missing woman tacked up to a wall?'

'We know who she is.'

'Yeah, and the only reason we know is because the son of a bitch sent the mother down here. And what do we do? We drop what we're doing, and now we've wasted part of the day looking into a woman who's been missing for twenty-six years. For all we know Fletcher consulted on this case years ago, and now he's rubbing our nose into it.'

'I'm not following.'

'It's bullshit. Fletcher is jerking us around.'

'I keep coming back to the statue. It's the same –'

'Darby, I know about the goddamn statue.' Bryson's face was mottled red. 'I was there with you, remember? I saw it with my own eyes.'

She didn't answer.

Bryson waved a hand in apology. 'I don't mean to take my frustration out on you,' he said. 'I'm operating on about four hours of sleep.'

'If it's any consolation, I'm feeling the same way. Fletcher's using the statue as a carrot, dangling it in front of us, and every time he calls or does something, we drop what we're doing and jump.'

'Maybe that's what he wants.'

'We need to find out what he's doing.'

'It's a waste of time.'

'We don't have much of a choice, Tim. Malcolm Fletcher is here, and he knows something. He's not going away.'

'Let's talk about your surveillance,' Bryson said.

44

'If Fletcher calls you at home or at the lab, we can trace his location in about forty-five seconds,' Bryson said. 'The moment your phone rings, the trace starts. Let it ring three times before you pick up.'

'What about my cell phone?' Darby asked.

'That's where it gets dicey. Cell signals bounce through towers.' Bryson reached into his pant pocket. 'It could take anywhere from one to three minutes to pinpoint his location. If he calls you on your cell, the key is to keep him talking as long as possible. Once we get a lock on his signal, we can trace it even if he hangs up, as long as he keeps his phone turned on. I also want you to carry this.'

Pinched between his fingers was a small rectangular piece of black plastic, thin, with a grey button in the centre. The device reminded Darby of the medical alert units some elderly people carried in case they fell and couldn't get up.

'This is what we call a panic button,' Bryson said. 'If something happens, if you believe you're in danger, you press the button – you have to do it hard enough to break the seal. Once that happens, we come running. There's also a GPS transmitter in there, so we'll know where you are at any given time.

You're to carry this with you, even when you go to bed.'

'Do you think Fletcher's going to attack me in my sleep?'

'I don't think you should take any chances. During the day, keep the device tucked inside your pant pocket. What time are you leaving work?'

'I don't know.'

'Let me know when you do. We need to install privacy devices on your phones. If you get a private call and don't want us listening in, you press the button on the privacy device and the trace stops, nobody hears a thing. When you're ready to leave, call and I'll meet you at your place.

'One other thing,' Bryson said. 'When you leave work, don't look around the streets to see if you can spot surveillance. If Fletcher is watching, he may suspect something and run. Keep up your normal routine and act natural. Do you have a boyfriend?'

'No.'

'Someone you're seeing?'

'I hope you're not asking to fix me up on a blind date.'

'I'm asking because I was hoping someone was staying with you.'

'Coop is.'

Something flickered across his eyes. Was it disappointment?

'He's not my boyfriend, just a very close friend,' Darby said. 'He's very protective.'

'The surveillance team will be watching you when you leave work today, when you leave your condo – eyes will be on you at all times. Again, just act natural. Try to relax. If there's a problem, we'll call and give you instructions.'

Bryson handed her his business card. 'My home phone number is on the back. Programme it into your cell phone. If you need anything, give me a call.'

'What's Hannah's address?'

'She never made it home, never got on the bus.'

'I want to look through her things.'

Bryson wrote the address down on a sheet of paper, tore it off and handed it to her. 'I'm going to head downtown and help Watts.'

'I'll call you if I find anything at Hannah's place,' Darby said. 'After that, I need to collect makeup samples.'

She told him about the makeup stain on Chen's sweatshirt.

'Sounds pretty thin,' Bryson said.

'It's the only evidence we have to work with at the moment.'

'Before you go, I have a present for you.'

He opened his desk drawer and handed her a small box. Inside was a tactical light for her handgun.

Darby smiled. 'You certainly know the way to a woman's heart.'

45

On her way back to her office, Darby called Coop and gave him a quick rundown of her meeting with Tim Bryson.

Coop was already driving back into town with the fingerprints he'd collected from Tina Sanders' mailbox. He agreed to meet her at Hannah Givens' home in Brighton.

The events of the day crowded her thoughts. Darby wanted to hit the gym. A run on the treadmill would sweep her head clean but there wasn't any time. She put on her coat, grabbed her forensics kit and headed out. Walking outside in the dark, frigid air, she wondered where the surveillance was. She also wondered if Malcolm Fletcher was watching.

Safe behind the wheel of her Mustang, her thoughts turned to the Virgin Mary statues. In her mind's eye she saw the Blessed Mother's sorrowful expression, arms held wide open, ready to embrace. The face vanished, replaced by Fletcher's strange black eyes. Darby thought she heard him laughing.

She didn't want to think about the former profiler. She focused her thoughts on the man who shot Hale and Chen. That man had placed a statue of the Virgin Mary in their pockets. He'd sewed them shut and tied the end off with a knot so the statues would stay with them. He'd placed a sign of the cross on Chen's forehead and dumped her body into Boston Harbor. Why? What was the significance of the statue and why was it so important that it stay with the two women after they were dead?

You cared for them, I know you did. Why did you keep them alive for so long only to turn around and kill them?

Darby wondered if the killer was possibly schizophrenic. Most schizophrenia was based on a specific delusion – UFOs, secret government organizations implanting microchips in people's brains to eavesdrop on their thoughts. A lot of schizophrenics believed God, Jesus or the devil spoke directly to them.

With Hale and Chen, there seemed to be an organizational element at work in the way both women were killed and dumped in water. And then there was the length of time between the abductions. Emma Hale had been held somewhere for roughly six months – half a year, Jesus – her body discovered in early November. Chen's body was found two days ago. It was February. Her stay had lasted only a couple of months.

As a general rule, schizophrenics weren't organized offenders. They were impulsive killers. The crime scenes were sloppy. With Hale and Chen, there was no crime scene.

Emma Hale, the first victim, had left a party at her friend's Back Bay apartment. It wasn't a long walk home but it had been snowing, so Emma had called a cab. She grabbed her coat and went outside to smoke. Twenty minutes later, the cab pulled up to the apartment building but Emma Hale wasn't there.

Judith Chen had studied late into the evening. She left the library and somewhere on her way home had disappeared.

Both women had not made it home. Had they been abducted by force? If a strange man had tried to grab Hale or Chen, both women would have tried to fight. They would have kicked and screamed. No witnesses had come forward to indicate this had happened.

Darby felt certain the killer didn't do this – he wouldn't want to draw attention to himself. He was more cunning. He *needed* these women. Before approaching them, he would have a plan in place to get them quickly inside his car as quietly as possible. Had the killer driven up to them and offered a ride? Darby considered the possibility. If this had happened, the killer wouldn't drive a clunker or a van – vans always sent a message of danger. Appearances would be important.

Both women were smart and well educated. Darby felt confident that neither of them would have accepted a ride from a stranger. Either they knew him or he had acted in such a manner as to make them feel comfortable about getting into his car. To do that, he would need to have known something about his victims. Had he followed them, observing their habits and routines, their friends and class schedules? Or were they randomly selected?

Random selections were desperate. If these women were randomly selected, they would be used and discarded. They wouldn't be kept somewhere for months. Maybe they were victims of opportunity. Maybe the killer simply approached a variety of women to see which one would climb inside his car. Maybe he had posed as an undercover cop and used a fake badge to lure them. Or maybe everything she was thinking right now was a complete waste of time and energy.

Darby spotted a Starbucks and pulled over. She was walking back to her car when her cell phone rang. The caller ID window said UNKNOWN CALLER. She waited until the fourth ring to pick up, just to be sure.

'Are you ready to discover the truth?' Malcolm Fletcher asked.

46

'I spoke to Tina Sanders,' Darby said.

'Did she tell you about her daughter?'

'She did. For some reason, the woman is under the assumption that I know what happened to her. Is there something you'd like to tell me?'

'If you want to know what happened to Jennifer Sanders and the others, drive to Sinclair,' Fletcher said. 'This time, I want you to come alone.'

'Why?'

'I've decided I want you all to myself.'

Click.

The phone call was short, less than thirty seconds. Did Fletcher know the call was being traced? This time he had asked her to come alone. Had he somehow already spotted the surveillance or was he merely anticipating it?

Darby pulled onto the highway and called Bryson. He promised to call her back and did, twenty minutes later.

'I just got through talking with Bill Jordan, the man heading up your surveillance,' Bryson said. 'Fletcher wasn't on long enough. They couldn't lock on to his signal.'

'Is there any way he could have found out about the trace?'

'No. My guess is he's playing it safe, trying to hedge his bets. I've got to run and coordinate with Jordan. He's still scrambling to get his people together.'

'What do you want me to do?'

'It's like you said – he left us the same Virgin Mary statue we found in Chen's and Hale's pockets. It's hard to ignore that fact.'

'He wants to meet me alone.'

'Jordan's using some undercover narcotics detectives. They'll pose as Reed's security people and escort you inside.'

'Tim, if Fletcher does, in fact, know something, maybe I should go in there alone.'

'I'm going to pretend I didn't hear that.'

'If the man wanted to hurt me, he's had ample opportunity,' Darby said. 'What does Fletcher have to gain by killing me?'

'If I let you go inside the hospital without any sort of protection, the commissioner will have my ass. If something happens to you – if you go in there and stub your toe, the city would be liable. You could sue me, the city.'

'You want me to sign a waiver?'

'I'm not going to debate this with you. You want to drive up to Sinclair, then go, but we're going to be there.'

'I'm driving there now.'

‘Okay. We’ll make sure all the exits are covered.’

‘How many are there?’

‘A lot,’ Bryson said. ‘This past weekend Reed showed me all the different places people can sneak inside. His security can only cover so much of the campus at any given time. When Fletcher calls, keep him on the phone and we’ll do the rest. Is your phone fully charged?’

Darby checked the battery level. ‘It’s still got some juice,’ she said. ‘I have a charger in my car.’

‘Good. Everyone will be in position by the time you arrive.’

‘What if he leads me into the basement? The cell won’t work down there.’ They had discovered that during their weekend search. The basement was too far underground, the walls too thick. The signals either dropped or cut out completely.

‘I’m hoping it doesn’t come to that,’ Bryson said.

47

Jonathan Hale sat on his office floor, elbows propped on his knees and hands buried in his unwashed hair as he stared at the pictures of Emma and Susan scattered across the rug.

All day Saturday he had scoured the house for the photo albums and removed each and every picture and arranged them on the floor. It was now Monday evening. He had spent the entire time holed up in here in his office drinking bourbon and reliving the memories buried in each of the pictures. Some were clear but most had either faded or dulled.

When he nodded off, sometimes he had flashes, clips of memory that didn't make much sense or carry any significant weight – Susan kneeling on the boat dock, rubbing sunscreen on Emma's pudgy little arms; Emma cutting off her doll's hair then crying after Susan told her it wouldn't grow back; Susan at a Rolling Stones concert sipping beer from a paper cup while Mick Jagger belted out 'Sympathy for the Devil'.

A phone rang. He thought it was his office phone, and when he stood, he realized the ringing was coming from inside his suit jacket. He only carried one phone with him now; the one Malcolm Fletcher had given him.

'Have you looked at today's mail?' Fletcher asked.

'No.'

'I placed an envelope inside your mailbox,' Fletcher said. 'Inside you'll find a DVD containing the garage surveillance video of the man who killed Emma. Call me after you've seen it.'

Hale opened his office door. His assistant had placed the day's mail inside the leather tray sitting on the small table, along with a new bottle of Maker's Mark bourbon. A small padded brown envelope was tucked into the bottom. Malcolm Fletcher's name was written as the return address. The envelope, Hale noticed, didn't contain any postage.

Standing at his desk, Hale grabbed the envelope's tab and ripped it open. A shiny silver DVD slid onto his blotter.

His office had a TV with a DVD player. He made sure the door was locked, then slid the disk inside the player and waited.

The garage surveillance tape is a grainy haze of colour without sound. On the TV screen, a man wearing jeans, a baseball cap and a windbreaker runs across the garage to the private elevator. He presses the button and then bows his head, his gloved hands making fists by his sides. His back is toward the camera.

The elevator doors open. The man steps inside. He doesn't turn around, just stands there with his head bowed. He knows the cameras are watching and recording.

The doors start to slide shut. He whips his head around and the camera catches a brief glimpse of his face as he presses the number for Emma's penthouse suite.

Jonathan Hale shifted his attention to the bottom right-hand corner of the TV screen, to the bold white lettering holding the date and time of the recording: July 20: 2:16 a.m. Emma had been missing for two months. The man who had abducted her had decided, for a reason known only to God, to come back to her home to retrieve a necklace.

Why? Why would this monster risk everything for a *necklace*? Why would he perform this seemingly kind act only to turn around and kill her?

The tape ended. The TV went dark.

Hale stared at the screen and imagined his daughter trapped in some rundown room with no windows or light, Emma alone, confused and scared, forced to do things only God could see. When she cried out in pain, when she asked God for comfort, did he listen or turn his back? Hale already knew the answer.

Fact: the man had entered in through the garage.

Fact: he had waited for the garage to open and then snuck inside.

Fact: Detective Bryson said he had people posted in front of the building. Why hadn't his people seen this man? If Bryson's men had done their goddamn job, they would have seen this man and caught him and Emma would be alive.

Fact.

Hale started the DVD again, pierced by a memory of Emma sitting in this same chair watching *The Sound of Music.* After Susan died, Emma watched the movie over and over again, insisted on watching it in here, in the office, so she could be close to him. Only now did he understand the connection – the mother died and the children found a new mother in the nanny. *Emma must have watched the movie for comfort because I was unavailable.*

Now Hale watched a movie for comfort. Again he watched the man who killed his daughter, the man who was last to see Emma alive, to speak with her, the last man to touch her.

Hale gripped the armchair as a new memory came to him: Emma, a little over a year old, sitting on his lap while he is talking on the phone. He doesn't remember what the call was about, although it was probably business related. What he remembers now, clearly, vividly, is the smell of his daughter's clean hair, the curve of her plump and downy cheek pressed up against his neck. He remembers the way Emma's mouth hangs open as she studies his pen. She holds it in her tiny hands, her eyes wide, amazed.

Hale knew he would spend the good part of whatever was left of his life wishing he could go back in time to that moment. If God would somehow grant him this impossible power to go back through time, he would hang up the phone and just stare at Emma playing with the pen. He knew he could stay wrapped up in that memory forever and be happy.

48

Malcolm Fletcher stood in front of a glassless window inside the dark, dusty remains of Sinclair's top floor, watching the main road. He had selected this location for its strong cellular signal and its sweeping view of the campus, one aided by the use of a pair of excellent night-vision binoculars equipped with infrared technology. With the flick of a switch he could locate the heat signatures of anyone sitting inside a car or van, conducting surveillance.

The binoculars pressed to his eyes, Fletcher surveyed the area. Reed's security staff patrolled the campus in shifts, focusing their attention on some of the more unorthodox ways one might enter the hospital. There were several points of entry, and many ways in which one could escape without being seen.

As he continued his campus search, Fletcher thought about the man he had seen on Emma Hale's garage surveillance tape. The man had made one critical mistake: he had turned around before the elevator doors shut. The security camera caught a brief glimpse of the man's face. It was enough. Fletcher captured the frame on his computer. The video-enhancing software did the rest.

The man who had retrieved the necklace from Emma Hale's home bore a striking resemblance to a patient named Walter Smith, a twelve-year-old paranoid schizophrenic burned in a gasoline fire. Drifting back through time, Fletcher replayed his first encounter with Walter.

The young boy sat on the bed inside his hospital cell, his head a hairless, red-clay mask of strips of scars and stitches and healing skin. A pair of glasses with thick lenses magnified the severe damage to his left eye. It was wide-open, unblinking.

Walter's arms were wrapped around his stomach. When he wasn't dry-heaving into the wastebasket, he gnawed on his tongue as he rocked back and forth, back and forth, trying to stop the trembling.

'I need Mary,' Walter said, pleading. 'I need you to take me to her.'

'Where is she?'

'At the chapel. Please bring me there so Mary can take away the pain.'

Hanging on the walls were pieces of construction paper holding remarkable, detailed drawings done in crayon and magic marker of a young boy free of scars and disfigurement holding the hand of or hugging a woman dressed in long, blue flowing robes with a red heart painted on the front of her white tunic.

'Mary's gone,' Walter said, his voice strangling on tears. Clutched in his good hand was a small plastic statue of the Blessed Mother of God. 'Dr Han put the medicine in my veins and it sent Mary away again. I need to talk to my mother, I'm lost without her. Please bring me to the chapel.'

Fletcher was snapped from the memory by the vibration of his cell phone. He answered the call but didn't take his eyes away from the binoculars. The heat signatures of four men were running through the woods, heading for Reed's heated trailer.

'Yes, Mr Hale?'

'I watched the DVD.' Hale's voice was thick with bourbon. 'Is this the man who killed my daughter?'

'I believe it is. His name is Walter Smith.'

'You know him?'

'I met Walter while he was a patient at the Sinclair Mental Health Facility in Danvers. He's a paranoid schizophrenic – the worst type, actually. His particular delusion is difficult to treat even with the proper medication, which, I'm sure, Walter is no longer taking. The medicine prevents him from hearing Mary.'

'Who's Mary?'

'The Virgin Mother of God,' Fletcher said. 'Walter believes the Blessed Mother speaks to him. Walter's real mother poured gasoline on him while he was sleeping. The burns covered over ninety per cent of his body, including his face. His mother died in the fire, and Walter was brought to the Shriners Burn Center in Boston for treatment.

'Walter survived two burns. His left hand was severely disfigured the previous year, when she put his hand into a pot of boiling water after she caught him masturbating. She didn't bring her son to the hospital. She treated him at home, where he was home-schooled.

'When it became clear that Walter was schizophrenic, he was placed at Sinclair. He was a patient there for many years. When it was forced to shut its doors, my guess is Walter was released into either a low-risk group home or back into the general population.'

'How do you know this?'

'I came to know Walter through his friendship with a sociopath named Samuel Dingle, a man the Saugus police believed to be responsible for the deaths of two women who were strangled and dumped along Route One. Saugus police asked me to interview Dingle because they had misplaced a key piece of evidence, a belt used to strangle one of the women. I had several sessions with Sammy. At the time, he wasn't ready to confess his sins. I had to wait until we spoke again, years later, in a more private setting.'

'How can you be sure the man on the tape is Walter Smith? It could be someone else.'

'Walter's been to Sinclair recently.'

'Why? The hospital is abandoned – I tried to buy the property years ago but it was tied up in legal tape. Why would he go there?'

'To visit Mary, his one true mother,' Fletcher said.

'Walter goes there to talk to the Virgin Mary?'

'Yes.'

'You've been to the hospital?'

'Yes. In fact, I'm here right now, waiting for the police to arrive.'

'How did they find out about Sinclair?'

'I called them here.'

'You *called* them?'

'They're already here.'

'Do they know about Walter Smith?'

'No. Mr Hale, I want you to listen to me very carefully.'

For the next ten minutes, Fletcher explained to Hale what was going to happen. When he finished, Hale was silent.

'There is no way the police will be able to connect you to this, but I can't prevent them from focusing their attention on you.'

'Does Karim know?' Hale asked.

'We've discussed the matter at length.'

'He approves?'

'He does. However, since we have no choice but to involve you, Dr Karim and I both agree that the decision is yours. If you change your mind, you know how to reach me, but don't take too long. The preparations have already been made.'

'How long do I have?'

'An hour,' Fletcher said. 'I'd suggest you leave for New York this evening. Dr Karim has searched through a national patient database called the Medical Information Bureau. Walter sees a doctor at the

Shriners Burn Center, but the MIB contains an old address.'

'Can you find him?'

'Karim can't access the Shriners database. I plan on doing that myself later this evening. I suspect I'll find Walter in the next few days. In the interim, you may want to give some significant thought as to what you asked during our initial conversation.'

'I haven't changed my mind.'

'After I hang up, I want you to call Detective Bryson and tell him about the DVD you received in the mail. Tell him what you saw, and please make sure to give him the mailer.'

'Your name is on it.'

'Along with my fingerprints,' Fletcher said.

'I don't understand.'

'The police already know I'm here. I want them to think I'm acting independently.'

'Won't the FBI find out?'

'By the time their task force arrives, I'll be gone.'

A black Mustang tore its way up the winding road.

'I'll contact you shortly,' Fletcher said. 'If you change your mind, you know how to reach me.'

Darby McCormick stepped out of the car and showed her ID to the two security guards standing outside their truck. Apparently she had called ahead to let them know of her arrival.

The young woman was, by all indications, bright and fearless; but would she keep pushing until she found the truth? It was time to find out.

49

Darby paced outside the room where she had found the photograph and statue. The two undercover Boston detectives who escorted her were somewhere in the dark, watching.

She pushed the button for the backlight for her watch. It was almost nine and Malcolm Fletcher still hadn't called.

The ancient building groaned around her. Down the hall, wind blew through a window, the sound like a high-pitched scream.

Darby felt the hospital's presence as though it was a living, breathing entity like the Overlook Hotel from *The Shining*. She didn't believe in ghosts but she knew there were places in this world that were haunted, where men had performed unspeakable acts of cruelty and violence against each other, where the cries of the damned lingered for eternity. As she waited, she wondered about the possible secrets waiting for her inside these walls.

Her phone rang. She grabbed it, heard silence on the other end of the line. Then she realized her phone was set to vibrate.

The ringing was coming from inside the patient room.

Darby had already mounted the tactical light on her SIG. She turned it on and found a cell phone lying on the floor behind the steel door.

'Step out of the room and turn to your left,' Malcolm Fletcher said. 'At the end of the hallway, you'll see a stairwell.'

Darby saw the stairs. They led only one way: down.

'Don't worry about the stairs or the landings,' Fletcher said. 'They're secure.'

Darby moved the beam of her tactical light around the cold, empty rooms. 'What happened to Jennifer Sanders?'

'Ask her yourself,' Fletcher said. 'She's waiting for you downstairs.'

'I know you're in here. I know you're watching me right now.'

Fletcher didn't answer.

'I'm alone,' Darby said. 'Show yourself. We'll go downstairs together.'

'I'm afraid you'll have to endure this journey alone.'

'I'm not going anywhere until you tell me your agenda.'

'I thought you wanted to know the truth.'

'Then tell me.'

'Telling you the truth doesn't carry the same impact as discovering it for yourself.'

'Tell me where you found the statue.'

'The historian Ian Kershaw said the road to

Auschwitz was paved with indifference,' Fletcher said. 'It's time for you to choose. You need to make your decision now.'

Darby looked back to the stairs, thinking of Emma Hale and Judith Chen. She thought about Hannah Givens. She wondered if the answer to Jennifer Sanders' disappearance was, in fact, waiting somewhere below her.

She thought of Jennifer's mother clutching the crucifix tucked underneath the cellophane wrapper of her cigarettes and took the first step.

Descending into the awful dark, Darby was aware of her physical senses – the hollow feeling in her legs; the sweat collecting underneath her arms and hardhat; the way her footsteps echoed and thumped along with the rapid beating of her heart.

'How are you feeling?'

'Nervous,' Darby said. 'Scared.'

'Are you claustrophobic?'

'I don't think so. Why?'

'You'll see in a moment.'

Darby reached the bottom floor. She saw the steel door marked 'WARD 8'. She hadn't searched this area over the weekend because it was locked. Reed had said the area was too unstable and refused to let anyone through, forcing the search teams to find alternate routes.

A padlock was lying on the floor. The lock had been sawed off.

'I'm here.'

'Open the door,' Fletcher said.

The corridors went straight ahead, to her left and right. They were narrow and pitch black and in the thin beam of her flashlight they seemed to stretch for miles.

'Your destination is straight ahead,' Fletcher said. 'When you reach the end of the corridor, turn left and travel halfway down the next hallway until you see a maintenance door.'

Exposed pipes ran along the walls, near the ceiling. Almost every door was shut. The floors were frozen with ice. Darby heard a humming sound and then realized it was her blood pounding against her ear drums.

The cold darkness pressing against her, she made her way down the main corridor, the ice slippery beneath her boots. She remembered a line from Dante, how hell wasn't burning with fire but rather a place where Satan was frozen in a lake of ice.

Darby turned left into another maze of corridors. On a wall of chipped white and blue paint was faded lettering with arrows pointing to the different locations inside the hospital. The frigid air smelled of dank pipes and mildew. She moved into the corridor, listening for sound and watching for movement.

Ten minutes later, she found the door marked 'MAINTENANCE'.

'I found the door,' Darby said.

Malcolm Fletcher didn't answer.

'Hello?'

No answer.

Darby checked the phone. The signal had dropped. She was too far underground.

She placed the phone on the floor. Leaning against the door, she pressed down on the handle with her elbow and pushed it open.

50

The maintenance room was empty.

Darby tucked the phone in her pocket. The room was a closet and held nothing but rusted shelves. The middle and bottom shelves were empty, but the top shelf held rusted tools, metal pails and old bags of cement. Under the centre bottom shelf and lying against the wall was a large metal ventilation grille, the kind used to heat and cool large buildings.

Darby got down on one knee and shined the thin beam of light against the grate. Beyond it was a vent about thirty feet long; it curved off to the left. Standing at the end of the vent was a small statue of the Virgin Mary.

There was no way Malcolm Fletcher had crawled through the vent. The man was too big, too wide to fit through this narrow space.

Are you claustrophobic? Fletcher had asked.

Was Fletcher waiting for her on the other side? Or had he led her here to find something?

Darby checked her phone. No signal. She could backtrack, locate a signal and call Bryson; or she could crawl through the vent now.

She saw the Blessed Mother's sorrowful expression in the beam of her flashlight. Darby removed the tactical light and holstered her SIG. She rolled her flashlight across the vent, then got down on her stomach and crawled inside.

Malcolm Fletcher waded through the knee-deep snow on the western part of Sinclair's campus. His Jaguar was strategically parked behind a grouping of dumpsters, safely out of view – at least for the moment.

His years of living on the run had taught him the importance of carrying only minimal possessions. A small suitcase held his clothes. His briefcase held the more important items – surveillance gear, listening devices, and GPS units. The false passports were practically worthless. Since 9-11, Interpol had stepped up its restrictions at airports.

Fletcher popped the trunk. He tucked his FBI badge and supporting credentials in his suit jacket pocket. He had already procured a new sidearm, a 9mm Glock, courtesy of a Roxbury gang-banger who suddenly became very eager to unload his illegal firearm after his wrist and nose were broken. Fletcher took the other items he needed and shut the trunk.

A laptop sat on the front seat. The padded cone of the headphone pressed against one ear, he typed on the laptop to activate the remote transmitters he had strategically placed inside the lower level. He heard the sound of a young woman's laboured breathing and the clang of metal. Darby McCormick was crawling through the heating vent.

So close, he thought, grinning.

Malcolm Fletcher started the car. Cecil's soft, haunting piano music played over the speakers as he drove away.

Tim Bryson sat in the cramped passenger seat of a Honda Civic parked at a Mobil gas station on Route One. His partner, Cliff Watts, stood outside, smoking.

Bryson had picked the location in case he needed to move to the hospital. If there was a problem, he could be at the front doors in less than three minutes.

For the past hour he had talked to Bill Jordan. His men had reported that Fletcher had left a cell phone inside the patient rooms. He had called Darby on this phone, so there was no way to listen in on the conversation.

The two undercover detectives watched Darby descend the stairs. Several minutes later they followed and found the sawed-off padlock on the floor.

Beyond the door was a maze of corridors. The last report was that they still hadn't found her.

Another troubling note: the panic button with its GPS unit was no longer transmitting. Jordan had lost her signal.

Darby was too far underground, Jordan said. He had sent her a text message asking her to check in but she still hadn't responded. Given her location, it was possible that she hadn't received the message. Jordan still couldn't hail either of his men.

Bryson's phone rang.

'Still no word from Darby,' Jordan said.

'Give her some time.'

'I don't like her wandering down there alone without knowing what's going on. We should move some more people inside.'

'And if Fletcher is watching, he'll see them and bolt.'

'Or he could be inside the basement with her,' Jordan said. 'We've already mapped out the terrain. The building plans are shit – half the passages are either sealed off with rubble or locked. The place is a goddamn maze, but we managed to find a way to the basement level. I can have them there in half an hour – Wait, hold on.'

Bryson heard mumbling. Then Jordan was back on the line: 'A black Jaguar just pulled out of the western part of the campus and it's moving fast. It was parked behind some dumpsters. The driver will be at your location in under a minute.'

'You just discovered this *now*?'

'We had to do this on the fly, Tim. This place is massive – we couldn't see that part of the campus from our location. You think it's your boy?'

'Last time he was here, he was driving a Jag. Who else could it be?' Bryson leaned forward in his seat, thinking fast. 'I won't be able to block off the main road by myself. How soon can you get someone here?'

'Lang's on his way. He should be there –'

'Shit, he's here.' Bryson watched the black Jag pull onto the highway. He banged on the window, got Watts' attention and motioned him inside the car. 'I'm going to follow. How many men can you spare?'

'The second van's already on its way. Call Lang, coordinate everything through him. He's got you on his GPS so he won't lose you.'

Watts started the car.

'Move inside the hospital,' Bryson said to Jordan. 'Pull Darby out of there.'

51

The heating vent was narrow and smelled of rust and decay. Darby crawled forward on her stomach. She reached the flashlight and rolled it ahead of her, feeling like the John McClane character Bruce Willis had played in the first *Die Hard* movie.

When she reached the statue, she placed it into an evidence bag and tucked it into her coat pocket. She picked up the flashlight.

The vent curved to the left. The second part was only ten feet long and led out to a floor covered in dust and rubble.

Turning onto her side, Darby edged her way around the corner, boots banging against the metal, and got stuck. Panic gripped her as she imagined being trapped here. *Why in the name of God am I doing this?*

Darby took in deep breaths, forcing herself to relax. She got her footing and pushed herself into the second vent, hearing her coat rip. Turning back onto her stomach, she crawled forward and pushed herself onto a floor covered with rubble.

A hole was in the ceiling and, beyond it, walls stretching up into the darkness. Sections of the floors above her were missing. She wondered what had caused such a massive amount of damage.

The door to the room was closed. Moving the beam of her light around the wooden shelves, most of which were still intact, she saw clear plastic vials full of water and cardboard boxes full of rosary beads and stacks of books. Darby wiped away the dust from the spines; bibles and hymn books.

Darby gripped the door, surprised to find it opened without effort.

She didn't know what she had expected to find but she hadn't expected this – an old chapel holding a dozen wooden pews covered in dust and debris. Some of the pews had been crushed from where the ceiling had caved in, and she saw a steel beam resting through what was probably a confessional.

To her left, dozens of footprints led down an aisle. At the end, inside an alcove, was a life-size statue of the Virgin Mary sitting on a bench, her son, Jesus, sprawled across her lap. The Blessed Mother was dressed in flowing white and blue robes, her facial expression frozen in eternal sorrow as she looked down at bloody holes in her dead son's feet and palms from the nails that had pinned him to the crucifix.

The Virgin Mary was clean – no dust, no grime.

Moving the beam of her light around the statue, Darby spotted rags and a bucket of water holding a sponge.

She carefully made her way to the centre aisle, not wanting to disturb the footprints. They appeared to be recent. The marks belonged to a boot or sneaker.

When she reached the centre aisle, Darby saw another set of footprints which were distinctly different. These shoeprints bore a strong resemblance to the one she had found on the floor inside Emma Hale's spare bedroom.

A woman cried out for help.

Heart leaping high in her chest, Darby swung around and in the beam of light saw an altar covered in debris. The wooden pulpit was crushed. A large statue of Jesus hanging on the cross lay on the floor in pieces.

There was no one here. She hadn't imagined the sound, she was sure of it.

Darby made her way to the aisle on the far right. No footprints. She moved down the aisle and heard a woman screaming, the sound faint, coming from the altar.

Darby ducked under the beam. Jesus' head, crowned in bloody thorns, lay on the floor, his sorrowful eyes staring at her as she moved up the altar steps. The woman's painful cries grew louder.

A broken door was behind the altar. Darby slipped inside as a man moaned, the sound mixed with the woman's pleading, begging for the pain to stop.

The adjoining room was not much bigger than the maintenance closet and held dusty shelves stacked with the same bibles and hymn books. The ceiling was intact.

On the floor was a cardboard box full of small plastic statues of the Virgin Mary – the same statues she had found sewn inside Emma Hale and Judith Chen's pockets. The same statue Malcolm Fletcher had left inside the vent and on the windowsill of the room.

Shoeprints stopped in front of a brick wall. At the bottom was a large, wide hole. The dust and dirt on the floor had been disturbed, as though someone had recently stood here.

A man laughed. Darby knelt on the floor, away from the footprints, and shined the beam of her flashlight inside another room. Lying against the debris was a skeletal set of remains.

52

Jonathan Hale stared at his daughter's pictures, searing Emma's face into his mind's eye, wanting to preserve every angle to keep her from fading.

But she *would* fade. The mind, he knew, was the most cunning prison, a ruthless warden. It would take these memories of Emma and, like Susan, blur them over time while torturing him with this singular, inescapable fact: he had taken each of these moments for granted.

His girls, the two most important people in what he had come to realize was a completely insignificant, hollow life, smiled at him. Husband and father. Now he was a widower, the father to a dead child.

Daddy.

Hale, drunk and numb, looked up and saw Emma sitting in the leather armchair. Her hair wasn't wet and mangled with twigs; it was neatly combed, thick and beautiful. Her face was alive, full of colour.

'Hey, baby. How are you doing?'

Mom and I are fine now.

'What are you doing here?'

We're worried about you.

Hale's eyes were hot and wet. 'I miss you so much.'

We miss you too.

'I'm sorry, baby. I'm so, so sorry.'

You didn't do anything wrong, Dad.

Hale buried his face in his hands and cried. 'I don't know what to do.'

You already know what to do.

'I can't.'

God answered your prayers. He sent someone to help you.

Yes, he had prayed to God for the truth, and the messenger was like a creature spawned from the Catechism books from his childhood – a man with strange black eyes holding terrible secrets, a man who had killed two federal agents and God only knew who else; a man who had given him the name and face of his daughter's killer.

Now that he knew the truth, he wished God would take it away. He didn't want to know. He didn't want to know.

It's not just about me any more, Daddy. You know about what happened to the others.

Hale checked his watch. He could still make the call. He still had time.

They can't speak for themselves. They need you to speak for them.

Hale stumbled across the room and scooped the cell phone from his desk.

You can't let them suffer in silence.

He dialled the number.

Look at me, Daddy.

He felt numb as Malcolm Fletcher answered the call.

'Yes, Mr Hale?'

Daddy, look at me.

Hale looked at the armchair where Emma sat, legs crossed, hands folded on her lap.

Think about the parents of all those young women. Don't they have a right to know the truth? Don't they deserve justice?

'Have you changed your mind, Mr Hale?'

You've been given an amazing gift, Daddy. God heard and answered your prayers. Are you going to refuse him?

Hale rubbed the whiskers along his face. 'Do it.'

'You are aware of the potential risks.'

'That's why I employ the best lawyers in the state,' Hale said. 'I want the son of a bitch to pay for what he did. I want him to suffer.'

53

Tim Bryson crunched a Rolaids between his teeth as traffic crawled past the Tobin Bridge tolls. Cliff Watts had the window down so he could smoke.

A battered plumber's van, complete with a ladder fixed to the top, was waiting in the left lane, two car lengths behind the Jag.

Bryson's phone rang. It was Lang, the man driving the plumbing van.

'I ran the plates. The car's registered to a man named Samuel Dingle from Saugus. I've got an address.'

Bryson felt a sick feeling crawling underneath his skin. 'Is it stolen?' he asked.

'If it is, nobody has reported it,' Lang said.

'Send someone over to the house. Call me back when you find out.'

The Jag drove fast across the new Zakim Bridge, heading for Boston's southeast expressway. *So close*, Bryson thought. *Too close.*

Fletcher merged onto Storrow Drive, heading west. A few minutes later he took the Kenmore exit.

The problems of tailing someone in a city without being spotted were numerous – the traffic lights, the maze of one-way streets and, in the case of Boston, the never-ending headaches of the Big Dig. If you didn't stick close to your mark, you could lose him.

Malcolm Fletcher wasn't acting like someone who knew he was being shadowed. No sudden turns down a narrow street, he didn't change direction – he wasn't doing any of the normal counter-surveillance manoeuvres to shake off a tail. The man stuck to the main roads and kept up with the flow of traffic.

Fenway Park was dark and deserted. Without the Red Sox playing, the place was dead. Traffic was light. Watts kept a good, safe distance.

Fletcher put on his blinker and turned left into a parking lot. Watts drove past him. Bryson turned in his seat, wondering if Fletcher had spotted the tail.

A guard rail lifted into the air. Fletcher pulled inside the parking lot.

Watts banged a U-turn at the lights and found an empty spot along the side of the street, in front of a fire hydrant. He killed the lights but not the engine. Bryson already had the binoculars in his hands.

The parking lot was well lit and, thankfully, there was no tree cover, just a chain-link fence. There. The Jag was parked in a corner on the far right.

Bryson looked past the Jag to Lansdowne Street. The dingy area – horse barns at the turn of the century that were later converted to warehouses – was now home to a string of popular bars and dance clubs set up inside brick buildings. Lines of young men and women stood behind velvet ropes in the freezing cold, waiting for the bouncers to usher them through.

'What the hell is he doing down here?' Watts asked.

Good question, Bryson thought. The Jag door opened.

Malcolm Fletcher was dressed in a dark wool overcoat. Sunglasses covered his eyes. He looked like a character from *The Matrix*. He didn't look around, just shut the door and jogged across the street.

The people in line stared at him, wondering if he was some sort of celebrity. He stepped up to a bouncer with a big, round head. The bouncer leaned forward to listen.

Bryson read the sign above the door: Instant Karma.

'I can't believe it,' Watts said. 'The son of a bitch is going dancing.'

Bryson's phone rang as he watched the bouncer pull back the velvet rope to let Fletcher pass.

'You think he spotted us?' Lang asked.

'If he did, the smart move would have been to try to shake us off,' Bryson said. 'He wouldn't lead us to a dance club. Have you ever been inside Instant Karma?'

'Hitting the clubs isn't my scene any more. I'm way too old.'

'We broke up an ecstasy ring about two years ago. The bottom level connects to other clubs. I'm going to head inside with Watts. I want you to coordinate the surveillance. Who else is with you?'

'Martinez and Washington,' Lang said. 'Tim, this guy attacked three federal agents.'

'He did it in the privacy of his own home, and he took his sweet time. Move your boys to the front. There's an alley around the back, near the fire exits. Park there. I'll escort Fletcher out through the alley.'

From the glove compartment Bryson pulled out a surveillance rig – an earpiece and lapel mike with encryption that allowed him to keep in constant communication with his team without the possibility of eavesdropping.

'I'll contact you once I'm inside,' Bryson said.

54

A small, portable Sony radio shaped like a bubble was set up on the floor. A cassette was playing, the reels going around and around as a woman screamed in pain.

Not wanting to disturb any fingerprints, Darby used the tip of her pen to press the player's STOP button. The only sound she heard was the wind howling above her.

The remains resting against the debris were skeletonized; no muscle or skin. All that was left were bones inside women's clothing: jeans, a black shirt and a long winter jacket covered in dust. The jeans were bundled down around the ankles, the white underwear inside them stained black with dried blood.

Darby peeled back the jacket to reveal a lab coat with 'Sinclair Hospital' embroidered on the breast pocket.

A grey winter scarf was wrapped around the woman's neck. Strips of duct tape had been used to secure the wrists and ankles.

Behind the skull was a hair mat – long, blonde hair covered in dust. The skull, with its sharp eye orbits, tapered chin and smooth cranium, were that of a female. The vertical teeth confirmed that the woman was Caucasian.

There were no breaks on the skull to indicate a head injury. Hopefully Carter, the state's forensic anthropologist, would be able to determine a cause of death. That wasn't always the case with skeletal remains.

Darby found maggot husks scattered inside the remains. Entomology would use the husks to pinpoint the time of death. She wondered how long the remains had been here.

A red purse lay next to the body. Darby looked inside. The purse was empty. She checked the jean pockets. Empty.

Darby moved the beam of her tactical light around the area. It was impossible to tell what this place was. Mountains of debris covered crushed hallways and doors. There was no ceiling. Looking past the missing floors, all the way to the roof, she saw the night sky.

Malcolm Fletcher didn't crawl through the vent. He must have come through one of these doorways. To do that, he would have to be familiar with the layout of the basement.

Darby took out her cell phone, relieved when she got a signal.

Her first call was to Tim Bryson. When he didn't answer, she left a message and called Coop.

'I'm inside Sinclair – I'll explain everything when you get here,' Darby said. 'Have you met the two new guys who are working in ID?'

'Mackenzie and Phillips,' Coop said.

'Which one of them is slim and small?'

'That would be Phillips. He's very slim because he watches his girlish figure.'

'Tell him to dress warm and to wear old clothes. It's dirty as hell in here, and I ripped my coat. I'll tell the security people to expect you.'

Darby looked back to the remains. The fear was gone, swallowed by the exhilaration of this new discovery buried deep in the earth.

The bouncer who let Fletcher bypass the waiting line had a young face – he was no older than twenty-five, Bryson guessed. Judging by the rolls under the young man's chin, most of the muscle had turned to fat.

Bryson flashed his badge and moved the young man away from the other bouncers.

'Don't be alarmed, you're not in trouble,' Bryson said. 'I just want talk to you alone for a moment. What's your name?'

'Stan Dalton.'

'The guy with the sunglasses you just let in, what did he say to you?'

'He didn't say anything, he just showed me his executive card and I let him through.'

'Executive card?'

'If you're willing to pony up a grand a year, you can apply for an executive card which means you get to bypass the waiting line. You also get free valet service and access to the VIP area with your own waitress and tab.'

'I'm assuming there's a security checkpoint past the front doors.'

'Every place has one.'

'Okay, Stanley, you're going to escort me past the security checkpoint, and then you're going to come back out here and do your job. You're not going to tell anyone about our conversation. Once I'm inside, you're not to get on the horn and call your boss. The guy I'm watching, I don't want to spook him. I need to play this nice and cool. If I go in there and find security hovering all over him, you're going to have a permanent problem with the IRS.'

The front doors opened to a hall blasting heat and techno music pounding behind black walls. Across from the coat check-in room was a security checkpoint consisting of two men with serious expressions holding metal-detection wands to frisk the patrons.

Stan Dalton had a private conversation with the security boys. They nodded and let them into the club without having to go through the ordeal of being frisked.

The dance club seemed like a party taking place in hell. Pounding techno music blasting from speakers, *boom-boom-boom*, the dance floor packed with pretty young women wearing revealing tank tops and half-shirts showing off their surgically enhanced tits and flat stomachs, tight pants hugging the sweet curves of their asses as they jumped and gyrated under mirrored disco balls, *boom-boom-boom*, hands waving in the oppressively hot air smelling of sweat and perfume and sex, hands holding drinks, bodies grinding together, men with girls, girls with girls, men with men, *boom-boom-boom*, everyone happy, smiling, drunk and high.

Set up in the corners, below the laser lights, were cages holding dancing girls in bikinis. One cage held two young muscular men dressed in black bikini briefs, their tanned, perfectly sculpted bodies glistening with oil and glitter to reflect the lasers and coloured lights. Bryson looked away, disgusted, his eyes drifting up to the ceiling where plasma TVs played music videos.

A bar was set up to his right. The counter was covered with Plexiglas, bright white lighting beneath it. Waitresses wearing black leather pants and matching bikini tops placed drinks on their trays and hustled off to a roped-off area behind the bar crammed with black leather couches and chairs – the VIP area. Malcolm Fletcher, still wearing his black-lens sunglasses, stood next to a jaw-dropping young woman wearing a tight black dress. She was tall and had long, dark red hair. She looked like Darby McCormick.

The woman whispered something in Fletcher's ear, then walked away.

A moment later Fletcher stood and followed, swallowed inside the crowd of gyrating bodies and groping hands.

Christ, where did he go? Bryson looked around the club. The techno music was deafening. One song blended into the next, *boom-boom-boom*, that same hideous beat playing over and over again, vibrating inside his chest.

There; there he was, standing on the opposite side of the dance floor with the redhead, who was talking to a security guard, a pissed-off looking gentleman sporting a long goatee and a lot of jailhouse tattoos inked on both forearms.

The guard nodded and stepped aside. The woman opened a door marked 'Private'. Fletcher followed.

55

So that's why you came here, Tim Bryson thought. Fletcher was heading downstairs to get laid. Perfect.

Bryson put on his earpiece. The lapel mike was already in place.

'Lang, can you hear me?'

'I hear you.'

'Stand by,' Bryson said as he pushed his way through the dance floor.

The bouncer guarding the door marked 'Private' put his hand out and asked for a password. Bryson flashed the badge and had to scream above the music to tell the guy with the goatee not to let anyone else down here.

Bryson descended the black-painted stairwell in the dim light, the shit music shut off by the thick metal door but the same hideous beat pounding inside his head, *boom-boom-boom*, Watts running behind him. No doors, the stairs kept leading down and down, Christ, how deep was this place buried?

Six flights of stairs and here was an archway leading into a room with a marble floor. Aquarium tanks were built into the walls, packed with bright coral and colourful fish. Standing behind a podium much like the kind in restaurants where they took your dinner reservation was a tall man with a shaved head. He was dressed in a black suit and silver tie.

'Good evening, gentlemen.'

Bryson looked to his right, to a change room with lockers. White terrycloth robes were neatly folded on the shelves.

The man with the shaved head smiled. 'You must be new. Welcome. My name is Noah. You can change into your robes or, if you prefer, you can go directly to a private room. Let me see what's available.' He looked down at the podium. 'Room sixty-two is available. Shall I give you a key? Or would you like to enjoy the bathhouse first?'

Bryson flashed his credentials. Noah cleared his throat.

'Officers, this is a private establishment. Our members pay for their –'

'I'm interested in only one member, a tall man with black-tinted sunglasses,' Bryson said. 'He came through here a few minutes ago with a redhead. Where did they go?'

'They requested a private room – room thirty-three.'

'Is it locked?'

'I would imagine so.'

'Do you have a spare key?'

'It's in the back office. Give me a moment.' Noah disappeared behind a black curtain. Watts followed.

Now Bryson had to figure out the logistics of removing Fletcher. Marching him up the stairs and through the crowded dance floor was not a viable option. Too many things could go wrong.

Noah returned with Watts and handed Bryson a key.

'Is there a separate, more private exit for your members?' Bryson asked.

'I was going to suggest using our elevator. It's next to room thirty-three. It will take you up to the main floor and out a private door that leads to the back of the club.'

'You're talking about the alleyway.'

'Yes. Our members value their privacy, as I'm sure you can understand.'

'We'll be very discreet, I promise. This room you're taking us to, are there any other doors in there?'

'No sir, just the single door which leads into the hallway.'

'What about cameras? Do you have anyone watching this level?'

'Certainly *not*,' Noah said. 'Security cameras would be a violation of our members' privacy.'

Bryson talked to Lang through the lapel mike. Lang didn't respond. *I must be too far underground*, Bryson thought. *The walls are blocking the signal.*

He had better luck with the cell phone. The signal was weak but it would do. He told Lang where he was.

'Repeat that?' Lang said.

'We're going to bring Fletcher out through the

alley. Move everyone into position. If you don't hear back from me within twenty minutes, storm the club.'

What to do with the bald man? Bryson didn't want to leave him here. He might call management. He might bring additional security. He could do any number of things to protect his job. Bryson wanted to play this nice and quiet.

'Lead the way.'

Noah escorted them into a hallway of white tile and dim lighting designed to hide faces. There was a steamy reek of chlorine from the bathhouse. Murmured conversations and moaning from behind each of the closed doors. From a room far down the hallway, a man screamed in either pain or ecstasy, maybe a combination of both.

Noah stopped in front of room 33. Grunting came from the room across the hall. The door had a mesh grating in it. Darkness in there but Bryson could make out the shape of a man. He was tied down to a table and wore a leather mask.

'Harder,' the man cried. '*Harder.*'

A woman laughed.

Bryson removed his handgun and listened at room 33. He heard running water. He motioned for Noah to step closer.

'Is there a shower in this room?' Bryson whispered.

'Each room has its own bathroom.'

'Where is it?'

'When you open the door, it will be to your left.'

'Locks?'

'Yes, each bathroom door has a lock. I don't have a key. If you'd like additional help, I could call security.'

'No. Please step back. Stay right here.'

Noah moved against the far wall, looking as though he might faint. Bryson turned to Watts.

'I'll go in first and you'll cover me. If he makes a move, take him down.'

Watts nodded, sweat dripping down his face. The hallway was uncomfortably humid from the steam. Bryson slipped the key inside the lock and held his breath for a moment before turning the handle. Don't throw the door open. If it banged against the wall, the sound would alert Fletcher, might give him enough time to reach for his gun. Okay . . . *now*.

56

Snapshots in the candlelight – a massage table in the corner, clothes piled on a fabric-covered bench, the assortment of toys, handcuffs and bottles of lotion lying on a shelf next to folded towels.

Clear. Bryson turned to the bathroom, the light on, relieved to see the door was cracked open. He threw his shoulder into the door and rushed into the thick steam. Clear. Watts moved past him and yanked the shower curtain aside.

The showerhead was running hot, steam everywhere, but nobody was standing under the water.

On the floor was a metal canister shaped like a soda can only it had the kind of handle and pin seen on a grenade. Underneath the pounding water Bryson heard a hissing sound.

From the bathroom doorway came a muzzle flash. Watts was hit in the back. He fell inside the shower as Bryson turned around to fire – a second flash and Bryson felt a force like a hot, metal fist slam into his stomach.

Bryson fell against the bathroom wall, gasping for air, saw the third flash from the doorway and the fist hit him again high in the chest as he tripped over Watts and crashed sideways into the shower stall.

Bryson's heart was pounding but his lungs felt as though they had shut off. He couldn't breathe. The gun was still gripped in his hand. Gasping for air, he brought the gun up, about to fire into the steam when a black-gloved hand gripped his wrist and twisted, *snap*. Bryson tried to scream but no sound came out. The Beretta fell. He tried to reach for it. The fabric of a pair of black pants whisked past his face and a foot kicked him in the stomach.

He threw up his coffee and parts of a bagel. A boot pressed his face against the shower floor. His arms were yanked behind his back, his fists bound with what felt like Flexicuffs. Bryson felt the plastic biting his skin, his eyes on the canister lying sideways on the floor, hissing.

Next his ankles were bound and then the gloved hand ripped the lapel mike from his coat. The hands grabbed him by the hair. Bryson felt a needle plunge into his neck. He tried to pull away, couldn't, felt a long, slow burn and then he was tossed out of the shower stall and onto the bathroom floor.

Bryson lay on his side, every muscle in his body straining as he dry heaved. Something was wrong. His eyes were burning and he felt another wave of nausea running wild through his stomach.

Fletcher dragged him into the adjoining room. Watts lay on the shower floor, hogtied by Flexicuffs, the water spraying his bloody face as he threw up onto the floor.

A fire alarm sounded. Fletcher shut the bathroom

door and dragged Bryson across the floor, the carpet burning his cheek as he kept dry-heaving. Then the burning stopped and his face was lying against the cool tile in the hallway. Men and women in towels and bathrobes were standing around to see what the commotion was.

A small, cylindrical object trailing thick grey smoke rolled down the hallway. A hissing sound behind him and then Bryson saw the same canister from the bathroom rolling across the floor as he was dragged into an elevator.

A whine of the motor and the clank of gears as the elevator lifted. Timothy Bryson lay on his stomach on the elevator floor of dirt and grime. He turned onto his side, dry-heaving, and looked down at his stomach. No blood.

That didn't make sense. He had seen the muzzle flash, had felt the gunshot tear through his stomach and then his chest. He should be bleeding.

Malcolm Fletcher stood above him, his voice muffled behind a small mask covering his mouth and nose.

'Do you know who I am, Detective?'

Bryson nodded then dry-heaved again.

'Then you know why I'm here.'

Bryson didn't answer. Fletcher took off the mask and tucked it inside his jacket pocket.

The elevator stopped. The doors slid open, the hallway dark.

Malcolm Fletcher flipped the emergency stop

button. A hunting knife was gripped in his gloved hand.

Bryson felt a surge of panic and then, strangely, the feeling vanished behind an odd sense of calmness. He knew he should be scared but his body seemed completely unaware of the danger.

'If you're a good boy and tell the truth, Timmy, I'll let you go. But if you don't tell the truth, if I don't feel you're truly sorry for your sins, well, you'll have no one to blame but yourself.'

The blade cut through the bindings on his ankles.

Fletcher helped him to his feet. Bryson coughed, tried to catch his breath. Hands cuffed behind his back, it was difficult to stand.

Fletcher gripped his arm and moved him into the hallway. As Bryson made his way up the stairs, wobbling like a drunk, that odd sense of calm transformed itself into something different, a feeling of bliss that took away the fear, the pain, everything.

A door opened and Bryson saw a flat roof that seemed to stretch for miles. Three drunken steps and then Fletcher shoved him back against a brick wall and pressed the blade of the knife underneath his chin.

'Say hello, Timmy. And remember our agreement.'

Fletcher pressed a cell phone against Bryson's ear.

'Hello?'

'Detective Bryson? This is Tina Sanders – Jennifer's mother. We met at the police station.'

Bryson heard a dim voice scream at him to run, run as fast as you can.

'I was told you have information on the man who killed my daughter.'

Where could he run? He wouldn't get far, not with a knife pressed to his throat, not with this peaceful, drunken dreaminess that made him feel like he was an angel floating on air.

'Please, I –' Tina Sanders' voice caught. She cleared her throat, collected herself. 'I need to know what happened. I've been living with this so long, I can't stand not knowing. Please tell me.'

'I don't know what happened to your daughter.'

'I was told a man named Sam Dingle killed Jenny.'

'I don't know anything about that.'

'This man . . . is he in jail?'

Bryson shivered underneath his wet clothes, his teeth chattering as he scrambled to recall the pieces of carefully constructed lies he had stitched together over the years in case this moment ever came.

Fletcher stuck the tip of the knife through his throat. 'Make a choice, Timmy.'

'My daughter was dying,' Bryson said. 'Emily had a rare form of leukaemia. My wife and I tried everything. The doctors wanted to give her an experimental treatment but my health insurance wouldn't cover it.'

'What's this have to do with Jenny?'

The truth floated to the surface. Bryson closed his eyes, surprised at how easily the words came.

'Sam Dingle used his belt to strangle one of the women. We found a fingerprint. That was the only evidence we had. We had no witnesses, and Dingle's mother said her son was with her the night those women disappeared. We were building a case against him when I approached Dingle's father. I told him I could make the belt disappear for the right price.'

In the distance was the sound of fire engines. *Just keep talking. Lang knows you're in here so just keep talking until he finds you.*

'I needed the money for my daughter's treatment,' Bryson said. 'I couldn't get any more loans, we were already maxed out. We couldn't borrow any more money. I was desperate. My daughter was looking to me to save her life and when Dingle's father agreed to pay, I made him promise me to get his son treatment at a psychiatric hospital. He went to Sinclair.'

'You son of a bitch,' Tina Sanders said. 'You rotten son of a bitch.'

'Emily was eight, she was only eight years old, and this treatment was supposed to save her life. She couldn't do any more chemotherapy, her body –'

Fletcher moved the phone away and pressed it against his ear. 'Hello, Miss Sanders . . . yes, it's me. Now about Detective Bryson, have you given any thought about our previous discussion? . . . I see. That is, of course, your choice. I'll call you back shortly.'

Malcolm Fletcher flipped the phone shut. Bryson ran.

57

Bryson took one step and his legs buckled.

Lying on the roof, hands cuffed behind his back and sirens blaring in the cold night air, he stared up at the sky bursting with the kind of bright stars that made him think of the warm summer evenings when Emily, as an infant, was cradled in his arms. He held her bottle, rocking back and forth on the front porch, back and forth until she finally fell back asleep.

Then he saw Malcolm Fletcher looming above him, his eyes as black as the night sky.

'I didn't kill her daughter,' Bryson said. His voice sounded so far away.

'Oh but you did,' Fletcher said. 'That belt would have sent Mr Dingle to jail or, depending on his legal representation, permanently confined him to a mental asylum like Sinclair. If you did your job, Jennifer Sanders would still be alive.'

'I'm sorry.'

'The sympathy in your voice is overwhelming.'

'I didn't have a choice.' In his mind's eye Bryson saw his bald daughter lying in the hospital bed, skin ashen from the chemotherapy, arms bruised from the IV lines. He saw Emily sucking on ice chips.

Emily throwing up in a pail and Emily crying out for her mother and Emily screaming as the nurse injected her with morphine to take away the pain.

'I didn't have a choice,' he said again.

'What day was Sammy released from Sinclair?'

'I don't know.'

'You didn't keep a close eye on him?'

'No.'

'Did you look for Sammy after his discharge?'

'No.'

'I didn't think so.' Fletcher picked him up by the arms. 'You know Sammy killed those women. Since Sammy *voluntarily* admitted himself under the guise of having a nervous breakdown, you knew he could release himself whenever he wanted, or at least until his parents stopped paying the hospital bill, which they did, incidentally, six months later.'

'I did what you asked. I told the truth.'

'You did, and I'm very proud of you. See the fire escape at the end of the roof?'

'Barely,' Bryson said. Everything was blurry.

'I'm going to escort you there now.' Fletcher helped him across the roof. 'That's it, watch your step. I wouldn't want you to trip and hurt yourself.'

Bryson wanted to get out of this terribly cold air. He couldn't stop shivering.

'In case you're wondering, Sammy wandered across the country performing menial construction and landscaping jobs,' Fletcher said. 'He did, however, manage to return east once to collect his portion of his parents' rather meagre estate. During his visit, he raped and tortured Jennifer Sanders over a period of days before strangling her and leaving her body to rot.'

Bryson wanted to close his eyes and go to sleep.

'Like you, Detective, I knew Sammy had killed those women he dumped along the highway. Unlike you, I never stopped searching for him. It took me years to find him, but I never gave up hope. I finally found him last year in Miami, where he had resumed his nocturnal activities. Sammy couldn't recall where he dumped their bodies, but he *did* remember all the names of his victims and could recall, in vivid detail, how he had killed them. I think his memory was aided by the recordings I found in his home. Sammy taped his . . . experiences with each of his victims. I'll spare you the grisly details. I would hate to place an additional burden on your conscience.'

Bryson closed his eyes and saw

himself at ten climbing the big oak in the backyard, he wants to reach the top and watch the homes on Foster Avenue, brick-faced houses with three-car garages and big backyards of nice lawns and swing-sets and dollhouses where kids in nice clothes played under the supervision of their nannies and au pairs – he feels like the way God must feel looking down on them, watching, learning their secrets. He almost reaches the top when he slips and falls, branches whisking past his face and flailing arms as he tumbles through the leaves, limbs pounding him before he comes to a hard, sudden stop. He is lying on the ground and he can't breathe. His ribs are broken and he can't call for help. His mother is standing at the kitchen window, washing her hands in the sink. He opens his mouth to scream but can't draw a breath, he is gasping for air. She doesn't see him, just keeps washing her hands, her apron streaked with flour.

'Wake up, Timmy.'

Bryson stood at the edge of the roof, near the fire escape. From this height, the parked cars and fire trucks looked like toys. People were streaming out into the street as firemen moved inside the club. Bryson wanted to wave to them but his hands were cuffed behind his back.

Directly below was the surveillance van. It was blocking the alley. He didn't see Lang or any of his men. *They must be inside the club now, looking for me.*

'Before I remove your cuffs, I want you to deliver this to Darby McCormick.' Fletcher stuffed something inside Bryson's coat pocket. 'Make sure you give that to her.'

'I will.'

'You promise?'

'Yes.'

'Thank you,' Fletcher said and shoved Bryson off the roof.

Falling through the cold air with his hands cuffed behind his back, Bryson screamed as he watched the roof of the surveillance van coming closer . . . closer . . . too close, his head landed on the roof, neck snapping as his body fell against the van in a sickening thud, denting the steel and shattering glass.

Bryson stared up at the building's roof. Malcolm Fletcher waved good-bye and disappeared.

Blurred faces crowded around him. One face came closer.

'Help is on the way.' A woman's voice. She gripped his hand, squeezed. 'I'll stay right here with you. What's your name?'

The woman's voice was soft and reassuring, like his mother's. The day he fell from the tree, he lay on the ground thinking he was going to die and here came his mother running out of the back door, running as fast as she could in her high-heeled shoes, her apron streaked with flour and cake frosting. 'The ambulance is on its way,' she said, kissing his forehead. Bryson watched the colourful leaves blow across the lawn. 'Relax, Timmy, just lie there and relax. Everything's going to be all right now. You'll see.'

58

Darby received the news from Bill Jordan, the man heading up her surveillance. He was waiting for her on the front steps of the hospital.

Jordan quickly filled her in on the Jaguar and Tim Bryson's last conversation with Mark Lang, an undercover narcotics detective and driver of the second surveillance van. Lang had followed Bryson into Boston. Bryson had entered the club along with his partner Cliff Watts, who had provided the details of the events inside the club's private basement but couldn't explain why Bryson was cuffed and dragged away or how Bryson had ended up on the roof of the second surveillance van. Jordan was taking his men into the city.

Darby stood alone in the dark, hands deep in her pockets as she stared off into the woods, allowing the news to sink past her skin. She had to deal with this. Now.

She left Coop in charge of the crime scene and drove to Boston.

One hand steady on the wheel, the Mustang's engine booming as she tore down the highway, she dialled the commissioner's home phone number.

Chadzynski had already received several updates

about the events in Boston. At the moment, details were sketchy. Darby briefed the commissioner on what she had discovered inside the hospital's chapel.

'These Virgin Mary statues you found inside the box are the same ones found on Hale and Chen?' Chadzynski asked.

'They appear to be the same. I'm more interested in the Virgin Mary statue standing next to the altar.' Darby told her about the rags she had found along the floor, the sponge in the bucket of water. 'The statue was spotless. He's been there recently. After we're done with the remains, I want to stake out the chapel, leave a couple of men inside there so we'll be ready the next time he returns.'

'You really think he'll go back?'

'He will as long as he thinks it's safe.'

'Okay, I'll find someone to organize the stakeout.'

'We can't involve Danvers PD.'

'Aren't they already involved?'

'They don't know about the remains. I'd like to keep it that way.'

'Darby, we can't –'

'I know we're playing in their backyard. But the more people we bring into this, the greater risk we run of having the information slip out. If the media gets wind of the remains found inside that chapel and decides to run with it, the man who killed Chen and Hale won't come back. If it's the same man who has Hannah Givens, he might kill her and run.'

'What about Reed's people? How are you going to keep them quiet?'

'We can't. Bill Jordan and some of his men are already working with Reed's people, so we're containing the situation the best we can. Finding this chapel might be the break we needed. I'd hate for us to lose it.'

'I'll talk to Jordan. Call me when you know more about Bryson. I want to be updated at every turn.'

Darby took the first empty parking spot she found on the street and ran the rest of the way, following the red, blue and white lights pulsing like distress beacons over the building rooftops on Lansdowne Street.

The streets were blocked off with sawhorses and cruisers. It seemed as though every emergency vehicle in the city had been summoned to the area. Patrolmen were everywhere performing crowd control.

Darby pushed her way past reporters and showed her ID to one of the patrolmen. A moment later she was snaking her way past cops, firemen and emergency medical technicians until she reached Tim Bryson's body.

59

Tim Bryson lay on the dented roof of a surveillance van, a pool of blood under him. Drip marks were frozen along the van's sides and back doors, blood smeared against the shattered front windshield where his crooked legs were splayed, one of them dangling near the dashboard. He stared up at the sky, his head tilted against his shoulder, as if puzzled. His neck was broken.

Two men from ID were photographing the body. She couldn't examine Bryson until ID had finished.

Darby looked up the brick building full of dark windows. *Offices*, she thought. The building was at least ten storeys high. *Why did Fletcher bring you up to the roof, Tim? If he wanted to kill you, why didn't he do it downstairs?*

She found Cliff Watts sitting in the back of an ambulance holding an oxygen mask to his mouth while an EMT stitched an ugly gash on his forehead. The front of his jacket and shirt was stained with blood and vomit.

He saw Darby, pulled away the mask and gave her a detailed report of the basement attack.

'He left an aerosol grenade inside the shower,' Watts said. 'Firemen said it contained some chemical that induces vomiting. I was staring at it when the next thing I knew I was hit. I thought I was gunshot – it sure as hell felt that way. I fell and cracked my head on the shower knob.' He inhaled on the oxygen mask for a moment as he reached inside his jacket pocket. 'He hit us with this.'

Watts came back with a blue ball the size of marble. 'It's a kinetic weapon,' he said. 'It looked like a shotgun. I don't know how he got it past security. You'll find shotgun-sized shells along with these rubber balls all over the floor.'

Darby rubbed the ball between her fingers. It felt hard.

Kinetic weapons were non-lethal devices used by police forces in riot situations. Boston police had used them up until a few years ago when working crowd control after a Red Sox game. A beanbag weapon was discharged and hit a college student in the head. The student died, and the parents sued the city and won a large settlement.

The weapon Watts had described contained more firing power than the traditional beanbag weapon. The shotgun round was designed to hit the target with maximum force. Unlike a bullet, this round exploded upon impact.

'I couldn't stop throwing up,' Watts said. 'Fletcher hogtied me and then dragged Tim into the next room and locked me inside the bathroom. The firemen had to chop down the door.'

Why hadn't Fletcher killed Watts? Darby tucked

the question away and said, 'Did he say anything to you, Cliff?'

'Not a word.'

'Did he speak to Bryson? Did you overhear anything?'

Watts shook his head as he brought the oxygen mask up to his face.

'What was the security like?' Darby asked.

'They had two guys waving one of those magic wands over you to see if you're packing a knife or gun. They said Fletcher flashed his badge and they let him through. I didn't see any security cameras, but I wasn't really paying attention.'

'Who's in charge of the scene?'

'Neil Joseph.'

Good. Darby knew the man. Neil was solid.

'Fletcher went downstairs with a woman, a red-head,' Watts said. 'We thought he was going down there to get his rocks off. It's one of those private sex clubs with a bathhouse and lots of rooms full of kinky toys that would make a good Catholic girl like you blush.'

A tired grin as he put the mask over his face again. He inhaled for several seconds. 'You can't get down there unless you have a gas mask,' he said. 'In addition to a smoke grenade, Fletcher threw another one of those aerosol containers. The place is sealed tight, so that chemical shit is still lingering in the air. It has a longer shelf life because of the steam from the bathhouse.'

Darby left to find Neil Joseph. A patrolman pointed her to a brick-faced club called Instant Karma.

All the lights inside the club were on, the dance floor crowded with witnesses being interviewed by patrolmen and detectives. Empty steel cages hung from the ceilings, the tables and counters were stacked with glasses and beer bottles, many of them still full of booze. Darby spotted Neil Joseph behind the bar, in a roped-off area with plush chairs and couches. He was talking to a group of young men built like linebackers, all of them dressed in black and wearing matching shirts with the word SECURITY silk-screened on the back.

Neil saw her, flipped his notebook shut and limped his way toward her. What was left of his black hair was damp against his scalp. With the exception of his limp from his bad knee, he still looked the same as when she had met him during her first days at the lab – an old-school cop with a no-bullshit attitude hidden behind layers of caustic sarcasm nurtured from his years on the job and growing up one of twelve boys in a strict Irish Catholic family.

'Have you found the woman who accompanied our suspect downstairs?' Darby asked.

'Not yet. When the fire alarm went off, they all went running. Do you know a woman named Tina Sanders?'

Darby nodded. 'Her daughter disappeared over two decades ago. We thought it might be connected to a current case.' She thought about the skeletal remains dressed in the Sinclair lab coat. The remains were definitely female. 'I think we might have found her.'

'When did you tell her?'

'I haven't.'

'So Tina Sanders doesn't know you found her daughter?'

'We haven't identified the remains yet. Why are you asking?'

'She's here. A taxi dropped her off near the commotion and the woman tried pushing her way through the crowd with her goddamn walker, screaming about her daughter's murder and Bryson's swan dive from the roof.'

'How does she know that? Did someone tell her?'

'I don't know anything else,' Neil said. 'The woman refuses to talk to anyone but you.'

60

Neil Joseph explained what to do as they walked.

Be patient, he said. If the woman doesn't answer a question right away, hang back for a moment. Silence can be your biggest ally. Most people want to talk, want to get things off their chest. It's important that they be heard. When she does talk, be an empathetic listener. Nod in the appropriate places. You want her to open up and share everything. Don't take any notes, just listen. You want her to trust you.

Tina Sanders sat in the back of a patrol car parked in a dark alley away from the commotion. She wore the same threadbare winter coat Darby had seen that morning at the lab.

Neil knocked on the driver's window. The patrolman left the motor running and walked with Neil into the alley to smoke.

Darby opened the back door. The interior light clicked on. Tina Sanders didn't look over, didn't look up. The woman's face was streaked with mascara, her grey hair dishevelled, as though she had rolled out of bed and into her clothes. The cigarette pack with the crucifix tucked under the cellophane was clutched in her arthritic hands, the gnarled fingers shaped like tree roots.

Darby slid into the seat and shut the door. The interior was uncomfortably warm and smelled of stale beer and cigarettes.

'I understand you wanted to speak to me.'

Tina Sanders didn't answer. In the soft blue glow from the dashboard lights, Darby could see the dark, hollowed pockets underneath the woman's eyes. Her cheeks, etched deep with grooves, were wet and shiny, but her voice was clear when she spoke.

'He said I can trust you,' Tina Sanders said.

'Who said this?'

'Malcolm Fletcher. He said his name was Malcolm Fletcher. He's one of those FBI-type cops. He called me today. Twice.' The woman paused between her words to take short, quick breaths. 'He's the same man who called and told me to go to my mailbox, to go to the crime lab to talk to you about Jenny.'

'You said he called you twice.'

Sanders licked her lips, nodded.

'When was the first time he called?'

'This afternoon,' Sanders said. 'He told me you found Jenny's body.'

Darby shifted in her chair.

'Did you find Jenny?'

'We found a set of remains, but I can't say for certain if it's your daughter,' Darby said. 'We have to do a dental comparison first.'

'How did she die?'

'I don't know.'

Jennifer's mother looked to the crucifix now

wrapped around her fingers, tears streaming down her cheeks.

'He said you would tell me. He told me to come down here and find you and you would tell me what happened to my daughter.'

'I don't know anything at the moment,' Darby said. 'I haven't examined the bones.'

'He said you would tell me the truth.'

'I am telling you the truth. If the remains we found belong to your daughter, I'll tell you. I promise I'll tell you everything.'

'Have you found Sam Dingle?'

'Who?'

Tina Sanders turned her head and stared out the window.

'Who's Sam Dingle?' Darby asked.

The woman didn't answer. Her blank expression reminded Darby of her mother – Sheila staring at Big Red's coffin, not believing he was lying in there, dead and waiting to be lowered into the ground as the priest talked about God's divine plan for all of us; Sheila looking inside the closet, afraid to touch Big Red's clothes; Sheila wandering around the house in the months after he was buried, wondering what went wrong, how she got to this place.

'He put Detective Bryson on the phone.'

Surprise bloomed on Darby's face. 'You spoke to Detective Bryson?'

Jennifer's mother nodded.

'When did you speak to him?'

'Tonight,' Sanders said. 'He confessed to everything.'

'How do you know you spoke with Detective Bryson?'

'I recognized his voice.' The woman's voice was eerily calm. She squeezed the crucifix in her hand and closed her eyes. 'I know the truth now. You people can't hide it any more. I won't let you.'

Darby's head was spinning. She wanted roll down the window for air. 'What did Detective Bryson tell you?'

'All these years . . . all these years I prayed to God to tell me what happened to Jenny. If I knew the truth, then at least I could grieve and move on, maybe get to some place where remembering Jenny wouldn't hurt as much. That need to know the truth – time doesn't take it away. It only sharpens the edges.'

Darby thought back to Fletcher's warning. What had he said? *I shouldn't have to warn you, of all people, that the truth is, more often than not, a terrible burden. You may want to give that some thought.*

'After I left the police station, I was angry,' Tina Sanders said. 'I didn't want to carry that hope again – that hope of finally coming close to knowing the truth. It's happened too many times over the years. I went to church and prayed to God to take it away. Father Murphy told me to have faith. "God will send his angels, Tina."

'And then this man Malcolm Fletcher called me

and he put Detective Bryson on the phone and he told me how Sam Dingle killed these women – Detective Bryson *knew* it and yet he went to Dingle's father and said he would throw away the evidence because he needed money to pay doctors to treat his daughter. He let Dingle go and then Dingle came back and killed Jenny. The man raped my daughter for *days* inside that basement and then he strangled her and left my baby to rot.'

'Detective Bryson *told* you this?'

Tina Sanders looked back to her rosary beads. 'Father Murphy said if I ever met the man who killed Jenny, I had to forgive him. It was the only way to let go of the hate. I had to forgive him.

'Malcolm Fletcher asked me how Detective Bryson should be punished. I said it was for God to decide. That's what I said. Those were my exact words.' She squeezed the rosary beads in her hand and closed her eyes. 'Is he dead?'

'Yes.'

'Did he suffer?'

Darby told the woman the truth. 'Yes,' she said. 'Yes, he did.'

Jennifer's mother took a deep breath. Opening her eyes, she exhaled slowly, choking back tears, and stared back out the window.

She refused to speak again.

61

Darby was placed in charge of the crime scene. The remaining members of the lab were called to the nightclub. It took considerable time to locate additional gas masks.

At 6 a.m., bleary-eyed and weary, she entered the lab and started logging the evidence. Neil Joseph called. He asked her to come to the morgue.

Her office door was open, the light on, spilling into the hallway. Darby heard the voice of a reporter.

'... don't know any details yet. Detective Timothy Bryson was the lead investigator for Boston Police's newly formed Criminal Services Unit, which was working on the murders of Emma Hale and Judith Chen. Both women were abducted and disappeared for several weeks before their bodies were found. Both women were shot execution-style in the back of the head. While the police have been uncharacteristically quiet on the murder of these two college students, Channel Seven has uncovered through a source close to the investigation that Hannah Givens, a sophomore at Northeastern University, is, in fact, missing and may be the next victim of this Boston-based serial killer. Boston Police Commissioner Christina Chadzynski is scheduled to hold a press conference sometime this afternoon. Stay tuned for more details.'

Darby stepped into her office and saw Coop and Woodbury sitting in chairs, watching a live newsfeed on the internet.

'Have they mentioned Malcolm Fletcher?' Darby asked.

Coop answered the question. 'I didn't hear anything, and I haven't had a chance to read the papers. We just got back from Sinclair.'

'Did the news mention anything about the remains?'

Coop shook his head. His eyes were puffy and bloodshot.

'The remains are at Carter's office,' he said. 'Keith and I are going to get started on the duct tape and clothes.'

'Okay, good.'

'The Sony player you found is a new model, one of those combo devices – radio, cassette, and CD player. There's even a jack to hook up an mp3 player. Did you notice anything strange about it?'

'It was the only thing inside that room that wasn't covered in dust.'

'Right,' Coop said. 'So either Malcolm Fletcher brought it there or the killer did.'

'The killer brought the radio there?'

'We found the box of Virgin Mary statues, and that statue of her inside the chapel was clean. We know this guy goes there, so while he's there, I don't know, talking to the Virgin Mary or whatever, maybe he goes inside that other room and listens to the tape so he can relive what he did to Sanders. That's what these perverts do, right?'

'Sometimes,' Darby said.

'But you don't buy it.'

'You saw the remains. The pants were pulled down. That woman, whoever she is, was most likely raped, maybe even tortured.' Darby recalled portions of the recording – the man grunting as the woman cried out in pain and fear, begging for it to stop. 'If it's the same killer, I don't see how he would evolve from rape to abducting women, holding them for weeks and then, after shooting them, dumping their bodies in water with a statue of the Virgin Mary sewn in their pockets.'

'Hale and Chen were held someplace for weeks. We don't know what this guy did to them.'

'You're right, we don't,' Darby said. 'If the killer didn't bring the cassette tape, that leaves only one other person – Malcolm Fletcher. Don't ask me why, I have no idea.'

'The cassette is old. The manufacturing stamp on the plastic is PLC. I forget what it stands for, but I remember buying them at record stores during the eighties. They were the cheapest tapes around. I'm pretty sure they don't manufacture them any more, but we'll run it down.

'As for analysing the tape – trying to isolate or enhance certain sounds, lift background noises – we don't have that kind of equipment, so we can either send it out to a private company or we can call the FBI,' Coop said. 'The Feds will probably turn it over to one of the audio wizards at the Secret Service.'

Woodbury said, 'I'd recommend using the Aerospace Corporation in Los Angeles. They're the ones who worked on the mother's 911 call in the JonBenét Ramsey case. Aerospace had better luck than the Secret Service.'

'Make the call,' Darby said. 'Can you make me a copy of the tape?'

'I can probably make an mp3 file and burn it to a CD.'

'That's fine. What's going on with the unknown makeup sample?'

'I'm still working on it with my friend at MIT,' Woodbury said. 'I was planning on heading there today, but given what's going on, our time and resources are going to be spread pretty thin.'

'Which is probably what Fletcher wants,' Coop said. 'He's burying us in evidence. It's probably going to take us the rest of the week, including overtime, to process what we found inside the hospital.'

'I want our focus on Hannah Givens,' Darby said. 'She's our top priority. Neil Joseph is working on Bryson's case. Fletcher is his responsibility now.'

'Keith and I lifted a partial latent print on Judith Chen's pant pocket,' Coop said. 'It's running through AFIS.'

'What about the thumbprint from her forehead?'

'It didn't find a match. The ballistics report came back. The slug retrieved from Chen's skull was fired from the same gun that killed Hale. What about your end? What's going on?'

Darby told them about the basement level of Instant Karma, an upscale members-only bathhouse where any sexual appetite could be indulged. The man who ran the operation, Noah Eckart, preferred the term 'private gentleman's club'. The yearly fee was $5,000. Malcolm Fletcher had joined the club two days ago, paying in cash, under the name Samuel Dingle. The paperwork listed an address in Saugus. Darby wondered if, during that initial meeting, Fletcher had planted the 'non-lethal' shotgun Watts had described. Had Fletcher planned all along to lure Bryson to his death?

The private club had no security cameras. Members flashed their ID and signed a sheet. The name Sam Dingle was on the list.

Fletcher had specifically requested room 33, which was conveniently located next to the elevator. His companion was an as-yet-unidentified young woman with long dark-red hair.

Eckart had escorted Bryson and Watts to the room, and when he heard the gunshots, he ran away and called security instead of the police – 'I wanted to handle the matter privately, as I'm sure you can understand,' he told Neil Joseph. Thick, grey smoke had started to fill the rooms and Eckart, believing there was a fire, had no choice put to pull the fire alarm.

Witnesses were hard to come by. Neil found two men who, after considerable prodding, reported seeing a man matching Bryson's description being dragged into the private elevator before a smoke grenade and aerosol container laced with a nausea-inducing chemical flooded the hallways.

'The aerosol and smoke grenades are used by SWAT teams in hostage situations,' Darby said. 'Both grenades contain serial numbers. The companies that manufactured them can use the serial numbers to find out which police agency purchased them.'

Malcolm Fletcher, Darby was sure, had most likely obtained the grenades from either a black-market dealer or at a gun show in a state where laws were lax and anything could be purchased for cash.

The blue pellets covering the bathroom floor came from three shell casings which also contained serial numbers. Neil Joseph was saddled with the unfortunate task of having to devote a significant amount of manpower to chasing down these leads which would most likely prove to be worthless.

'You think Fletcher is still lingering around Boston?' Coop asked.

'If he is, he won't be for long. He just killed a cop. Everyone in the state is going to be looking for him.' Darby checked her watch. 'I have to get to the morgue.'

Waiting for the elevator, Darby wondered why Malcolm Fletcher had decided to make a public spectacle of Bryson's death. Doing so ensured intense media coverage. Maybe he wanted Bryson's sins to have a national audience. Chadzynski was probably already meeting with her media advisor, working on spin control.

Darby couldn't blame her. If what Tina Sanders said was true – that Tim Bryson had thrown a critical piece of evidence in exchange for money – what other cases had he contaminated? Had he planted, destroyed or removed evidence on the Emma Hale case?

62

Tim Bryson's body lay on a steel table underneath a blue sheet spotted with blood.

Darby headed to the back of the autopsy suite. Cliff Watts, arms folded across his chest and face swollen from the stitched gash on his forehead, looked over the shoulder of Neil Joseph, who was hunched over one of the benches examining a clear, Ziplock bag smeared with blood. Lying next to the bag was a cell phone with a cracked screen.

'This was inside his jacket pocket,' Neil said to her, tapping his pen against the bag. It held Jennifer Sanders' driver's licence, hospital ID and credit cards. 'I understand you found a purse next to the remains.'

Darby nodded. 'It was empty,' she said.

'Bryson searched the hospital last weekend, right?'

'We split into teams. The basement is a maze.'

'Was Bryson with you?'

'No.'

Neil looked to Watts and said, 'How was the search organized?'

'Three people on each team – two cops and someone from Sinclair security,' Watts said. 'Danvers PD loaned us some people.'

'I talked with Bill Jordan. He said there are several ways to get inside the hospital. Bryson was well aware of them.'

'Meaning?'

'Maybe your partner went back for this evidence here and didn't get around to disposing of it.'

'Cut the shit, Neil, you know as well as I do Fletcher planted this bag before he tossed Tim off the roof.'

'I don't know that. The only thing I know is that this bag here was found inside Tim Bryson's jacket. Maybe there's some truth to what Bryson told Tina Sanders about that piece of missing evidence – what was it again, a belt?'

'You're taking sides with a psychopath?'

'No, Cliff, I'm trying to figure out why Fletcher tossed Bryson off the roof – in a public place, no less. I'm trying to figure out if your partner was dirty.' Neil straightened and looked Watts directly in the eye. 'You two worked together in Saugus, right?'

'I don't have to put up with this shit.' Watts stormed out of the room.

'Don't go too far,' Neil called after him. He caught the expression on Darby's face and said, 'Something you want to add?'

'I was thinking about a quote Fletcher told me, a line from George Bernard Shaw: "If you cannot get rid of the family skeleton, you may as well make it dance."'

'Well, it looks like the son of a bitch is going to get

his wish. Bryson's all over the news. How long do you want to bet it will be until his conversation with Tina Sanders gets out? My guess is the end of the week.'

'A cassette was playing when I found the remains,' Darby said. 'If Bryson went back there and cleaned out her purse, why would he leave the cassette?'

'That's a good question. You got an answer for me?'

'Not yet, but if I were you, I'd shitcan the attitude.'

Darby left to change into scrubs. She ran cold water over her face until her skin was numb.

When she came back into the room with her equipment, ID was taking pictures. Tim Bryson's mangled, crushed body lay under the harsh autopsy light, still dressed in his bloody clothing. Bags were tied around his hands.

Neil walked up next to her and leaned against the counter. 'Tina Sanders still won't speak to us,' he said. 'You think Fletcher threatened her?'

'I don't know. My guess is she's in shock. All these years go by and then in the course of two days she not only discovers her daughter's remains, she's given the name of the man who killed her.'

'Have you spoken to Jonathan Hale recently?'

'Bryson and I went to talk to him on Saturday.'

'So you haven't talked to him since?'

'No. Why?'

'I took a look through Bryson's cell phone. Hale's name is listed on Bryson's call log. Hale called twice last night. Bryson got a voicemail, but I don't know his password so I can't unlock it. You mind if I speak to Hale?'

'Be my guest.'

ID finished the first round of pictures. Darby collected grit samples from underneath Bryson's fingernails. There were no marks on his palms; he hadn't fought off Fletcher. His right wrist was broken.

Collecting fibres and pieces of glass from the clothing, Darby spotted a bruised area on Bryson's neck.

'It looks like an injection site,' she told Neil. 'We'll have to wait until the tox screen comes back.'

Darby went to work cutting the clothing. She replayed her conversation with Tina Sanders, remembering the framed picture of the young girl she had seen on Bryson's desk.

I had one, my daughter, Emily, Bryson had told her that morning after visiting Jonathan Hale. *She had this really rare form of leukaemia. We took her to every specialist under the sun. Seeing everything she went through, I would have sold my soul to the devil to spare her life. I know that sounds overly melodramatic, but it's the honest-to-God truth. You'll do anything for your kids. Anything in the world.*

Was Bryson made so desperate by his fear and love for his daughter that he orchestrated a plan to throw away the key piece of evidence in a murder investigation in exchange for money he used in a final attempt to save his daughter's life?

Darby slipped into that private place where she

carried her true feelings about people, the same part which demanded a fierce, almost childish fairness in all human transactions; that constantly fought to separate everyone and everything into clearly labelled categories of right and wrong, good and evil. What side did Bryson fall? Darby considered the question and was surprised, even slightly appalled, to feel a cold, grim satisfaction.

To wash it away, Darby thought of the framed picture of the young girl. She focused on Emily Bryson's smile to summon some measure of sympathy and still she felt empty.

63

Boston's Forensic Anthropology Unit was a small suite of windowless, cluttered offices crammed with government-issued steel grey bookcases and matching filing cabinets. Except for an anatomical chart, the white walls behind Carter's desk were bare.

'Sorry to keep you waiting,' Darby said.

'It's fine. It gave the students more time with the bones. It's rare to get a full set of remains.' Carter, short and stocky with grey stubble and thick glasses from some bygone era, grunted as he stood. 'You look exhausted.'

'I haven't slept yet.'

'I don't know if the remains belong to Jennifer Sanders. I'm still waiting for the dental records to be sent over.'

Carter escorted her to the locker room. Darby changed into surgical scrubs and followed him down the hall to the bone room.

She passed the small room containing a sink and stove. The majority of bones sent here for examination more often than not were covered in decomposing soft tissue. In such cases, bones were placed in Crock-Pots and roasting pans holding water and detergent and brought to a gentle boil in order to allow the bones to adjust to the heat. The process, called thermal maceration, sloughed off the remaining tissue.

The remains were assembled on an adjustable steel gurney similar to the ones used in the morgue. As always, the room was very cool.

'The remains are definitely female,' Carter said. He pointed to the pelvic bones. 'We have a raised sacroiliac joint and the wide sciatic notch. Given the blonde hair mat and the characteristics of the skull, our Jane Doe is definitely Caucasian.'

'What about age?'

'The medial ends of the bones aren't completely fused to the shafts, so she's at least twenty-five. The pelvic bones are dense and smooth. Because they don't show any grain, and given the fact that the cranium's intermaxillary sutures aren't fused, she's no older than thirty-five.'

'Cause of death?'

'Look at the hyoid bone.'

Darby checked the horseshoe-shaped bone in the neck. It was broken.

'She was strangled.'

'Yes,' Carter said. 'Now take a look at this.'

He pointed to the scapula. Darby saw a large fracture.

'That was caused by a serious blow,' Carter said. 'Either he kicked her or he hit her with something like a bat or a long piece of wood.'

'What about a brick?'

'That might do it. She's got some other fractures. The poor girl was beaten.' Carter sighed, shook his head. 'The femur is just under forty-eight centimetres. Our Jane Doe is between five-six and five-nine.'

The office phone buzzed.

'Excuse me,' Carter said. He took the call, listened for a moment and without answering hung up. 'Jennifer Sanders' dental records are here. I'll be right back.'

While Carter compared the dental records, Darby stared at the remains, wondering how long they had lain inside the room full of brick and plaster. Was she kept alive for days, beaten and possibly raped before she was strangled? How long had she cried out for help?

Carter pushed his glasses up his long, beak-like nose.

'It's Jennifer Sanders,' he said.

64

Walter calmly set the tray on the kitchen counter. Hannah had finished most of her dinner. She had been with him for nearly five days and she still refused to speak to him.

Emma Hale had screamed the first two weeks, calling him every name in the book while demanding to be let go immediately. At the beginning of the second month, she had tried to attack him with one of the kitchen chairs inside her room. To prevent that from happening again, he used chains with brackets and locks to secure chairs to the kitchen table legs. As punishment, he turned off the electricity to her room and left Emma alone in the dark, without food, for several days, to teach her a lesson.

It worked. For the next three months Emma was well behaved. She acted friendly and kind. She seemed interested in what he had to say. She opened up and shared things about her life – personal, intimate things like her mother's death. They had many long, pleasant conversations. They even watched movies together – *When Harry Met Sally* and *Pretty Woman*. To show his appreciation, he brought her to the upstairs dining room for a special romantic dinner and served everything on fine china. Emma had repaid his kindness by hitting him over the head with the dinner plate. She almost made it to the front door.

In the beginning, he had been dazzled by Emma's beauty, had fallen under her spell and was willing to do anything in the world to make her love him – he had gone so far as to sneak back inside Emma's home to retrieve a special necklace. He had given it to Emma as a surprise and she still refused to love him and Mary told him it was time to send Emma away.

The first week, Judith Chen hadn't screamed or yelled; that came later. When he offered to buy her clothes, any clothes she wanted, she had said yes and thanked him. She had modelled the clothes for him, said how nice they were, and thanked him. He bought her the books she wanted, DVDs and magazines; he cooked her favourite meals and always she thanked him.

With her soft voice and disarming manner, Judith had seductively manoeuvred him into walks outside to get fresh air. He always took her out late at night, when the rest of the world was asleep. Blindfolded, she sat in the passenger seat and he drove her a mile away, to an isolated section of woods, and walked with her. She never complained about the gag or the handcuffs. When he returned Judith to her room, she thanked him, she always thanked him.

The night she tried to escape, they were out for one of their lovely walks. This time he hadn't gagged her but her wrists were cuffed. On the way back to the car, she asked if she could kiss him. She leaned forward, smiling, and drove her knee into his crotch.

The pain was like a white-hot supernova; it exploded across his vision and the next thing he knew he was down on the ground among the dry pine needles gasping for air. She kicked him in the stomach and kicked him in the head once, twice, three times. Then she was sitting on the ground and, like an acrobat, moving her cuffed wrists across the back of her legs and over her feet. She grabbed the car keys from his coat pocket and ran through the woods.

Bleeding and dizzy, he managed to get to his feet and run after her. Mary told him to relax – everything would be fine, she said, and Mary was right; she was always right.

Walter caught up to Judith just as she reached the car. He pulled her away from the door and Judith screamed and he shoved her face against the hood and she kept screaming and again he smashed her face against the hood and windshield until Mary told him to stop.

Judith didn't talk after that. Then she got sick and she . . . she had to leave.

Why wouldn't Hannah speak to him?

This morning, when he delivered breakfast, he had asked her if there was anything she would like: a book, movie, a CD by her favourite band – anything, just name it. Hannah didn't answer.

Walter came back an hour later and knocked on

the door. She didn't answer. He collected the dishes from the sliding tray and carried them upstairs. He worked out extra hard and took a long shower.

He brought her lunch and knocked. When Hannah didn't answer, he let himself in. She was sitting in the leather chair again.

Unable to stand the silence any more, Walter decided to tell Hannah about the accident, how he had woken up in bed with his skin and hair on fire and Momma already collapsed on the burning bed. He stressed how he didn't blame Momma for hurting him. Momma was angry because Daddy had left them when Walter was still in her belly and Momma had to work two jobs to keep a roof over their heads and food on the table. Momma talked about how angry she was at God for having him take away her dreams and sticking her with a bad child – and he had been bad, oh yes, he had done bad things to get Momma's attention. He didn't tell Hannah about the time he was caught choking the little girl. It was an accident. All he wanted was to hug her. She was so pretty and she smelled so good.

Walter told Hannah how he had learned, through patience and prayer, lots of prayer, to forgive Momma even after all the terrible things she did to him, like the time she dunked his hand in a pot of boiling water. He still loved her now, even though Momma was gone and in heaven.

And now it was time for Hannah to forgive him. It was time to move forward. It was time for Hannah to be thankful for all the wonderful blessings in her life.

As a show of good will, Walter gave her a present – a sheet of beautiful Crane stationery and a matching envelope. He handed her a pen and told her to write a letter to her parents. He promised to mail it. Again he said he was sorry for hurting her. It was an accident. Forgive me, Hannah. Please.

Hannah didn't answer.

Walter gripped the edge of the kitchen counter. He had opened up to Hannah, shared his most painful secrets, and she hadn't said one word, just sat in the damn chair, waiting for him to leave. Her silence mocked him. He felt like slapping her right then but he didn't. Walter was proud of his self-control. He washed the dishes and shut off the lights in the kitchen.

For the next two hours he worked on a client's website. Then he hit the weights until his muscles were depleted.

Walter felt lighter, much better. He sat down with the wedding album.

The first picture was a wonderful black-and-white photograph of Hannah dressed in a stunning Vera Wang wedding gown. Walter wore a classic black tux. They were holding hands. The people sitting in the pews were smiling, admiring them. Everyone was clapping.

Here was another picture of them on their honeymoon in Aruba. Hannah stood on a beach of white sand, wearing a breathtaking black bikini that barely covered her tanned body. Her hair was wet, smelling of the ocean, and she was smiling and happy as she looked down on him, her husband, lying on a towel under the bright, hot sun, his skin perfectly tanned and sculpted with muscle, not a blemish or scar anywhere.

Walter was very good with computers. Using Photoshop, he had transferred the digital pictures he had taken of Hannah walking to her job and class and pasted her face on the various photographs he had found on the internet. The results were spectacular.

His favourite picture was the last one – Hannah holding their newborn son.

65

For the next three days, Darby searched through Hannah Givens' cramped bedroom cluttered with notebooks and textbooks piled on a thrift-store desk. She hunted through Hannah's receipts, pictures and scraps of paper jumbled with notes and 'to-do' lists. She examined Hannah's Day Runner and interviewed Hannah's two roommates, friends, classmates and professors, and her parents, who had flown into Boston and were staying in Hannah's apartment.

Three long days and this was all Darby knew: Hannah Givens was last seen leaving her shift at Downtown Crossing's Kingston Deli on the day of the snowstorm. The bus driver for that route confirmed Hannah Givens never got on the bus. A canvas of local businesses owners, as well as the extensive media coverage, had failed to bring forth any witnesses.

Given the amount of media attention, the taped pleas from the parents and the toll-free number set up by Commissioner Chadzynski playing in heavy rotation on all the news cycles, some people believed Hannah's abductor might let her go. Boston PD had traps on all the phone lines. As of this morning, they had logged thirty-eight calls, all cranks.

CNN's Nancy Grace, ringleader for the freak media circus, had stirred up the trash journalists, and they had adopted the college girl's plight with a fevered, Anna Nicole-like intensity. Hannah's high-school graduation picture screamed from the supermarket tabloids, her story the lead item on shows like *Inside Edition*. Darby wondered if the national exposure would scare Hannah's abductor, prompt him to panic and kill her.

The twenty-six-year-old mystery of what had happened to Jennifer Sanders was, at the moment, only regulated to the New England news outlets. Tina Sanders refused to speak to the police. Her lawyer, Marshall Grant, an ambulance-chaser with a bad toupee who ran successful TV commercials during daytime soap operas promoting his firm's extensive legal services, had swooped in and somehow convinced Sanders to allow him to take up her case.

Grant had no problem speaking to the press. The exposure landed him an interview with Larry King.

'The police have officially identified a set of remains belonging to Jennifer Sanders but refuse to tell us where she was found for reasons we don't understand,' Grant said. 'We do, however, have reason to believe Jennifer's murder might be connected to a man named Samuel Dingle, who was the prime suspect in the strangulations of two Saugus women in 1982. Unfortunately, Larry, one of the few people who can provide us with clues, Detective Bryson, was murdered by a former FBI profiler named Malcolm Fletcher.'

Tim Bryson's 'alleged' involvement in disposing of the belt wasn't mentioned or hinted at in any newspaper articles or on TV. Darby wondered if Chadzynski was negotiating with Tina Sanders' lawyer to keep the matter quiet. Chadzynski and her PR machine had, at least for the moment, prevented information about Sinclair from being leaked to the press.

The morning after Bryson's death, Chadzynski held a press conference and released Malcolm Fletcher's name to the media. The former profiler, Chadzynski said, was wanted in connection with the murder of Detective Timothy Bryson, who was thrown from the roof of a popular Boston nightclub. Fletcher's picture was printed on the front pages of almost every major newspaper along with the picture from the FBI website. Chadzynski kept stressing the $1 million reward the federal government was offering for information leading to the arrest or capture of the former profiler.

Chadzynski didn't mention Fletcher's visit to Emma Hale's home, his conversations with Tina Sanders or the DVD he had mailed to Jonathan Hale.

Darby had processed the mailer. It contained a single fingerprint which matched Malcolm Fletcher's; AFIS identified the print on Wednesday night. The

FBI, she was sure, would be arriving in Boston any day now.

Darby hadn't spoken to Jonathan Hale. According to his lawyer, Hale was out of town on business and unavailable for comment.

Sam Dingle's whereabouts were still unknown, but this morning's *Boston Globe* contained a quote from his sister Lorna, who was divorced from her third husband and living in Baton Rouge, Louisiana: 'The last time I saw my brother was when he came home to collect his share of my parents' estate back in 1984. He said he was living somewhere in Texas. That was the last time I spoke to him. I don't know where he is, I have no idea what he's doing. I haven't heard a word from him in decades. For all I know, he's dead.'

Darby sat on Hannah Givens' sagging mattress. She rubbed the dryness from her eyes and, taking a deep breath, focused her attention on the student's bedroom.

Hannah had covered up the cracks in the pink wall with framed pictures of her parents, the family Labrador and her friends back in Iowa. Milk crates doubling as shelves held CDs and paperback books with missing covers. An old radio/cassette Walkman sat on a denim beanbag chair. The closet was stuffed with clothes from Old Navy and American Eagle Outfitters.

Hannah Givens had been missing for a week. Had her abductor panicked and killed her? Was Hannah's body floating somewhere along the bottom of the

Charles? The thought left a cold, hollow pocket in the pit of Darby's stomach.

Three victims. Two were dead and one, Hannah Givens, was possibly still alive. What did all three women have in common? They were young women enrolled in *Boston* colleges. That was the common trait these three women shared.

Tim Bryson had investigated the college admissions angle. Darby, along with a team of detectives, had revisited it, checking to see if the three women might have possibly applied to the same school at one point in time. When the search came up empty, she tried to find a common point where all three women might have intersected – a bar, a student group, anything. So far, she had come up empty handed.

The first victim, Emma Hale, rich and white and extremely attractive, grew up in Weston and went to Harvard. The second victim, Judith Chen, middle-class and Asian, was plain and frumpy, a tiny, almost frail young woman born and raised in Pittsburg, Pennsylvania. She came to Boston's Suffolk University to take advantage of their generous financial-aid package.

Now here was Hannah Givens, another college student, the only child of a lower-middle-class farming family from Iowa, a big-boned girl with plain-Jane looks and a kamikaze attitude toward her studies, her free time, what little of it she had, spent working at either the deli or Northeastern's campus library.

Why did the killer focus on *Boston* colleges? Was he a student? Did he pose as a student?

Darby opened her backpack, grabbed the files and flipped through the pictures of all three college students, trying to see them the way their killer did – possessing something he needed. *Why did you keep them for so long only to turn around and kill them?*

Three college women, at least one of whom, Emma Hale, seemed to be tied to Malcolm Fletcher, a former FBI profiler who had been on the run for twenty-five years only to resurface – again in Boston – inside Emma Hale's home. Was Jonathan Hale using Fletcher to hunt down his daughter's killer?

Like Tim Bryson, Jonathan Hale was a father crippled by grief. Unlike Bryson, Hale was a powerful, wealthy man. If Fletcher had approached Hale with either information about the man who had killed his daughter or a plan to find him, wouldn't Hale jump at the opportunity? And why would Fletcher come out of hiding to help a grieving father find his daughter's killer?

Maybe Fletcher hadn't approached Hale. Maybe Fletcher's agenda was simply to expose Tim Bryson's sins. Fletcher had made a public spectacle of Bryson's death, throwing him off the roof of a crowded nightclub with a plastic bag holding Jennifer Sanders' licence and credit cards. Fletcher had also contacted Tina Sanders. He put Tim Bryson on the phone and Bryson confessed to throwing out evidence that would have implicated Samuel Dingle in the rape and murder of two women from Saugus.

And where was Sam Dingle? Had he moved back east? Was he responsible for the deaths of Emma Hale and Judith Chen? Did he now have Hannah? His name was all over the news. Had he killed Givens, dumped her body in the river and disappeared?

Everything pointed back to Sam Dingle. It seemed too neat, too easy.

Bryson had mentioned that Fletcher was trying to throw them off the scent. Maybe Bryson said it to try to protect his ass. Maybe Bryson was telling the truth.

What if Fletcher's real agenda was to shift the focus of the police away from the real killer so he could find him first? According to Chadzynski's FBI contact, Malcolm Fletcher was a one-man judge, jury and executioner. If Sam Dingle was, in fact, the man who had killed Hale and Chen, Darby doubted Fletcher would leave town without finding him.

Darby's cell vibrated. The caller was Christina Chadzynski.

66

'It seems Malcolm Fletcher mailed CDs containing a recording of Tim Bryson's conversation with Tina Sanders to every reporter in the city,' Chadzynski said. 'I'm sure they'll be playing it over the news tonight.'

'Have you heard a copy?' Darby asked.

'Not yet. I'm afraid I have more bad news. A reporter for the *Herald* knows Sanders' remains were found inside Sinclair. The reporter is amenable to stalling the story in exchange for an exclusive interview with you after you've solved the case.'

Darby leaned back against the wall. Stuffed animals from Hannah's childhood were arranged around the pillows and cheap comforter.

'I'm not suggesting you do it,' Chadzynski said. 'It's only a matter of time before other reporters find out. I'll try and stall him as long as I can.'

'I spoke with Bill Jordan. He's brought in some men with SWAT experience. When our man shows up at the chapel, Jordan and his men will take him down.'

'Do you really think this person is going to show up?'

'I do. At some point, he *will* return. The statue of

the Virgin Mary I found was clean – remember the bucket of water and towels I found? That statue and the chapel hold a special connection for this person. He could go to any church but he specifically goes to this chapel that's buried under the ground. It's not easy to find. He must have found a special route.'

'Darby, I've been on the phone with the federal task force assigned to track down Malcolm Fletcher. The task force coordinator is a man named Mike Abrams. He met Fletcher while he was working the Sandman case. Abrams was a site profiler for the Boston office. He suspects Fletcher is long gone, but Abrams still wants to speak to us. They're scheduled to arrive at Boston sometime tomorrow afternoon. His people want to look at the DVD Fletcher sent to Hale as well as the audio tape you found.'

'Maybe you should have him talk to Jonathan Hale while he's here.'

'I'm sure they'll want to talk to him. Have you read Bryson's toxicology report?'

'I didn't know it was available.'

'I received a copy this morning. Tim was injected with GHB and Ketamine. If he was alive, his drug-induced confession would be thrown out. It wouldn't have a leg to stand on during trial.'

Maybe that's why Fletcher threw him off the roof, Darby thought.

'Have you made any progress with Sam Dingle?' Chadzynski asked.

'The address Fletcher left on the sign-in sheet at the club and the registration for his Jaguar, which still hasn't been found – all of it points back to the house where Sam Dingle grew up. It's like Fletcher's shoving it in our faces.'

'I agree. Where do you think he is?'

'Who knows? If you're serious about finding him, you need to put people on Hale.'

'Malcolm Fletcher is a loner. He doesn't work for anyone.'

'The locks for Emma Hale's doors weren't picked. He didn't force his way in there.'

'Darby –'

'At least put Hale under surveillance.'

'I'm not going to do that.'

'Why? Because he's rich?'

'Because there is *no* evidence to suggest that Fletcher is working for or is in collusion with Jonathan Hale,' Chadzynski said. 'For God's sake, we have a security tape showing the man sneaking inside the parking garage.'

'Fletcher didn't break into Emma Hale's home; he had a key.'

'Have you considered the possibility that maybe Fletcher's working for Tina Sanders? Fletcher's spoken to her several times. Maybe I should put her under surveillance.'

'I would.'

'You can make your recommendations to the federal task force,' Chadzynski said. 'Have you found any indication that Bryson tampered with evidence on either the Hale or Chen case?'

'Both Neil and I reviewed the chain of custody on all the evidence. It doesn't appear Bryson tampered with any of our cases. I can't say what happened in Saugus.

'I got the state lab's report on the two Saugus women. Both were raped and strangled. There were no traces of semen, no blood under the fingernails, but they found a lubricant that's used with some condoms. Coop's reviewing the evidence files right now.

'NCIC doesn't contain any listing for Samuel Dingle,' Darby said. 'There is no DNA profile in CODIS under that name. Same goes for AFIS. Dingle could possibly be using an alias.'

'I heard something about a fingerprint being recovered from the duct tape used to bind Sanders' wrists.'

'It's a palm print. Have you spoken to Dr Karim?'

'I did this morning. He was very cooperative. He didn't have anything new to add.'

'Maybe we should dig a little deeper.'

'What's going on with Hannah Givens? What new developments do you have?'

'I don't have anything at the moment. Neil told me Bryson did, in fact, pay for an experimental stem-cell treatment for his daughter.'

'I want your focus on Givens.'

'I'm at her place right now.'

'Good. I need to get going. We're holding another press conference. We can talk more after Bryson's wake.'

'I'm going to stick around here for a while.'

'Keep at it,' Chadzynski said. 'I believe you have a real talent for this.'

Darby hung up. From behind the closed bedroom door she heard the TV playing down the hallway, the murmured voices of Hannah's parents. They were parked in the living room hoping for a phone call from their daughter's kidnapper.

For the next hour Darby walked around the bedroom examining Hannah's things, feeling certain she had overlooked something valuable. That feeling, she knew, was her frustration speaking. There was nothing here.

Darby put on her coat. She opened the door and walked down the hallway to the living room where Hannah's parents were waiting.

67

Hannah's parents sat on the couch watching a recording of last night's Nancy Grace show. The so-called victim's rights crusader was talking about the abduction of Hannah Givens, the apparent third victim of a Boston-based serial killer who abducted college women and, after holding them for a period of weeks, shot them in the back of the head and dumped their bodies.

After rehashing the gory details of Emma Hale and Judith Chen's murders, Nancy Grace consulted a criminal psychologist and a former FBI profiler, both women, and asked them if Hannah's abductor, given the heightened media attention, might panic and decide to kill her. There was much discussion about the possibility.

Tracey Givens, her eyes bloodshot and puffy from crying, turned away from the TV, saw Darby and stood.

'You find anything in my daughter's bedroom, Miss McCormick?'

'No, ma'am, I didn't.'

Hannah's mother seemed surprised. Hannah's father stared at the stains in the well-worn carpet.

'You were in there an awfully long time today, I thought you . . .'

'I wanted to get to know your daughter better,' Darby said.

Tracey Givens glanced back to the TV where Nancy Grace was shouting at Paul Corsetti, the media rep for the Boston police. By not telling the truth to the public, Nancy Grace yelled to the camera, Boston PD had put Hannah's life in danger.

No, you dumb, self-centred piece of shit, you're the one who's putting Hannah's life in danger.

Darby couldn't stomach it any more. 'Thank you for allowing me to examine Hannah's things,' she said, opening the front door. Hannah's father followed.

Michael Givens had the face of a man who had spent too many years in the sun. His skin, sagging and leathery, was carved with deep grooves. He looked frail in the afternoon light. The street was quiet now. The Boston media and national tabloids were downtown at Chadzynski's press conference.

'The experts on TV, they're saying all this attention Hannah's getting might egg this man on – might encourage him to, you know, do something,' he said. 'But those TV people, these so-called experts, they're looking at it from the outside. You're on the inside, Miss McCormick. You've got all the facts.'

Darby waited, not sure what the man was asking.

'They said on the news you worked on the other two cases where the women disappeared.'

'I've only read the case files.'

'Those two girls . . . they were gone for a long time, right?'

'Mr Givens, I'm going to work day and night to find a way to bring your daughter home. That's a promise.'

Hannah's father nodded. He was about to open the door when he decided to lean against the doorway. He crossed his arms over his chest and looked to the corner of the porch, at the recycling bins filled with beer cans.

'Hannah . . . she wanted to stay home with us and go to a local school, a community college about ten minutes away,' Michael Givens said. 'Schools in the northeast are real good. Hannah got this real nice financial aid package from Northeastern, so I pushed her. Sometimes you've got to push your kids. You've got to give them a shove 'cause sometimes that's the only way to help them.

'I told Hannah I couldn't afford to send her to the local college, which was the truth. We don't make much. Getting a degree up here would open all sorts of doors for her. Hannah didn't like it much – she missed her friends, didn't care for the weather here. Too cold, she said. My wife, she sort of relented, said she'd pick up an extra job to help see Hannah through a local college but I said no. I kept pressing Hannah to come here. My daughter's shy – she's been that way since she was wee-high – and I thought, my thinking was being up here, surrounded by all these smart people, it would do Hannah a world of good, help break her out of her shell. She may be shy but she's a persistent bugger when it comes to studying.

'Hannah kept on telling me how unhappy she was, how she wanted to come home, and I kept telling her no. I'd hang up and every time there'd be a knot in my stomach. I always shook it off. Maybe God was trying to tell me something.'

'Mr Givens, I know this is easy for me to say, but you can't blame yourself for what's happened. Sometimes . . .'

'What?'

Sometimes things just happen, Darby said to herself. *Sometimes God doesn't care.*

'We're all working real hard on this, sir.'

Michael Givens stood with his hands in his pockets, unsure of what to say or where to look.

'What do you think of her?' he asked.

'I think your daughter is –'

'No, I meant Nancy Grace. She wants us to come on TV and talk about Hannah, says it will help find her. My wife wants to do it, says anything we can do to help Hannah we ought to. Truth be told, I don't feel too good about it. There's something about the way that woman carries on that gives me a bad feeling all over. If we go on TV, you think it will make this person who's got Hannah decide to . . . hurt her?'

Darby told him the truth. 'I don't know.'

'What would you do, if you were in my situation?'

'I think you should do what you feel is right.'

'What's your opinion of that Nancy Grace woman?'

'Personally, I think the only thing she gives a shit about is ratings.'

'You're blunt. I admire that. You and Hannah would get along real good. Thank you, Miss McCormick.'

Hannah's father turned around but he didn't open the door.

'She's our only child. We couldn't have any other children. It was a miracle we had her. I don't know what we'd do if she . . . Just bring my baby girl home, okay?'

His hands fumbled for the doorknob. Michael Givens stumbled back inside, forgetting to shut the door behind him. He took the seat next to his wife and stared at the phone, willing it to ring.

68

Keith Woodbury had taken the cassette tape and created an mp3 file which he burned onto a CD.

The first time Darby had listened to it she had to excuse herself. She went outside and walked around the building several times until the fresh air had purged the sick, clammy feeling that wrapped itself around her skin.

The second time was just as difficult, but with the initial shock over, Darby concentrated on the recording, forcing herself to ignore the woman's screaming and listen for background noises. Darby listened to the CD again as she drove back into the city.

Jennifer Sanders screamed out in pain, screamed for it to stop, begged for it to stop. The man on the tape grunted and moaned. Sometimes he laughed. He didn't speak. If he had said something, then maybe Dingle's sister could have identified her brother's voice. At least then Darby would know for sure that the man on the tape was, in fact, Sam Dingle.

The traffic leading into Boston was awful. There was some sort of road construction. Darby took the nearest exit, her mind focused on the sounds playing over her car speakers. She didn't hear anything in the background. The tape needed to be analysed by an audio expert, a process that would take months.

Half an hour later she found herself driving through the Back Bay. Trinity Church, one of the oldest in Boston, stood in the shadow of the Prudential Center. Every Christmas season, for as long as Darby could remember, her mother had brought her here to Copley Square for the candlelight carols. Sometimes the Trinity Chamber Choir sang.

Darby spotted an empty parking space and, without a moment's thought, pulled in as daylight died behind the Prudential Tower.

A Catholic church is a sinister place. Sin and salvation. A life-size statue of Jesus hanging on the cross was mounted on the wall behind the altar. In the dim light Darby saw the painted drops of blood running from his crown of thorns and the nails driven through his palms and feet.

The original church, founded in 1733, was burned in the Great Boston Fire of 1872. The architect H. H. Richardson rebuilt the church in the style which became popular in a number of European buildings – massive towers of stone with clay roofs and arches. Darby was always mesmerized by the stained-glass windows behind the altar. She saw David's Charge to Solomon, designed in 1882 by Edward Burne-Jones and William Morris.

Darby sat in a pew, wondering about the generations of people who had sat in this same spot and prayed to God out of desperation and fear. Please, Jesus, my son has cancer. Please help him. Mary,

Mother of God, please keep my children safe. Please don't let anything happen to my family. Please help me, God. Jesus, please help me.

Did God hear their prayers? Did he listen? If he did, did he pick and choose at random? Did he even care?

Did the victims go to church?

Darby set her backpack on the pew and removed the copy of Emma Hale's murder book. She hunted through the text with the aid of a pen light.

Emma Hale was born and raised Catholic. She went to Mass every Sunday with her father. What about Judith Chen? She, too, had been raised Catholic. Her roommates didn't know if she attended church.

Darby called the number for Hannah's apartment. Michael Givens answered.

'What is your daughter's religious affiliation?'

'We raised her Catholic,' Hannah's father said. 'That was my wife's doing. Me, I didn't really have much use for it.'

'What about Hannah?'

'She went through the motions for her mother, but I don't think it really took hold.'

'Do you know if Hannah ever attended Catholic services in or around Boston?'

'Hold on.'

Michael Givens conferred with his wife for a moment. Tracey Givens mumbled something to her husband and then she came on the line.

'Hannah hasn't attended church for a while now. I wasn't too happy about it, but Hannah wasn't afraid to speak her mind. She wasn't real religious, and whatever faith she had left went out the window when that *awful* sexual abuse scandal broke out here – you know the one I'm talking about, where the priests molested those boys and Cardinal what's-his-name covered it up?'

'Cardinal Law,' Darby said. 'What about any local charity work?' Bryson hadn't investigated that item.

'My daughter didn't have a lot of free time between her classes and two jobs – Hannah kept complaining about it to both me and her father, saying she wished she had more of a personal life. If she was doing any charity work, she didn't tell me.'

'What about a boyfriend? Was she seeing anyone?' Darby felt desperate, reaching for straws.

'Hannah was seeing a nice boy back home but that fell by the wayside after Hannah left for college,' Tracey Givens said. 'She wasn't dating anyone here. It was a real sore spot for her.'

'Thank you for your time, Mrs Givens.'

Darby stared at Jesus' sorrowful expression and for some reason her thoughts drifted to Timothy Bryson. His body was lying inside a casket at a funeral home in Quincy. Tomorrow morning he would be buried. She wondered who had made the arrangements.

Darby recalled the framed picture of his daughter and held it in her mind's eye while she examined her feelings.

I'm sorry for what happened to your daughter, that cold, analytical part said. *But I don't feel sorry for what happened to you, Tim. I know I should, but I don't.*

Darby thought of her own mother. Out of habit, or maybe out of faith, she knelt, and with her back ramrod straight, just as the nuns at St Stephen's had taught her, made the sign of the cross and closed her eyes. First she said a prayer for Sheila. Then she prayed for Hannah.

Her phone vibrated against her hip. The display said UNKNOWN CALLER. Darby let her phone ring three more times before she answered.

69

'Are you praying to God to help you find Hannah?' Malcolm Fletcher asked.

Darby reached inside her coat pocket and undid the strap of her shoulder holster as she looked around the church. The pews were empty, the walls with their stained-glass depictions of the stations of the cross covered in shadows.

'I didn't think I'd hear from you again, Special Agent Fletcher.'

'That was a long time ago.'

'Jonathan Hale told us everything.'

'A clever lie,' Fletcher said.

'I know what you're doing. I know why you're here.'

'Aren't you going to ask me about Detective Bryson?'

'You're admitting you killed him?'

'I did you a favour. Who knows what sorts of schemes he was planning? You might want to check your evidence locker.'

'Why didn't you just tell me?'

'I wanted Timmy to deliver a message and decided to send it air mail.' Fletcher laughed, a deep, guttural sound that made her feel cold all over. 'Aren't you glad he's dead?'

'I don't think he deserved to suffer.'

'Another lie. That's part of the reason you're at church now, isn't it? You wanted to lay down your guilt at the altar and beg the Almighty for mercy. I forget how much you Catholics enjoy the rack. Did He decide to end his insufferable reign of silence and answer your prayers?'

'I'm still waiting.'

'Don't you know your god deals in silence and ash?'

'We identified the remains.'

'I'm sure Tina Sanders is relieved. She's been praying for this moment for a long time.'

'She still won't speak to us.'

'I wonder why.'

'Let's talk about Sam Dingle.'

'I'm afraid I'm going to have to end this conversation. I don't entirely trust the phone. You never know who might be listening in. Oh, and Darby?'

'Yes?'

'Despite what you've read or heard about me, I have no intention of harming you now or anytime in the future. Hannah is in excellent hands. I hope you find her soon. Goodbye, Darby.'

Click.

Darby was standing outside the church, looking around the streets when her phone rang again. It was one of the surveillance technicians.

'We couldn't trace his call,' the tech said. 'If he calls again, just keep him talking. At some point he'll slip and we'll find him.'

'Don't bet on it,' Darby said.

70

Hannah Givens was thinking about the letter again, wondering if she had made a mistake.

Three days ago Walter had presented her with a nice sheet of stationery and matching envelope with postage. He gave her a pen and told her to write a letter to her parents. He promised to mail it.

Hannah knew full well Walter would never mail the letter. It was too risky. The way forensics worked now, the police could trace a postage stamp to the exact post office where it had been purchased. She had seen it done on a TV show.

The letter, Hannah knew, was a peace offering, a way to get her to speak. Walter *needed* her to talk. He had tried to get her to open up by sharing a horrible story about how his mother had almost burned him to death and then followed it up with all that religious talk about the importance of forgiveness.

When she didn't speak, when she continued to sit there, silent and staring, she could tell he wanted to hurt her. To his credit, he didn't, but that didn't mean Walter would wait forever. He'd hurt her once. There was no question in her mind he'd do it again.

Walter had left the felt-tipped pen. For a good amount of time she had played with the idea of using the pen as a weapon – stab him in the throat, if possible. At the very least, she could take out an eye. She had played through the scenarios in her mind and noticed that not once did she feel any fear. She had never injured another human being before but felt certain, if and when the time came, she could do it.

Walter, though, was smart. He wouldn't forget the pen. At some point he would ask for it back.

Another idea had taken root in her mind, one with possibly even greater potential: What if she could use the letter as an opportunity to gain some leverage? The question consumed her waking thoughts.

Hannah came up with a plan. She concentrated on what she would say, creating several drafts in her mind before committing the words to paper.

> Walter,
>
> The Virgin Mary came to me in a dream last night and told me not to be afraid. She told me what a good, caring person you are. She told me how much you love me, that you wouldn't do anything in this world to hurt me or my family. Your Blessed Mother also said that you would allow me to call my parents and tell them not to worry.
>
> After I talk to my parents, I was thinking that maybe you would join me for dinner, and we could talk and get to know each other better.

Hannah had set the envelope and pen in the sliding food carrier along with the dirty paper plates from today's lunch. Now she had to wait to see what Walter would do.

To pass the time, she reread the short diary written by a woman named Emma. Hannah flipped to the last page and began to read:

I don't know why I'm bothering to keep this journal. Maybe it's a coping mechanism, this need to leave something behind – to leave my mark. Maybe it's the fever. I can't stop shaking; I'm cold and hot at the same time. Walter, of course, thinks I'm faking. I told him to take my temperature and he did. He said my temperature was a little high but nothing to worry about. He said he wouldn't let anything happen to me.

When my fever didn't break, Walter came into my room holding two big white pills – penicillin, he said. He came back at lunch with two more pills, then two more at dinner. This went on for days (at least it seemed like days; time has no meaning down here). Finally I said to him, 'Do you want me to die?'

'You're not dying, Emma.'

'The pills aren't working. There's something wrong with me. I can't keep any food down. I need a doctor.'

'You have to give the medicine a chance to work. Keep drinking water. I bought you the fancy kind you like, the Pellegrino. You need to stay hydrated.'

'I don't want to die here.'

'Stop saying that.' Walter then launched into another story about how 'his' Blessed Mother came and told him how I would be fine.

'Please listen to me, Walter. Will you listen to me for a minute?' He didn't answer so I kept talking. 'I've been giving this a lot of thought. I don't know where you live. You can blindfold me, put me

in the car and drive me to a hospital in some other city. Just drop me off and leave. I swear to God I won't tell anyone who you are.'

His face changed and, I don't know, he looked disgusted, as though whatever was wrong with me was somehow my fault.

'I don't want to die alone,' I said. 'I want to see my father.' I begged, I cried – I did it all.

Walter waited until I was done, and then he gripped my hands and said, 'Pray with me, Emma. We'll pray together to Mary. My Blessed Mother will help us, I promise.'

Walter has just left the room. I try not to think about what will happen to me when I die.

Maybe God gives you a second chance. Maybe he lets you come back until you leave your mark. Or maybe there is no such thing as a soul. Maybe you're just like everything else that wanders the earth, alive for a short amount of time only to die alone, only to be forgotten. Please God, if you're there and you can hear me, please don't let that be true.

Hannah skimmed over the next paragraph, a long, delusional rambling of a repeated fever dream where Emma found herself wandering around dark streets at night, wondering why the sun wouldn't come out, why there weren't any lights on inside the houses, why the streets didn't have any names.

And here were the last words the woman named Emma wrote:

I keep thinking about my mother. She died when I was eight. The day of her funeral, when my father and I were finally alone, I remember how he kept reassuring me that my mother's death was a part of God's divine plan. The image that comes to my mind over and over again from that day is how the traffic kept moving past us, the people in those cars going about their lives, going to their jobs, going to see their families and friends. Life just keeps moving forward. It doesn't stop for you. It doesn't even pause to offer you an apology. What scared me then – what scares me now – is how small you really are. In the grand scheme of things, you don't matter. If you're one of the lucky ones, you'll get a nice obituary and maybe a handful of people will pause to remember you for a while, but in the end they just go on, keep on moving forward and force themselves to forget until you've faded just a bit – you have to fade just enough so when they remember you you're not as sharp. You're easier to carry.

My father won't be that lucky. He'll leave my pictures up and he'll stop and stare at them and wonder what happened to me, what my last moments were like. I wish I could give him this diary or whatever it is I'm writing here so he could have some, I don't know, some final peace, I guess. I want my father to know

The entry ended.

I want my father to know. Emma's last words.

What happened to her? Had she died here, in this room? On this bed? If she died here, what had Walter done with her body?

Had he killed her?

Walter knocked on the door.

71

Hannah shoved the notebook underneath the sheets. She waited for the door to open. It didn't. The card reader didn't beep and the lock didn't click back.

Walter knocked again. Then she realized he was waiting for her to speak.

Don't speak unless he allows you to talk to Mom and Dad.

Two more knocks and when Hannah didn't answer, he opened the door.

Walter was dressed in a crisp white shirt and grey pinstriped dress pants. He was holding two items – a gift-wrapped box and, folded on top, a white terrycloth robe. He placed both items on the table.

'I thought you might want a clean robe,' he said. 'You can wear it on your way to the bathroom. You can take a shower or, if you prefer, a bath.'

Hannah didn't answer.

'I read your letter,' Walter said. 'I've prayed long and hard, and I've decided to let you call your parents.'

'Thank you.'

Walter smiled. His face changed, became more relaxed.

'It's good to hear your voice,' he said.

‘I’m sorry I haven’t been too talkative, but I thought . . .’

‘You thought I was going to hurt you again.’

Hannah had anticipated the question. She knew what to say.

‘I know what happened in the car was an accident. I forgive you.’

Walter placed the gift-wrapped present on the bed.

‘You didn’t have –’

‘I wanted to,’ he said. ‘Go ahead and open it.’

Hannah tore off the paper. Inside the box, wrapped in tissue paper, was the black Calvin Klein cocktail dress she had admired in the Macy’s store window the night of the snowstorm.

‘Do you like it?’ Walter asked.

‘It’s beautiful.’ Hannah shivered beneath her pyjamas. She forced a smile. ‘Thank you.’

‘I was hoping you’d wear it tonight, at dinner. I’m making veal cutlets. The first course is braised scallops served in a white wine sauce.’

‘It sounds wonderful.’ Hannah took a deep breath and plunged. ‘I’d like to talk to my parents now. I don’t mean to be pushy; it’s just that I’m worried about my father. He’s very sick. He has cancer.’

That was a lie. Hannah had watched a *Forensic Files* show about a man who raped and killed prostitutes. The killer had snatched one woman and handcuffed her inside the back of his van. She kept talking about her father, how he had cancer and if she died nobody would take care of him. Her abductor raped her and let her go. After he was caught, he told police he didn't kill the woman because his mother also had died of cancer.

'Why don't you shower first?' Walter said. 'Change into the robe, and I'll escort you to the bathroom. Knock on the door when you're ready.'

Hannah wondered if Walter was watching through the peephole. She stepped behind the curtain that hid her toilet and changed quickly. She pulled the robe tightly around her, knotted the belt around her waist and knocked on the door.

Walter stepped into the room. He was holding a pair of handcuffs.

'To make sure you don't run away or, you know . . .'

Go along or try to fight him? If she fought him now, on this issue, he might not let her make the phone call.

'They'll be off in a moment,' Walter said.

Hannah needed to push past her fear. She needed to be brave. She turned around and Walter slipped on the handcuffs. Hannah wondered if he did this because of Emma. Had she tried to run away during her first visit to the bathroom?

Walter stepped up next to the card reader. It beeped and the lock clicked back. The card reader was set up next to his waist, she noticed. *The card must be in his pocket. That way he can keep his hands free.*

Hannah stepped into the hallway of a half-finished cellar. To her left was a linen closet. He turned her around and she saw, at the end of the hallway and to the right of the stairs, a bathroom of white tile. The door had two padlocks on it.

Hannah walked slowly, wanting time to process everything she was seeing. The concrete floor was cold beneath her bare feet.

'May I take a bath?'

'Of course,' Walter said.

'How long do I have?'

'Take as long as you want.'

Good. Not only did she want some time to soak in the hot water – she hadn't bathed since her arrival – she wanted to poke around and see if she could find anything. If she did, through some miracle of God, find something useful, would Walter know it was missing? She'd have to give it some thought.

Heading past the cellar steps, Hannah glanced to her left and saw a washer and dryer. The clothes she had worn to the deli that day were folded neatly on top.

'I don't know what kind of shampoo or soap you like, but if you tell me, I'll be more than happy to get them for you,' Walter said. 'Whatever you need, whatever you want, just ask and I'll gladly –'

The doorbell rang.

72

Walter shoved her up against the wall and jammed the stump of his disfigured hand against her mouth. 'Say one word and I'll lock you in the dark with no food. Do you want that? *Do you?*'

Hannah shook her head.

The doorbell rang again. Looking past his horribly scarred face, she saw the basement steps leading up to an opened door; saw kitchen cabinets and the ceiling of another room. Less than a dozen steps. If only she wasn't handcuffed . . .

What if the police were at the door?

Bite his hand, get it away from your mouth and scream DO IT.

Walter yanked her away from the wall, spinning her around and wrapping his arm around her throat, squeezing as he dragged her back down the hallway. She couldn't breathe and she couldn't fight him. He was too strong.

He stepped up next to the card reader. It beeped and he pressed 2 followed by 4 and 6. She didn't see the last number.

The door opened. Walter shoved her inside. Hannah tripped and fell against the floor. A moment later, the room went dark. Hannah hugged her knees close to her chest and rocked back and forth, trying to stifle her tears.

Walter grabbed the .22 Bulldog from the kitchen cabinet. He kept the gun behind his back as he moved inside the living room and looked through the window.

Standing on his front porch was a heavyset woman bundled up in a bulky winter coat, hat and scarf. Walter didn't recognize her. She was holding a dish wrapped in tinfoil.

He checked the street and didn't see any cars. His was the only house on this street. He looked back to the woman.

Answer the door or let her leave?

She rang the doorbell again.

The woman smiled as the door opened. The smile faltered a little when she saw his face. It took her a moment to recover.

'Hello, I'm your new neighbour, Gloria Lister.'

Walter didn't answer. He stared at the snow melting against her boots, knowing she was shocked by his face, knowing she was judging him. He wanted to swing the door shut and hide.

When he didn't introduce himself, the woman broke the uncomfortable silence. 'The lights were on, and when I saw your car in the driveway, I thought you were home,' she said. 'I didn't want to leave this pie out here, so I rang the doorbell a few times. It's apple. I'm a baker –'

'I'm allergic to apples.' A lie. He wanted her to leave. Now.

'Oh . . . okay, well, I'll take it back then.' She waited a moment, and when he didn't answer, she said, 'I didn't mean to disturb you. Have a good night.'

Walter slammed the door shut. He put on the padlocks and shut off all the lights. He felt dizzy.

He should have said hello. He should have taken the pie. Tomorrow, when his new neighbour went to work, she would tell all her friends at the bakery about her strange neighbour, the man with the ugly, scarred face. *I was glad to go, really, he looked like a monster*, Gloria would say, and they would all have a good laugh. People would talk. Word would get around – it always did in small towns – and sooner or later the police would get wind of Gloria Lister's strange neighbour who didn't invite her inside his home, who left her standing outside in the cold with her pie. Maybe the police would pay him a visit, decide to come inside and take a look around. You never knew.

He should have at least said hello.

Using the wall for support, he stumbled into the living room and looked out the window again, watching his new neighbour carefully manoeuvring her way over the icy patches on the street. Walter wondered what it would be like to invite a woman inside his house. That would be a first.

73

Darby was reviewing the DVD Malcolm Fletcher had sent to Jonathan Hale when she heard a knock on the door.

'I've got some news on the unknown makeup sample,' Keith Woodbury said. He wore a winter coat and his face was red from the cold. 'Follow me to my office.'

Seated behind his desk, Woodbury removed a sheet of paper from a folder. He handed her the FTIR graph showing the breakdown of the chemical compounds and their individual concentrations.

'For the past week, I've been playing the chemical version of Scrabble with my MIT friend, rearranging the compounds,' Woodbury said. 'What threw us off were the levels of titanium dioxide. It's a mineral. You can find traces of it in everything from food to cosmetics. You don't need to take notes. This will all be in my report.

'One of the products found in the sweatshirt sample is called Derma. It's a cosmetic concealer used to hide severe facial scarring caused by acne, surgery or burns. The product comes in a variety of shades so the patient can match it to their individual skin pigmentation. A good number of plastic surgeons and dermatologists recommend it to their patients. It's not a prescription item any more – it used to be, until the late nineties – but you can't buy it at a store, at least not yet. The company is manufacturing a new line of cosmetics that, starting next year, will be carried nationwide in department stores like Macy's. At the moment, you can only order Derma through the company website.'

Woodbury handed her another graph. 'This is the unknown sample,' he said. 'It's LYCD, shorthand for live yeast cell derivative. It's a relatively new chemical – that's the reason why FTIR couldn't identify it. LYCD isn't listed in any of the cosmetics databases.'

'What is it?'

'To put it simply, LYCD provides oxygen to the skin, allowing it to breathe. It's a facial cream but not a traditional one. LYCD is supposed to help facilitate the healing. You apply it to either a fresh incision or a severe burn. It's also supposed to help relax scar tissue. Did Judith Chen have any facial scarring?'

'No.'

'What about Emma Hale?'

'Her face was flawless.'

'Did either woman get a chemical peel?'

'I don't know. Judith Chen didn't make enough money to afford something like that, but I wouldn't be surprised if Emma Hale did.'

'The sweatshirt sample contained *both* Derma and

LYCD. As I said, LYCD is designed for fresh incisions, burns or scars. You apply the LYCD cream to your face in the morning and then at night, before bed. A container lasts about thirty days. Derma is used to camouflage the scarring. It's for people who have sensitive or problematic skin. It doesn't contain any alcohol. Most over-the-counter cosmetic concealers contain some alcohol-based preservative which, for some people, can irritate the face.'

'Let me ask you this,' Darby said. 'Could someone with normal skin use it as a beauty treatment?'

'You mean younger, healthier looking skin in thirty days or your money back?'

'Exactly.'

'I suppose you could use it for that purpose, but there are better products on the market, ones you can readily purchase in high-end specialty stores. What do you ladies call it? Hope in a jar?'

'I wouldn't know.'

'Don't you watch *Oprah*?'

'No.'

'I thought all women watched *Oprah*. It's like a law or something.' Woodbury grinned as he leaned back in his chair and folded his hands behind his head. 'Okay, let's say you wanted to use LYCD because you believed it would help make your skin more youthful. You'd have to go to a dermatologist's office or a burn clinic. I doubt they'd sell it to you on that basis. Did you find any evidence of recent facial trauma on either victim?'

'Given the advanced state of decomposition, it was impossible to tell.'

'If Chen and Hale didn't have any facial scars, if they hadn't suffered some sort of facial burn, then there was no reason they would be carrying either product in, say, their purse or backpack when they were abducted. The other problem is Derma. The shade doesn't match Judith Chen or Emma Hale's skin colour. That leaves us with two possible scenarios. The first is that these products belong to another victim. The second is that their attacker uses both of these products. If Chen's killer was wearing Derma and LYCD, it's possible he might have accidentally transferred the products to her shoulder when he picked up her body.'

'How would I go about finding out who sells this LYCD cream?'

'That's where we're in luck,' Woodbury said. 'Only one company manufactures an LYCD product – Alcoa, based out of Los Angeles. The product is called Lycoprime. You can't buy it at a drugstore or purchase it legally online. You have to find a dermatologist or burn clinic that sells the product. Lycoprime is relatively new. Alcoa started manufacturing it less than two years ago.'

'So we're talking limited distribution.'

'I took the liberty of speaking to one of their sales reps this afternoon. Eli – that's the name of the sales rep I talked to, Eli Rothstein – he faxed me a list of doctors and clinics who sell the product in New England. I assumed you'd want to start there.'

'You assumed correctly.'

Woodbury handed her a sheet of paper.

The list of New England doctors was surprisingly small. Shriners Burn Center was a major customer, as were the burn centres in Boston's two major hospitals, Beth Israel and Mass General. A handful of local dermatologists also prescribed the product. There were fewer than a dozen dermatologists in Rhode Island and New Hampshire that used Lycoprime.

Boston hospitals and doctors' offices wouldn't release any patient files without a court order. Neil Joseph could get the court order, but it would take time. Darby checked her watch. It was coming up on 4 p.m. If Chadzynski asked for the court order, people would jump through hoops.

Darby stood. 'This is amazing work, Keith. Thank you.'

'I'm sorry it took so long.' Woodbury's expression turned serious. 'Hannah Givens . . . Do you think she's still alive?'

'I hope so.' Darby said a quick prayer as she reached for Woodbury's phone to dial Chadzynski's number.

74

For the rest of the day Walter worked on his client websites. His thoughts kept drifting back to Hannah, trapped alone in the dark.

Hannah had finally spoken to him and then the doorbell rang and he had panicked and now everything had turned to shit. Now Hannah thought he was a monster. He needed to figure out a way to fix this and start over.

Walter went downstairs into the kitchen and found the phone book. The closest florist was in the next town, Newburyport. He called the number. The man who answered the phone said it was too late for a delivery, but the store was open until five. He thanked the man and hung up.

Walter didn't like to leave his house. Thanks to the wonders of the internet, there was no need. Clothes, medicine, movies and books, even groceries, were delivered to his doorstep. The only time he left the house was to see Mary.

Mary knew how lonely he was. She told him to be brave. He had prayed for months for strength. Then one day Mary told him to drive to Harvard Square. She didn't tell him why. It was a surprise, she said.

Walter sat in his car and from behind the tinted

windows watched the college students. It was spring, sunny and warm. He wished he could be outside, mingling with the crowds. If he got out of the car, people would see his face in the unforgiving light. People would stop and stare. Some would laugh.

The piercing loneliness Walter had felt for as long as he could remember stirred inside him, awakened, and then disappeared, replaced by Mary's love. His Blessed Mother told him he was beautiful and made him look to his left.

A sexy woman with long blonde hair was crossing the street, heading in his direction. She wore heels, a short skirt and a tight-fitting shirt. Her face was flawless. Men were eyeing her, turning their heads to watch, and she knew it. She was the most beautiful woman Walter had ever seen.

This is my gift to you, Mary had said. The spirit of the Blessed Mother moving through him, Walter started the car and followed the woman he would come to know as Emma Hale. Mary said Emma was a special woman. In time, Emma would grow to love him. Mary told him what to do.

He had tried everything to make Emma love him, and when that failed, Mary told him to drive back to Boston and introduced him to Judith Chen.

Now Walter had Hannah and she refused to speak. He needed to make it right. He grabbed his car keys and headed out.

The heavyset man working behind the counter and a young woman doing floral arrangements stared when he opened the door, tracked him as he walked to the refrigeration unit and examined the roses. Walter could feel their gazes, as hot as fire, on his neck.

He decided to go with a colourful bouquet of mixed flowers. A chime as the door opened behind him. Flowers in hand, Walter turned and saw a boy no older than five standing in the aisle.

'Are you a good monster?' the boy asked.

The boy's face became a great, bright white blur, like a star staring down on him from space.

Walter put his hand inside his pocket and gripped the small statue. His Blessed Mother shrouded him with her love.

'I'm not scared of monsters,' the boy said. 'My daddy reads me a book every night about the monsters that live inside my closet. They're not scary. You just have to be nice to them.'

The boy's mother apologized and whisked him away. The man behind the counter smiled thinly as he wrapped the flowers. Walter thought of Hannah while he waited, remembered her skin, so warm and soft, pressed against his scarred body.

When he arrived home, Walter immediately went downstairs. First he turned on the electricity for Hannah's room. Then he placed the flowers inside the rolling food carrier, pushed them through and looked through the peephole. Hannah lay in her bed. Her back was to the door.

'I brought you a gift,' Walter said.

Hannah didn't answer, didn't move.

'Hannah, can you hear me?'

She didn't speak.

'I was hoping we could talk.'

No answer.

'Hannah, please . . . say something.'

No answer.

'If you want to eat, you need to talk to me.'

Walter waited. Minutes passed. She wouldn't speak.

Walter stormed upstairs and paced around the kitchen, hands shaking. When he'd calmed down, he went to the closet to pray to Mary for guidance.

His Blessed Mother's voice was faint; he could barely hear her. Mary's voice grew fainter, as though she was dying, and finally she stopped talking.

He needed to go to Sinclair. He needed to pray in front of Mary – the real, true Mary, the one who had saved him. He needed to get down on his knees, press his head against the chapel floor and with his hands clasped together and tucked against his stomach, pray until his Blessed Mother spoke and told him what to do.

75

'I don't believe Sam Dingle killed Hale and Chen,' Darby said in greeting.

Commissioner Chadzynski sipped coffee from a fancy china cup. She was wearing a sharp Chanel suit. The lights in her office were dimmed. A radio set up on a bookcase played soft jazz music.

Darby gripped the back of a chair and leaned forward as she spoke. 'Dingle's sister said he left New England after his release from Sinclair. Then he came back once to collect his portion of the sale of his parents' estate, and while he was here he abducted Jennifer Sanders and brought her to that room next to the chapel, where he raped and eventually strangled her to death.

'Now, twenty-something years later, Fletcher wants us to believe Dingle's come back to his original hunting ground, only instead of strangling and raping women, Dingle is now abducting female college students, keeping them for weeks before shooting them in the back of the head and dumping their bodies with a statue of the Virgin Mary in their pockets. I'm not buying it.'

'Tell me why,' Chadzynski said.

'Margaret Anderson and Paula Kelly were

strangled and dumped along the road like trash. Jennifer Sanders was strangled, raped and tortured and left to die. Emma Hale was kept alive for six *months*. Judith Chen was kept alive for several weeks. We also know that at some point the killer went back into Emma Hale's home to retrieve her necklace. In addition to being a considerable risk – he could have been easily caught – it shows a remarkable degree of empathy, even love.'

'From my understanding, serial killers evolve. Isn't it possible Dingle –'

'Strangling someone is an intimate, sexual act,' Darby said. 'Hale and Chen weren't strangled. They were shot in the back of the head. The first method is intimate, the second distant. Shooting the victims in the back of the head suggests the killer felt shame at having to kill them. A psychopath doesn't evolve into a killer who develops empathy for his victims. Dingle may very well have murdered Anderson, Kelly, and Sanders, but I don't believe he killed Hale and Chen. I believe we're dealing with a distinctly different killer.'

'I just got off the phone with the Saugus detective in charge of the Anderson and Kelly cases,' Chadzynski said. 'He's retired now, but he remembers management brought in a profiler to help build the cases against Dingle – Malcolm Fletcher. He supposedly visited Dingle at Sinclair.'

'Bryson believed that Fletcher was trying to throw us off the scent.'

'Tim also lied to us. I heard a copy of his confession. There may be some truth to it.'

'Fletcher called me again.' Darby told the commissioner about the phone call. 'I think Dingle is a smoke screen.'

'Do you think Fletcher will come after you?' Chadzynski asked.

'He's had plenty of opportunity.'

'Do you think he'll harm you?'

'No.'

'Did he threaten you in any way?'

'No,' Darby said.

'I'll keep the traps on your phones, but at some point, we'll have to pull your surveillance.'

'I think you should put them on Jonathan Hale.'

'Every expert I talked to says Malcolm Fletcher works alone.'

'Your FBI contact said Fletcher murdered the killers he hunted,' Darby said. 'I wouldn't be surprised if Fletcher already found Dingle.'

Chadzynski stared at the blinking lights on her phone for a long moment.

'If you want to find Fletcher,' Darby said, 'you need to put people on Jonathan Hale.'

There was a knock on the door. Chadzynski's secretary came in and placed the court order on the edge of the desk.

The commissioner waited until the door was shut before she spoke. 'The *Herald* reporter has decided to run the story about the remains being found at Sinclair.'

'Did you remind him it might cause Hannah's abductor to panic and kill her?'

'I did. The story will be on the front page of tomorrow's paper.'

Darby picked up the copies of the court order. 'If there isn't anything else, I'd like to get to work on this.'

'Where are you going to start?'

'The Shriners Burn Center,' Darby said. 'Coop and Woodbury are going to hit the dermatologists' offices before they close for the day.'

'I'll see if I can locate Jonathan Hale,' Chadzynski said, reaching for her phone.

Malcolm Fletcher had traded his hotel room for a safe house in Wellesley, a suburb twenty minutes outside of Boston. Ali Karim had made all the arrangements.

The place was fully furnished. Fletcher sat at a small antique desk reading a computer printout of Walter Smith's patient file from Shriners. He had managed to hack his way past the hospital's firewall and into the patient database. Once Walter's file was printed, Fletcher deleted it from the hospital's computer system.

Walter's last corrective surgery took place in 1987, when he was eighteen. The address listed in the file was an apartment building in Cambridge, Massachusetts.

Fletcher had checked the address earlier in the day. Walter had moved out in 1992. The forwarding address was a studio apartment in the Back Bay. The landlord had faxed Karim a copy of the rental agreement. Walter didn't leave a forwarding address, but his social security number was listed on the application.

The quickest way to find Walter's current address would be through tax records. That meant hacking into the IRS's computer network.

At the moment, a UNIX program was running, quietly searching for a back door past the IRS firewall. To slip in and out without leaving a digital footprint or, worse, triggering an alarm, required a tremendous amount of patience and skill. One wrong move and federal agents would be standing on his doorstep.

Malcolm Fletcher picked up the Virgin Mary statue he had removed from inside the cardboard box at the Sinclair chapel and moved it between his fingers as he reached for the phone.

'Have you changed your mind about meeting Walter, Mr Hale?'

'No.'

'Make sure your phone is charged,' Fletcher said, watching the computer screen. 'I'll have Walter's address tonight, tomorrow at the latest.'

76

The hospital director for the Shriners Burn Center, Dr Tobias, sat behind his cluttered desk and watched Darby over his bifocals. He hadn't read the court order. He had handed it off to the hospital's legal counsel, who took his sweet goddamn time reviewing it. *Jesus Christ, hurry up*. Finally, the lawyer gave Tobias the go-ahead.

Tobias, round and bowlegged, escorted her through gleaming white hallways. Behind the closed doors Darby heard the steady beep of machinery and murmured conversations. Some doors had small windows built into them. Most of the patients lying in the beds wore pressure-garments over their faces and arms. It was impossible to tell if they were male or female. Many of the burn patients were children.

Some patients wandered through the hallways. Darby looked away from their mangled faces and limbs.

The hospital pharmacy had a computer system which allowed searches based on a patient's name or the name of a particular medication. Darby searched for 'Samuel Dingle.' No one named Dingle was listed in the pharmacy database.

The list of male patients using Lycoprime totalled 146.

The man who had Hannah Givens would be young, white and probably in his late twenties to early thirties. Physically, he would have to look and appear young. A college student would be reluctant to climb inside the car of an older man, but they might be more inclined to do so if they believed the person appeared to be a college student too, possibly one who said he was attending the same college. Darby believed the killer was local. He wouldn't want to live too far from Sinclair. She would pay close attention to those who had criminal records.

For that she would have to rely on Neil Joseph, who was sitting at his desk waiting for her to call. Neil could easily find a criminal record provided it wasn't a juvenile offence. Those records were sealed and couldn't be accessed without a court order. Darby hoped that wouldn't be the case.

'Can you sort the Lycoprime list by the patient's age?' she asked Tobias. 'I'd like to review the younger patients first.'

'I can't print out a single, definitive list starting with age – you'd have to examine each file to find that information. We could, however, print out the list of all male patients using Lycoprime.'

'What about patients using Lycoprime in conjunction with Derma?'

'The problem is you won't get an accurate sampling. We stopped selling Derma, oh, I'd probably say at least four years ago. It's no longer a prescription item.'

'If a patient is using Derma, would it be listed in their file?'

'In the older files, yes,' Tobias said. 'We recommend Derma to all of our patients. It's an excellent product. We give out trial samples to our patients to see what colour best matches their skin tone, and then they can order the particular shade over the company website.'

Meaning there's no way to track recent Derma orders from the pharmacy records, Darby thought.

'I know you're anxious to get to this,' Tobias said, 'so in the interest of saving time, I'd recommend Craig – that would be the gentleman to your left, Craig Henderson, our pharmacist – I can have Craig send the Lycoprime patient files to my office printer. They'll start alphabetically by the patient's last name. You can use my office computer to access the actual patient files. You can't access the patient database through the pharmacy's computer. The patient files are on a separate system.'

Tobias' laser printer was dreadfully slow. Each pharmacy file contained the patient's name, date of birth, address and health insurance information. The patient's entire prescription history was listed.

It took an hour to print Lycoprime patients A through H. The ages ranged from five to fifty.

Dr Tobias helped her sort the patients into two

piles – one for ages up to fifteen, the other pile for ages sixteen and older.

Most of the patient records were of young male children or teenagers who had been burned in a house fire caused by a parent falling asleep with a lit cigarette. Some had been accidentally scalded by boiling water left on a stove. One boy, a ten-year-old, had decided for some ungodly reason to light firecrackers near a plastic gas jug in his parents' garage. The fire was so severe he couldn't breathe without the aid of a ventilator. He later died.

And then there were the other files, the ones dealing with parents who had dumped their screaming infant or meddlesome toddler into a tub of scalding water; parents who, in a moment of anger or drunken rage, shoved their son into a fireplace or wood stove. Jesus, here was a file on a father who, wanting to teach his eleven-year-old a lesson about the dangers of fire, lit a match and held it to up to his son's hand. The flame caught on the boy's polyester pyjamas. They melted against his skin, covering him with permanent burn scars.

One patient seemed promising: a twenty-nine-year-old white male named Frank Hayden. In 1996, at age seventeen, Hayden was jumping a faulty car battery when it exploded. The battery acid burned his face. His patient file listed the dozens of reconstruction surgeries Hayden had endured over the past decade.

Hayden also had a criminal record. In 2003 he had been arrested for attempted rape. He served two years in Walpole. After his release, he went back to live with his mother in Dorchester.

Coop called as Darby was examining another patient file. Coop was at a Cambridge dermatologist's office who was the third largest supplier of Lycoprime.

'Nothing on Sam Dingle, but I found six male patients who use Lycoprime,' he said. 'The oldest is twenty-eight. Ten years ago, this guy's father was in massive debt and took out insurance policies on his family. The asshole lit the house on fire, tried to make it look like they were victims of arson. The whole house went up in flames, and when the fire department arrived, they managed to save this kid. His parents and four other siblings burned to death.' Sighing, he added, 'I think I need to find another profession.'

'What about a criminal record?'

'Drug offences,' Coop said. 'Kid's both a user and a dealer. The other five patients are clean. No criminal records.'

'Who's next on your list?'

'I was thinking of tackling Mass General's Burn Center.'

Massachusetts General Hospital was the second largest supplier of Lycoprime in New England.

'Head over,' Darby said. 'Depending on what time I finish up here, I'll either join you at Mass

General or we'll head over together to Beth Israel.'

An hour later her phone rang again.

'I think you can scratch Frank Hayden off your list,' Neil Joseph said. 'I just got off the phone with the guy's mother. Hayden's been living in Montana for the past year. He's an auto mechanic.'

'Hold on.' Darby shuffled through her papers, found Hayden's pharmacy records. 'He refilled his Lycoprime prescription two months ago.'

'Yeah, I know. The mother says she goes to the hospital, picks it up and mails it out to him. He can't get his hands on it down there.'

'What about Derma?'

'She didn't mention it. I have people looking into Hayden just to be sure. Do you have any more names?'

'Not yet.'

The hum of the printer filled the room. It was after eight and the windows were dark.

Darby picked up the fresh stack of patient files and started reading. *Please God, give me something.*

77

Walter parked his car in the back lot of the Sleepy Time Motel on Route One. He never drove into the hospital campus. Security trucks patrolled the area day and night. Walking through the woods behind the motel was long and hard, especially in the snow, but he always made the journey because he never wanted to do anything to put his Blessed Mother at risk.

The access tunnel was on the south side of the Sinclair campus, an ancient water duct built sometime after the turn of the twentieth century. Walter reached it after a long hike up a steep, snow-covered hill.

When the hospital officially closed in 1983, the security staff in charge of monitoring the property installed a metal gate with a lock across the tunnel's opening. Walter came back with a pair of bolt-cutters and a lock of his own – the same make, model and size. Security never found out about the replacement lock because they never came out this way.

Walter shook the snow off his boots. He turned on his flashlight and unlocked the gate.

During his stay at Sinclair, Walter had become very well acquainted with the hospital. Danvers City Hall had a copy of the original architectural blueprints on file. For a cost of only twenty dollars, they printed out the several colour pages detailing each floor.

The problem was the amount of decay and ruin. Many of the basement hallways had collapsed. It had taken Walter several weeks to chart the best route to the chapel.

As he walked down the tunnel, his thoughts drifted back in time to his stay at Sinclair, the nights he had spent alone inside his room rocking back and forth on his bed, sweating, the medicine burning inside his veins. He would look to his drawings of the Blessed Mother holding his hand and sometimes the pain became manageable. Sometimes Nurse Jenny took him to the chapel.

It was during his first visit to the chapel that Mary revealed herself to him.

Mary's dead son, the saviour, the Lord Jesus Christ, was sprawled across her lap. Mary's sorrowful expression pierced Walter's heart. He felt the weight of Mary's unbearable loss.

Kneeling, Walter closed his eyes and prayed to his mother.

I know I wasn't a good boy. You were good to me and I know you did the best you could. I forgive you. I love you, Momma.

A new voice spoke to him: *Your mother is safe. She's here with me in heaven.*

Walter opened his eyes. Mary, the Blessed Mother of God, was looking directly at him.

I know how much you love your mother, Walter. She wants me to look after you. Come here.

The Blessed Mother stood. Jesus tumbled from her lap, dropping to the floor, and Mary stood there in her flowing blue and white robes, arms wide open, ready to accept him, to bring him closer to the secret world held inside the red-painted heart glowing in the centre of her chest.

There's no reason to be afraid. I love you so much. Come here and let me hold you.

Walter obeyed the Blessed Mother. He left the pew and went to Mary and she held him in her arms.

You're a brave boy. I'm very proud of you.

Surrounded by Mary's love, Walter cried.

You'll never be alone, Mary said, kissing the top of his head. *I'll always be with you. I love you so much.*

Walter came back to the chapel and visited Mary often. When they were alone, she would reveal herself to him. The crippling loneliness, the pain, fear, isolation and loss – it vanished every time Mary held him in her arms.

In time, Mary shared all of her secrets. They had many wonderful conversations. When the hospital closed, Walter found a way back to his Blessed Mother.

Walter walked through the abandoned hallways of paint-chipped walls. He didn't like the dark but he wasn't scared. Mary was close; he couldn't hear her voice yet but he could feel her love stirring inside his heart.

He put the flashlight in his back pocket and climbed the rusted ladder bolted to the wall. When he reached the top, he ran through the cold hallways. He was almost in tears when he slipped through the final door and into the last hallway.

Mary's love swelling inside him, Walter picked up the wooden ladder and walked carefully over the debris to a hole in the floor. He slid the ladder through, and when he set foot on the gravelly bottom, he pushed open the door and moved inside the chapel. He grabbed his flashlight.

His Blessed Mother stood at the end of the aisle. Her expression of eternal sorrow disappeared, turning into a smile when she saw him.

Walter, you came.

Sweet relief flooded through him. His legs buckled. He grabbed the edge of a pew to keep from falling.

I'm so glad you're here. I missed you.

'I missed you.' His eyes were burning, wet.

Come talk to me about Hannah.

Walter stumbled down the aisle. He couldn't hold his Blessed Mother's love any longer. It was too strong, too powerful. He dropped to his knees, weeping. He closed his eyes.

Hail Mary, full of Grace, I am with thee ...

Mary screamed. Walter blinked, and through his tears saw a bright light aimed at him. Walter raised his hands.

'Down on your stomach and put your hands behind your head.'

The voice came from the man holding a flashlight and moving up the aisle fast – a short, wide man wearing a knit hat. He was holding a gun.

Walter looked over the man's shoulder, at Mary standing tall, her face twisted in anger.

Don't let him take you away, Walter. The doctors will pump you full of those awful chemicals and you won't be able to hear me and they'll take you away and you won't be able to see me.

The man with the gun spoke into a walkie-talkie pinned to his jacket. 'Brian, it's Paul, I need backup.' Then to Walter: 'Lie down on your stomach and put your hands behind your head.'

Walter felt his mother's love bleeding away. The man with the gun was going to take him to a hospital room and the doctors would pump him full of the medicine and he would never see Mary again and without his Blessed Mother he would be lost in limbo for eternity – he would *die* without her.

Walter turned off the flashlight and tossed it into the air as he rolled into the pew.

A gunshot, the muzzle flash jumping like lightning inside the chapel, and Walter was on his feet.

'Brian, get in here, he's running!'

Walter knew every inch of the chapel by heart. His hand was on the back of the pew and he saw the beam of the man's flashlight moving through the chapel. Another man was shouting, another flashlight beam crisscrossing through the darkness. Walter ran up the centre aisle, heading for the back of the chapel, and heard another gunshot, the muzzle flash lighting up the door to the room holding the ladder, and he ran inside and threw the door shut.

A gunshot splintered the door. Walter climbed the ladder, legs shaking, rubbery. He reached the top and scrambled to his feet as another gunshot blew apart the wood. Walter gripped the ladder and pulled it up. Below him, the door flew open, banging against the wall. Walter tossed the ladder into the hallway. The man with the knit hat moved into the room, saw the hole in the ceiling and fired. The man started to climb the mountain of debris and Walter grabbed a brick and threw it down the hole, the man screamed and Walter threw another brick, then another. A gun fired again but Walter was gone, running through the dark.

78

'Walter Smith isn't here,' Darby said.

Dr Tobias looked over his bifocals. 'What's that?'

'Walter Smith's entire pharmaceutical history is listed in the pharmacy database but his name doesn't appear in your patient database.'

The hospital director groaned as he got out of his chair. Darby handed him the printed sheets listing Walter Smith's medications.

At the beginning of the year a physician named Dr Christopher Zackary had renewed Walter Smith's prescription for Lycoprime. Walter Smith had been using the product for the past year and a half. He had used the Derma camouflage concealer steadily since the early eighties. The medical entries for Derma stopped in 1997, the time when it no longer required a prescription.

Tobias scanned the pages then set them aside and typed on the keyboard 'Smith, Walter'. The search came up empty.

'That's not possible,' Tobias said. 'If he's in the pharmacy database, then his patient file should be in our system.'

'I'd like to see his paper file.'

'Dr Zackary has most likely gone home for the

day. Let me see if I can find someone to unlock his office.'

Darby leaned back in her chair, stretching as she stared up at the ceiling tiles. It was after 10 p.m.

Why was Walter Smith's patient file missing? Was it some clerical oversight or computer glitch? A hospital of this size would have a system in place to perform weekly if not daily backups of its computer systems.

Her cell phone rang.

'You were right,' Bill Jordan said. 'He came back to the chapel.'

Darby stood, almost knocking over the chair. 'You've got him in custody?'

'Not yet. Look, I don't have much time, so let me give you a quick rundown. Quinn – he's one of the guys I have stationed inside Sinclair – Quinn said someone entered the chapel about half an hour ago. The guy he saw, his face was all messed up, like it was burned. The guy decided to run. Shots were fired and the guy made it into a room located in the back, behind the pews. There's a hole in the ceiling.'

Darby knew the room. She had seen it after she crawled through the vent.

'Quinn and his partner, Brian Pierra, they swear they saw a ladder,' Jordan said. 'Next thing they know, the ladder is pulled up. Quinn fired a shot and got a brick thrown at his head.'

'Can you cover all the exits?'

'We're covering all the exits we know about.

Danvers PD is here and they're pissed. One of Reed's security guys heard the gunshots, panicked and called in the locals. I've got to go.'

'I'm on my way.'

'No, I want you to stay right where you are. This place is a goddamn zoo, and I've got a tactical nightmare on my hands. I'll call you as soon as we have this guy in custody, I promise. Good work, Darby. You were right.'

And then Jordan was gone.

Darby wanted to run for her car, tear up Route One North and then what? Jordan's men had SWAT experience. If she drove up to Danvers, what could she do? She couldn't do anything.

She paced the cheap carpeting, surrounded by papers and steamed heat. She wanted to be there when they dragged this person out of the hospital. She wanted to see the face of the man who had shot Emma Hale and Judith Chen – and what about Hannah Givens? Was the college student still alive or was her body at the bottom of a river?

Darby was staring out the office window when Dr Tobias walked into the office. He handed her three bulky folders. Tobias checked his watch and excused himself to get coffee.

Darby leaned back on a desk and read the patient file.

Walter Smith had been admitted to Shriners during the early morning hours of 5 August 1980 with third-degree burns covering ninety per cent of his body.

His mother, who had died in the blaze, had doused his bed in gasoline and set him on fire because he was 'the son of the devil'. Walter Smith was eleven years old.

Walter had undergone psychiatric evaluation and been diagnosed as a paranoid schizophrenic. An orphan, with no access to medical insurance, Walter was refused acceptance at the McClean Hospital, famous for its treatment of mental illnesses. The Sinclair Mental Health Facility, a well-regarded psychiatric institution run by the state, offered the boy free treatment.

Darby looked back to the pharmacy records. Walter Smith had moved well over a dozen times during the past twenty years. His most recent address was in Rowley – two towns away from Danvers, where Sinclair was located.

She called Neil Joseph and gave him a quick rundown of Walter Smith.

'The name isn't appearing in any of our local cases,' Neil said. 'Do you have any other names for me?'

'No.' Darby told him what was going on with Sinclair.

Next she called Coop and relayed the same information. He was still searching through patient records.

'What do you want me to do?' he asked.

'You might as well keep looking.'

Darby hung up and stared at the close-up photographs taken of the boy's burned face. Was Walter

Smith the man who had killed Emma Hale and Judith Chen? On paper, he looked like the perfect suspect. Was the man trapped inside Sinclair?

She checked the clock. 11:35 p.m. Forty minutes had passed since her conversation with Bill Jordan. Was Walter Smith in custody? Or were Jordan's men still hunting for him? It was maddening to wonder.

A search warrant would be needed to get inside Walter Smith's Rowley home. That would take time.

Was Hannah Givens inside the Rowley house or was she being kept somewhere else? Did Walter Smith live with someone? A roommate or a girlfriend? If he did live with someone, this person might be able to provide additional information about him.

Darby made a copy of Smith's medical files. She stuffed the pages inside her backpack and ran through the corridors, heading for the front door.

Walter looked around the motel parking lot. The police hadn't followed him here – they hadn't followed him through the access tunnel but they were all over the hospital. He had locked the gate behind him and was off and running through the woods when he heard sirens. A moment later, blinking blue and white lights pierced the darkness.

The police hadn't found him but they had found Mary and she was gone, his Blessed Mother was *gone*.

Sitting behind the wheel, his clothes soaked with sweat, Walter rocked back and forth, back and forth, telling himself he wasn't going to cry.

He couldn't hold it any longer. He let it out, sobbing like a little boy, his whole body shaking.

Can you hear me, Walter?

Mary's voice was loud and clear. Walter stopped rocking, listened.

'I can hear you.'

I want you to listen to me very carefully. I'm going to help you. Are you listening?

Walter wiped his face. 'Yes.'

Mary explained what he needed to do.

'I can't,' Walter said.

There's no reason to be afraid. I'll be with you at every step. You're my special boy, and I love you so much. You can do this. Now drive home and get Hannah.

His Blessed Mother's love strong inside his heart, Walter started the car.

79

Hannah sat on her bed, a statue of the Virgin Mary clutched between her hands.

Mom was the believer, the one who had pushed the family into Mass every Sunday and sacrificing during the season of Lent. Dad didn't have much use for church. He confided in her once, when it was just the two of them: 'You want good things to happen in your life, you're not going to find it sitting on a pew. You've got to use that thing sitting between your ears.'

Still, Dad went along for the ride, paying the usual lip service – bow and stand, kneel, stand and bow, give thanks for all the wonderful things in your life, now go off and be good and don't you *dare* question the Good Lord's motivations. Hannah always felt caught in the middle – wanting to believe in some higher purpose or calling but not really buying into the whole invisible man in the sky thing watching everything you did, good and bad, and marking it in the appropriate columns.

The last time she prayed was the summer before college. Her cousin Cindy had a baby boy born with a heart defect. Little Billy lived in an incubator for six months and had undergone every type of procedure imaginable, including the installation of a pacemaker. A company made one specially to fit inside Billy's tiny chest. Donations were raised, churches prayed for Billy's recovery, and in the end God said no, sorry, Billy's got to go. All part of God's divine plan, the priest said.

Bullshit.

What part could an infant play in God's mysterious divine plan? Why let Billy be born in the first place? Why would a loving God make an infant go through all that pain and suffering? And why would a caring God turn a deaf ear to the thousands of starving Jews in the concentration camps? To the Jews who were marched into the ovens and shot in the head as they stood over a mass grave? How did *that* fit into the Almighty's divine plan?

Hannah didn't know the answers, but she couldn't deny that holding the statue brought some measure of comfort. The Blessed Mother of Jesus Christ kept the tears at bay and provided a sliver of hope.

Maybe there was a purpose to suffering, but if she was going to survive, Hannah knew she was going to have to use that thing between her ears.

The locks to her room clicked back and the door opened.

Hannah jumped off the bed and saw Walter holding the clothes she had worn the night she was kidnapped. The jeans and sweatshirt were neatly folded in his hands. A plastic shopping bag holding her boots was wrapped around his wrist.

Walter tossed the bag and clothes onto the floor. 'Get dressed.'

Something was wrong. The makeup Walter used to hide his scars was smeared in several places. She saw thick, rubbery patches of crimson and brown coloured skin. His eyes were wet. Had he been crying?

'Get dressed,' Walter said again. His hair was dishevelled, sticking up at odd angles as though he had just climbed out of bed. He was wearing his coat.

'Where are we going?'

'I'm taking you home.'

Hannah was about to ask the question, stopped. *Don't say anything. Just do what he says.*

She had to ask. She needed to know. 'Why are you letting me go?'

'Mary said it's the right thing to do.'

Hannah picked up her clothes. They smelled of fabric softener. Walter had cleaned them.

Walter didn't leave the room. Hannah took the clothes behind the curtain hiding the toilet and changed quickly.

When she came out, Walter was holding a pair of handcuffs.

This time he didn't ask her to turn around. He yanked her hands behind her back and handcuffed her. She didn't fight him. When he wrapped a black blindfold over her eyes, she didn't fight him. Walter grabbed her by the arm and quickly dragged her down the hallway as though the house was on fire.

Walter helped her up the stairs. Hannah took the steps one at a time, heart pumping with fear, the handcuffs biting into her wrist. Why was he rushing? Something was wrong. Hannah couldn't see, couldn't make out any shapes. She was trapped in the dark.

The stairs ended. Hannah stepped into the kitchen. Walter held onto her arm and led her down what felt like a narrow hallway. She kept bumping into walls.

Walter told her to stop. She did. He grabbed her by the shoulders and then moved her to the left and told her to take three steps forward. She did.

Walter was breathing hard. 'I'm going to take off your handcuffs and then help you put on your jacket,' he said. 'After your jacket is on, I'm going to cuff you again.'

Coat on and zippered, the handcuffs back in place, Walter put his hands on her shoulders and moved her to the right. Something hard bumped up against the tips of her boots.

He slipped something inside her jacket pocket.

There was a long moment of silence. She heard him sniffle and clear his throat several times.

Was he crying?

'You're so beautiful, Hannah.'

He *was* crying.

'You're the most beautiful woman I've ever met,' Walter said. 'I love you so much.'

In some strange, bizarre way, she wanted to thank him for his kindness – to tell him he was doing the right thing. She wanted to say she wouldn't tell anyone about him or what had happened, cross her heart and hope to die, swear on a stack of bibles, whatever he wanted. But she didn't want to risk breaking whatever spell he was under by saying something that might cause him to change his mind.

'Stay still,' Walter said. 'Don't move.'

80

With Emma and Judith, Walter fired one shot in the back of their head and quickly pushed them over the bathtub before their legs buckled. He never stayed inside the bathroom – seeing their bodies thrashing inside the tub, limbs kicking, hearing the gurgling sounds they made as their brain died . . . it was too upsetting. He went to the closet to pray to Mary, waiting for them to bleed out, Mary reassuring him that they hadn't felt anything. What he was witnessing was their bodies dying. The body didn't matter. It was just a vessel for the soul, and the soul was what mattered.

The difficult part done and out of the way, he came back to the bathroom and turned on the shower to rinse away the blood. Then he made a sign of the cross on their foreheads with their blood, baptizing them as he prayed, and transferred the bodies to the plastic tarp lying on the floor. The pocket holding the statue was then sewn shut – Mary needed to stay with them until their souls were finally released three days later – and before he dumped them into the water to be baptized all over again, he prayed again.

When he arrived home, he cleaned the shower and floors with bleach, wiping everything up with the towels, and then he'd go to the closet again to pray.

Tonight would be different.

Hannah Givens stood facing the shower wall. No plastic tarp under her feet. No towels or bottles of bleach to clean out the tub. The statue was in her pocket but there was no need to sew it shut. Mary didn't want him to deliver Hannah into the water. After he shot Hannah, he was to place the gun against his temple or the roof of his mouth and pull the trigger. Those were Mary's instructions.

Walter brought the handgun up and pointed it at the back of Hannah's head. His hand was shaking. He couldn't stop crying. Mary spoke to him.

Don't be afraid. I'm here with you.

I'm scared.

It's painless. You won't feel a thing, I promise.

Help me.

Remember when I took you into my arms for the first time and pulled you close to my heart?

Yes.

You were surrounded by my love. I took the pain away. Do you remember?

He did.

Do you feel my love for you, Walter?

Yes.

You'll forever be surrounded by my love. Now do it.

He couldn't pull the trigger.

Your mother is here with me. Emma and Judith are excited to see you. They love you, Walter. Deliver Hannah to me and then come and join us.

The doorbell rang.

Hannah's head turned to the sound. Lightning quick, Walter wrapped his arm around her throat, the good hand coming up, pressing the muzzle of the gun against her head.

'Say one word and I'll kill you.'

The doorbell rang again.

Who was at the door? Had his new neighbour Gloria Lister come back with another one of her pies?

You're my special boy, Walter. I love you.

The bathroom door was open. The lights were on, as were the kitchen lights.

Come home to me. It's time.

The doorbell rang again, followed by a knock on the door. Hannah was crying, shivering against him.

'Shut up.'

I love you, Walter.

It was hard to hear Mary over Hannah's bawling.

'Shut up.'

Pull the trigger.

Hannah didn't stop. He placed his good hand over her mouth.

There's no reason to be afraid, Walter. Can you feel my love? Can you feel –

Hannah bit his thumb.

Walter screamed and Hannah pushed him backwards. He hit the bathroom vanity, the back of his head shattering the mirror. Hannah twisted her head side-to-side like a rabid dog, tearing skin from his hand, and Walter kept screaming as the gun dropped into the sink.

81

The front door had a thick pane of glass covered with lace curtains. Someone was home. A light was on inside the kitchen, and Darby could see a round table and a wool jacket lying over the back of a chair.

Darby was about to lean on the doorbell again when she heard a man screaming.

She reached one hand inside her coat, the other gripping the doorknob, turning and finding it locked. She kicked the window with the heel of her boot. The glass splintered and she kicked it again and it shattered – a woman was screaming for help. *Oh Jesus, Hannah Givens is in there and she's screaming.*

Darby crawled through the pane, jagged pieces of glass cutting her coat and cheek, and stepped into the foyer. SIG gripped in her hand, she moved down the hall and stared down the target sight, ready to shoot, the screaming growing louder as she spun into the kitchen and checked her left side, her blind spot – clear. To her right, a well-lit hallway of checked green and white linoleum stretching down to an opened door with stairs leading into the dark garage. At the end of the hallway and to the left, another opened door, the light inside blazing. Shadows moved across the hallway wall and Darby moved fast. *Get ready to shoot. Keep shooting until he falls.* Mouth dry and adrenaline pumping, she crouched low and turned the corner.

A man with a mangled face smeared with makeup had one arm wrapped around Hannah Givens' throat, squeezing, pressing her close to him. Darby couldn't fire. Hannah's head was too close to the man's face – the man was Walter Smith, there was no question; the man Darby had seen in the hospital photographs, the face with slabs of scarred meat stitched back together and smeared with the same shade of makeup found on Judith Chen's sweatshirt.

Hannah's nose was broken. Blood poured down her face and a blindfold of black cloth covered her eyes. Walter Smith stood behind her, his head partially shielded behind Hannah's, his bloody hand coming out of the sink holding a revolver. *He's going to kill her, you can't risk a shot. Do something.*

An idea came and she had to try it, roll the dice and pray.

'The Virgin Mary sent me here to help you,' Darby said. 'She's in danger.'

A single, lidless eye stared at her.

'Mary called for me, Walter. She told me to go to Sinclair and help her.'

'You talked to Mary?' Walter didn't lower the gun, kept it aimed at her, but the caged, desperate glare in his good eye disappeared, replaced by confusion, maybe even hope. *Use it.*

'Yes,' Darby said. 'I spoke to her. She told me what

happened. She told me to come here and help you.'

'Why do you have a gun?'

'I had to protect Mary.'

'Are you an angel?'

'Yes.' Darby didn't want to lower the gun. If she lowered the gun, she'd expose herself. Walter might panic and start shooting. Keep talking. 'The Blessed Mother was in great danger, but I saved her. She told me to come here to help you. Your hand is bleeding. Are you hurt?'

'They have her.' Walter was crying. 'They're going to hurt my Blessed Mother.'

'They can't hurt her. I took care of them.'

'What did you do?'

'They're gone. They can't hurt you. Mary's safe but she needs your help. We have to move our Blessed Mother to a safe location.'

'Mary said I had to do this.' Walter moved the gun to Hannah's head.

'Mary wants you to give Hannah to me. Do not disobey her.'

'Mary told me what to do. She told me but I can't . . . I can't do the other thing. I can't kill myself, I'm too scared.'

'You don't have to be afraid any more. I'm here to help you. Mary sent me here to help you, but first, you need to help her.'

'I love her.'

'She loves you too, Walter. That's why she sent me here.'

‘I love her so much.’

‘I know you do.’ *Get him to put down the gun.*

‘I can’t live without her,’ Walter said.

‘Mary has given us both so much and now it’s our turn to help her.’

‘Where are we going to take her?’

‘I don’t know. Mary said she would tell me when I brought you back to the chapel. Let Hannah go and I’ll take you to Mary.’

Walter eased Hannah into a sitting position on the tub’s side and then collapsed to his knees, sobbing, hands in his hair. The gun slid from his fingers and dropped to the floor covered with shards of broken glass.

‘I love her,’ Walter said.

‘I know.’ Darby kicked the gun away, grabbed Walter by the hair and smashed his face against the floor.

Walter cried out in surprise, his muscles tensing, ready to fight. She pressed a knee into the base of his spine, grabbed the back of his collared shirt and dug the muzzle of her gun against his neck.

‘Move and I’ll kill you.’ Darby could taste it on the back of her throat, that burning satisfaction of killing the monster that lived beneath his human skin.

A shot to the head was too kind. She wanted him to suffer.

Then do it. Make him suffer.

Walter’s muscles went limp. He collapsed back against the floor.

He didn't fight her when she yanked his hands behind his back and cuffed them. If he had tried to put up a fight, she could have shot him. She could have done anything. Darby felt a curious disappointment seeping through her limbs as she reholstered the SIG.

She rifled through his pockets for the handcuff key.

'You're safe, Hannah, he can't hurt you.' The college student was lying sideways inside the tub, shaking and crying. 'I'll have those cuffs off in just a moment.'

Walter lay motionless on his stomach, eyes blank as he stared off into space mumbling what sounded like a prayer.

Darby found the handcuff key. She reached inside her jean pocket for the phone. She felt it along with the small panic button Tim Bryson had given her.

Behind her, the sound of a heavy footstep crunching over glass and then the feeling of two cold metal prongs pressed against her neck.

'I'd prefer not to use the Taser,' Malcolm Fletcher said, 'so please sit still.'

82

The SIG was tucked inside her shoulder holster. There was no way Darby could reach it.

'Special Agent Fletcher,' Darby said, gripping the panic button between her fingers. 'I thought you'd left town.'

'I missed you so much I decided to come back.' Fletcher stood behind her. 'Please put your hands behind your back.'

Darby pressed the button, felt the seal break. 'May I stand?'

'If you wish,' Fletcher said. 'But please, no sudden movements.'

Darby slowly removed her hand from her pocket. Leaning forward, she placed both hands on Walter's lower back, tucked the panic button in his back jean pocket and stood. The Taser's metal prongs never left her neck.

'Nice job deleting the patient file from the Shriners computer system,' Darby said, placing her hands behind her back. 'Did Jonathan Hale pay you extra for that?'

Malcolm Fletcher wrapped a pair of Flexicuffs around her wrists and motioned to the hallway. 'After you,' he said.

'I'd like to stay here with Hannah.'

'Miss Givens will be joining you in the living room momentarily.' He gripped Darby's forearm gently and whispered against her ear. 'Don't be scared. I won't harm you.'

Darby wasn't afraid. For some reason, she believed him.

Malcolm Fletcher, murderer of Tim Bryson and two federal agents, escorted her into a living room with shabby grey carpeting. A framed oil painting of the Virgin Mary hung on the wall above the fireplace.

'Tell me about Sam Dingle,' Darby said.

Fletcher brought her to an armoire holding a TV, turned her around and asked her to sit on the floor.

'Did Dingle kill Jennifer Sanders?' Darby said.

'You'll have to ask him yourself when you find him.'

'You promised me the truth.'

'Sit on the floor,' Fletcher said. 'I'm not going to ask you again.'

'Can't keep Mr Hale waiting, can we?' Darby sat.

'Sammy raped and strangled Jennifer Sanders,' Fletcher said, looping another pair of Flexicuffs inside the ones fastened around her wrist. 'He also strangled the two women from Saugus.'

'Is that Jennifer's voice on the audio tape?'

'Yes.'

'Where did you get it?'

Fletcher tied a second pair of cuffs around the

armoire's legs. 'I found the cassette and many more inside Sammy's home.'

'Did you kill him?'

'No.'

'Then what did you do to him? Where is he?'

Malcolm Fletcher left the room without answering.

Darby sat on the floor with her arms behind her, wrists cuffed and fastened to the armoire's leg. Fletcher was talking to Hannah. He was speaking too softly. Darby couldn't hear what he was saying.

On the fireplace mantel was a small clock. Darby watched the time, hoping Bill Jordan or someone from his team had noticed she had set off the panic button. Driving from Danvers to Rowley would take an hour. Jordan wouldn't wait; he would call the locals. Had he already placed the call? How long would it take Rowley PD to arrive? She would have to try and stall Fletcher.

Ten minutes later Fletcher came back into the room carrying Hannah Givens in his arms. She was still blindfolded and handcuffed. He gently placed her on the couch, then grabbed an old afghan from a chair and draped it over her. He turned to Darby.

'You won't be here long. I'll call nine-one-one from the road.'

'Why don't you just kill Walter now?' Darby said. 'That's why you're here, isn't it?'

'Why didn't you kill him? Isn't that what you wanted?'

'You don't have the right –'

'I watched you in the bathroom. You *wanted* Walter to suffer, Darby. Were you hoping to turn him into a paraplegic? Or did you want to kill him because, deep down, you know he's beyond redemption?'

Fletcher knelt on one knee, his strange black eyes hovering in front of her face. Behind them was infinite darkness.

'That appetite, you'll soon discover, is hard to suppress.'

'Are you speaking from personal experience?'

'We'll have to discuss the matter another time.' Fletcher's eyes roamed over her face and body. 'Maybe one day we can talk about it. Privately.'

'Let's talk about it now.'

Fletcher stood. 'When you think back to that moment inside the bathroom, you'll wish you'd pulled the trigger.'

'Where are you taking Walter?'

'I'm going to give him what he truly wants,' Fletcher said, tossing the handcuff keys on the table. 'I'm going to deliver him to his mother.'

'I'll find you.'

'Better men have tried, mate. Goodbye, Darby.'

83

Walter was trapped in pitch-black darkness. There was no floor beneath his feet, and he didn't feel anything as he waved his hands around in the air – it was like he was floating in outer space, without stars, without sound.

He had been to this place, whatever this place was, once years ago, after the fire. At first he thought he was trapped in hell and then a woman's voice, soft and reassuring, had called out from somewhere in the darkness and told him not to be scared. He wouldn't be here for long. Great and wonderful miracles were about to happen.

Walter didn't know the voice belonged to Mary. It was only when the Virgin Mother of Jesus revealed herself inside the chapel had he realized that the voice belonged to Mary, his Blessed Mother.

Walter came to his senses as he was dragged out of the bathroom. His feet bounced down the steps and then he was lifted into the trunk of a car. His body was stiff with terror.

A devil with black eyes and pale skin looked down on him before the trunk shut, plunging him into darkness.

Mary was calling for him. Walter shut his eyes and,

curling himself into a ball, recited his special prayer, waiting for Mary to save him.

Darby talked to Hannah Givens, encouraging her to get off the couch and grab the handcuff keys from the coffee table, but the young woman refused to move. Either she was in shock or Fletcher had said something to scare her.

Eventually, Darby heard sirens and saw flashing lights. Rowley police had arrived. She called to them as they ran up the front steps.

The patrolman who cut off her cuffs said a 911 call had been placed by an unidentified male who stated that Hannah Givens and a member of the Boston Crime Lab were being held inside the home of Walter Smith. The caller gave the address and hung up.

Hannah Givens sat on the couch, sobbing into the chest of a female officer. Darby tried speaking to Hannah, wanting to know what Fletcher had said inside the bathroom, but the young woman refused to speak.

Darby's first call was to Bill Jordan. When he didn't answer his phone, she left a message, telling him it was an emergency and to call her back.

Neil Joseph answered his cell phone. Darby explained what she needed and asked him to drive to Danvers to find Jordan.

Hannah's father called as the ambulance pulled away. He spoke in a strangled voice.

'Detective Joseph just left. I told him about your partner, but he wanted me to call and tell you.'

'Tell me what?'

'Your partner called me about an hour ago and said you found Hannah. He said that she was okay and told me not to worry. I asked to speak to Hannah and he apologized and said he had to get off the phone and help you. He hung up and forgot to give me your number. Detective Joseph gave it to me. Can you put Hannah on the phone, Miss McCormick? I just need to hear my baby's voice, just for a moment, please. My wife and I have been sitting here worried sick.'

'Your daughter's on her way to the hospital.' Darby had to keep reassuring Hannah's father that his daughter was alive.

'This man said one other thing before he hung up,' Mr Givens said. 'He told me not to worry, that justice was going to be done. That's what he said. What's your partner's name? Tracey and I would like to thank him.'

In the basement, mounted inside a wall, was a rolling food carrier and next to it, a door locked by a magnetic keycard unit.

Darby helped Rowley police search the rooms. When a keycard wasn't found, the fire department was called to dismantle the door.

She gave her statement to two Rowley detectives. Phone calls were made. Forensic investigators from the state lab were called but wouldn't arrive for a few hours. In the interest of saving time, Rowley PD agreed to let lab technicians from Boston help process the crime scene. Everyone agreed to share.

Word of what happened to Hannah Givens had reached the media, and by 2 a.m., the small, quiet street was filled with news vans and reporters hoping to get an exclusive, behind-the-scenes interview. Darby watched them from the bedroom window, wondering if Walter Smith was still alive.

84

Jonathan Hale stood in the cold room of an old mill building just outside of Vernon, Connecticut. Malcolm Fletcher had selected the location for its privacy. There were no surrounding buildings, no street lights. The nearest house was ten miles away.

Dr Karim had seen to the travel arrangements. One of his men had driven Hale from his hotel to this location. As far as the authorities were concerned, Hale was sleeping inside his New York hotel room.

'Nobody knows you're here,' Fletcher said. 'Walk straight down this hall and turn to your left.'

The abandoned building had no lights but Hale could see well enough in the moonlight. He took off his overcoat and handed it to the former profiler.

'Aren't you coming?'

'This is something you have to do alone,' Fletcher said.

Jonathan Hale wore sneakers, jeans and an old Harvard sweatshirt similar to the one Emma had given him for his birthday. Fletcher had instructed him to wear old but comfortable clothes. The former profiler had also given him latex gloves to wear underneath his leather ones. The clothes, gloves and jacket, everything he was wearing, would be collected in a trash bag and given to Malcolm Fletcher to be thrown into an incinerator.

The hallway ended. Hale turned left and stepped inside a cold room lit up by patches of moonlight.

Walter Smith, the man who killed Emma, was bound to a chair set up on a large plastic tarp, the corners weighed down by rocks. A blindfold covered his eyes. He mumbled underneath the gag secured across his mouth.

The man's face was horribly scarred. He looked like a monster.

He is a monster, Daddy. He abducted me, he abused me and shot me in the back of the head and dumped me into the Charles River. He killed Judith Chen and he was going to kill that other woman, Hannah Givens. He's a monster.

A hammer, revolver and hunting knife were lying on the tarp. The gun, Malcolm Fletcher said, was the same one used to kill Emma and the second college student, Judith Chen.

Hale picked up the revolver. It felt incredibly light in his hands.

For weeks now, he had rehearsed this moment in his mind, playing out different scenarios to see which would be the most rewarding. Shooting the thing in the back of head was too merciful. Hale wanted him to see the gun, wanted to see the look of terror and hopelessness in the thing's eyes and drink it all in until the pain faded. Then he would say Emma's name and shoot the thing in the face.

Or maybe he would prolong it a bit.

Hale walked across the tarp. The thing didn't move its head at the sound but it kept mumbling underneath the gag. Hale pulled off the blindfold.

There was something wrong with the creature's expression. Its eyes were wide, unblinking, staring off in the distance. Hale turned around and saw the corner of the room. There was nothing there.

The thing didn't move, didn't look up, but kept talking underneath the gag. Hale untied it.

'Hail Mary full of grace I am with thee blessed is me and blessed are you among mothers and blessed is the fruit of your womb, Walter –'

It was praying – a bastardized version of Hail Mary.

'– Holy Mary Mother of God and Walter pray for the sinners now at the hour of their death amen. Hail Mary full of grace I am with thee –'

Hale pressed the gun against the monster's head. It didn't flinch; it didn't scream or cry. It had no reaction. Every muscle in its body was rigid, frozen, but it kept praying.

'Look at me,' Hale said.

The creature didn't look.

With his free hand, Hale reached underneath his sweatshirt and clutched Emma's locket in his fist. The hate he had been nursing over the past year burned inside his chest along with his love for his daughter. His love for Emma would not go away. His loss would not go away. His hatred for this man –

this monster, this thing . . . It had to suffer. It *deserved* to suffer.

Kill it.

Hale's heart was beating so fast he felt dizzy.

That thing killed me, Daddy. It put a bullet in my head and dumped my body in the river. You saw the picture. You saw what he did to me.

Hale stared at the gun. His gloves were covered in blood.

Startled, he dropped the gun and instead of picking it up stumbled back through the hallway.

Malcolm Fletcher stood with his back to him, staring out of one of the broken windows.

'What's wrong with him?' Hale said.

'He's catatonic.'

'He wouldn't look at me but he kept praying.'

'Walter is waiting for his mother, Mary, to come to him. Incidentally, Walter told me Mary chose Emma and the other women for him.'

'Why?'

'The Blessed Mother promised him love.'

Hale looked back down the hallway. 'When will he come out of it?'

'Impossible to say,' Fletcher said. 'Walter could remain in his current catatonic state unless he's given the proper medication. Even then, there is no guarantee.'

'Why didn't you tell me this earlier?'

'Would it have made a difference?'

Hale looked at his gloves. There wasn't any blood.

'I can't do it.'

'Do you mean you can't kill him yourself or you don't want him killed?'

'I can't kill him myself.'

'Would you like some time to reconsider?' Fletcher asked. 'We have all night.'

'No. I've made up my mind.'

'What would you like me to do?'

'You told me what you did to Sam Dingle. You said you had the same thing in mind for Walter.'

'Yes.'

'Have you made the necessary preparations?'

'I have.'

'Then take care of it,' Hale said, tossing his gloves to the floor.

At 4 a.m., Darby sat on the unmade bed where Hannah Givens, Judith Chen and Emma Hale had slept and checked her watch. Bill Jordan still hadn't returned her phone call. She tried calling Neil Joseph but there was no answer. Was he still looking for Jordan in the maze of crumbled rooms where no cell-phone signal could penetrate?

An investigator had found a spiral notebook wedged underneath the seat cushion of the leather chair. Darby read Emma Hale's diary as crime scene investigators processed the room, tagging potential evidence.

The spare bedroom on the top floor held stacks of barbells and a lifting bench. Walter Smith had taped several photographs of Hannah Givens to a full-length mirror.

In the corner was a desk with a computer and a multifunction printer that operated as a fax machine and scanner. Darby made a copy of the diary. She placed the folded sheets inside her jacket pocket and grabbed her car keys.

85

Jonathan Hale woke to bright sunlight. The breeze coming through the hotel window was pleasantly cool. He wondered if spring was coming early this year.

Inhaling deeply, he remembered the dream where Emma stood on the front steps of the ranch-style house where he grew up. The front door was open. He heard his dead wife's voice as he walked up the porch steps. There were other voices whispering in the darkness, voices he didn't recognize. Emma was standing next to him. When he saw her face, he realized he didn't need to be scared. She held his hand and the fear disappeared. He remembered feeling content, at peace.

That feeling was still with him as he rolled over and checked the clock. 7:15 a.m. Despite having slept for only a few hours, he felt remarkably rested. Hale called his driver. When he checked out of the hotel, the limo was waiting. Hale drank coffee and on the way home read newspapers and listened to the news.

The limo's privacy screen was up. Hale took out the phone Malcolm Fletcher had given him. There was only one number to call now. Hale didn't speak, just listened.

Tony carried the bags into the house. Today was Sunday. Hale checked his watch. If he hurried, he could still make the noon Mass. He drove alone to the church.

Showered and shaved and dressed in a suit, Jonathan Hale sat in a pew surrounded by his neighbours and their children, some grown, some still growing. Father Avery gave a sermon on the importance of helping the less fortunate. God had blessed everyone here with good fortune, he said. Hale listened, his attention fixed on the cross hanging on the wall behind the altar.

After Mass, friends and neighbours stopped to shake his hand. Some pulled him aside and asked how he was doing. Do you need anything, Jonathan? We're here for you.

Father Avery also wanted a private word with him.

'It's good to have you back, Jonathan. Your daughter was a very special young lady. I miss her terribly – the whole community does. The church's fundraising committee was thinking of doing something special to honour Emma's memory. Maybe you'd like to talk to them?'

What Father Avery wanted was access to his list of friends and business associates who would come out for a good cause. By using Emma's name, the church would most likely double if not triple last year's charity contributions. Tragedy always made people reach deep into their wallets.

'I'll be more than glad to help out,' Hale said.

'Thank you so much for thinking of me, Father.'

Hale pulled onto his street and saw a young woman with pale skin and shockingly dark red hair leaning against a black Mustang parked a few feet from the main gate. Hale pulled the Bentley up next to her and rolled down his window.

Up close and in the sunlight, Darby McCormick's green eyes were striking. She didn't seem that much older than Emma.

'May I talk to you for a moment, Mr Hale?'

'Of course,' Hale said. 'I'll drive you up to the house.'

'Let's talk out here. I'm enjoying the weather.'

Hale stepped out of the car but left it running.

Dr McCormick's face was friendly when she said, 'I want to talk to you about Malcolm Fletcher.'

'The former FBI profiler.'

'You know who he is.' It wasn't a question.

'It's been all over the news. He killed Detective Bryson and now they're saying he abducted Walter Smith.' Hale placed his hands in his jacket pockets. 'Did that man kill my daughter?'

'I think you already know the answer to that question.'

'I'm sorry?'

The young woman turned her attention to the house, to the limo and vintage cars parked in the driveway. The maintenance staff, taking advantage of the warm weather, were cleaning and waxing the vehicles.

Hale remembered the day of Emma's high-school graduation. He had given her a car, a convertible BMW, as a gift. A big red bow was affixed to the car roof. He could remember her breathless gasp when she saw it, the sound of her laugh. He remembered lots of things now.

'Someone I know decided to take the law into his hands,' Darby McCormick said. 'This person believed, deep in his heart, he was doing the right thing. At first, this person felt good about having his revenge, but over time, the guilt of what he did ate him alive.

'Mr Hale, what you've done or whatever it is you're doing, I know it feels right. Now. But this feeling of peace or justice or whatever you're calling it, it will turn on you. Time won't wash it away, and you can't pay someone to remove it for you. It will be with you forever. It's a heavy burden to carry, that guilt. You're not equipped to live with it. It will eat you alive.'

The dream from this morning came back to him and he saw Emma's face clearly in his mind's eye. He felt her hand gripped in his.

The young woman's next words were startling.

'If you tell me where Walter Smith is, I'll blame it on Fletcher,' Darby said. 'I'll say he called me again and told me where to find Walter's body. This conversation stays strictly between you and me. I give you my word.'

'With all due respect, Miss McCormick, you've overstepped your bounds.'

'I'm trying to save you from making a terrible mistake, sir. This is a one-time offer. When I leave, it's off the table.'

'I can't help you.'

'So you don't know where Walter Smith is?'

'No.'

'For your sake, Mr Hale, I hope you're telling the truth. The FBI will be paying you a visit. I hope you have a good lawyer.'

'Enjoy the rest of your day.'

'Before you go, I wanted to give you this.' She handed him some folded papers. 'It's Emma's diary. We found it at Walter's home. I made you a copy.'

Hale took the folded pages and held them gently in his hands.

'Is there anything you'd like to tell me, Mr Hale?'

'Please let me know when you find Walter Smith. I'd like to speak to him. Thank you for this.' Hale held up the pages as he opened the car door.

Hale went to his office and shut the door.

After he finished reading, he sat in the chair, staring out the back windows. He sat for a long time, thinking.

He stood slowly, using the chair for support, lit a fire and filled a glass with bourbon. He drank the first glass empty and poured himself another.

He was on his third glass when he took out the cell phone and dialled the number he had called inside the limo.

The line rang once. The phone on the other end picked up.

'I'm sorry,' Walter Smith said. His voice was raw from screaming.

The thing's cell phone could only receive calls. It couldn't call out for help.

'I loved Emma. I loved her so much.' It was sobbing again. 'Do you know what that feels like? To love someone so much you can't breathe? Like your heart is about to burst?'

I do, Hale thought.

'I want to see my mother.'

Looking at the back lawn, at the patches of wilted grass peeking out from the melting snow, Hale saw Emma chasing after a ball – she was two, her legs wobbly, uncertain. She wore a beautiful pink dress. The expression on her face was pure joy.

I wish I could reach down and pick you up, Emma. I wish I could hold you in my arms and hold you and kiss you and tell you how much I love you just one more time, just one more time, one last, final time. I wish . . .

'Please, Mr Hale, please let me see my mother.'

'I suggest you pray to God. He's the only one who can help you now.'

Jonathan Hale disconnected the call. He removed the cell phone battery, threw it in the trash, and then tossed the phone into the fire. He opened the balcony doors to get rid of the unpleasant odour.

86

Bill Jordan called as Darby was pulling onto the Mass Pike. Darby explained what she needed.

'You're in luck,' he said. 'The panic button is transmitting. The GPS signal is about a quarter of a mile north of number eight Old Post Road in Sherborn.'

The town, located south of Boston, was less than a half-hour's drive from Weston.

'That's all I can tell you right now,' Jordan said. 'When I get closer I can lock onto the signal and we'll walk right up to him – or whatever's left of him.'

'Where are you?'

'I'm already on the road. I should be there in Sherborn in forty minutes.'

'I'll meet you there.' Darby pulled over to enter the address into her car's GPS unit.

'I don't think we have to rush,' Jordan said. 'The signal hasn't moved in fifteen minutes.'

Like Weston, the small town of Sherborn was another high-end suburb of cold McMansions and renovated antique farmhouses separated by miles of trees and dense woods to give owners the illusion of privacy.

Old Post Road was long and steep, bordered by

rolling fields of melting snow. Darby drove ten miles and passed two homes.

The mailbox for number 8 was still standing, but the home at the end of the driveway had been demolished to make way for a new foundation. An excavator, backhoe and two dump trucks sat in a wide open field across from a pair of horse barns, the wood grey and rotting.

Standing under the warm afternoon sun, listening to the tick of her car engine, Darby shielded her eyes and stared into the distance at the woods. Jordan said the GPS signal was a quarter of a mile away from here, but which route had Fletcher taken?

Walter Smith was too heavy to carry. Did Fletcher drive him somewhere into these woods? A car couldn't drive out here, not with all this snow, but a truck might work.

Darby walked into the open field. Tyre tracks left by a heavy piece of machinery were in the snow. The tracks led back to an excavator. The ignition had been hotwired.

Weapon in hand, she followed the tracks into the woods, wading through the wet, knee-high snow. The overhead tree branches were bare, and she could feel the sun on her face and hair.

A quarter of a mile in, she found a large open space of recently overturned dirt. Darby looked around the woods and didn't see any additional tyre tracks. They ended here. She called Bill Jordan.

'I think I found the spot where Fletcher buried the

body,' Darby said. She told Jordan about the excavator tracks and poked the ground with her boot. The dirt was loose. 'We're going to need shovels.'

'See you in twenty.'

Sticking out of the ground was an inch of white PVC pipe. In the slant of sunlight, Darby saw that the white tubing extended deep into the earth. Kneeling, she took out her flashlight.

A ruined eye stared back at her.

'Help me,' Walter Smith croaked. 'I can barely breathe.'

Darby backed away, stumbled, and fell against the cold ground.

'I'm sorry!' Walter's raw, terrified voice echoed up the pipe from his crudely made coffin. *'I don't want to die in here. PLEASE!'*

Darby tried to get to her feet and stumbled again. She knelt on all fours, heart hammering as she gasped for air.

Malcolm Fletcher had cut a hole into the coffin and fitted it with a PVC pipe that ran up to the surface so Walter wouldn't suffocate. He could breathe until he died of starvation or insanity.

'I told Mr Hale I was sorry! I'm sorry! I'm sorry!'

Did Hale know Walter was buried here? Did he plan to come out to this spot and drop food down the pipe to prolong Walter's torture?

You wanted *Walter to suffer*, Malcolm Fletcher had said. *When you think back to that moment inside the bathroom, you'll wish you'd pulled the trigger.*

In her mind's eye Darby saw herself pressing the handgun's muzzle against Walter's head. The cold, alien voice that spoke to her inside the bathroom was speaking to her now: *Block the pipe and let him suffocate to death.*

'Please,' Walter screamed. 'Please don't leave me here, I'm sorry.'

Darby recalled the photograph of Emma Hale's body lying on the bank of the Charles, buried under snow, discovered by a dog. Judith Chen's body lay on the autopsy table, the woman's face picked apart by fish. Walter Smith killed both women and he was going to kill Hannah Givens before turning the gun on himself.

'Please get me out of here,' Walter cried. 'I'm so scared. I don't want to die here alone without Mary.'

Block the pipe and cut off his air. Let him suffer.

Walter Smith deserved to suffer. She *wanted* him to suffer.

Do it. Nobody will know.

The wind blew through the woods, shaking the branches. Darby scrambled back across the ground and looked down the pipe.

'Hang on,' she said, reaching for her cell phone. 'Help is on the way.'

Acknowledgments

This book could not have been written without the insight of criminologists Susan Flaherty and Kevin Kershark; Randy Moshos, from the Boston Medical Examiner's Office; Meigan Dingle, a burn specialist; and Keith Woodbury, who helped guide me through the minefield of chemistry. These people patiently answered all of my technical questions. All mistakes are mine.

One of the perks of being a writer is having the opportunity to discuss the craft with some of the best. With that in mind, I'd like to thank the following writers: John Connolly, Gregg Hurwitz, Laura 'Mrs Mooney' Lippman, Mike Connelly, Joe Finder, Tess Gerritsen, George Pelecanos, and Jodi Picoult.

Thanks to Pam Bernstein and the wonderful Maggie Griffin.

If you liked the book, you can thank my editor, Mari Evans, for all of her hard work; and my agent, Darley Anderson, and his wonderful staff – Emma White, Madeleine Buston, Camilla Bolton and Zoe King.

What you have in your hands is a work of fiction. That means I made most of it up.

If you enjoyed
The Secret Friend,
read on for a taster from the first
Darby McCormick novel,

The Missing

Out now in paperback

1

The Man from the Woods (1984)

Chapter 1

Darby McCormick grabbed Melanie by the arm and pulled her into the woods with no trails. Nobody came out this way. The real attraction was behind them, across Route 86, the biking and hiking trails along Salmon Brook Pond.

'Why are you taking me out here?' Melanie asked.

'I told you,' Darby said. 'It's a surprise.'

'Don't worry,' Stacey Stephens said. 'We'll have you back at the convent in no time.'

Twenty minutes later, Darby dropped her backpack on the spot where she and Stacey often came to hang out and smoke – a sloping wall of dirt littered with empty beer cans and cigarette butts.

Not wanting to ruin her new pair of Calvin Klein jeans, Darby tested the ground to make sure it was dry before sitting down. Stacey, of course, just plunked her butt right down in the dirt. There was something inherently grubby about Stacey, with her heavy mascara, hand-me-down jeans and T-shirts always worn a size too tight – nothing was ever quite able to mask the sense of desperation that hovered around her like Pig-Pen's dirt cloud.

Darby had known Melanie since, well, since

forever, really, the two of them having grown up on the same street. And while Darby could recall all the events and stories she had shared with Mel, she couldn't for the life of her remember how she had met Stacey, or how the three of them had become such good friends. It was as if Stacey had suddenly appeared one day. She was with them all the time during study hall, at football games and parties. Stacey was fun. She told dirty jokes and knew the popular kids and had gone as far as third base, whereas Mel was a lot like the Hummel figurines Darby's mother collected – precious, fragile things that needed to be stored in a safe place.

Darby unzipped her backpack and handed out the beers.

'What are you doing?' Mel asked.

'Introducing you to Mr Budweiser,' Darby said.

Mel fumbled with the charms on her bracelet. She always did that when she was nervous or scared.

'Come on, Mel, take it. He won't bite.'

'No, I mean, why are you doing this?'

'To celebrate your birthday, dumbass,' Stacey said, cracking open her beer.

'And for getting your license,' Darby said. 'Now we have someone to take us to the mall.'

'Won't your dad notice these cans are missing?' Mel asked Stacey.

'He has six cases in the downstairs fridge, he won't miss six lousy beers.' Stacey lit a cigarette and tossed the pack to Darby. 'But if he and my mom came home and caught us drinking, I wouldn't be able to sit or see straight for a week.'

Darby held up her can. 'Happy Birthday, Mel – and congratulations.'

Stacey drained half her beer. Darby took a long sip. Melanie sniffed her beer first. She always smelled anything new before tasting it.

'It tastes like soggy toast,' Mel said.

'Keep drinking, it will taste better – and you'll feel better too.'

Stacey pointed to what looked like a Mercedes snaking its way up Route 86. 'I'm going to be driving one of those someday,' she said.

'I can totally see you as a chauffeur,' Darby said.

Stacey shot Darby the finger. 'No, shitbird, some-body's going to be driving *me* around in one of those 'cause I'm going to marry a rich guy.'

'I hate to be the one to break this to you,' Darby said, 'but there are no rich guys in Belham.'

'That's why I'm going to New York City. And the man I marry is not only going to be drop-dead gorgeous, he's going to treat me right. I'm talking dinners at nice restaurants, nice clothes, any kind of car I want – he's even going to have his own plane to fly us to our fabulous beach house in the Caribbean. What about you, Mel? What kind of guy are you going to marry? Or is your heart still set on being a nun?'

'I'm not going to become a nun,' Mel said and, as if to prove her point, took a long sip.

'Does that mean you finally gave up the goods to Michael Anka?'

Darby nearly choked on her beer. 'You've been making out with *Booger Boy*?'

'He stopped that back in the third grade,' Mel said. 'He doesn't, you know, pick it anymore.'

'Lucky for you,' Darby said, and Stacey howled with laughter.

'Come on,' Mel said. 'He's nice.'

'Of course he's nice,' Stacey said. 'Every guy acts nice in the beginning. Once he gets what he wants from you, he'll treat you like yesterday's garbage.'

'That's not true,' Darby said, thinking about her father – Big Red, they used to call him, just like the gum. When her father was alive, he always held open the door for her mother. On Friday nights, her parents would come home from dinner and Big Red would put on one of his Frank Sinatra records and sometimes dance with her mother, check to cheek, as he sang about how those were the days.

'Trust me, Mel, it's all an act,' Stacey said. 'That's why you've got to stop being so mousy. You keep acting that way, they'll take advantage of you every time, trust me.'

Then Stacey started in on another one of her lectures about boys and all the sneaky things they did to trick you into giving them what they wanted.

Darby rolled her eyes, leaned back against a tree and looked off in the distance at the big, glowing neon cross overlooking Route 1.

As Darby drank her beer, she watched the traffic zipping across both lanes of Route 1 and thought about the people inside those cars, interesting people with interesting lives off to do interesting things in interesting places. How did you become interesting? Was it something you were born with, like your hair color or your height? Or did God decide for you? Maybe God chose who was interesting and who wasn't, and you just had to learn to live with whatever you were handed.

But the more Darby drank, the stronger and clearer that inner voice of hers grew, the one that told her, with some sense of authority, that she, Darby Alexandra McCormick, was destined for bigger things – maybe not the life of a movie star but something definitely better and a whole lot bigger than her mother's Palmolive world of cleaning, cooking and cutting coupons. Sheila McCormick's biggest thrill was the greedy hunt for bargains on the clearance racks.

'You hear that?' Stacey whispered.

Snap-snap-snap – the sound of dry twigs and branches being crunched by footsteps.

'It's probably a raccoon or something,' Darby whispered.

'Not the branches,' Stacey said. 'The *crying.*'

Darby put her beer down and poked her head up over the slope. The sun had gone down a while ago; she saw nothing but the faint outline of tree trunks. The dry, snapping sound grew louder. Was someone really out there?

The snapping and cracking sounds stopped, and then they all heard the woman's voice, faint but clear:

'Please let me go, I swear to God I won't tell anyone what you did.'

Chapter 2

'Take my purse,' the woman in the woods said. 'There's three hundred dollars in there. I can get you more money, if that's what you want.'

Darby grabbed Stacey by the arm and pulled her back behind the slope. Melanie huddled up against them.

'This is probably just a mugging, but he might have a knife, maybe even a gun,' Darby whispered. 'She'll hand over her purse, and then he'll run away and it will be over. So let's just keep quiet.'

Both Mel and Stacey nodded.

'You don't have to do this,' the woman said.

As scary as it was, Darby knew she had to look over the slope again. When the police came with their questions, she wanted to be able to recall everything she saw – every word, every sound.

Heart beating faster, she poked her head back over the slope and looked around the dark woods. Blades of grass and dead leaves brushed against the tip of her nose.

The woman started crying. 'Please. Please don't.'

The mugger whispered something Darby couldn't hear. *They're so close,* she thought.

Stacey had decided to take a look, too. She moved closer to Darby.

'What's going on?' Stacey whispered.

'I don't know,' Darby said.

A car was heading up Route 86. The headlights formed a pair of eerie white circles that were now sliding and bouncing across the tree trunks and the sloping ground full of rocks, leaves, and downed tree limbs and branches. Darby heard music – Van Halen's 'Jump,' David Lee Roth's voice growing louder along with the worrisome voice in her head telling her to look away, look away *now*. God knows she wanted to, but some other part of her brain had taken control, and Darby didn't look away as the headlights washed over her, David Lee Roth's booming voice singing to go ahead and jump, and she saw a woman dressed in jeans and a gray T-shirt kneeling by a tree, her face a deep, dark red, eyes wide and fingers desperately clawing at the rope tied around her throat.

Stacey jumped to her feet and knocked Darby backward against the dirt. A rock smacked the side of her head hard enough that she saw stars. Darby heard Stacey pushing her way past branches, and when she rolled onto her side, she saw Mel running away.

Next came the dry crack of branches and twigs snapping – the mugger was coming toward them. Darby scrambled to her feet and ran.

*

Darby caught up with Stacey and Mel at the corner of East Dunstable. The closest pay phones were the ones around the corner from Buzzy's, the town's popular convenience store, pizzeria and sub shop. They ran the rest of the way without talking.

It seemed to take forever to get there. Sweating and out of breath, Darby picked up the phone to dial 911 when Stacey slammed down the receiver.

'We can't call,' Stacey said.

'Have you lost your goddamn mind?' Darby shot back. Behind her fear was a severe and growing anger directed at Stacey. It shouldn't have come as a shock that Stacey had pushed her aside and run off. Stacey always put herself first – like last month, when the three of them made plans to go to the movies only to have Stacey cancel at the last minute because Christina Patrick called and invited her to some party. Stacey was *always* doing stuff like that.

'We were drinking, Darby.'

'So we won't tell them.'

'They'll smell the beer on our breath – and you can forget about chewing mint gum or brushing your teeth or gargling with mouthwash, because none of that works.'

'I'll risk it,' Darby said, and tried to yank Stacey's hand away from the receiver.

Stacey wouldn't let go. 'The woman's dead, Darby.'

'You don't know that.'

'I saw the same thing you did –'

'No, you didn't, Stacey, you couldn't have seen the same thing I did because you ran away. You pushed me aside, remember?'

'It was an accident. I swear I didn't mean –'

'Right. As usual, Stacey, the only person you care about is yourself.' Darby ripped Stacey's hand away and dialed 911.

'All you're going to get is punished, Darby. Maybe you won't get to go down the Cape with Mel, but your father won't –' Stacey stopped herself. She was crying now. 'You don't know what goes in my house. None of you do.'

The operator came on the line: 'Nine-one-one, what is the nature of your emergency?'

Darby gave the operator her name and described what had happened. Stacey ran behind one of the Dumpsters. Mel stared down at the hill where they used to go sledding as kids, her fingers touching each of the charms on her bracelet.

An hour later, Darby was walking back through the woods with a detective.

His name was Paul Riggers. She had met him at her father's funeral. Riggers had big white teeth and reminded Darby of Larry, the slimy next-door neighbor from *Three's Company*.

'There's nothing here,' Riggers said. 'You kids probably scared him off.'

He stopped walking and shined his flashlight on a blue L.L. Bean backpack. It was unzipped all the way and she could see the three Budweiser cans lying inside the bottom.

'I take it that's yours.'

Darby nodded as her stomach flipped and squeezed and flipped again, as if it were trying to tear itself away to find a place to hide.

Her wallet had been removed from her backpack. It was now lying on the ground, along with her library card. The money was gone, and her learner's permit, printed with her name and address, was missing.

Chapter 3

Darby's mother was waiting for her at the police station. After Darby finished giving her statement to the police, Sheila had a private talk with Detective Riggers for about half an hour and then drove Darby home.

Her mother didn't talk. Darby didn't get the sense Sheila was mad, though. When her mother got this quiet, generally she was just deep in thought. Or maybe she was just tired, having to pull double shifts at the hospital since Big Red died last year.

'Detective Riggers told me what happened,' Sheila said, her voice dry and raspy. 'Calling nine-one-one – that was the right thing to do.'

'I'm sorry they had to call you at work,' Darby said. 'And I'm sorry for the drinking.'

Sheila put her hand on Darby's leg and gave it a squeeze – her mother's signal to let Darby know everything was okay between them.

'Can I give you a piece of advice about Stacey?'

'Sure,' Darby said. She had an idea what her mother was going to say.

'People like Stacey don't make good friends. And if you hang out with them long enough, at some point they'll end up dragging you down with them.'

Her mother was right. Stacey wasn't a friend; she was dead weight. Darby had learned the lesson the hard way, but the lesson was learned. As far as Stacey was concerned, good riddance.

'Mom, the woman I saw . . . Do you think she got up and ran away?'

'That's what Detective Riggers thinks.'

Please God, please let him be right, Darby said to herself.

'I'm glad you're okay.' Sheila squeezed Darby's leg again, only this time it felt harder, the way you grip something to keep from falling.

Two days later, on a Monday afternoon, Darby came home from school and found a black sedan with tinted windows parked in her driveway.

The door opened and out stepped a tall man wearing a black suit and a stylish red tie. Darby spotted the slight bulge of a sidearm under his suit jacket.

'You must be Darby. My name is Evan Manning. I'm a special agent with the Federal Bureau of Investigation.' He showed his badge. He was tanned and handsome, like a TV cop. 'Detective Riggers told me about what you and your friends saw in the woods.'

Darby could barely get the words out. 'You found the woman?'

'No, not yet. We still don't know who she is.

That's part of the reason why I'm here. I'm hoping you can help me identify her. Would you mind taking a look at some pictures?'

She took the folder and, with a sense of falling, opened it to the first page.

The word MISSING ran across the top sheet. Darby looked at a Xeroxed picture of a woman wearing a nice string of pearls over a pink cardigan sweater. Her name was Tara Hardy. She lived in Peabody. According to the information printed under her picture, she was last seen leaving a Boston nightclub on the night of February 25.

The woman in the second picture, Samantha Kent, was from Chelsea. She had failed to report to her shift at the Route 1 IHOP on March 15. Samantha Kent had a painfully toothy smile and was the same age as Tara Hardy. Only Samantha was heavily into tattoos. She had six of them, and while Darby couldn't see any of them in the picture, the description and location of each of the tattoos were listed.

Both women, Darby sensed, carried the same desperate quality as Stacey. You could see it in their eyes, that bottomless need for attention and love. Both women had blond hair – just like the woman from the woods.

'It might be Samantha Kent,' Darby said. 'No, wait, it can't be her.'

'Why not?'

'Because it says here she's been missing for over a month.'

'Look at her face.'

Darby studied the picture for a moment. 'The woman I saw, her face was thin and her hair was real long,' she said. 'Samantha Kent's face is round and she has short hair.'

'But it looks like her.'

'Kind of.' Darby handed the folder back and rubbed her hands on her jeans. 'What happened to her?'

'We don't know.' Manning gave her a business card. 'If you remember anything else, even the smallest detail, you can call me at this number,' he said. 'It was nice meeting you, Darby.'

Her nightmares didn't stop until about a month later. During the day, Darby rarely thought about what happened in the woods unless she happened to bump into Stacey. Avoiding her was easy enough – too easy, really. It just went to prove how they'd never really been true friends.

'Stacey said she was sorry,' Mel said. 'Why can't we go back to being friends?'

Darby shut her locker. 'You want to be friends with her, that's your business. But I'm done with her.'

One thing Darby had in common with her mother was a love of reading. Sometimes on Saturday mornings she'd join Sheila on her yard sale trips, and while her mother was busy haggling over the price of another stupid knickknack, Darby would be on the prowl for cheapo paperbacks.

Her latest find was a book called *Carrie*. It was the cover that had grabbed her attention: a girl's head floating above a town in flames. How cool was that? Darby lay on her bed, deep in the part where Carrie was going to the prom (only the popular kids were going to play a sick, cruel joke on her) when the living room stereo kicked on and Frank Sinatra's booming voice started singing 'Come Fly with Me.' Sheila was home.

Darby glanced over at the clock on her nightstand. It was almost eight-thirty. Her mother wasn't supposed to be home until eleven or so. Sheila must have knocked off work early.

What if it isn't your mother? Darby thought. *What if the man from the woods is downstairs?*

No. This was the writer's fault; that stupid Stephen King had gotten her imagination all worked up. Her mother was downstairs, not the man from the woods, and Darby could prove it by simply taking a walk down the hallway to her mother's bedroom and looking out the windows at the driveway where Sheila's car would be parked.

Darby dog-eared her page and walked into the hallway. She leaned over the banister and looked into the foyer.

One dim light was on, and it was coming from the living room – probably the banker's lamp on the table next to the stereo. The kitchen lights were off. Had she turned them off on her return trip upstairs? Darby couldn't remember. Sheila had this thing about leaving lights on in empty rooms, always made it a point to say she wasn't working all these extra hours to put Lester Lightbulb through college –

A black-gloved hand gripped the downstairs banister.